Praise for *Iron Wolf*

"**T**he action's relentless. . . . High-tension, all-out
action-adventure . . . Brown out-Clancys Tom."
Kirkus Reviews

"**T**he action, the technology, the politics,
and even the personal stories make this tale
one of Brown's best in some time."
Booklist

"**B**rown stays true to form. . . . Highly recommended."
Library Journal

Praise for Dale Brown

"**D**ale Brown is a superb storyteller."
W.E.B. Griffin

"**B**rown puts readers into the cockpit. . . .
Authentic and gripping."
New York Times

"**B**rimming with action and political
intrigue . . . First-rate."
San Francisco Chronicle

By Dale Brown

DALE BROWN

IRON WOLF

A NOVEL

wm
WILLIAM MORROW
An Imprint of HarperCollins*Publishers*

This is a work of fiction. Names, characters, places, and incidents are products of the author's imagination or are used fictitiously and are not to be construed as real. Any resemblance to actual events, locales, organizations, or persons, living or dead, is entirely coincidental.

WILLIAM MORROW
An Imprint of HarperCollins*Publishers*
195 Broadway
New York, New York 10007

Copyright © 2015 by Air Battle Force, Inc.
ISBN 978-0-06-226241-7
www.harpercollins.com

First William Morrow premium printing: April 2016
First William Morrow hardcover printing: August 2015

William Morrow® and HarperCollins ® are registered trademarks of HarperCollins Publishers.

Printed in the United States of America

10 9 8 7 6 5 4 3 2

This novel is dedicated to all who rise up against tyranny, intimidation, and aggression, not just in Eastern Europe but around the world.

The violence we are seeing in 2015 rivals anything we have seen since the end of the Cold War, and the world needs leaders who have the strength, courage, and vision to lead others to engage and defeat the aggressors.

Whether it is by massive armies or navies, by small teams of special operations forces, or by an entirely new class of high-tech weapons and tactics, free nations and those praying for freedom need a leader to devise a plan, lead warriors into battle, and get the job done.

ACKNOWLEDGMENTS

Thank you to author and visionary Patrick Larkin for his hard work.

You gain strength, courage and confidence by every experience in which you really stop to look fear in the face.

—Eleanor Roosevelt, First Lady

WEAPONS AND AIRCRAFT

ADM-160—Medium-Range Air-Launched Decoy (MALD), a heavy aircraft defensive cruise missile

AGM-154A—Joint Standoff Weapon (JSOW), GPS-inertial navigation guided glide weapon

AGM-158—Joint Air-to-Surface Standoff Missile, advanced long-range precision strike weapon

AGM-88 HARM—High-Speed Anti-Radiation Missile, air-launched antiradar missile

ALQ-293 SPEAR—Self-Protection Electronically Agile Reaction, an integrated aircraft defense suite

AN/APG-81—advanced air-to-air and air-to-ground aircraft radar

AWACS—Airborne Warning and Control System, an airborne radar that can detect aircraft from hundreds of miles and vector interceptor aircraft

Beriev-100—Russian AWACS aircraft

BLU-97B—Combined Effects Munition antipersonnel mine

BTR-80—Russian armored personnel carrier

CID—Cybernetic Infantry Device, an advanced manned combat robot

CLAM SHELL—Russian antiaircraft radar

DTF—Digital Terrain Following, using a global terrain and obstacle database for extreme low-level flying

F-22 Raptor—U.S. Air Force air superiority fighter aircraft

F-35 Lightning II—U.S. medium bomber and attack aircraft HEMI, 520

HUD—Heads-Up Display, an electronic device that presents important flight data in front of a pilot

IRSTS—Infrared Search and Track System, a sensor that detects heat and can feed targeting data to a computer

KAB-500L—Russian laser-guided bomb

M320—forty-millimeter grenade launcher

MH-47—American heavy-lift helicopter

MiG-29—third-generation Russian air superiority fighter, used by a number of former Soviet countries

MQ-55 Coyote—advanced unmanned air weapon launch platform

MSBS Radom—Polish assault rifle

OSCE—Organization for Security and Cooperation in Europe, an intergovernmental organization promoting peace, security, and human rights

RDX—Research Department Explosive, a widely used military explosive

ROCC—Remote Operations Control Center, a location with many unmanned aircraft control stations

RPG-22—shoulder-fired antitank weapon

RQ-20 Vedette—small, stealthy unmanned airborne threat-warning aircraft

SNR-125—Russian air defense radar system

SPY-1 Aegis—American air defense radar system

Su-34—Russian modernized second-generation fighter-bomber

Su-50—Russian fifth-generation multirole stealthy fighter

Sukhoi-30—Russian fourth-generation multirole fighter

Sukhoi-35—Russian advanced air superiority fighter

T-72—Soviet second-generation main battle tank, widely exported around the world

T-80—third-generation Soviet main battle tank, widely exported

XV-40—unmanned tilt-rotor aircraft used for covert, rapid supply and insertion

REAL-WORLD NEWS EXCERPTS

EMERGING ALLIANCE IN EUROPE—
George Friedman, Stratfor.com, June 12, 2014— . . . The term "Intermarium" itself comes from a Polish general and founder of modern Poland, General Pilsudski. He was dealing with the same geopolitical problem that exists now. He had a Russia, a Soviet Union that was in the 1920s, increasingly assertive and pressing on his frontiers and the frontiers of the rest of what we now call Central Europe. Behind him he had a Germany that at that time was unclear with its intentions. Poland had emerged from World War I with these two empires clearing the way, so his question was how to preserve Polish independence.

He had really two strategies since he wasn't strong enough to defeat them. One had somebody from the outside guarantee their security and that was France for him, but he didn't really trust that this would be sufficient, so he imagined an alliance that ran from the Baltic Sea to the Black Sea, including countries at the time like Poland, Czechoslovakia, Hungary, Romania, Bulgaria and possibly Turkey. This group would serve to contain Russia and would have, instead of an east-west orientation, a north-south orientation . . .

But what I started thinking about was the fact that today Russia was reasserting itself, was going to be reclaiming its priority within the former Soviet Union, repressing on them, and the fact that Germany is once again uncertain. I thought this might be something that would emerge and in a kind of very early protostage, that seems to be what is happening right now . . .

NATO: TOP COMMANDER WARNS AGAINST CRIMEA METHODS IN ALLIED COUNTRIES—© Stratfor.com, August 18, 2014—If Russia does in a NATO state what it did in Crimea, it would be considered an act of war against the alliance, Philip Breedlove, NATO's top military commander, said Aug. 17, EU Observer reported Aug. 18, citing Die Welt.

Breedlove said NATO nations are prepared for the intervention of armed military without insignia who seek to create unrest, as well as separatists who give military advice and help destabilize a country. If NATO sees such an approach in an allied country and deems it an aggression, it will entail a military response, he said.

NATO: SEVEN MEMBER STATES CREATING NEW RESPONSE FORCE FOR UKRAINE CRISIS—© Stratfor.com, August 30, 2014—Seven NATO member states will create a new response force of 10,000 troops to improve the group's capabilities as the crisis in Ukraine continues, RIA Novosti reported Aug. 30. Britain will join Denmark, Latvia, Estonia, Lithuania, Norway, and the Netherlands in contributing air, land, and sea units, while Canada may join in . . .

RUSSIA: POLAND WILL ONLY RECEIVE MINIMAL AMOUNTS OF NATURAL GAS FROM GAZPROM—© Stratfor.com, Tuesday, September 16, 2014—Gazprom, Russia's state-controlled energy company, is only capable of supplying Poland with the minimal contracted amount of natural gas and not the quantity requested, a Gazprom spokesperson said, The Warsaw Voice reported Sept. 16.

The spokesperson did not say why the company was reducing natural gas levels to the country. Last week, Poland claimed it was receiving 45 percent less natural gas than expected, but current levels represent an estimated 20 percent drop. Austria and Slovakia have also reportedly experienced a drop in Russian energy imports.

RUSSIA'S AIR POWER CONSOLIDATES CONTROL IN UKRAINE—December 3, 2014 | 1913 GMT—Russia has deployed a significant number of air defense systems to eastern Ukraine, reports from local sources and the Ukrainian security services say. Medium ranged Buk M1M2 air defense systems cover most of the separatist held areas, and shorter ranged systems such as the Pantsir S1, Osa, and Tor cluster around the strategic supply lines running from the Russian border into the main cities of Luhansk and Donetsk. The systems combine to create a layered air defense infrastructure that prevents the Ukrainian air force from using its assets over separatist held areas.

Even though a Sept. 5 cease-fire agreement explicitly rules out Ukrainian air operations over separatist held areas, and the Ukrainian military has not attempted any such operations since then, the Russian move to establish this air defense presence indicates strong commitment to defending the separatist held territory.

The deployment of these air defense systems, as well as measures by artillery units to prevent the Ukrainian military from massing forces for an attack on separatist held areas, seem to serve a mostly defensive objective. However, separatist units continue to fight to expand their territorial hold over smaller areas along certain positions on the front line. They have continued to encircle and then take over Ukrainian checkpoints in areas near Luhansk, while bitter fighting between both sides continues at the Donetsk airport. The Ukrainian military's positions at Debaltseve, a strategic town that controls the main highway directly connecting Donetsk and Luhansk, have also been contested. As the separatist and Russian forces seek to consolidate their positions there, they may still make significant attempts to seize this location.

Even though the cease-fire has not been completely implemented and skirmishes continue to break out along the front line, the shape and posture of Russian reinforcements do not necessarily indicate a further escalation of the conflict between Ukrainian forces and separatists. Instead, Russia seems to be consolidating the gains made prior to the cease-fire declaration, securing the separatists' hold on the territory they currently control . . .

CAST OF CHARACTERS

AMERICANS

STACY ANNE BARBEAU, president of the United States of America

TIMOTHY SPELLING, general, U.S. Air Force, chairman of the Joint Chiefs of Staff

THOMAS TORREY, CIA director

EDWARD RAUCH, president's national security adviser

KAREN GRAYSON, secretary of state

LUKE COHEN, White House chief of staff

KEVIN CALDWELL, admiral, U.S. Navy, director of the National Security Agency

ROWLAND HALL, brigadier general, U.S. Marine Corps, top aide to General Spelling

HUNTER "BOOMER" NOBLE, Ph.D., chief of aerospace engineering, Sky Masters Aerospace Inc.

DEKE CARSON, Sky Masters student pilot, U.S. Air Force (ret.)

FRANK TALBOT, officer, U.S. Customs and Border Patrol

COMMANDER RUSS GERHARDT, U.S. Navy, air operations officer, CVN-77 USS *GEORGE H. W. BUSH*

FIRST SERGEANT MIKE IKEDA, U.S. Army, 75th Ranger Regiment

CAPTAIN DANIEL ROJAS, U.S. Army, 75th Ranger Regiment

FIRST LIEUTENANT WILLIAM WEBER, U.S. Air Force, Special Operations Command

IRON WOLF SQUADRON AND SCION

KEVIN MARTINDALE, president of Scion, former president of the United States of America

BRAD MCLANAHAN, commander of the Iron Wolf Squadron's XF-111 SuperVark bomber unit

PATRICK MCLANAHAN, Cybernetic Infantry Device (CID) pilot, Iron Wolf Squadron ground operations unit, former lieutenant general, U.S. Air Force (ret.)

WAYNE "WHACK" MACOMBER, commander, Iron Wolf Squadron CID operations, former major, U.S. Air Force Special Operations Command (ret.)

MARK DARROW, XF-111 pilot, Iron Wolf Squadron, former Tornado fighter-bomber pilot, Royal Air Force (ret.)

JACK HOLLENBECK, XF-111 weapons officer, Iron Wolf Squadron

BILL SIEVERT, XF-111 pilot, former F-15E Strike Eagle pilot, U.S. Air Force (ret.)

GEORGE "SMOOTH" HERRES, XF-111 weapons officer, former B-1B offensive systems operator, U.S. Air Force (ret.)

KAREN TANABE, XF-111 pilot, former B-52 pilot, U.S. Air Force (ret.)

IAN SCHOFIELD, commander, Iron Wolf deep-penetration unit, former captain in Canada's Special Operations Regiment

SAMANTHA KERR, operative, Scion's security and countersurveillance division

MARCUS CARTWRIGHT, operative, Scion's logistics division

RUSSIANS

GENNADIY ANATOLIYVICH GRYZLOV, president of the Russian Federation

SERGEI TARZAROV, president's chief of staff

GREGOR SOKOLOV, minister of defense

VIKTOR KAZYANOV, minister of state security

DARIA TITENEVA, foreign minister

IVAN ULANOV, president's private secretary

GENERAL MIKHAIL KHRISTENKO, chief of the General Staff of the Russian armed forces

LIEUTENANT GENERAL MIKHAIL VORONOV, commander of Russia's 20th Guards Army

COLONEL GENERAL VALENTIN MAKSIMOV, commander of the Russian Air Force

IGOR TRUZNYEV, former president of the Russian Federation and former head of the Federal Security Service (FSB)

MAJOR GENERAL KONSTANTIN ZARUBIN, commander, 9th Motor-Rifle Brigade

LIEUTENANT GENERAL MIKHAIL POLIVANOV, new commander of Russia's 20th Guards Army

MAJOR VIKTOR ZELIN, Su-34 fighter-bomber pilot

CAPTAIN NIKOLAI STARIKOV, Su-34 fighter-bomber navigation and weapons officer

CAPTAIN KIRILL ARISTOV, commander, 2nd Spetsnaz Brigade Quick Reaction Force

SENIOR SERGEANT IVAN CHAPAYEV, scout, 2nd Spetsnaz Brigade

CAPTAIN LEONID DAVYDOV, Su-24M2 fighter-bomber pilot

CAPTAIN STEPAN NIKOLAYEV, Su-24M2 fighter-bomber pilot

LIEUTENANT YURI BELINSKY, Su-24M2 fighter-bomber weapons officer

CAPTAIN TIMUR PELEVIN, 2nd Spetsnaz Brigade

REAR ADMIRAL ANATOLY VARENNIKOV, task force commander, Russian aircraft carrier *ADMIRAL KUZNETSOV*

CAPTAIN LEONID YAKUNIN, chief intelligence officer, Russian aircraft carrier *ADMIRAL KUZNETSOV*

MAJOR VLADIMIR CHERKASHIN, Su-35 fighter pilot

CAPTAIN OLEG BESSONOV, Su-35 fighter pilot

COLONEL VITALYI SAMSONOV, senior air controller, Beriev-100 AWACS plane

COLONEL ALEXEI FILIPPOV, Su-35 fighter pilot and fighter strike force commander

MAJOR YEVGENY KUROCHKIN, MiG-29M fighter pilot

CAPTAIN IVAN TEPLOV, T-72 tank company commander

COLONEL KONRAD SARATOV, commander, 72nd Tactical Missile Brigade

LIEUTENANT KARARINA KIROV, deputy action officer, 72nd Tactical Missile Brigade

MAJÓR GENERAL ALEXANDER KORNUKOV, commander, Western Military District

CAPTAIN PAVEL IGNATYEV, Su-30 pilot

SENIOR LIEUTENANT VIKTORIA GREF, Su-30 weapons officer

UKRAINIANS

MAJOR FEDIR KRAVCHENKO, second-in-command of Kaniv Volunteer Battalion, later partisan leader

Colonel Romaniuk, commander of Kaniv Volunteer Battalion

Sergeant Pavlo Lytvyn, senior noncom, Kaniv Volunteer Battalion, later second-in-command of Fedir Kravchenko's partisan unit

Hennadiy Vovk, partisan fighter

Dmytro Marchuk, former colonel in Ukraine's special police, the Berkut

POLES

Piotr Wilk, president of Poland, former general in the Polish Air Force and commander of the First Air Defense Wing

Klaudia Rybak, Polish prime minister

Janusz Gierek, minister of national defense and deputy prime minister

Andrzej Waniek, foreign minister

Irena Malinowski, minister of the interior

Captain Nadia Rozek, military aide to President Piotr Wilk, pilot in Polish Special Forces, 7th Special Operations Squadron

Major General Tadeusz Stasiak, Polish Land Forces

Major General Milosz Domanski, Polish Land Forces

Colonel Paweł Kasperek, F-16 pilot and commander of the Polish Air Force's 3rd Tactical Squadron

Major Dariusz Stepniak, head of presidential security detail, Bureau of Government Protection (BOR)

Sergeant Konrad Malek, Polish Border Guard

Captain Marek Kaczor, MiG-29 fighter pilot

Lieutenant Milosz Czarny, MiG-29 fighter pilot

Staff Sergeant Teodor Górski, support division, Polish armed forces

Captain Kazimierz Janik, liaison officer, Iron Wolf Squadron, Polish Special Forces, *Jednostka Wojskowa Grom* counterterrorism unit

BALTIC STATES

Lukas Tenys, prime minister of Lithuania

Sven Kalda, prime minister of Estonia

Kunnar Dukurs, prime minister of Latvia

ORGANIZATION FOR SECURITY AND COOPERATION IN EUROPE (OSCE)

Captain Stefan Covaci, Romanian Military Police, co-commander of OSCE Starovoitove Arms Control Station

CAPTAIN VITALYI YUREVICH, Belarussian Border
   Guards, co-commander of OSCE Starovoitove
   Arms Control Station

CHINESE

QIN HENG, regional managing director for the
   Kiev branch, Shenzen Merchants Bank, and
   senior intelligence agent for the ministry of
   state security

PROLOGUE

> *Destiny is not a matter of
> chance, it is a matter of choice;
> it is not a thing to be waited for,
> it is a thing to be achieved.*

— WILLIAM JENNINGS BRYAN,
AMERICAN POLITICIAN

SOUTHWEST OF DONETSK, UKRAINE
Late Summer 2014

The Russian shelling had stopped. An eerie silence descended on the shattered and burning village.

Smoke drifted through the bomb-cratered streets, curling past wrecked homes and shops. A battered convoy made up of commandeered civilian trucks and cars and a few wheeled BTR-80 armored personnel carriers lined the main road. White truce flags fluttered from their radio antennas.

Wearily, Major Fedir Kravchenko pulled himself

up onto the rear deck of one of the APCs. Even in his midthirties, the Ukrainian officer had kept himself fit and trim. But now, after months of brutal combat against separatist rebels and Russian "volunteers," he felt more dead than alive.

"Major!" His radio crackled. "This is Colonel Romaniuk. The Russians are giving us just another thirty minutes to begin our evacuation before they open fire again. Get your troops moving!"

"Understood," Kravchenko acknowledged tersely. Though they had no real choice, accepting defeat still left a bitter taste in his mouth.

Sighing, he stripped off his American-made Kevlar helmet and ran a grimy hand through his stiff, short-cropped hair. Then he filled his lungs and began shouting orders. "Men of the Kaniv Battalion! Let's go! Form up! We're pulling back."

Ukrainian soldiers wearing torn and tattered camouflage uniforms climbed warily out of slit trenches and foxholes, slowly assembling in squads and then platoons. Lightly wounded men, wrapped in blood-soaked bandages, hobbled toward the waiting vehicles. Others, more seriously injured, were carried out on stretchers and carefully loaded onto flatbed trucks. All of them, whether wounded or unhurt, were haggard, dirty, and gaunt. Bloodshot eyes stared out of sunburned, unshaven faces.

Led by a handful of regular officers, the enthusiastic volunteers of the Kaniv Battalion had fought hard for weeks—grinding the Russian-backed separatists out of village after village as they closed in on the rebel stronghold of Donetsk. Casualties had been high, but they had been winning. Final victory seemed only days away.

And then Moscow had entered the war openly.

Massed columns of Russian tanks, infantry fighting vehicles, self-propelled artillery pieces, and rocket launchers poured across the border, defying every call from the United States and the West to withdraw. And all of Kiev's pleas for military aid had been rebuffed by the Americans and NATO. Outnumbered and outgunned, Ukraine's regular forces and volunteer units had been smashed in a series of bloody pitched battles.

Like so many others, the Kaniv Battalion had found itself surrounded, trapped in this burned-out village under constant shelling by Russian artillery batteries. Although they had repelled several enemy attacks, Kravchenko and his men knew they faced certain annihilation once their supplies and ammunition were exhausted. And so, early this morning, their commander, Colonel Romaniuk, had reluctantly accepted Moscow's radioed offer of a temporary cease-fire and safe-conduct back to Ukrainian-held territory.

"So that's it? We're just cutting and running?" a voice rasped.

Kravchenko looked down, meeting the angry eyes of Sergeant Pavlo Lytvyn. Before the war, Lytvyn had been a professor of classics. Weeks of fighting had turned him into a ruthless, determined killer—and one of the best soldiers in the battalion.

The major shrugged. "For now, Pavlo." He donned his helmet again. "But we'll be back."

Sourly, Lytvyn spat to one side. "Not in our life-times, Fedir. You'll see. What those bastards in the

Kremlin take, they hold. We're not coming back here. Not ever."

Thirty minutes later, perched uneasily atop the swaying deck of the BTR as it lurched south, Kravchenko pondered the sergeant's grim prophecy. He craned his neck, staring back past the exhausted, silent soldiers crowded around him. Columns of smoke coiled upward from burning buildings, staining the blue summer sky. A distant rumble of guns off to the northeast signaled that other Ukrainian units were still fighting—still desperately trying to hold off the Russian onslaught.

For a moment, he wondered whether they should have spurned the Russian president's offer of safe-conduct, instead choosing to sell their lives in a heroic last stand. Could such an act have inspired his countrymen to even greater patriotism in the face of Moscow's aggression?

Then he shrugged. It was too late for suicidal heroism.

Obeying the withdrawal instructions signaled by the local Russian commander, the ragtag Ukrainian convoy of trucks, cars, and battle-scarred APCs turned off the main highway and onto a rutted dirt road paralleling the railroad to Mariupol. The BTR he was riding on was fourth in line, and the ruined village they'd abandoned was soon lost to sight. Thick woods hemmed them in on both sides.

Spewing a blue haze of exhaust fumes, the column moved slowly southward. Their white truce flags hung limp in the stagnant, humid air. Every rut jolted groans from the wounded men crammed into trucks and cars.

Suddenly the shrill roar of a gas turbine engine echoed off the surrounding trees. It was coming from ahead of the convoy.

Kravchenko scrambled to his feet to get a better look. He was in time to see a massive T-80 main battle tank clatter out onto the railroad tracks. The white, blue, and red tricolor of the Russian Federation streamed from its whip antenna.

"What the devil is that idiot doing?" he muttered. "He's blocking the damned road."

The T-80's turret whined round, bringing its 125mm smoothbore gun to bear.

"Christ!" Lytvyn swore wildly. "It's a fucking ambush!"

KA-BLAAMM!

One round from the T-80 blew Colonel Romaniuk's prized UAZ Hunter staff car into a blazing, mangled wreck. Razor-edged fragments sleeted outward from the blast, smashing windshields and shredding men in nearby cars and trucks.

Seconds later, the convoy's tail-end vehicle, a flatbed truck crowded with wounded Ukrainian soldiers, exploded in a ball of flame. It has been hit by another high-explosive tank round—this one fired by a T-72 tank marked in separatist colors. The rebel tank had roared out behind them to cut off any escape to the north.

With a chattering, rippling crackle, both tanks opened up with their 7.62mm coaxial and heavier 12.7mm turret-mounted machine guns. More stalled vehicles burst into flame or were torn open from end to end. Screaming men scrambled out of the wreckage and were cut down. Crumpled bodies piled up on the dirt road.

The Russian T-80 rumbled around Romaniuk's wrecked staff car, maneuvering for clearer shots with its main gun. Its squealing treads crushed wounded Ukrainians writhing desperately to escape.

Wide-eyed in horror, Kravchenko grabbed Lytvyn and dragged him off the BTR-80 APC. They landed heavily in the tall grass growing beside the road and went prone. Most of those who'd been riding with them on the deck reacted too slowly. A hail of machine-gun rounds laced the BTR, ricocheting off its armor, but ripping through flesh and bone. Dead and dying soldiers tumbled down around the two men.

"Get to the woods!" Kravchenko shouted into the sergeant's ear. "We've got to break out of this killing zone!"

Nodding, Lytvyn slithered ahead through the grass, hugging the earth to stay beneath the machine-gun bullets whipcracking just over their heads.

Kravchenko lagged behind, waving other survivors into the trees. "Move it! Go! Go! Go!"

A few yards away, the BTR's gunner hand-cranked his turret around, desperately trying to bring his own heavy machine gun to bear on the Russian tank. His rounds wouldn't be able to penetrate its thick armor, but they might knock out its optics and lighter weapons.

Kravchenko saw the turret turning and glanced to his left. The Russian tank's big gun was whirring round, too, coming on target faster. "Oh, hell," he snarled, scrambling to his feet and turning to run.

WHAAMM!

The T-80's 125mm high-explosive antitank round slammed into the BTR, penetrated, and blew up.

Kravchenko had just enough time to see searing tongues of orange and red fire lance out of the APC's open hatches and firing ports. And then the blast caught him. It picked him up, squeezed the air out of his lungs, and hurled him into the woods.

Everything went black.

Fedir Kravchenko swam slowly up out of darkness into a world of blinding light and searing pain. Every part of his body seemed wrapped in agony— his arms, his legs, his chest, his face. Every shallow, gasping breath he took turned the world around him red.

But his eyes were closed.

He struggled to open them.

"Calmly, Fedir. Calmly," he heard a voice saying. It was a voice he recognized. It was the voice of Pavlo Lytvyn. "You must not move too fast or you will rip the dressings open and bleed out."

Moaning, Kravchenko forced an eye open. But only one eye. There were bandages covering half his face.

Slowly, Lytvyn's own grim face swam into focus. It was framed by tall sunflowers, bright yellow against the sky.

"I need to see," he mumbled, tasting blood in his mouth.

"Yes," the sergeant agreed slowly. "You must see." Carefully, he propped Kravchenko up.

The major stared, trying to understand what he saw through the waves of anguish surging through his mangled body. They were deep in a field of sunflowers, hidden among the tall plants. A few other Ukrainian soldiers, most spattered in blood and ashen-faced, squatted near them.

Thick plumes of oily, black smoke billowed above the distant trees. Each pillar of smoke marked the pyre of a wrecked vehicle and dead men.

Slowly, painfully, Kravchenko turned his head away. He stared at Lytvyn. "Where is the rest of the battalion?"

"The battalion?" The sergeant shook his head. His eyes were sad and distant. He nodded at the tiny handful of frightened men around them. "This, Major, *is* the battalion. All that survives."

Kravchenko closed his eye. Part of him wanted to let go, to fall away from this place of pain and horror and humiliation into sheer nothingness. But then he felt a flood of rage buoying him up. It was not a blinding, maddening frenzy. Instead, it was as though he were gripped by a tide of ice-cold fury that cut through all pain and all confusion—laying open the real world in all its stark cruelty.

He looked again at Lytvyn, this time seeing the other man with crystalline clarity. He forced a twisted smile, knowing how strange and terrible it must look on his maimed, bandaged face. "Hear me, Pavlo."

"Sir?"

"We will take our vengeance on those treacherous Russian bastards," Kravchenko said coldly. "We will make widows of their wives and orphans of their children. We will kill them by the hundreds and the thousands and the tens of thousands. We will kill them here on our native soil and on the streets of Moscow itself. They will learn to fear us. And they will beg for mercy, but still we will kill them. This I swear to you, and to our fallen comrades." He fell silent, sliding back into unconsciousness.

Pavlo Lytvyn stared down at the gruesomely disfigured man who had been his commanding officer. "And so Nemesis awakes," he murmured, recalling the ancient myths he had once studied and treasured. Then he remembered the scenes of slaughter he had just witnessed. His big, capable hands tightened on the AK-74 assault rifle he'd saved from the massacre and rout. "So be it."

CHAPTER 1

*Bring ideas in and entertain
them royally, for one of
them may be the king.*

—Mark Van Doren,
American poet and scholar

SKY MASTERS AEROSPACE, INC.
XF-111 SUPERVARK BOMBER,
OVER "WESTERN RUSSIA"
July 2017

"*Big Bird radar detected at twelve o'clock. Estimated range forty miles,*" the XF-111 SuperVark's computer said in a calm female voice. "*Detection probability high.*"

"Activate SPEAR," Brad McLanahan ordered, tweaking his stick to the left. The bomber banked slightly, following the visual cues shown by its digital terrain-following system. Blinking lights on a towering factory smokestack flashed past the right side of the canopy and vanished in the darkness. The XF-111 juddered slightly, hitting turbulence created by warmer air rising from the ground just two hundred feet below.

"ALQ-293 SPEAR activated," the computer told him.

Brad relaxed slightly. If the computer was doing its job right, his XF-111's Self-Protection Electronically Agile Reaction system was busy transmitting precisely tailored signals that would fool the enemy radar into believing his bomber was somewhere else in the sky over Russia. And that might make the very real difference between living awhile longer and "catastrophic mission failure"—that dry little phrase used by his Sky Masters tactics instructors to describe what happened when a missile hit turned an aircraft into a tumbling ball of flame and shredded metal.

Then he tightened up again. That radar detection was an indication that he was flying straight into the zone where Russia's air defenses formed what was supposed to be an impenetrable barrier of overlapping radars and surface-to-air missile batteries. The 91N6E radar, code-named Big Bird by NATO, was the acquisition and battle management radar for Russia's first-line S-400 Triumph SAM battalions. Equipped with eight launchers, each S-400 battalion could fire up a mix of up to thirty-two highly accurate, long-range surface-to-air missiles. That was more than enough to make a very bad day for any attacking aircraft.

"Search radar broke lock," the computer reported.

Brad really hoped the XF-111's defensive programs were running smoothly. He didn't especially like having to rely entirely on the computer this way. Ordinarily, a separate weapons system officer would closely monitor its operations, but he was stuck flying this mission alone.

But this was one awesome bird to fly even without a weapons systems officer—it was so highly automated that it almost flew itself. Each crewmember had two large color multifunction computer monitors that could display a dazzling array of information, from engine and systems readouts, navigation, weapons status, and even a virtual depiction of the outside world that was so detailed and clear that it seemed like a color photograph. The center of the instrument panel had a large multifunction display that mostly showed engine, fuel, electrical, and other system readouts, although data could be displayed and swapped around to any other monitor in case of damage or malfunction.

The original F-111 "Aardvark" was very advanced in its time, but the SuperVark was a digital masterpiece, in line with the latest bizjets and spacecraft: flight controls were triple-redundant digital fly-by-wire; voice-command redundant computers controlled navigation, flight control, attack, defensive systems, and weapon release. The SuperVark had an AN/APG-81 active electronically scanned array radar for air-to-air and air-to-ground attack, and the radar could even be used in a high-power, narrow-beam mode to attack and disrupt enemy aircraft and incoming missiles. It employed four infrared detectors to provide warning and track enemy aircraft and missiles, and the sensors interfaced with the ALQ-293 SPEAR defensive system and the flight control computers to track and evade attackers.

Controlled by its digital terrain-following radar and computers, the SuperVark pitched up slightly as it popped up over a wooded hill and then descended again—speeding low across the hilly, forested landscape at nearly six hundred knots. Glowing numbers counting down on his HUD showed that he was still more than one hundred miles from his primary target, the headquarters of Russia's 4th Air-Space Defense Brigade in Dolgoprudny, a suburb just north of Moscow.

For a moment, Brad was tempted to pop up off the deck and launch his cruise missiles now. The two AGM-158 JASSMs (Joint Air-to-Surface Standoff Missiles) slung in his XF-111's internal weapons bay had a rated range of around two hundred nautical miles. Once he launched them, he could turn and get the hell out of Russian airspace. But he fought down that urge.

Technically, JASSMs were low-observable, semi-stealthy weapons designed to penetrate to defended enemy targets. But semistealthy didn't mean invisible, especially not up against equipment like that Big Bird positioned up ahead. It was a powerful phased array radar, the land-based equivalent of the U.S. Navy's SPY-1 Aegis. If he launched now, the flight path for his subsonic cruise missiles would take them straight over the Russian S-400 battalion, and the JASSMs would be detected and shot down in seconds.

No, Brad decided, feeling his heart rate accelerate, there was only one way this mission was going to work. He was going to have to blow a hole through the Russian air defenses *before* he launched the JASSMs.

Keeping his right hand on the stick, he keyed in a new target on the large color multifunction display set below his HUD. Another quick button press selected a different weapon, one of the two AGM-88 HARMs hanging from launch rails beneath his XF-111's wings.

"Range to Big Bird radar," he asked aloud.

"*Fifteen miles,*" the SuperVark's voice-command system said.

Good enough, Brad thought. His HARMs, High-Speed Anti-Radiation Missiles, could reach out and smack enemy radars at ranges of up to eighty nautical miles. He squeezed the "DTF DIS-ENGAGE" paddle switch on his control stick with his right little finger, temporarily disengaging the digital terrain-following system, and pulled back slightly. His left hand pushed the throttles forward a bit, feeding more power to the XF-111's brand-new turbofan engines. The big fighter-bomber climbed, roaring up past two thousand feet.

"*Warning, Big Bird radar has a lock,*" the computer reported in a maddeningly calm voice.

"Crap," Brad muttered. But that was no real surprise. There were limits to what any defensive electronic countermeasures system could do, even one as sophisticated as the ALQ-293 SPEAR. Now that they had a solid lock on him, those Russian SAM launchers would start flushing their own missiles in seconds.

Heart pounding, he toggled the weapons button on his stick and squeezed his eyes shut to avoid being dazzled by the HARM's rocket plume.

WHOOSH!

The antiradiation missile he'd selected streaked out from under the XF-111's right wing. It curved slightly, already guiding on the Russian SAM radar's emissions.

Brad released the paddle switch and watched the terrain-following system yank the SuperVark's nose down, heading for the deck again in the hope that he could break that radar lock by getting down in the clutter. He banked hard right and then jinked back left. No point in making it easy for them, he thought.

A huge white flash lit the night sky directly ahead.

"Big Bird radar off-line," the voice-command system said.

"Sweet," Brad said, rolling back onto his preplotted attack course. He shoved the throttles forward, going to full military power. The XF-111 responded instantly, accelerating fast. With their primary battle management radar blown to hell, it would take the officers and men of that Russian S-400 battalion a minute or two to power up their replacement systems. Time to git while the getting's good, he told himself.

"Command not understood," the computer said.

Oops. Brad colored briefly, embarrassed. The SuperVark's voice-command system was a high-tech marvel, but it had limitations where English-language idioms were concerned. "Disregard."

"Disregard last command. Fifty miles to primary mission target."

Brad glanced ahead out the XF-111's canopy. A pale yellow and white glow on the far horizon marked the city lights of Moscow. Almost there, he thought. Once he got within forty miles of Dolgoprudny, he'd pop up again to launch the JASSMs and break away at high speed.

"EXODUS threat detected at four o'clock," the voice-command system said sharply. *"Range is one hundred and sixty feet."*

What the hell? Brad swung his head sharply, straining to look out the right rear quadrant of the XF-111's canopy. There was nothing there, just the black of a clear Russian night sky speckled with cold bright stars. Reacting instinctively, he turned hard into the threat. But what was this EXODUS thing? Some new surface-to-air missile? A new-type Russian fighter? And how had whatever it was gotten so close that it was practically scratching the paint on his SuperVark?

"Query EXODUS," he demanded. He kept the fighter-bomber in a tight turn while frantically scanning for some visual on this unidentified threat that would explain things.

"EXODUS confirmed," the computer said. *"Still at four o'clock. Range one hundred and sixty feet."*

Brad frowned. Somehow, this unknown object was holding a static position relative to his aircraft, even while he maneuvered wildly. How was that possible?

Suddenly all the cockpit displays went out, leaving him sitting in absolute darkness. The noise and rumble of the XF-111's twin turbofan engines died. The night sky outside the cockpit went black. With a whine of hydraulics, the floor tilted back to level. After a split second, red emergency lighting flickered on, outlining a door at the rear of the compartment.

"*Simulator power loss*," the computer reported. "*Mission incomplete.*"

Not cool, Brad said to himself through gritted teeth. Doing all the grunt work and manual labor expected of summer interns at Sky Masters and keeping up with required classes in aerospace engineering, business management, and air combat tactics left him scrambling just to eat, stay in shape, and occasionally sleep. And now, just when he'd committed a whole hour of his incredibly limited free time to this XF-111 mission simulation, the darned thing had gone dead less than halfway through. It was like getting all the *interruptus* without any of the *coitus*.

Sky Masters Aerospace operated some of the most advanced full flight simulators in the world, enabling the Nevada-based private company to train pilots to fly almost any kind of aircraft. Its programs and instructors could teach you to handle everything from lowly little turboprops to fifth-generation fighters like the F-22 Raptor. Sky Masters even trained astronauts to fly the incredible S-series advanced spaceplanes, which delivered passengers and cargo to Earth orbit from ordinary commercial runways. For Brad, the chance to grab occasional sim time was one of this unpaid internship's biggest perks.

Still pissed, he unstrapped himself from his seat and stood up, stretching out the kinks in his shoulders and legs. His build was one of the few disadvantages he'd inherited as a McLanahan. Most of the time there was nothing wrong at all with being tall and powerfully built, but it kind of sucked when you had to squeeze yourself into a crowded cockpit for hours on end. Getting the chance to lob some ordnance into a computer-generated building full of virtual bad guys would have made up for the physical discomfort.

It was only when he stepped out onto the narrow platform attached to the huge, full-motion simulator that the penny dropped. There, off at his four o'clock and about a hundred sixty feet away, was the exit door for the huge converted hangar Sky Masters used to house its simulators. It was at the same range and bearing as that weird threat warning he'd been given just before the simulator's power failed.

EXODUS wasn't NATO shorthand for a new Russian SAM or fighter plane, he suddenly remembered. It was one of a series of code words created by his father, retired Air Force Lieutenant General Patrick McLanahan, and by former U.S. President Kevin Martindale, now the owner of Scion, a private military and intelligence company. They had wanted a means to communicate quickly, securely, and secretly with Brad in an emergency. *EXODUS* was essentially shorthand for "make an excuse and get out of Dodge fast."

Which meant there was trouble brewing some-where.

His hands balled into fists. What the hell was going on now? he wondered.

For years, he had been caught up in events well beyond the pay grade of any trained military officer, let alone an ordinary college student barely into his twenties. In 2015, together with his father and other Sky Masters pilots under government contract, he'd flown an unauthorized retaliatory strike against the People's Republic of China after Chinese bombers attacked the U.S. Air Force base on Guam. Almost everyone thought his father had been killed during that mission. The fact that Patrick McLanahan, though terribly wounded, had survived was known only by a tiny handful of people.

Then, last year, funded by a grant from Sky Masters, Brad and a team of fellow students from Cal Poly had worked hard to build and deploy an experimental orbital solar power plant called Starfire. It used a microwave laser to beam all the power they collected back to Earth. Despite their peaceful intentions, the Russians and Chinese claimed they were building space weapons and launched an attack on Starfire and Armstrong Station. With salvos of S-500 air-to-space missiles streaking toward them, Brad's team had been forced to convert their laser into a real fighting weapon. And it had worked—helping defend Armstrong Space Station success-fully right up to the moment when a Russian EMP blast knocked out their electronics.

That would have been way more than enough danger and excitement for anyone. Unfortunately,

Brad had also found himself hunted by Russian assassins, narrowly escaping being murdered more times than he liked to think about. It seemed that Russia's president, Gennadiy Gryzlov, had embarked on a personal vendetta against anyone bearing the McLanahan name. It was a vendetta that went back more than a decade, all the way back to the day when Gryzlov's own father had been killed by American bombs—bombs dropped in a raid commanded by Patrick McLanahan.

Things had been quieter in the months since the tangled wreckage of Armstrong Station fell burning through the atmosphere. The press, quickly bored by old news, had stopped hounding him for interviews. The survivors of his Starfire team had drifted apart—drawn back to their own academic challenges and lives. Even Jodie Cavendish, the Australian exchange student with whom he'd fallen in love, or maybe just lust, and shared the secret that his father was alive, had gone back to Brisbane. Then, after the school year ended, the higher-ups at Sky Masters, impressed by his work and leadership skills, had offered him this summer internship. And even the Russians seemed to have stopped trying to kill him. Brad had been hoping that destroying the Starfire Project had satiated that nut case Gryzlov's rage.

His father and Martindale weren't so sure. Both men suspected Brad was still under close surveillance—certainly by the U.S. government and probably by Russia's SVR, its Foreign Intelligence Service, and the PRC's Ministry of State Security. If so, none of his phone calls or e-mails were secure. That was why they'd ginned up a number of code words and phrases for different situations and made him memorize them.

So now his father and Martindale were privately signaling him to bail out of his Sky Masters internship and head for the hills. Fair enough, Brad thought. The trick was going to be how to do that without tipping off the FBI and various Russian and Chinese intelligence agents that something weird was up. If he just waltzed into the personnel office and said he was quitting, he might as well send up a flare. Nobody who knew anything about him would believe he'd walk away from this gig with Sky Masters without a darned good reason.

Still thinking about that, he slid the last few feet down the ladder from the XF-111 simulator and dropped lightly onto the hangar floor. The massive Hexapod system's huge hydraulic jacks towered above his head.

"Well, shit, look who's been hogging the sim again, guys," a voice jeered from behind him. "It's Boy Bomber Jock McLanahan and his trusty sidekick, Ego Fricking Mania."

Brad spun around.

Deke Carson and two other Sky Masters test pilots were about twenty feet away, loitering near the control consoles that ran the simulators. Carson, the biggest of the trio, leaned back against one of the consoles with his arms folded and an unpleasant sneer plastered across his face. His two friends, slightly smaller and lighter but wearing obnoxious smirks of their own, hovered at his elbows.

Brad's eyes narrowed. Mostly he got along pretty

well with the fliers who worked for Sky Masters and with the other professional pilots who flocked here for advanced training. Carson and his cronies were the exception. They'd been riding him all summer.

Carson was the worst. Like many Air Force pilots, he'd been "involuntarily separated" from the service in the last round of budget cuts. Sky Masters was retraining him to fly big commercial jetliners, but he was still pissed off about losing his military career. And even the sight of Brad McLanahan was like waving a matador's red cape in front of a bull. Knowing that a kid, and a civilian kid at that, had more flight time, even time in space, and real-world combat experience than he did struck the former Air Force captain as proof that politics and family clout counted for more than talent and training.

"Did you cut the power to my sim, Deke?" Brad snapped, moving toward the other men.

Carson raised an eyebrow. "*Your* sim, McLanahan?" He snorted. "Last time I looked, you were just a jumped-up broom jockey with a big mouth. Or did somebody in corporate promote you to CEO because you did such a good job cleaning toilets?"

His two friends snickered.

Encouraged, Carson unfolded his arms and stepped right up to Brad, crowding inside his comfort zone. "Look, Bradley McDumbshit. These guys and me . . ." He nodded at his cronies. "We're paying the freight here, to the tune of ten thousand bucks apiece per goddamned month. And we're getting sick of seeing you waltz around like you're God's Own Aviator. Hell, you're not even a nugget.

You're just a little piece of crap with delusions of grandeur."

"I've paid my dues," Brad said tightly. "I've flown enough to—"

"Bull," Carson interrupted. "The only reason anyone's ever let you sit in a cockpit is because your dad, the late and totally unlamented General McLanahan, knew how to kiss political ass in Washington, D.C., and corporate ass here at Sky Masters."

For a moment, Brad saw red. Then he breathed out slowly, forcing himself to regain self-control. He had nothing to gain from getting into a fight with a dick like Carson. Three years ago, losing his temper with an instructor had gotten him bounced out of the U.S. Air Force Academy in the middle of cadet basic training. Though he'd never said so, Brad knew that was the one time he'd genuinely disappointed his father.

"Nothing to say, McLanahan?" Carson asked loudly. His sneer grew deeper. "I guess that's because you know it's the truth." He glanced at his friends, saw them grinning in encouragement, and swung back to Brad. "Hell, the only other thing you've got in common with your dad is the nasty habit of getting other people killed for your own goddamned glory! How many people were left sucking vacuum when you ditched from Armstrong Space Station and hightailed it for home? Four? Five? More?"

On the other hand, Brad thought coldly, he *did* need a good reason for leaving Sky Masters before his internship was up. Maybe this was his chance to create one. He looked hard at Carson. "I strongly suggest you shut up, Deke," he said.

"Or what?" Carson asked, still sneering.

"Or I will kick your sorry Hangar Queen ass," Brad told him. "And right in front of your little friends, too."

For a second, he thought the other man would play it smart and back down. That would be . . . disappointing. But then he saw Carson's nostrils flare and knew he'd jabbed the right nerve with that Hangar Queen crack. Maybe it wasn't fair to rub Deke's face in the fact that his beloved Air Force had treated him like a broken-down bird useful only for spare parts, but this wasn't exactly a time to be fair.

Carson shoved his shoulder hard. "Screw you," he snarled.

One, Brad thought. He just smiled.

Furious now, Carson started to shove him again.

Now.

Brad slid to the left, deflecting the other man's arm up and away with a right fan block.

Off balance, Carson stumbled forward.

Moving swiftly and fluidly, Brad swung in behind him, sliding his left hand under and around the other man's jaw to bring Carson's throat into the crook of his elbow. At the same time, he brought his right hand over to grip the back of the former Air Force pilot's head and pushed forward, exponentially increasing the force on his carotid arteries.

Within seconds, deprived of any blood flow to his brain, Carson sagged, unconscious. Brad dropped him to the hangar floor. The self-defense training he had received from Chris Wohl and his countersurveillance operatives of Scion, even though long discontinued, still stuck with him.

"Who's next?" he asked, stepping over the other man's limp body. He grinned. "I'll be nice. You can both come at me at the same time."

But Carson's two cronies were already backing away. One of them had his cell phone out. "Sky Masters Security?" he stammered. "We've got a big problem in the Simulator Building. We need help, right now!"

The other looked at Brad with an odd mix of fear and curiosity in his eyes. "You know you're totally fucked, McLanahan, don't you?"

Brad shrugged. "Well, yeah, I guess I probably am."

OSCE ARMS CONTROL STATION, NEAR STAROVOITOVE, URKAINIAN-POLISH BORDER
That same time

Lieutenant General Mikhail Voronov, commander of Russia's 20th Guards Army, leaned forward in the Kazan Ansat-U helicopter's left-hand seat, studying the ground flashing below at 250 kilometers per hour. This part of western Ukraine was covered in tiny lakes, narrow rivers, and marshland. Patches of pine and oak forest alternated with small fields sown in rye, potatoes, and oats. There were relatively few roads, most of them running east toward Kiev and west toward the Polish frontier.

A poor countryside, Voronov thought. But a useful place to keep a choke hold on the Ukrainians.

"We are five minutes out, sir," the pilot told him. "Captains Covaci and Yurevich report they are ready for your inspection."

"Very good," Voronov said.

Stefan Covaci, a Romanian military police officer, and Vitalyi Yurevich, a member of Belarus's border guards, jointly commanded one of the OSCE arms control posts sited at every border crossing into Ukraine. Since Romania was friendly to Ukraine and Belarus favored Russia, the dual command arrangement kept each national contingent reasonably honest and efficient.

In theory, under the cease-fire agreement between Ukraine's government and the separatists allied with Moscow, these stations were supposed to stem the flow of weapons and military technology that might trigger a new conflict. In practice, their work helped keep the Ukrainians militarily weak and under Moscow's thumb. Weapons sought by Kiev were deemed contraband, while Russian arms shipments to Donetsk, Luhansk, and other rebel-held cities easily evaded the OSCE's inspectors.

The Russian general smiled, remembering the carefully crafted English-language quip his president had used at a recent meeting: "So the West thinks OSCE stands for the 'Organization for Security and Cooperation in Europe,' eh?" Russian Federation President Gennadiy Gryzlov had said with a wolfish grin. "How very high-minded of them. Fortunately for us, we know that it really stands for the 'Organization to Secure Our Conquests and Empire.'"

It was the kind of darkly ironic gibe Voronov greatly enjoyed.

Since the tank, motor-rifle, and artillery brigades of his 20th Guards Army were based closest to Ukraine's eastern border, Voronov acted as Moscow's de facto satrap for the rebel-controlled regions. He made sure that the Kremlin's carefully expressed "wishes" were obeyed to the letter. If necessary, separatists who balked were discreetly eliminated by special hit teams under his orders—as were other Ukrainians still living in those areas who were too stupid to understand who now ruled them.

As the senior Russian commander in this region, he also made a habit of periodically inspecting the OSCE's arms control posts. These inspection tours added up to long, dreary hours spent flying from place to place, refueling when necessary, but his visits kept the monitors on their toes. And that was useful. Arms and ammunition they confiscated were arms and ammunition his own troops would not have to face when the day finally came to finish the job and reconquer all of Ukraine.

For now, President Gryzlov seemed content with the status quo, but the general suspected that would soon change. The NATO powers, led by the United States, were increasingly weak. Just last year the Americans had effectively stood aside while Russia first destroyed an S-19 spaceplane with their vice president aboard, and then blew their prized Armstrong orbital military station into a million pieces. And if anything, their new president, a woman of all things, seemed even less likely to get in Moscow's way.

Voronov's sly grin slipped.

Poland was the one real remaining obstacle. It, too, had a new president, Piotr Wilk. But this Pole, a former air force commander, seemed made of sterner stuff than the American, Stacy Anne Barbeau. His sympathies plainly lay with Ukraine's democratic regime. And he was already proposing a program of significantly increased defense spending to boost Poland's military capabilities. If left too long to his own devices, Wilk seemed likely to make trouble for Moscow.

Which gave Voronov all the more reason to keep a close eye on this particular arms control post. Sited at the busiest border crossing between Poland and Ukraine, it was just the place the Poles might use for clandestine shipments to Kiev.

"The Starovoitove arms control station is in sight," the helicopter pilot reported. He reduced collective and pulled back on his cyclic joystick to begin slowing the Ansat. He keyed his mike. "*Opekun* flight, clear us into the landing zone. Acknowledge."

Another voice crackled through their headphones. "Understood, Lead. Guardian flight complying. Out."

Two narrow-bodied Ansat-2RC light helicopter gunships flashed past and descended, spiraling into orbit ahead at low altitude. The pilot and gunner aboard each helicopter were using their nose-mounted infrared sensors to scan for potential threats. If anyone was concealed in the surrounding forests, their heat signature would stand out against the cooler vegetation.

Voronov looked through the windscreen. They were coming up on the Bug River, a shallow, meandering waterway that marked the border between Poland and Ukraine. Two bridges spanned the river, one for the Lublin-Kiev railroad and the other for the E373 highway. Sunlight glinted off slanted glass and metal roofs, pinpointing the twin checkpoints where the Poles and Ukrainians conducted their own hunt for illegal immigrants, cigarettes, drugs, and other contraband.

Long lines of semitrailer trucks and cars were backed up on the highway in both directions, waiting for clearance across the frontier. More vehicles filled the large lots adjacent to each customs and border inspection plaza or were parked nose to tail along the various connector roads.

The OSCE had erected three plain, prefabricated buildings just beyond the Ukrainian border crossing. One was a headquarters and communications center. Another provided living quarters for the twenty Romanian and Belarusian arms inspectors. The third building, larger than the others and the only one surrounded by a barbed-wire-topped fence, served both as a storage area for any confiscated weapons and an armory. There were no other defenses.

Voronov's thick lips pursed in disgust. This was his second inspection of the Starovoitove Station in the past twelve months and nothing had changed. The Romanian military police captain and his Belarusian counterpart refused to consider fortifying their post, insisting that maintaining good relations with the locals required a more open approach. Good relations with the Poles and the Ukrainians? *Kakaya yerunda*, the general thought. What bullshit!

Then he shrugged. Their carelessness about their own safety wasn't his problem.

"Lead, this is *Opekun One*," the senior gunship pilot radioed. "You are clear to land."

The driver of a huge MZKT Volant truck parked along the road watched the Russian utility helicopter fly low overhead and flare in for a landing next to the OSCE headquarters. His refrigerated semi-trailer carried the logo of a Donetsk-based frozen foods company.

He leaned forward and spoke softly into an intercom rigged between the cab and its trailer. "Our fat friend is arriving."

"And the two whores keeping him company?"

"Still circling, but I think they'll follow him in soon," the driver said, peering through his windshield to watch the two shark-nosed Ansat gunships orbiting over the border checkpoint.

"Very good," the voice from the trailer said. "Keep me informed."

Less than two hundred meters away, the helicopter carrying Voronov settled smoothly onto the landing pad. Its twin turboshaft engines spun down and stopped. Four soldiers in light blue berets, bulky body armor, and pixelated camouflage uniforms jumped out, bending low to clear the slowing rotors. Each carried a compact 9mm Bizon submachine gun. They fanned out across the pad, staying between the helicopter and the group of unarmed Romanian and Belarusian arms control monitors already lined up to greet their distinguished visitor.

Those were Voronov's Spetsnaz bodyguards, the truck driver realized. The Russian lieutenant general was a cautious man. Then he snorted softly. But perhaps not cautious enough.

Two Russian junior officers, clearly military aides, followed the bodyguards. They snapped to attention as Voronov himself clambered out of the helicopter cockpit and dropped heavily onto the tarmac. Straightening up, the general marched forward to exchange salutes with the two young officers assigned to command the OSCE station. Decked out in his full dress uniform, complete with peaked cap, jangling medals, and highly polished black boots, the burly, thickset Russian looked more like an overstuffed toy soldier than a cold-blooded killer.

If so, his looks were deceiving, the truck driver decided grimly. Both directly and indirectly, the commander of the 20th Guards Army was responsible for thousands of deaths.

One after another, the two Russian helicopter gunships settled onto the far end of the pad and cut their engines.

Trailed by his Spetsnaz bodyguards, Voronov and his hosts moved off toward the headquarters building. Behind them, the other Romanian and Belarusian arms control monitors dispersed, with some heading for their posts at the Ukrainian customs plaza and others to their off-duty living quarters. Voronov's pilot climbed out of the Ansat-U's cockpit and stretched, easing shoulders cramped during the long flight.

The truck driver clicked the intercom again. "The whores are in bed. It's time." Then Pavlo Lytvyn popped open the cab door and dropped lightly onto the grass verge running along the road. He carried an AKS-74U carbine wrapped in a lightweight windbreaker.

Inside the semitrailer, Fedir Kravchenko stood up. He turned to the others crowding its otherwise empty interior. A quick, warped grin flitted across his scarred face. "Right. Keep it nice and easy, boys. You're just getting some fresh air, remember? Stretching your legs during a short break from a long drive, eh?"

His men nodded. Most wore the set, grim expressions of those who had already killed enemies in battle and seen friends and comrades die. A few of the youngest, those without combat experience, looked pale but determined.

He unlatched one of the heavy back doors and stood aside. "Then off you go. Remember the plan. Follow your orders. And good luck!"

They filed out past him, ambling along the road toward OSCE post in scattered ones and twos. A few had leather jackets thrown over their shoulders to hide slung submachine guns—a mix of Israeli-designed UZIs, older Czech-made Skorpions, and newer Polish PM-84s. Others carried duffel bags carefully unzipped to allow quick access to the assault rifles and other weapons stashed inside.

Kravchenko was the last one out. Appreciatively, he slapped the thick insulation that had hidden them from the thermal sensors carried by the Russian helicopters. Voronov's flying guard dogs had gotten lazy, he thought. They'd switched on their high-tech IR gear and switched off their brains.

Pavlo Lytvyn joined him and together they strolled along the edge of the highway, bitching amicably and loudly about the lousy roads and the extortionate price of petrol.

Fifty meters from the front entrance to the OSCE headquarters building, Kravchenko knelt down, pretending to tie a shoelace. He risked a glance ahead. The Russian general's bodyguards were bunched around the door, joking and smoking cigarettes.

Sloppy, the Ukrainian thought coldly. With their boss safely tucked away inside that building, those supposedly elite commandos were acting as though they were off duty until it was time to escort the general back to his helicopter. He looked up at Lytvyn. "Everything set?"

The bigger man nodded, his eyes roving along the highway and around the OSCE compound. Their strike force was in position—carefully dispersed around the perimeter of their target. Some were prone in a drainage ditch that paralleled the road. Others crouched behind trees or had concealed themselves among the vehicles parked next to the compound's buildings, white official SUVs assigned to the joint Romanian and Belarusian arms control team.

"*Rozkryty peklo*," Kravchenko said stonily. "Unleash hell."

Still down on one knee, Kravchenko reached into his jacket pocket and pulled out a metal egg shape. It was a Russian-made RGN offensive fragmentation grenade. Without hesitating, he pulled the pin, making sure to keep a tight grip on the arming lever. Then he stood up and started walking steadily toward Voronov's bodyguards, holding the grenade low at his side.

Lyvtyn walked beside him, now grousing loudly about the crummy food at their last rest stop. "So I told that stupid cow of a waitress if I wanted to die of food poisoning, I'd eat my wife's cooking. I wouldn't pay fifty *hryvnias* for your slop!"

Kravchenko forced a laugh.

Forty-five meters.

His right hand ached from the strain of holding the grenade lever closed. A droplet of sweat stung his one good eye. Impatiently, he blinked it away.

They were forty meters away.

One of the Spetsnaz soldiers, turning away from his friends to light another cigarette, finally noticed them. Startled, he stared at the two Ukrainians for a long moment and then hurriedly nudged his closest comrade.

"*Stoi!* Hold it!" this one shouted, unslinging his submachine gun.

Thirty-five meters. Close enough.

Still moving, Kravchenko hurled the grenade toward the bunched-up Russian bodyguards. As it flew through the air, the arming lever popped off in a hissing shower of sparks and smoke.

Kravchenko and Lytvyn threw themselves flat.

The grenade hit the pavement right in the middle of the Russians and went off in a blinding flash. Ninety-seven grams of RDX explosive hurled jagged shards of aluminum outward at more than two thousand meters per second. All four soldiers were knocked down. Fragments that hit their body armor failed to penetrate the titanium and hard carbide boron ceramic chest- and backplates. Fragments that hit arms, legs, faces, or skulls punched through in a gruesome spray of blood and bits of shattered bone.

Before the echoes of the blast faded, the two Ukrainians were up and running toward the headquarters building. Lytvyn tossed his windbreaker aside and opened fire with his AKS carbine on the move, hammering the fallen Spetsnaz troops with short bursts. Hunks of bullet-shattered concrete danced and skittered away. Kravchenko drew a Makarov pistol from his shoulder holster and thumbed the safety off.

Off to their right, a rifle cracked—dropping the pilot of Voronov's helicopter with a single shot.

Across the pad, twin turboshaft engines whined shrilly as the crews of both Ansat gunships went for emergency starts. Slowly at first and then faster, their rotors started turning.

Two of Kravchenko's men broke cover and dashed

to the edge of the tarmac. They carried RPG-22 antitank rocket launchers. Both men stopped, braced, and fired almost simultaneously. Finned, rocket-propelled grenades streaked across the pad and slammed into the gunships.

The Ansat-2RCs blew up, torn apart by the RPG warheads and the detonation of their own fuel and ammunition. Twisted pieces of rotor and fuselage spiraled outward. Clouds of oily black smoke lit by fire boiled away from the heaps of blazing wreckage.

Pavlo Lytvyn charged into the OSCE headquarters building without slowing down. Kravchenko followed him.

Two ashen-faced Russian officers spun away from the windows looking out across the helicopter landing pad. They frantically clawed for the pistols holstered at their sides.

Lytvyn shot them at point-blank range and moved on down the central corridor.

The wide hallway ended in a door marked *BIROU DE COMANDĂ* and *KAMANDA OFIS*—"Command Office" in Romanian and Belarusian.

The big man kicked the door open and slid inside, moving sideways to cover the three stunned men—the two young officers who commanded this OSCE post and Lieutenant General Mikhail Voronov—grouped behind a large conference table covered with official documents and maps. He settled the stock of the AKS firmly against his shoulder. "Stay very still, gentlemen. And, please, keep your hands where I can see them."

Fedir Kravchenko entered the room. He heard the shocked, indrawn breaths when they saw the mutilated left side of his face. Kiev's best plastic surgeons had done their utmost to repair the damage, but there hadn't been much left for them to work with.

He moved behind Voronov and the others, deftly relieving them of their sidearms. He tossed the pistols across the room and stepped back a pace.

"What do you want from us?" one of the two OSCE officers asked stiffly, keeping his eyes locked on the unwavering muzzle of Lytvyn's carbine.

"From you? Nothing," Kravchenko said. He shrugged. "We are not your enemies. Once we're done here, you will be released safe and sound. Why, with a bit of luck, none of your men have even had their hair mussed."

"Then I suppose you want *me* as your hostage," Voronov growled.

With a faint smile, Kravchenko raised his Makarov and shot the Russian in the back of the head. "Wrong, General," he said quietly. "Dead men are useless as hostages."

Two minutes later, he led his strike team at a steady lope northwest across the tarmac. Skirting the burning Russian helicopters, they entered the forest, heading toward the Bug River several hundred meters away.

"You know those arms inspectors are going to start screaming for help over their cell phones any second now," Pavlo Lytvyn said.

"Yes, I know." Kravchenko nodded. He glanced

at his subordinate with another quick, humorless grin. "In fact, I'm counting on it."

OFFICE OF DR. HUNTER "BOOMER" NOBLE, CHIEF OF AEROSPACE ENGINEERING, SKYMASTERS, INC., BATTLE MOUNTAIN, NEVADA

"Thanks, guys!" Brad said cheerfully to the stone-faced corporate security guards who had just ushered him into the office. "I probably would have gotten lost without you."

The tall, lanky man sitting on the other side of the desk frowned. "Put him in a chair and get out," he told the guards. "I'll handle this."

Once the security personnel were gone, Brad looked across the desk with a wry grin. "Hey, Boomer! Long time no see."

Hunter "Boomer" Noble shook his head in disgust. "Christ, Brad. I thought you had a handle on that dumb-ass McLanahan temper of yours. And then you pull a stunt like this?" He leaned forward. "Do you have any idea of the kind of money Sky Masters is going to have to lay out to keep this son of a bitch Carson from filing criminal assault charges against you?"

"A lot?" Brad guessed.

"Yes, a lot," Boomer said. "As in free tuition for his courses and probably at least a six-figure, tax-free settlement."

"Ouch."

"Yeah. Ouch," Boomer agreed. He sighed. "Look, I went to bat for you with Richter and Kaddiri for this internship. They admired your dad, but they didn't always see eye to eye with him. And they are not going to be real happy to hear that his son shares his less appealing qualities."

Brad nodded. As chief executive officer and chairman of the board respectively, Jason Richter and Helen Kaddiri ran Sky Masters as a tight-knit team. They didn't exactly manage business matters with a nakedly iron hand, but there was definitely a touch of something hard and inflexible inside the velvet glove. According to the corporate rumor mill, they were also a heck of a lot more than mere business associates, but nobody had any hard evidence of a romantic affair.

"Sorry, Boomer," he said, trying to put a little sincere contriteness into his voice. In truth, he was genuinely sorry. Despite the long hours and lack of pay, this internship at Sky Masters had been a dream come true. In two months, he had picked up more about the subjects he really loved—flying, aerospace technology, and tactics—than he could ever have learned in four years at the Air Force Academy in Colorado Springs or at Cal Poly–San Luis Obispo, where he was a student of aerospace engineering.

"I bet you really are," Boomer said. He shook his head again. "But you still couldn't stop yourself from going apeshit crazy on that asshole."

"I *was* provoked," Brad pointed out.

"Maybe by the letter of the law," Boomer agreed. "Too bad that's not the way the corporate world works, even here at Sky Masters."

"Which means what exactly?" Brad prompted.

"Which means you're out," Boomer told him. "Canned. Axed. Terminated with prejudice. Pick your own favorite phrase." He sighed again. "Look, Brad, ordinarily I don't do shit for someone I'm firing, especially not some jackass intern. But I respected your dad a hell of a lot . . . so I'm giving you a onetime severance package." He tossed a manila folder across the desk. "There. Don't waste it."

Brad flipped open the folder and found himself staring at his passport, a plane ticket to Mexico, and several thousand dollars in cash. Caught by surprise, he looked up at Boomer.

"Go spend some time hanging out on the beach with the señoritas and get your head screwed on straight, before you restart school," the other man said. "Just don't plan on blowing the next forty years playing around in the sand, okay?"

This time Brad caught the twinkle in Boomer's eye. Forty years in the desert. EXODUS. Right. Now he knew who had relayed his father's signal through the simulator program. He grinned back across the desk. "I'll be a good boy, Dr. Noble," he said. "I promise I won't cause any more trouble."

"See that you don't," Hunter Noble said with a wry smile. He cocked his head to one side. "But I hope you won't mind if I don't hold my breath on that promise of yours. Because I sure don't hear any ice freezing over down in hell."

CHAPTER 2

*Every adversity, every failure,
every heartache carries with it the
seed of an equal or greater benefit.*

—Napoleon Hill,
American author

OVER UKRAINE
Thirty minutes later

Two Russian Air Force Su-34 fighter-bombers in black, white, and light blue camouflage streaked west, flying low over the flat Ukrainian countryside. Precision-guided bombs, antiradiation missiles, and air-to-air missiles hung from their external hardpoints.

The lead pilot, Major Viktor Zelin, caught sight of smoke from the wrecked helicopters rising on the horizon. He throttled back as he banked into a hard turn and climbed—a maneuver copied by his wingman, flying in loose formation aft and about two kilometers off his right wing. He craned his neck to get a quick look at the Starovoitove station as it flashed below, catching a fleeting glimpse of flashing blue lights on the highway and around the OSCE post. It looked like the Ukrainian police were on the scene, he thought. *Nu i chto?* Well, so what? What good were ordinary policemen going to do against a murderous terrorist gang? Especially one that was probably made up of their bastard countrymen?

"Inform Voronezh Control that we have the attack area in sight," he told the navigation and weapons officer in the right-hand seat.

"Sending now," Captain Nikolai Starikov acknowledged. He transmitted the message using a series of short, three-figure Morse codes, and then checked the glowing multifunction map display in front of him. "We're right up against the border," he warned. "We're going to stray across into Polish airspace."

"No shit," Zelin grunted, continuing the turn and bleeding off more speed. Even with its superb maneuverability and flying just fast enough to stay in the air, the Su-34 had a turning radius measured in kilometers. There was no way his flight could orbit close enough to the OSCE post to keep it in sight and stay entirely on the Ukrainian side of the frontier.

Suddenly a warning tone sounded in both men's headsets.

"Search radar spike," Starikov said, studying his displays. "L-band. Single emitter. Computer evaluates it as a long-range Polish RAT 31DL radar. Strength is sufficient to detect us."

"No surprise now that we're off the deck," the major commented. He showed his teeth. "But I bet some fucking Pole just crapped his pants when we popped up onto his screen." Then he shrugged against his harness. "Let's hear what they have to say."

"Switching to GUARD channel," Starikov reported. The international emergency channel was commonly used for communication between aircraft and ground stations belonging to different nations.

"This is the Warsaw Operations Center calling the two aircraft now turning two hundred and twenty-five degrees over Starovoitove at one thousand meters, identify yourselves. Repeat. Identify yourselves," a Polish-accented voice said in their earphones.

"Nice of him to speak Russian," Zelin snorted. He keyed his mike. "Warsaw Operations Center, this is Sentinel Flight Leader."

"Sentinel Leader, you are on course to violate our airspace!" the Polish air defense controller radioed. "Withdraw to the east immediately. Repeat. Turn east immediately!"

The major glanced at his subordinate. "Find out what Voronezh wants us to do. Meanwhile, I'll try to buy us some time."

Starikov nodded, already tapping out another series of short Morse codes that would alert their own commander to their situation and ask for new orders.

"Warsaw Center, this is Sentinel Leader," the Su-34 pilot said. "Regret unable to comply with your request. We are conducting an emergency antiterrorist operation."

"That is not a request, Sentinel Flight!" the Polish air defense controller snapped.

Zelin and his comrade stiffened as another warbling tone, shriller this time, sounded in their headsets.

"X-band tracking and fire control radar. Forward right quadrant," Starikov said tightly. "Source is an SNR-125 and it has a lock!"

"Damn it," the major muttered. That was the radar used by S-125M Neva surface-to-air missile system, the type NATO code-named the SA-3B Goa. Though old, it was still a highly capable weapon, especially with the digital component upgrades the Poles had made. Plus, circling like this left them sitting ducks against a SAM attack. If he stayed, he was risking two billion-ruble fighter-bombers.

He shook his head. It was a losing proposition. And no one in Moscow would thank him for triggering a shooting war with Poland without positive orders.

Followed by his wingman in the second Su-34, Zelin banked harder and dove, turning back to the east. The radar warning faded away.

"Voronezh approves a withdrawal to an ACP thirty kilometers east of the frontier," the navigator told him, entering coordinates on one of the keypads at his station. "Cue up."

Faintly glowing bars appeared on Zelin's HUD, above and to the right of his current course. He pulled back on the stick and turned, centering the bars on his display. These flight-director bars were a navigation cue that would lead them toward the

ACP, the air control point, selected by the staff back at Voronezh's Malshevo Air Base. Once there, the two Su-34s would fly a racetrack holding pattern designed to conserve their fuel.

"And when we get there, Nikolai? Then what?" he asked angrily, still furious at having been forced to turn tail and run. "Do we just fly around and around while those bastard Poles practice their radar search techniques against us?"

Starikov ignored his commander's ill-tempered outburst. He was too busy reading their new orders, freshly decoded by the Su-34's computers, as they scrolled across his display. "No, sir," he told Zelin. "We're ordered to provide on-call air support for a Spetnaz quick reaction force. They've been tasked to hunt down and kill these terrorists, and their transport helicopters and Mi-24 attack helicopters are only ten minutes out. Vornezh is also vectoring two Su-35 fighters to the ACP to back us up. Further orders will come straight from the Kremlin."

Major Viktor Zelin took that in and then smiled broadly. "*Otlichno!* Excellent! Maybe somebody in the high command just grew a pair!"

2ND SPETSNAZ BRIGADE QUICK REACTION FORCE, AT THE BUG RIVER
Thirty minutes later

Spetsnaz Captain Kirill Aristov saw his lead scout's silent hand signal and dropped prone. The rest of his command group did the same, taking cover among the bushes, moss-covered stumps, and saplings crowding the forest floor. Off on either flank, his other squads also halted and went to ground.

Carefully cradling his AN-94 assault rifle in both arms, he wriggled quietly forward to the scout's position behind a stunted pine tree. "Well, Chapayev?" he hissed. "What is it?"

The scout, a grizzled long-term professional soldier with combat experience in Chechnya, Georgia, and Ukraine, jabbed a thumb at a spot about a meter up the trunk of the pine tree. Something or someone had brushed up against one smaller branches, more a twig really, and almost snapped it off. The branch dangled loosely, hanging by a thin strip of bark.

Aristov reached up and rubbed his fingers across the torn bark. The break was fresh, still smelling strongly of pine sap. The scout raised a single eyebrow. *You see?* he mouthed silently.

The Spetsnaz officer nodded his understanding. The terrorists they were chasing were probably not far ahead.

Cautiously, he peered around the tree trunk.

They were very close to the river, within a dozen meters or so. The ground, still covered by trees and clumps of brush, sloped gently to the water's edge. But everything was still, motionless except where a light breeze stirred the forest undergrowth. Then Aristov looked closer. At several places along the bank, flattened patches in the tall grass showed where heavy objects had been dragged along the ground.

He laid his assault rifle down and took a pair of

binoculars out of one of the pouches on his tactical vest. Raising the binoculars to his eyes, he swept them slowly from side to side—scanning the opposite bank of the river. Along this stretch, the Bug was only about thirty meters wide.

Aristov could see more spots where the vegetation had been disturbed. And he just barely could make out something odd a little deeper among the woods, something dark-colored among the lighter green of the grass and bushes. He focused his binoculars on that spot.

The shape of a black rubber inflatable boat jumped out at him, roughly camouflaged with tree branches, uprooted bushes, and swaths of torn grass.

He swore under his breath. The terrorists had crossed into Polish territory.

Still scowling, Aristov crawled back to the waiting command group. He motioned his radioman over and grabbed the handset. "Hunter Group One to Hunter Command Prime."

"Prime to Hunter One, go ahead." Despite the hiss and crackle of static, that deep resonant voice was unmistakable. "Make your report!"

The Spetsnaz captain swallowed hard. "I'm afraid that we have a serious problem, Mr. President."

THE KREMLIN, MOSCOW
That same time

President of the Russian Federation Gennadiy Gryzlov tightened his grip on the secure phone as he listened to Aristov's reluctant confession of failure. The terrorists who had murdered Lieutenant General Voronov and his men had escaped—crossing into safe haven on Polish soil. When the Spetsnaz officer finished his report, Gryzlov said nothing for several moments.

This uncharacteristically calm reaction made his national security staff extremely uneasy.

In public, Russia's forty-one-year-old president was confident, always unruffled, and charming. Those qualities, plus his youthful good looks and the vast wealth he'd earned from his family's oil, gas, and petrochemicals companies, had brought him to power in a landslide election victory three years before. In private, however, Gryzlov was known for his fiery temper, towering rages, and utter disdain for anyone he believed had failed him.

So now the hastily assembled group of aides, cabinet ministers, generals, and intelligence chiefs waited nervously for their leader's inevitable tirade.

It did not come.

"Very well, I understand," Gryzlov said into the phone. He checked the nearest clock, an action slavishly imitated by his cabinet ministers and top aides. Just over an hour had passed since the terrorists butchered Voronov and the others. "Hold your force in position, Captain. I will call you back shortly with new instructions."

He hung up and stood tapping his fingers on the table, deep in thought. Then he turned to his minister of defense, Gregor Sokolov. "Show me a map of that sector, at the largest scale you have."

"Yes, Mr. President," Sokolov said hurriedly. He

was all too aware that Russia's chief executive might soon be looking for a scapegoat. He motioned frantically to one of his staff officers, an elderly, grayhaired colonel from the Military Topographic Directorate. "Get it up on the big screen, Isayev! Now!"

The colonel flipped open his laptop, quickly and efficiently sorted through a series of digitized maps, selected one, and then sent it wirelessly to the conference room's enormous flat-screen display.

Whistling tonelessly to himself, Gryzlov moved closer to the display, peering intently at the patterned landscape of woods, bogs, farmland, small villages, and roads it showed. With one finger, he traced the meandering line of the Bug River. He turned toward the colonel. "These depth markings for the river? They are accurate?"

"To a degree, Mr. President," the staff officer agreed. He hunched his narrow shoulders, thinking out loud. "The Bug's depth varies significantly from season to season—depending on rainfall and runoff. But those figures are a reasonable approximation. In fact, given the dry summer so far, it is probable the river is even shallower than depicted."

"*Ochen' khorosho!* Very good!" Gryzlov said drily, fighting down the urge to rip the other man apart for lecturing him as though he were a schoolboy. This cartographic colonel might be a dreary pedant, but at least he was competent.

He swung away from the map and picked up the secure phone. "Hunter One? This is Hunter Command Prime. Listen carefully. You and your troops will ford the river and continue your pursuit. You will find those terrorists and destroy them! Understood?"

"Yes, Mr. President!" Aristov's taut voice came through the crackling background static. "It is possible that the terrorists had vehicles waiting for them on the other side of the river. If so, my men will not be able to catch them on foot."

"Then you will follow them by air, using your helicopters."

"And if the Poles interfere?" the young officer asked.

"You will use whatever force is necessary to clear them from your path," Gryzlov told him. "Including the use of the fighter and bomber aircraft already on scene. Clear?"

"Very clear!" the Spetsnaz captain said crisply. "Your orders will be obeyed."

Gryzlov hung up and turned to look at the stunned faces of his national security advisers. A predatory smile flickered across his face and then vanished. "Do any of you doubt my decision?" he asked.

"I do not doubt your right to make this decision," Foreign Minister Daria Titeneva said slowly. "I only wonder if such haste to invade the territory of a member of the NATO alliance is wise. Poland will not turn a blind eye to the presence of our commandos."

Gryzlov's cold-eyed gaze caught hers for a moment and then ran up and down her lush, full body. She reddened slightly. They were occasional lovers, but apparently his dark-haired foreign minister still had a mind of her own. "Our need to act quickly is precisely *why* the Poles cannot stop us!" he snapped.

"You are claiming the right of hot pursuit," Sergei Tarzarov, his chief of staff, realized. "The right to chase criminals and terrorists across international borders."

The Russian president nodded smugly. "Exactly. The Americans have used this doctrine to excuse their intrusions into Mexico, Pakistan, and dozens of other weaker countries around the world. Now we shall apply their own legalistic reasoning against one of their own allies."

It was no surprise that thin, plain-looking Tarzarov was ahead of the others, Gryzlov thought. The shrewd old man had been a power inside the Kremlin for decades, first as an intelligence officer, then as minister of the interior, and now as his top aide. Rumor said that Tarzarov knew where all the bodies were buried in Russian politics. Other rumors, darker ones, said that was true because he'd buried most of them personally.

"We may have such a right in law," Tarzarov cautioned. "But this situation could easily escalate."

"Perhaps," Gryzlov agreed. He shrugged. "If so, we have sufficient force in hand to prevail in any localized conflict. And by the time larger Polish forces can intervene, our quick reaction force will be long gone."

He turned back to Titeneva. "Contact the Poles. Tell them what we're doing. Make it clear that we are *not* asking for their permission, and that we expect their full cooperation in this matter."

"No matter how it turns out, Warsaw will protest

vigorously," the foreign minister told him. Her dark eyes were troubled. "They will undoubtedly contact NATO and the European Union as well."

Gryzlov showed his teeth. "Oh, I hope the Poles do," he said. "I would enjoy watching their new president squirm and wriggle while he whines about us going after terrorists operating from Polish soil!"

WEST BANK OF THE BUG RIVER
That same time

Captain Kirill Aristov waded the last few meters of the river with his assault rifle and equipment vest held high over his head. With water dripping from his soaked fatigues and boots, he came sloshing up onto the opposite bank and dropped to one knee. The rest of his commandos were close behind. Moving rapidly, they fanned out, forming a defensive perimeter around the crossing site.

He unzipped the waterproof case containing his tablet computer and pulled up the map file Moscow had transmitted moments before they crossed the Bug. At first glance, this part of the west side of the Bug River seemed much like the Ukrainian side of the border, but that was deceptive. Beyond a narrow belt of pine trees and scraggly oaks, the countryside opened up into a mix of ponds, shallow streams, and flat meadows and pastureland.

The lieutenants and senior sergeants who commanded his four ten-man teams formed a circle around him, watching closely while he sketched out their orders.

"Berezin, Dobrynin, and Larionov, take your men and scout west," Aristov said, tracing a line with his stylus. "My command group will follow you. Look for signs of foot or vehicle traffic. Stay sharp. The terrorists who hit Voronov and our guys might not be too far ahead. So get moving!"

They nodded once and darted off, already waving their commandos into action. Soldiers bent low under the weight of their gear and weapons slipped off through the trees.

Aristov turned to his remaining team leader. "Milekhin, split your section in two. Deploy them at the north and south edge of these woods. You're my reserve and flank guard, clear?"

"*Da*, Captain!" the lieutenant said. "Don't worry. We'll keep everyone off your back."

Once the last of his troops were in motion, the Spetsnaz captain looked for Chapayev. The veteran scout was squatting silently a few meters away, methodically checking over his rifle and equipment.

He glanced up with a quick flash of tobacco-stained teeth. "And my orders, Captain?"

"Take a good hard look at those rubber boats and the ground around them," Aristov said. "See if you can pick up anything that might let us identify these terrorists. But watch out for booby traps. These bastards seem to know what they're doing."

The scout nodded once and vanished among the trees and bushes.

Surrounded by his command group, Aristov headed west, advancing deeper into Poland.

"To szalone, Panie Poruczniku!" Polish Border Guard sergeant Konrad Malek shouted into his cell phone. "This is crazy, Lieutenant! I've got eight men with me and we're mostly trained to arrest smugglers and illegals. How in hell am I supposed to stop what looks like a full-scale invasion by fucking Russian commandos?"

"No one's asking you to *stop* them, Konrad," his commander said calmly, still safely ensconced back in his cozy office at the Dorohusk Border Control Point. "We only want you to slow them down while the bigwigs in Warsaw get through to the Kremlin."

"And how the devil do I slow them down?" Malek growled. "Write them a ticket for trespassing?"

"See if you can contact their leader and—"

"Sergeant!"

Malek turned to see one of his men pointing east across the meadow. They had parked their two patrol cars on a rutted farm track about two hundred meters west of the woods lining the Bug River. Heavily armed Russian soldiers in camouflage battle dress were exiting the trees there and shaking out in a long skirmish line.

"Never mind, Lieutenant," said Malek grimly. "We're out of time here. Our uninvited guests from the east have arrived." He disconnected and turned to his corporal. "Hand me that bullhorn,

Eryk. Let's find out if we can talk some sense into these people."

Gritting his teeth, he walked out into the open pasture. He raised the bullhorn. "*Uwaga, Rosyjscy żołnierze!* Attention, Russian soldiers! This is Sergeant Malek of the Border Guard. You are in violation of Polish national territory—"

Suddenly a rifle shot rang out, echoing off the distant trees and across the open fields.

AT THE BUG RIVER
That same time

Spetsnaz scout Ivan Chapayev crouched down to look more closely at the black inflatable boat his captain had spotted earlier. It had been dragged up from the riverbank and back into the shadows under the trees. Broken branches, clumps of brush, and bundles of grass were heaped across the boat in a crude attempt to conceal it.

Lips compressed in concentration, Chapayev used the thin blade of his combat knife to gently edge aside heaps of the tangled plant debris. Careful, Ivan, he told himself. Take it nice and easy. If he missed just one little booby-trap detonator wire, his wife would get a fancy embossed letter of condolence with President Gryzlov's signature on it, suitable for framing. He chuckled. Hell, that sour bitch Yulia would probably just pawn it for a cheap bottle of vodka.

Nothing.

He sat back, frowning.

The terrorists who had tried to camouflage this boat had done a pretty piss-poor job of it. Even his captain, a decent enough officer but not the most observant of men, had picked it out from all the way across the river. On the other hand, those terrorists must have heard the clattering rotors of Russian helicopters pounding in their ears while they sculled across the water. That had probably pushed them right to the edge of panic. So it was no surprise that the terrorists had just heaped whatever vegetation they could grab on top of the boat in a frantic bid to hide it.

Then he looked more closely at the bundles of long grass he had pushed away. They were withered, already turning brown in the summer heat. Those bundles had been cut and put in place hours ago.

Chapayev's eyes widened. He scrambled to his feet, reaching for the short-range tactical radio clipped to his collar. The terrorists had *not* been in a hurry when they'd hidden this boat. They'd heaped all this crap across it long before they slaughtered Voronov and his men. Which meant the inflatable raft had never been used as part of an escape across the Bug River into Poland.

Which meant—

A 7.62mm round moving at 830 meters per second hit the veteran Spetsnaz scout in the face and tore out through the back of his head.

Crack!

Ivan Chapayev was dead before the sound of the shot arrived.

* * *

Several hundred meters to the north, lying prone in a clump of brush on the Ukrainian side of the river, Pavlo Lytvyn peered through the SVD Dragunov sniper rifle's telescopic sight for another few seconds. "No movement," he said finally with grim satisfaction. "My target is down."

Fedir Kravchenko clapped him on the shoulder. "Nicely done!"

The sudden crackle of automatic weapons fire brought a smile to his face. The trigger-happy Poles and Russians were shooting at each other. Killing that fat pig Voronov had been satisfying, but it was only part of a larger plan—a plan that was unfolding successfully. He had lured the Russian Federation into a direct armed confrontation with a member of the NATO alliance. Perhaps now the West would push back against the Kremlin's domination of his beloved country!

"Time to go, Pavlo," Kravchenko said. "We're finished here."

Nodding, the bigger man packed up his sniper rifle and followed his leader back through the carefully camouflaged entrance of their hideout, a concrete bunker dug deep into the riverbank. Originally built by the Soviets as part of the so-called Molotov Defense Line during their 1939–1941 occupation of eastern Poland, the half-buried bunker had moldered away for decades—forgotten by everyone except the odd Romany tramp or occasional kayaking tourists taking refuge during a thunderstorm. By the time anyone official stumbled across it, Kravchenko and his men would be long gone.

AIR CONTROL POINT ALPHA, OVER THE UKRAINE
That same time

Four thousand meters above the Ukrainian countryside, Major Viktor Zelin jogged his Su-34 fighter-bomber's stick slightly left, beginning another lazy, slow racetrack turn. His eyes flicked to the fuel indicator. They still had plenty of flying time left before they would have to break away and refuel.

He glanced out the canopy, making sure his wingman was still in position. The other Su-34 was right where it was supposed to be, hanging back about a kilometer off his wing tip. Two mottled green, brown, and tan specks were just visible off to the north, circling low above the mosaic of woods and fields. The two single-seater Su-35 fighters sent to back them up were staying well down on the deck, avoiding Polish radar detection.

"*My popali v zasadu!* We've been ambushed!" The Spetsnaz captain's frantic radio call broke into his headset. "A sniper just killed one of my men and now we're taking fire!"

In the seat beside him, Starikov keyed his mike. "This is Sentinel Leader, Hunter One. Do you need air support? Over."

"Hell, yes!" the Spetsnaz commander shouted. They could hear gunfire in the background, rising steadily in volume. "We're pinned down at the edge of the trees along the river, with terrorists to our front. Range is between two and three hundred meters. I can paint the target for you with a laser!"

Zelin frowned. That was awfully close for an air strike, even with precision-guided munitions. One little equipment or computer glitch could strew their bombs across friendly troops, not the enemy.

"Can you break contact?" Starikov asked, obviously thinking the same thing.

"Negative! Negative! We've practically got our backs up against the river as it is!"

"Understood, Hunter One," the navigation and weapons officer said with a shrug. If the commandos were willing to take the risk, so be it. He saw Zelin's confirming nod and added, "Start lasing your target. We're approximately three minutes out from your position."

"Did you get that, Sentinel Two?" Zelin asked his wingman.

"Two," a laconic voice said, responding with his position in the formation.

"I'll make the bomb run," Zelin told the other pilot. "You hang back about five kilometers. If the Poles bring up that damned SAM radar again, get ready to nail it on my command! Clear?"

"Two."

The major switched his attention to the leader of the Su-35 flight. "*Drobovik* Lead, cover us. But stay low for now."

"Shotgun Lead acknowledges," the fighter commander replied. "Just don't leave us down eating dust too much longer, Major. I've already practically harvested some clodhopper's wheat field for him the hard way."

Zelin grinned. "Very good, Shotgun. Out." He glanced at Starikov. "Let's use two KAB-500Ls."

"I concur," the weapons officer said. "They're the best option." He began entering commands into his attack computer.

New flight-director bars appeared on Zelin's HUD, marking the course selected by the computer's bomb program. He pulled back on the stick and increased power to the Su-34's two Saturn turbofan engines. The fighter-bomber climbed fast, soaring toward an altitude of seven thousand meters at more than eight hundred kilometers per hour.

The KAB-500L was a five-hundred-kilogram laser-guided bomb. In service for more than three decades, it was a powerful and accurate weapon—able to deliver its high-explosive warhead within a few meters of a chosen target. But it had weaknesses, ones it shared with other laser-guided weapons. Attacking with full precision required dropping the bomb within a relatively small "basket." This was a zone that met two basic requirements: the KAB's seeker head had to be able to see the targeting laser, and the bomb itself had to be high enough and falling fast enough to guide itself all the way to the laser-designated target.

In this attack, Zelin and Starikov would have to drop their bombs from an altitude of at least seven thousand meters, which meant their Su-34 would be more vulnerable to attack by Polish SAMs if Warsaw decided to escalate the situation.

"Ten kilometers to estimated release point," Starikov reported, echoing the data shown on Zelin's HUD.

A shrill radar warning warbled in both crewmen's headsets.

"X-band. Single emitter," Starikov said, peering at his displays. "It's that same SNR-125."

"Sentinel Lead, this is Two," their wingman radioed. "Shall I take it out?"

"Negative," Zelin said. "We're still well outside Polish airspace. They're not going to risk firing first."

Or so he hoped.

Technically, of course, he and Starikov were not going to be attacking from inside Polish territory. Since their bombs would have to fly more than nine kilometers to reach the terrorists shooting up those Spetsnaz troops, they would be released in Ukrainian airspace. Somehow, though, he doubted the Poles would care much about that little legal nicety once bombs starting exploding on their side of the river.

Sweating now, he focused on flying his aircraft right down the path selected by the attack computer, making small adjustments with the stick and throttles to stay on course and speed.

"Five kilometers," Starikov told him. The weapons officer keyed his mike, radioing the Spetsnaz team they were supporting. "Hunter, this is Sentinel. Keep that laser on target, but get your heads down now! We are attacking!"

Twin growling bass notes sounded in their earphones. The KAB seeker heads "saw" the targeting laser. Ten seconds later, the flight-director bars on Zelin's HUD flashed bright green. They were in range. He punched the release button on his stick. "Weapons away!"

The Su-34 bounced upward slightly as two laser-guided bombs fell away from under its wings. Zelin yanked the stick left, rolling the aircraft into an immediate tight, high-G turn to the southeast. If the Poles reacted badly, he wanted a lot more maneuvering room.

"Weapon impact!" he heard Starikov yell.

Fighting against the g-forces they were pulling, the major turned his head all the way to the right, straining to see through the canopy beyond Starikov's white flight helmet. There, low on the horizon, a huge cloud of smoke and tumbling debris and dirt marked the point where their bombs had slammed into the ground and exploded.

"On target! On target!" they both heard the Spetsnaz officer yelling over the radio. "The terrorists are dead! We are advancing!"

"Lead, this is Two!" their wingman snapped, drowning out the excited commando captain. "SAM launch! Two S-125s inbound at your six!"

Zelin slammed the stick even harder left and shoved his throttles into full afterburner. Accelerating past the speed of sound, the Su-34 turned tightly, breaking northeast across the path of the incoming missiles.

Beside him, Starikov frantically punched buttons to activate their countermeasures systems. The large jammer pod mounted below their fuselage went active, pouring out energy to degrade the accuracy of the Polish radars. Automated chaff dispensers fired, hurling cartridges into the air behind the fast-moving Su-34. They exploded, spewing thousands of small Mylar strips across the sky.

He looked to his left. Two plumes of dirty white

smoke were visible against the light blue sky, curving toward them. Shit. Their jammer and chaff blooms weren't working. The Polish SAMs were still locked on to their aircraft.

The major rolled the Su-34 inverted and dove for the ground. "Two, this is Lead," he said. "Hit that goddamned radar!"

"Kh-31 away!" his wingman yelled.

Zelin rolled out of his dive at less than a thousand meters. He risked another glance to the left.

A tiny bright dot trailed by smoke streaked northwest and then winked out. Then it flared again, slashing even faster across the sky. The Kh-31P antiradiation missile had a first-stage solid-rocket motor that kicked it up to Mach 1.8 just after launch. At burnout, its rocket motor fell away and a kerosene-fueled ramjet boosted the missile past Mach 4.

Seconds later, Zelin saw a blinding flash far off in the distance.

"That SNR-125 is off the air," Starikov reported.

And probably dead, the major thought coldly. Even if the Poles had detected his wingman's ARM launch and switched their radar off, the Kh-31 had an inertial guidance system that would take it all the way home to the target.

Zelin glanced aft. Without command guidance from their fire control radar, the Polish SAMs were going ballistic, corkscrewing wildly high into the atmosphere.

He breathed out, starting to relax.

And then swore bitterly as another shrill radar warning sounded in his headset.

"Two airborne radars operating in the X-band," Starikov said. "Computer evaluates them as pulse-Doppler N-O19 Phazotrons. Signal strength is weak, but increasing."

Zelin keyed his mike, calling the two Su-35 fighters attached to his force. "Shotgun Flight, this is Sentinel Lead. It looks like you're going to have to earn your pay after all. We have Polish MiG-29s inbound."

LYNX FLIGHT, 1ST TACTICAL SQUADRON, POLISH AIR FORCE, OVER EASTERN POLAND
That same time

Two Polish MiG-29 Fulcrum fighters, camouflaged in dark and light gray, raced southeast toward the border with Ukraine.

Inside the cockpit of the lead aircraft, Captain Marek Kaczor was trying very hard not to let his increasing exasperation boil over into rage. "Say again, Warsaw Operations Center. Exactly what kind of mess are you ordering us into?"

"The situation is unclear, *Ryś* Lead," the controller said. Kaczor could almost hear the man's apologetic shrug. "We have confused reports of Russian troops on the ground west of the Bug River. And now a SAM battery of the Sixtieth Rocketry Squadron says it has fired on Russian fighter-bombers."

"Fired on the Russians!?" Kaczor exclaimed. "Jesus Christ! Are we at war?"

"This situation is—"

"Unclear," the MiG-29 pilot growled, interrupting. "Fine. Great. Wonderful. Look, did the SAMs hit anything?"

"We've lost communication with the battery," the controller admitted.

Briefly, Kaczor closed his eyes, fighting down the urge to cut loose with a wave of profanity that would probably deafen anyone listening in and earn him yet another reprimand from his squadron commander. Just as quickly, he opened them again. His MiG-29s were already flying blind in a figurative sense. There was no point in doing the same thing literally.

"Well, what *can* you tell me, then?" he asked with exaggerated patience.

"We have intermittent radar contact with two rapidly maneuvering unidentified aircraft over the border area," the controller told him carefully. "We evaluate them as Russian Su-34s."

Kaczor absorbed that in silence. According to the best intelligence he'd seen, the Su-34 carried a multimode phased-array radar that could pick out fighter-sized targets at up to ninety kilometers in all aspects. That was a hell of lot better than the old Soviet piece-of-shit Phazotron in his MiG-29 could do. He'd be lucky to spot the Russians at seventy kilometers and that would only be if they were flying right out in front of him. Against aircraft coming up behind, he wouldn't get pings until they were within thirty-five kilometers.

In a short-range aerial knife fight, the Polish pilot was sure his Fulcrum and its AA-11 Archer heat-seeking missiles could defeat the bigger, somewhat less maneuverable Russian planes. The problem would be surviving long enough to get into close range. He wished again that the air force had installed a better radar as part of the major avionics upgrades they had applied to the MiG-29s.

"So . . . what are my orders, Center?" he asked finally.

"We need you to clarify the situation," the controller said. This time there was no mistaking the embarrassment in his voice. "Do not engage the Russians unless you are fired upon. Observe and report only, if possible."

"Understood, Center," Kaczor said through gritted teeth. "Lynx Flight Leader, out."

He checked his American-made digital navigational display. He and his wingman, Lieutenant Milosz Czarny, were already within one hundred kilometers of the border. At this speed, they should be able to detect those Russian Su-34s in just a couple of minutes.

"You heard the man, Milosz," he radioed the other pilot. "Finger off the trigger, okay?"

"*Jak dla mnie, w porządku!* Fine by me!" Czarny said. "You know this stinks, right?"

"*Stinks* is too nice a word," Kaczor replied. "So we do this carefully. We go in. We take a peek. And if this is a real shooting war and not some diplomatic clusterfuck, we bug out and wait for backup. Okay?"

Czarny waggled the wings of his MiG-29 in emphatic agreement. "Copy that—"

BEEP-BEEP-BEEP.

For a split second, Kaczor froze in horror. Then his eyes flashed to the readout from his radar warning receiver. They were being painted by Irbis-E phased-array radars—the kind of radar system carried by Russia's ultra-advanced Su-35 fighters. That was bad. Very bad. What made it worse was realizing that the Su-35s were already *behind* them. And they were well within missile range.

"Break! Break! Break!" he screamed into the radio.

Captain Marek Kaczor threw his MiG-29 into a radical, high-G diving turn while simultaneously punching out chaff and flares to decoy radar-guided and heat-seeking missiles.

Deceived by the chaff blooms or thrown out of lock by his wild maneuvering, three long-range R-77E missiles streaked past his canopy and vanished. But three more got close enough for their laser proximity fuses to detonate. Lacerated by dozens of hits from razor-edged shrapnel, the Fulcrum tumbled out of control and then blew up. Burning fuel and fragments drifted north on the prevailing wind.

Milosz Czarny's MiG-29 died the same way seconds later.

Against an ordinary opponent in a stand-up fight, the evasive tactics adopted by Kaczor and his wingman might have worked—or at least bought him enough time to retaliate. Unfortunately for the Poles, this was not a stand-up fight. This was a brutal and thoroughly effective ambush.

Alerted by Zelin's Su-34s, the Russian Su-35s had swung wide to the north and then turned back southwest, darting just above trees, buildings, and power lines to come up undetected behind the Polish fighters. Once in position, they climbed fast,

acquired the Poles on their radar, and fired six Mach
4+ R-77E radar-guided missiles, known to NATO
as AA-12 Adders, at each Fulcrum.

The two Polish pilots never had a chance.

THE KREMLIN, MOSCOW
A short time later

President Gennadiy Gryzlov paid close attention to
the young Spetsnaz captain's radioed report. The
large-scale map displayed on the conference room
monitor made it easy to follow the quick reaction
force's movements. After laser-guided bombs wiped
out the gunmen who had ambushed them, Aristov
and his troops had advanced southwest, pushing
across open cropland toward a small village close to
the Polish customs inspection plaza. All local farm
tracks led in that direction, which strongly suggested it was the path taken by the surviving terrorists.

Scratch that *suggested*, Gryzlov told himself, listening to the crackle of small-arms and automatic
weapons fire in the background. The Spetsnaz
troops must have run straight into a terrorist hideout. After all, who else could be stupid enough to be
shooting at his troops from those farmhouses and
cottages?

"We're meeting stiff resistance, Mr. President,"
Aristov said, raising his voice to be heard over the
sound of battle. "I have three men seriously wounded

and one more dead. I've deployed a team to flank
the village, but the ground is very difficult—"

"Mr. President?" a hesitant voice interrupted.

"Hold a moment, Captain," Gryzlov said. Impatiently, he turned away from the map. Viktor Kazyanov, the minister of state security, stood there
looking worried. "Yes? What is it?" he snapped.

"I am not sure that our troops are fighting terrorists," his intelligence chief said reluctantly. "Our signals intelligence units have intercepted cell-phone
calls which strongly suggest that village is being defended by elements of the local Polish Border Guard
detachment."

"Bullshit!" Gryzlov growled. "Since when do
customs inspectors carry assault rifles and machine
guns?"

"Many of the border-guard units have paramili-
tary training and equipment," Kazyanov told him.

"And if these bastards killing our men *are* wearing nice, neat, official-looking uniforms?" Gryzlov
asked coldly. "What difference does that make?"

The minister of security stared at him. "But then
we are attacking forces of the Polish government,
not just some ragtag band of terrorists," he stammered.

The Russian president felt his temper rising.
He stepped closer to Kazyanov, feeling some satisfaction as the taller, heavier-set man flinched and
backed away. "What the hell do you think is happening out there, Viktor?" he asked.

Without waiting for an answer, he swung around
and jabbed a finger at the map display. "We chase

a bunch of murdering bastards back across the Polish border and they ambush our men. So what do the goddamned Poles do? They fire missiles at *our* planes when we strike the terrorists! *Then* they send MiG-29 fighters to hunt down our bombers! And now, just when we're tracking these terrorists to their lair, they deploy so-called border guards armed with heavy weapons to stop us?" Gryzlov scowled. "How much more evidence do you need? It's obvious that someone high up in Warsaw is in bed with these terrorists. For all I know, it could be their whole damned, stinking government!"

An uncomfortable silence fell across the crowded conference room.

The minister of defense, Gregor Sokolov, cleared his throat. "That is certainly a strong possibility, Mr. President. But if so, Captain Aristov and his men face grave danger."

"How so?"

"Clearing defended buildings is a difficult and lengthy military task," Sokolov said. "Regrettably, I do not believe our commandos will be given the necessary time."

Gryzlov raised an eyebrow. "Oh? Why?"

"Even our closest bases are several hundred kilometers from this battle," Sokolov explained. "We cannot possibly reinforce our quick reaction force before they face overwhelming odds. If elements of the Polish government *are* in fact siding with the terrorists who murdered Lieutenant General Voronov, they can bring heavy armor and artillery into the battle within a matter of hours. Aristov and his commandos are highly trained light infantry, but they aren't equipped to fight tanks."

"What about our fighters and bombers?" Gryzlov asked. "We can destroy their armored vehicles and artillery from the air."

Sokolov shook his head. "I am afraid not, Mr. President. Major Zelin's Su-34s will have to break off to refuel within a matter of minutes. Our Su-35s have already expended most of their long-range missiles and much of their fuel is also gone, expended in low-altitude flight. We can sortie more planes from Voronezh, but they may not arrive before it is too late."

"I see," Gryzlov said flatly. His cold-eyed stare let Sokolov know this most recent evidence of poor military planning and preparation would be "discussed" later.

Seething inside, but unable to deny the seeming logic of his defense minister's argument, the Russian president spun back to the map display. Red arrows showed the positions held by Spetsnaz teams. Other symbols depicted their helicopters, three troop-carrying Mi-8s and two Mi-24 attack helicopters, currently parked in open fields across the Bug River.

He nodded to himself. So be it. If Aristov's men did not have time to flush the terrorists out of their defenses, there was another alternative. "Sokolov!" he snapped.

"Yes, Mr. President?"

"What armament is carried by those Mi-24s?"

The defense minister quickly consulted a tablet computer handed to him by a senior staff officer.

"Gun pods with twin-barrel 23mm autocannons, 80mm rocket pods, and 9K114 Storm antitank missile systems."

Gryzlov smiled thinly. "Good. That should be sufficient."

He turned to face Sokolov and the others. "Tell Captain Aristov to pull back. You will then order our attack helicopters to wipe that village off the map. I do not want a single building left standing! Tell them to make the rubble bounce!"

The Russian leader hardened his expression. "We will teach these terrorist-loving Poles a lesson they will not easily forget."

SPETSNAZ QUICK REACTION FORCE, OVER UKRAINE
An hour later

One by one, the heavily loaded Mi-8 transport helicopters staggered off the ground and into the darkening sky.

Aboard the lead helicopter, Captain Kirill Aristov sat slumped near the open side door, weary beyond imagining. Behind him, blank-eyed Spetsnaz soldiers filled the tip-up seats lining the cabin walls. Blankets shrouded two dead comrades lying motionless on the metal floor at their feet. Farther aft, their medics were hard at work, trying to stabilize some of the more seriously wounded for the long flight back to Russian territory.

Rotors beating, the Mi-8s climbed slowly, spiraling up as they gained altitude.

One of their escorting Mi-24 gunships loomed up out of the gathering darkness, bristling with rocket, cannon, and missile pods. The attack helicopter veered away, taking up its assigned post on their flank.

At least the sight of the gunship gave Aristov a feeling of grim satisfaction. He leaned carefully out through the open door—peering back along their flight path.

Beneath clouds of billowing black smoke, rippling sheets of orange-red flame danced and crackled among the shattered ruins of what had once been a Polish village called Berdyszcze. The fires were bright enough to outshine even the setting sun.

No, the Spetsnaz officer decided. The Poles will not soon forget us. He sat silently in the helicopter's door, watching the fires burn until they vanished beneath the curve of the earth.

CHAPTER 3

THE WHITE HOUSE SITUATION ROOM, WASHINGTON, D.C.
The next day

U.S. President Stacy Anne Barbeau frowned at the image of her younger Russian counterpart, Gennadiy Gryzlov. In other circumstances, she might have enjoyed the view. The Russian leader's rugged good looks came across clearly through the secure video link with Moscow. Unfortunately, this was not an appropriate time for the more informal personal diplomacy her own lingering beauty and carefully cultivated charm sometimes made possible.

"Mr. President, I share your concerns about this attack on the OSCE post, and I deeply regret the deaths of Lieutenant General Voronov and his men," she said. Then she hardened her voice. "But I must strongly protest the subsequent incursion of your troops and aircraft into Poland. No amount of provocation can justify the damage your forces inflicted on the Polish armed forces and on innocent civilians."

Gryzlov snorted. "Innocent, Madam President? I

think not. Innocents do not willingly harbor murderers and terrorists."

"I have been assured by the Polish government that none of its citizens were involved in this incident," Barbeau said.

The Russian president snorted. "Of course that is what Warsaw says. But only a fool would believe such a preposterous claim." His gaze turned cold. "The reports and recordings made by my commanders and pilots leave no doubt that the terrorists who committed this atrocity fled into Polish territory. They also prove that armed Poles attacked my troops while they were in hot pursuit of these terrorists. Given these facts, our retaliatory actions were not only justified—they were entirely proportionate!"

"Proportionate?" Barbeau shot back. "Your armed forces destroyed an entire Polish village, killing dozens of men, women, and children!"

Gryzlov shrugged. "Your outrage is misplaced. By giving the terrorists sanctuary, the Poles were playing with fire. And those who play with fire get burned."

"You can't just—"

"Do not presume to tell me what I cannot do, Madam President," Gryzlov interrupted. He scowled. "I had hoped your new administration would avoid the mistakes made by your predecessor. President Phoenix did not understand something very simple: I will do *whatever* is necessary to safeguard Russian lives and Russian national interests."

He brought his fist down hard on the table in front of him. "Listen closely! I will *not* tolerate the deliberate murder of Russian soldiers. And I will *not* allow Poland or any other Western-allied nation to provide safe haven for terrorists. My armed forces will seek out and destroy anyone who attacks us *wherever* they hide. Is that clear?"

"Your anger is clear enough," Barbeau said tartly. "What isn't so clear is whether you understand that your actions could force the Polish government to invoke the mutual defense clause in the NATO charter. And that would put us all in a very awkward situation."

"Naturally, your NATO alliance must do what it thinks best," the Russian president said. He smiled icily. "But I would strongly advise against a foolish overreaction. It may be summer now, but winter is coming. And your European allies will find it very cold and very dark indeed without our natural gas and oil."

Barbeau kept her face carefully blank. Russian oil and natural gas exports provided more than a third of Europe's energy. If Moscow shut down its pipelines to the West, it could wreak havoc on economies that were already teetering right on the brink of a new recession. Doing that would also cost the Russian badly needed income, but she didn't doubt that Gryzlov's authoritarian regime could stand the pain a lot longer than could the European democracies.

She supposed that things might have been different if the "green" interests in her own political party hadn't blocked U.S. energy exports to Europe, but that was not important right now. Unlike Kenneth Phoenix, she was a realist. You had to play the cards you were dealt instead of pretending that you could change the rules whenever you wanted. Phoenix had never figured that out, which was why she'd kicked his ass in the last election.

Right now it was quite clear that Gryzlov was not bluffing. If she backed him into a corner over this incident, the Russian would do exactly what he threatened to do. And nobody in Berlin or Paris or Rome would thank her for imperiling their economies and political stability—especially not when the situation was so unclear. Warsaw swore that it wasn't involved in this attack on that Russian general, but everybody knew Poland hated and feared the Russians. How sure could she be that the Poles were telling the truth?

Barbeau made a decision. The American people had not elected her to start a new round of tit-for-tat pissing matches with Moscow, which is what Phoenix did repeatedly and which cost the life of his vice president, Ann Page. It was up to her to find a diplomatic solution that would stop this mess from spiraling further out of control.

"I have a suggestion, Mr. President," she said carefully. "One I think is in all of our best interests."

"Go on," Gryzlov said. He allowed a bit more warmth to seep into his smile, though it never reached his eyes. "No one can say that I am unwilling to be reasonable."

The sheer audacity of that statement almost made Stacy Anne Barbeau choke. But she mastered herself quickly. Russia's leader might be a son of a bitch, but he was also the son of a bitch she still had to cut a deal with.

"I propose that we convene immediate high-level talks to de-escalate this unfortunate situation," she told Gryzlov.

"To what end?" the Russian asked skeptically.

"We must find ways to rebuild trust between us," Barbeau said quickly. "Solid, practical measures to persuade our NATO allies that your punitive raid on Poland will not be repeated. And equally important, steps that will assure your government that no such attacks will be necessary in the future."

"I am intrigued, Madam President," Gryzlov said. His smile broadened. "I had not thought it possible that an American government would show itself to be so reasonable and responsible. Very well, I agree to your proposal. My foreign minister and your secretary of state can arrange the details of any negotiations."

"This will only work if you restrain your forces," Barbeau warned. "No serious negotiations will be possible if your planes are busy dropping bombs on NATO territory—no matter what your excuse is."

"Naturally," the Russian agreed. His expression turned colder again. "But such forbearance comes at a price, Madam President."

"Oh?"

"You must assure *me* that the NATO countries will do everything possible to police their own borders," Gryzlov said. "Your allies, especially the Poles, must begin rooting out the terrorists who are targeting my country and its vital interests. And we must see this being done. Trust but also verify, is that not what one of your most famous presidents once said?"

"Yes, it is," Barbeau admitted, trying to hide the distaste in her voice. Ronald Reagan had never been a political leader she particularly admired. She looked at the Russian. "Do we have an agreement to begin these talks?"

He nodded. "We do, Madam President." He smiled more genuinely this time. "Let us hope these negotiations will signal the beginning of a new era of détente between our two proud nations, one which recognizes the true limits of our respective spheres of influence."

For a moment, but only for a moment, Barbeau was tempted to ask just which countries Gryzlov considered within the Russian sphere of influence. Then she decided it didn't matter. As always, the facts on the ground would matter more than rhetoric. And if she could pull off an agreement that would keep the peace in Europe and elsewhere, nobody she cared about would sweat the minor details.

THE KREMLIN, MOSCOW
A short time later

Gennadiy Gryzlov made sure the secure video link to Washington, D.C., was broken before turning to his closest advisers. "Incredible, eh? To think that the Americans have entrusted the fate of their nation to someone so shortsighted?"

"Her offer of negotiations seemed sincere," Foreign Minister Daria Titeneva pointed out.

Gryzlov waved that away with one hand. "I'm sure it was." He shook his head. "This President Barbeau has all the tactical skills of a successful politician, but she lacks the strategic vision of a true statesman."

"So you don't think these talks she wants to hold will be useful?" Chief of Staff Sergei Tarzarov asked.

"On the contrary," Gryzlov told his chief of staff. "I think they will be very useful to us—if only as an opportunity to drive a wedge between the Americans and their remaining European allies. But I do not believe diplomacy will solve our Polish problem."

"Oh?" Tarzarov raised an eyebrow.

"Come now, Sergei," the president said. "You know the Poles better than I do. We've just slapped them across the face as a warning to stop supporting our enemies. Do you really think that will make them more reasonable?"

Tarzarov frowned. "Probably not," he admitted. "They have always been a hotheaded, combative people. Their leaders may see our action as a challenge to a duel, as an affront to their honor."

"Exactly," Gryzlov said. "But I have no intention of sitting around waiting for their seconds to politely inform us of their choice of weapons. Only a fool fights fairly." He turned to the minister of defense. "I want additional fighter and bomber patrols over Belarus and the territory we control in Ukraine. The next time these terrorists attack us, I want aircraft ready to hit them immediately—not loitering uselessly out of reach."

"Yes, Mr. President."

"I also want additional Spetsnaz teams and GRU agents deployed into Ukraine and along the Polish-Belarusian frontier," Gryzlov said. "If necessary, you are authorized to conduct covert reconnaissance missions into Poland."

"Sir?" Sokolov asked.

"You will find these terrorists, Gregor," Gryzlov said flatly. "You will find their hiding places and weapons caches. You will identify those in Warsaw who support our enemies. And when you do, we will destroy them. All of them."

THE WHITE HOUSE, WASHINGTON, D.C.
That same time

"You all heard Gryzlov," President Barbeau said, looking around the table at her national security team. The chairman of the Joint Chiefs, Air Force General Timothy Spelling, and the CIA director, Thomas Torrey were the only holdovers from the Phoenix administration. Everyone else owed their appointment and their loyalty to her. "Besides the negotiations I've proposed, what are our other options?"

"They're pretty limited," her national security adviser, Edward Rauch, admitted. Gray-haired, pale, and ascetically thin, Rauch had spent half a lifetime writing about U.S. defense policy for a number of different Beltway think tanks. "For one thing, it's clear that NATO has no realistic military means of deterring the Russians from hitting Poland again."

"What?" Secretary of State Karen Grayson didn't even try to hide her astonishment. The petite former senator from Montana had spent most of her congressional career focused on agriculture issues and international trade. "You're telling me that the alliance we've spent sixty-plus years supporting as a counter to the Russians is a total bust? How is that possible?"

"Most of our NATO allies have been cutting their armed forces since the Berlin Wall came down, and their cuts have gone well beyond the fat and deep into muscle and bone," Rauch explained. "Heck, Germany is supposed to be the linchpin of the alliance. But their air force is so short of spare parts that they're cannibalizing frontline fighter aircraft just to keep the rest flying. Most of their cargo planes and helicopters are fit only for the scrap heap. Their navy has ships that can't steam, and Berlin would have to deactivate half of its armored brigades just to bring the others up to wartime strength."

Rauch looked around the table. "The plain fact is that Moscow has more available combat power—aircraft, tanks, artillery, infantry, and tactical missiles—than all of the European NATO countries combined. Right now the alliance is a busted flush."

"The Poles have been increasing their defense spending for several years," General Spelling objected. "Ever since the Russians annexed the Crimea and started screwing around in Ukraine."

"Which may be part of the problem," Rauch said. "Warsaw hasn't been shy about telling the world that its defense buildup is aimed at the Russians.

That's not the kind of challenge a guy like Gryzlov can ignore."

"Are you saying this so-called terrorist attack was a fake, Ed?" Barbeau asked carefully. "That the Russians staged it so they could have an excuse to go after the Poles?"

Her national security adviser shrugged his narrow shoulders. "I don't know. It seems a little farfetched, I guess. And those reports from the OSCE team sure made it sound real enough. But the fact is that we're awfully short on good firsthand intelligence sources inside the Kremlin."

Barbeau looked across the table at Thomas Torrey. "Tom?"

The CIA director nodded slowly, plainly uncomfortable at talking so openly about something so highly classified in front of so many others. Top-level clearances or not, whatever more than two or three people knew in D.C. was likely to leak to the press. "Ed is right, Madam President. The signals our satellites picked up strongly suggest the Russians were *reacting* to an attack, not following some scripted plan. On the other hand, our HUMINT in Moscow is thinner than I would like right now."

"HUMINT?" the secretary of state asked, evidently confused.

"Spies, Karen," Barbeau said patiently. "HUMINT is short for 'human intelligence.' We've got to get you up to speed on the jargon." She turned back to the CIA director and the chairman of the Joint Chiefs. "Look here, I'm tired of stumbling around in the dark. Right now we don't know anything concrete about the people who killed that Russian general and triggered all this mayhem. We don't know if they were Poles. Or Russians. Or Ukrainians. Or men from Mars, for that matter. True?" They nodded. "So get your intelligence assets in gear over there," Barbeau ordered. "Put some people on the ground in Warsaw and see what you can dig up in Moscow. Get me some hard data, understand?" They nodded again.

"There are some precautionary measures we could take in the interim," General Spelling said.

"Such as?"

"We could rotate a squadron of F-22 Raptors to Poland for NATO air defense exercises," the chairman of the Joint Chiefs told her. "At the same time, we could temporarily assign a battalion from the 173rd Airborne Brigade in Vicenza, Italy, to duty in the region. Once you give the order, our paratroops can be on the ground in seventy-two hours. Plus, we have enough sealift in position to ship a battalion from the First Cavalry Division to Gdansk, complete with M1A2 Abrams tanks and Bradley Fighting Vehicles."

There was a very uncomfortable silence around the table. "To what end, General?" Barbeau asked finally.

"Sending American troops and aircraft to Poland might make the Russians think a lot harder about pushing this situation over the edge," the chairman of the Joint Chiefs said. "Plus, it'll give the Poles some confidence that we're sticking by our alliance. I imagine Warsaw is pretty rattled right now."

"No," Barbeau said decisively. She shook her head. "President Gryzlov and his government are on a hair trigger already. I'm not going to give them the slightest excuse to escalate this mess."

"But, Madam President—"

"But nothing, General," she snapped, cutting Spelling off in midsentence. She smiled sweetly. "I'm enough of an Air Force brat to know that a dozen fighter planes and a thousand paratroopers, tank crewmen, and infantry grunts are not going to change the strategic equation in Eastern Europe. That's a trip wire, not a fighting force. And I am definitely *not* going to put American soldiers and airmen in unnecessary harm's way just to make the Poles feel safer!"

Sighing, Stacy Barbeau pushed her chair back from the table and stood up. "That's all for now, ladies and gentlemen. We'll reconvene when we know more." She shook hands with them as they filed out of the Situation Room. But she stopped Luke Cohen on his way out the door. "Hang on for a second, Luke."

Cohen, a tall, thin New Yorker who had managed her campaign for president and who was now her White House chief of staff, nodded. He dropped into the closest seat and sat crouched over, rapidly scanning through e-mails while she finished saying her good-byes.

She turned away from the door. "You were awfully quiet, Luke."

Cohen looked up with a lopsided grin. "It didn't seem like you needed any help." He shrugged. "Besides, you know my forte is politics, not bombs and missiles. That's why you have pointy-headed arm-chair strategists like Rauch."

"Well, what about the politics of this mess?" Bar-beau asked pointedly. "From a domestic point of view, do you think we ought to move more force-fully to help the Poles?"

"No way," Cohen said. He put his tablet to sleep and set it down on the table. "Politically speaking, we do not need a confrontation with the Russians right now. Sure your poll numbers are down a bit now that the inaugural honeymoon is over, but not enough to lose any sleep over. We still have enough clout to move your legislative program through the House and Senate."

He spread his hands. "Besides, you were elected to accomplish three things: to restore federal social spending after all this 'fiscal austerity' BS; to strengthen the Army, Navy, and Air Force by build-ing real ships, tanks, and planes—not all that pie-in-the-sky high-tech space garbage; and to mend all the diplomatic fences Ken Phoenix and his gung ho space cowboys knocked down with their stupid Starfire Project. Going toe-to-toe with the Russkies isn't part of the plan."

"Nice speech, Luke, but Gryzlov may have plans of his own," Barbeau said with a slight smile.

Cohen shrugged again. "So what?" He looked up at her. "Do you really want to risk a shooting war for a bunch of Poles? Especially if it turns out they've been dumb enough to turn a blind eye to terrorists gunning for the Russians?"

"You think Gryzlov is telling the truth?" Barbeau asked.

"Does it really matter?" her chief of staff countered.

"No," Barbeau admitted slowly. "It doesn't."

PRESIDENTIAL PALACE,
WARSAW, POLAND
That same time

Moving at his usual rapid pace, Polish President Piotr Wilk strode into the Blue Room and took his seat in the middle of the long conference table. In ordinary times, Poland's president served as the head of state and commander of the armed forces—leaving routine government business to his appointed prime minister and council of ministers.

But these were not ordinary times.

Today Wilk had convened an emergency Cabinet Council meeting, calling together the ministers most directly charged with Poland's defense, economy, and foreign affairs. Their task was to craft an official response to Russia's brutal surprise attack on the little village of Berdyszcze.

Grim, serious faces met his gaze. The usual hubbub of friendly greetings among colleagues was gone, replaced by a dead, unnerving silence.

For just a millisecond, the Polish president was tempted to break the almost unbearable tension by repeating Ronald Reagan's famous wisecrack about "bombing Russia in five minutes." But he resisted the temptation. Given the deep and abiding anger felt by the Polish people and armed forces over Moscow's latest act of aggression, too many of the men and women gathered here might be willing to turn his "joke" into reality. For that matter, Wilk bitterly admitted to himself, he was one of them.

Wiry, middling tall, and barely into his midforties, Poland's president still looked very much like the fighter pilot he had once been. Before being lured into politics, Wilk had flown Russian-made MiG-29 Fulcrum and American-made F-16 Fighting Falcon fighters. Marked as one of the new Third Republic's most promising officers, he had risen first to the rank of general and then the position of commander of the First Air Defense Wing, responsible for the defense of the capital itself. Taking on Russians was a task he had practiced almost his whole professional life.

Unfortunately, briefly satisfying though it would be, going to war with Moscow would be an act of irrational and suicidal defiance. Once the Cabinet Council began its work, the cold hard figures provided by the minister of national defense, Deputy Prime Minister Janusz Gierek, made that all too clear:

"Our rearmament program has made good progress," Gierek said. His dry, precise presentation and shock of unruly white hair were constant reminders that he had been a highly regarded professor of mathematics before entering government. "But the Russians still significantly outnumber us in every category—by better than six to one in raw troop strength, three to one in tanks and armored fighting vehicles, and six to one in heavy artillery." He paused briefly to let that sink in, then pushed his reading glasses back up his nose and went on. "In a defensive war, fighting on our home ground and in our cities, our forces *might* be able to slow any Russian invasion, perhaps even prolonging the fight for some weeks, until NATO reinforcements arrive."

"Delay is not a path to victory," Wilk said flatly.

"No, Piotr, it is not," Gierek agreed sadly. "And even achieving that much is unlikely, given Moscow's overwhelming superiority in modern aircraft and tactical missiles. Russia's recent de facto alliance with the People's Republic of China would give it the freedom to mass large numbers of its most advanced fighters and fighter-bombers against us. My analysts estimate their likely strength at several hundred frontline aircraft."

"While we have fewer than seventy," Wilk said.

"A third of which are MiG-29 Fulcrums," the defense minister reminded him. "And we saw how well they performed against Russian Sukhoi-35s yesterday."

Wilk frowned. Captain Kaczor and Lieutenant Czarny had both been brave, competent pilots. They had been killed from ambush, caught by surprise in peacetime. Still, Gierek's point was valid. Poland's upgraded MiG-29s were no real match for Russia's Su-27s, Su-30s, and Su-35s, with their superior radars and longer-range missiles.

"Then what can we do?" the prime minister, Klaudia Rybak, asked quietly. She was one of the brilliant economists whose work had helped transform Poland from a drab Marxist failure to a booming free-market nation.

"We must protest this murderous attack to the United Nations Security Council," Foreign Minister Andrzej Waniek replied.

"Which will accomplish what?" the prime minister wondered.

"Precisely nothing," Wilk said heavily. He shook his head. "Let's not fool ourselves. The UN is a laughingstock. And even if it were not, the Russians would veto any serious move to punish them."

"Then we must take our case to the NATO Council and the European Union," Waniek argued.

"Yes, we must, Andrzej," Wilk agreed. "For the sake of public and international opinion, if nothing else." He shrugged. "But I do not believe either NATO or the EU will come riding to our rescue. Nor will the Americans on their own, for that matter."

"Why not?" the foreign minister asked.

"Because those bastards in Moscow have effectively poisoned the well by claiming we are giving sanctuary to terrorists," Wilk said. "We all know this is false, but—"

"Do we?" Gierek said suddenly. "Can we be sure?" Surprised heads turned toward him. "I don't mean Moscow's assertion that our government supports those who killed their general," the defense minister added quickly. "That is quite obviously absurd." He looked troubled. "But can we be completely certain these gunmen were not operating from our territory?"

Wilk thought about that. Statements made by the OSCE commanders, the Romanian Covaci and his Bulgarian counterpart, had indicated the attackers were Ukrainians—probably war veterans embittered by Ukraine's defeat at the hands of the Russians back in 2014. But the Polish-Ukrainian border was porous and thinly policed. There were not many Ukrainians living in Poland, but those who did tended to live close to the Bug River. Could some of them have provided shelter for their fellow countrymen, perhaps even unwittingly?

He turned to the minister of the interior. "You'd better check that possibility out, Irena."

"I already have investigative teams on the ground," Irena Malinowski said crisply. Prim, good-looking, and always efficient, she ran her department, which included Poland's national police and border-guard forces, with an iron hand. "If evidence of any such involvement still exists in the ruins left by those Russian savages, we *will* find it."

The cabinet meeting dragged on for another hour, but it limped to an end without being able to do much more than vote against "precipitous" military retaliation for Russia's raid into Polish territory. The consensus was that President Wilk should stay in close communication with NATO and with the White House—passing along intelligence about Russian military activities while seeking whatever military and diplomatic aid he could obtain. Finally, they all agreed that more troops and police should be deployed to seal the border. No one wanted to give Moscow any more easy excuses for further aggression.

"Half measures!" Piotr Wilk muttered later to the tough-looking, slender young woman in uniform keeping pace at his side. They were heading for the armored limousine that would take him back to his working office in the Belweder Palace, a few kilometers south. Four plainclothes bodyguards kept station to their front and rear. "Nothing but half measures!"

"What else can we do, sir?" Nadia Rozek asked quietly. Newly assigned as one of the president's personal military aides, she wore the four stars of a captain on her shoulder boards—along with the insignia of Poland's Special Forces and her pilot's badge, the *gapa*, a silver eagle with a golden laurel wreath clutched in its bill.

"That's the devil of it, Captain," Wilk admitted. "We have no good options. Only a choice between those which are bad and those which are even worse! Which is precisely where Moscow wants us."

"You think the Russians will hit us again, sir?" Nadia said.

Wilk nodded. "I do." He grimaced. "For all his so-called sophistication, Gennadiy Gryzlov is a predator and a thug, just like all his predecessors. Having once tasted Polish blood without punishment, I believe he will look for other opportunities to test our resolve. To weaken and damage us."

Nadia said nothing for a moment. But her blue-gray eyes darkened at the thought of more civilians lying dead or maimed in the ruins of their cities and towns. Her mouth tightened into a thin line. Her parents had wanted their only child to pursue a career as a scientist or a doctor or an engineer. Instead, she had joined the armed forces to help defend her beloved country. She would not sit by and see Poland left helpless at the feet of another enemy—especially not the barbarous Russians.

She glanced at the president. "What about our allies, sir? The other NATO powers?"

"NATO will be useless, I suspect," Wilk said bitterly. "The Germans and the others are too weak—and too dependent on Russian energy—to risk coming to our aid with anything more than words. Or perhaps weak sanctions at best. As though Gryzlov and his backers in the Kremlin will be swayed by threats to their petty cash reserves!"

"And the Americans?"

Wilk shrugged. "I do not trust the new American president, Stacy Barbeau. Or rather I trust her all too well. President Phoenix may not have been the wisest of men, but he was a man of honor. His successor seems more likely to care about her popularity at home than doing what is right abroad. I do not believe she will rush to our aid if she believes her voters will not support her."

"Then we must strengthen our own defenses," Nadia said fiercely. She felt her cheeks turn red immediately, embarrassed at having spoken so bluntly to her country's elected leader.

The president only smiled. "Very true, Captain." He sighed. "Unfortunately, there is very little that we can do in the short term. We are spending tens of billions of *zlotys* on new aircraft, antiair defenses, helicopters, tanks, submarines, and other weapons. But fully modernizing our forces will take many months if we are lucky, and, more probably, several years."

"And you are afraid we will not be given the time we need," Nadia finished for him.

Wilk nodded. "Not with the Russian bear, its claws unsheathed, already prowling so close to our borders." He frowned again. "Somewhere, somehow, we must find an alternative!"

Nadia risked another glance at the president. He was staring off into the distance, deep in thought.

Suddenly Wilk stopped, spinning to face her so abruptly that the bodyguards coming up behind almost crashed into them. "We need what the Americans call a quick fix, Captain Rozek!" he said. "A means of acquiring more combat power immediately, within weeks—not months or years!"

"As a deterrent?" she asked.

"Perhaps," he said. "But also as some means of ensuring Poland's survival if deterrence fails." He looked closely at her. "Did you ever read about the last weeks of the American occupation of Iraq? Back about seven years ago? Those stories about a major Turkish incursion against the Kurds in northern Iraq?"

Nadia searched her memory. She had been a cadet at the Air Force Academy in Deblin then. That was a long time ago, what seemed a lifetime of rigorous training, hard work, and painful experience. But one of her instructors had insisted that his students pay attention to events in the outside world—especially to events that could be signs of a revolution in military tactics and technology. "The Turks were forced to retreat," she said slowly.

"Yes," Wilk agreed. "But not by regular American or Iraqi military units. The American military had all but deserted northern Iraq in their draw-down. They hired civilian contractors for surveillance as the military forces withdrew."

"That's right," she said, remembering more now. "Most of it was just rumors. Very little was ever officially admitted. But some observers claimed the Turks were defeated by a very unconventional force, one composed of special infantry with remarkably powerful weapons and a mix of advanced unmanned aircraft. It was also reported that this elite force was created by one of those private civilian security corporations."

"Exactly," the president said, smiling. "And do you remember the name used by this corporation?"

She bit her lip, concentrating, digging deep into her memories. "*Dziecko.* Child. No, that's not quite right. *Potomek!* Scion! That's it. Scion."

"Correct," Wilk said approvingly. He looked around carefully and then lowered his voice. "I will need your help in this matter, Captain. And your discretion."

She stiffened to attention. "I am at your service, sir."

"I would like to contact this American company, this Scion. But first I need more information about them. And about what they can do."

"Sir?" Nadia asked.

"But I can't do this myself," Wilk said. "Not officially. Not without approval by the Council of Ministers."

"You want me to research Scion," Nadia realized.

"And to make contact with them," Wilk said. "Discreet contact. Nothing about this initiative must leak out, especially not to the Russians. You understand?"

Captain Nadia Rozek nodded firmly, already contemplating the work she would need to do and the circuitous digital paths she would need to follow. "Yes, Mr. President. I understand. You can rely on me."

CHAPTER 4

*It is always our own self that we
find at the end of the journey. The
sooner we face that self, the better.*

— ELLA MAILLART,
SWISS TRAVEL WRITER

**THE ROYAL MAYAN RESORT,
CANCÚN, MEXICO**
A few days later

"So, are you just a beach bum here on your family's dime, or are you really a brilliant young
Internet billionaire in disguise?" a husky voice
asked, pitched just high enough to be heard over the
sound of the surf curling up on the beach.

Brad McLanahan looked up from the e-book
science-fiction thriller he'd been reading. He tipped
his sunglasses up to get a better look at the young
woman who'd stopped by his shaded beach chair.

She was a good-looking redhead in a bikini that left little to the imagination, including the fact that she was in incredibly good shape. Silhouetted against the white sand beach and the emerald-green waters of the Caribbean, she stood looking down at him with a faint smile. His pulse quickened. Play it cool, he told himself. Well, a little cool anyway.

"Neither," he said gravely. "I'm actually a lonely fugitive on the run from an international spy ring."

"Not likely," she said with a laugh. "If you'd said you were fleeing a paternity suit, I might have bought it."

Brad grinned.

"Mind if I sit down?" the woman asked, nodding to the empty beach chair next to his.

"Not at all." Brad laid his e-book reader aside and sat up a little straighter.

Maybe this day would be more interesting than the past several, he thought hopefully. Since arriving in Cancún, he'd done nothing but swim, sit on the beach, read, catch up on his sleep, and wait for the next signal from his father or Martindale. At first, after the rigors of his Sky Masters internship, he'd welcomed the chance to relax and rest. But now it was getting kind of boring. A little light vacation romance, or at least a fun, no-strings-attached roll in the sack, might be just the ticket to break the monotony.

"Samantha Kerr," the woman said, holding out her hand. "My friends call me Sam."

Brad shook it politely. "John Smith," he said. "My friends call me John."

She raised an eyebrow in disbelief. "John Smith? Really? That's what you're going with?"

"International fugitive. On the run. Remember?" he said, grinning wider now.

"Silly me," the redhead said. "It slipped my mind."

"Can I get you a drink, Sam?" Brad asked. "The guy at the beach bar makes a really good margarita."

"Sorry, but no." She shook her head. "It's getting a bit hot out here for my taste, so I think I'll head indoors."

Brad hid his disappointment. Oh, well, he thought, nothing ventured, nothing gained.

"But I do have a comfortable air-conditioned suite," she went on, with a heavy-lidded glance up and down his body. "And a fully stocked bar. Care to join me?"

"Oh. Er, yeah. Absolutely. I mean, yes." Keep it together, Brad told himself, quickly helping her up from the beach chair. Her fingers felt cool and dry in his hand. "That sounds like a great idea, Sam."

"I was hoping you'd say that, Mr. McLanahan," the woman said even more quietly. She smiled sweetly. "It'll make things so much easier."

Brad froze. He narrowed his eyes, tightening his grip on her hand slightly. "Who the hell are you? And what do you really want?"

"Easy, tiger," the woman said. "My name really is Samantha Kerr." With a quick twist of her fingers, she broke his grip. "As to why I'm here, let's just say that I'm Pharaoh's daughter come to pull your reed basket out of the Nile."

Oh, Christ, Brad thought, flushing slightly in embarrassment. EXODUS again. She must be a contact with word from his father or from Martindale. "You're with Scion," he guessed.

She nodded. "I work in the security and counter-surveillance division." Smiling again, she took his hand and brought it around her waist. "Which is exactly why we're going to saunter off this beach to my room—acting for all the world like we're heading in for an afternoon of really wild sex."

"Which isn't going to happen," Brad said sadly.

She laughed. "Maybe another time, McLanahan." Then she turned serious and gently urged him into motion, bringing him along with her toward the steps leading up off the beach and deeper into the resort. "But, no. Not right now. I prefer my personal pickups to be a little less public. And definitely *not* made right in front of a bunch of strange guys peeping through zoom lenses and binoculars."

Ah, Brad thought. He looked down at her. "I'm tagged."

"Oh, yeah. That you are. It took us a couple of days to zero in on the surveillance team dogging you, which is why you've had such a lovely, restful vacation. But now it's time to go."

"Who are they?"

"Mexico's CNI," she told him. "Their National Intelligence Center is the equivalent of our FBI and CIA."

That surprised him. "The Mexicans?"

"They're acting for the FBI," she said.

"Oh."

"And the Russian SVR."

Brad stopped dead. "You're kidding me."

"Nope." She shook her head and started walking again. "Double-dipping is an old game in the intelligence trade, McLanahan—especially in a routine operation like this. It looks as though both Washington and Moscow only want to keep tabs on your whereabouts right now, with nothing darker in mind. So the locals are perfectly comfortable getting paid twice for the same work."

"Jesus." Brad glanced at the beautiful woman nestled in his arm. "No offense, Ms. Kerr, but you work in a very weird world."

"That I do," she agreed.

Back in her suite, Samantha Kerr quickly bolted the door and made sure all the blinds were closed. Satisfied they could not be seen, she reached into her purse and handed him a sheaf of documents. "Welcome to your new and very temporary life, Mr. Jackson."

Quickly, Brad leafed through the papers. Right on top was a Canadian passport made out in the name of Paul Jackson. He flipped it open and stopped. The face staring back at him from the passport photo was his . . . only it wasn't, somehow. Instead of his own natural blond hair, the photo showed him with dark brown hair. And the face in the picture was, well, fatter. He looked up at Sam and showed her the photo with a raised eyebrow.

"Ah, the wonders of Photoshop," she told him cheerfully. "And a little hair dye and a couple of cheek pads will put you in the right shape to clear international customs and board your flight."

"My flight?"

"Air France direct to Paris," Sam said. "Lucky

you." She glanced at her watch. "You leave in about four hours."

"And what happens after I get to Paris?" Brad asked.

"That's above my pay grade, Mr. McLanahan," she said. "But I'm sure you'll be met and briefed more extensively on arrival."

"Hold on," Brad said, raising a hand in protest. "You say I'm under surveillance, right?"

"Yes."

"So when I just up and disappear, both the FBI and the Russians are going to go nuts trying to find me," he pointed out.

Samantha only grinned. "Who says you're going to disappear?"

"Huh?"

She turned toward the bedroom door and raised her voice slightly. "Time to make your appearance, Brad."

Moving quietly, a man moseyed out into the suite's living room. He leaned back against the nearest wall with his hands in his pockets. He didn't say anything. But there was just the faintest hint of a shit-eating grin on his face.

Brad suddenly realized they were just about the same height and had the same build.

"See?" Samantha said impishly. "You're not going anywhere, Mr. McLanahan . . . rather, Mr. Smith. You're going to be having the time of your life here in Cancún. With me." She shrugged her tanned shoulders and sighed dramatically. "It is a rough job, but I guess someone has to do it."

MCLANAHAN INDUSTRIAL AIRPORT, BATTLE MOUNTAIN, NEVADA
That same time

Hunter "Boomer" Noble stood off to the side of the long runway, scanning the sky through a pair of binoculars. He squinted, fiddling with the focus as he zoomed in on a small flying-wing aircraft turning toward the field at low altitude. Heat rolling off the tarmac shimmered in the air. Summers in the high desert of north-central Nevada were always hot and bone-dry.

A voice sounded in his earbud. "McLanahan Tower, Masters Five-Five, level at one thousand, airspeed one-eight-zero knots. Five miles southeast of runway three-zero, full stop."

Boomer hid a grin. Tom Rogers always sounded so serious on the radio, just as if he were really up there in the aircraft instead of sitting in an air-conditioned office in front of a remote piloting console.

"Masters Five-Five, McLanahan Tower, winds calm, cleared to land straight-in runway three-zero," the controller responded.

Boomer stood watching while the remotely piloted plane slid lower, touched down gently with a small puff of gray smoke from its landing gear, and taxied past him. Its wing-buried turbofan engines were already spooling down. Seen up close, the aircraft was tiny, about the size of a small business jet. No windows or cockpit canopy broke its smooth lines.

"I assume this little bird is what you wanted to show me, Dr. Noble?" a smooth, resonant voice said suddenly from over his shoulder.

Startled, Boomer swung around. He found himself staring into the amused eyes of a much shorter man with long gray hair and a neatly trimmed gray beard. Two bigger men, wearing sunglasses, suits, and ties, were posted about twenty feet away. Slight bulges marked the holstered weapons concealed under their jackets. Kevin Martindale, former president of the United States and the current president and CEO of Scion, never went anywhere without armed bodyguards.

Boomer finally noticed the big black limousine parked next to the airport tower and shook his head ruefully at the newcomers. How the hell does Martindale do it? Boomer wondered. How does he manage to pop up unannounced whenever and wherever he likes? Sky Masters didn't run ordinary flight operations with total military-grade security, but there were still fences, sensors, and guarded gates. Somebody should have spotted Scion's CEO on his way in and notified him.

He felt his pulse settle and forced a smile of his own. Spooky son of a bitch or not, Martindale was one of Sky Masters best customers, and he was closely tied in with the company's head honchos.

"That's right, sir," he said. He nodded toward the unmanned aircraft as it swung slowly off the runway and rolled to a stop on a nearby ramp. "Meet the MQ-55 Coyote."

"Give me the basic rundown, Dr. Noble," Martindale said. He looked the small aircraft over with a critical eye. "From the shape and engine placement, I assume it's designed for stealth?"

"Reasonably so," Boomer told him. "Besides using a flying-wing configuration and wing-buried turbofans, we've also covered it with a special radar-absorbent coating created by an Israeli company, Nanoflight. This coating sucks up most of the electromagnetic energy from a radar wave and shunts it off as heat. Some energy gets back to the emitter, of course, but only in a really reduced and scattered form."

"Interesting," Martindale said.

"Oh, yeah," Boomer agreed. "The stuff's not cheap, but it's a lot less expensive than most of the other stealth materials on the market."

"So how stealthy is this Coyote of yours?" Martindale asked. "Could it penetrate heavily defended airspace without being detected?"

"On its own? Nope." Boomer shook his head. "But the MQ-55 isn't designed for that mission. It's designed to operate in a combat environment full of violently maneuvering aircraft all emitting like hell with every radar and ECM system they've got. In the middle of a fight like that, the Coyote doesn't *have* to slide through the air like it's not really there. It just has to be less visible and quieter than everything else."

"Which makes it what exactly?" Martindale wondered.

"The MQ-55 is a missile truck, sir," Boomer said. "A low-cost platform built with mostly off-the-shelf components and designed for one primary task—dumping a lot of long-range missiles out into the sky in a hurry for our fighter jocks to control. We started working on the concept right after that Chinese sneak attack on Andersen Air Force Base on Guam a couple of years ago."

"I remember," Martindale said softly. "We were bushwhacked in the air, blinded when they knocked down our AWACS plane, and then our base took heavy damage and terrible casualties from Chinese supersonic cruise missiles. If Patrick McLanahan and a few of our other XB-1F Excalibur bombers hadn't gotten off the ground first and been able to hit back, we might have lost everything in the Pacific."

Boomer nodded. "We analyzed every piece of data we could get from that first fight, the one between the two F-22A Raptors that were on patrol west of Guam and the Chinese strike force. Unfortunately, the picture we put together matched up right down the line with the results of a computer war simulation Rand Corporation ran way back in 2008. Plane for plane and pilot for pilot, our Raptors were superior to those Chinese J-20 fighters they tangled with, but the Raptors ran out of missiles before the Chinese ran out of jets . . . and that was it. Game over."

Boomer headed toward the parking ramp. Martindale came with him. "We figured there was no way the Air Force or the Navy could afford to build enough F-22s or F-35s to match the Chinese or the Russians in numbers," Boomer said. He pointed to the Coyote. "So this was the answer we came up with. The MQ-55 is relatively cheap, reasonably fast, has decent range, and it can carry enough long-range, air-to-air missiles to even up a fight against superior numbers of enemy aircraft."

"Go on," Martindale said, clearly intrigued.

"The airframe is new, but we modeled it closely after our other successful flying-wing designs," Boomer said. "That cut our development and flight-testing costs dramatically. Since it's remotely piloted, we don't need a lot of complicated avionics—just enough so that a ground- or air-based pilot can fly it safely and perform a few basic maneuvers. The engines are off-the-shelf Honeywell TFE731s, the same kind flown on most business jets."

"What about sensors?" Martindale asked. "What kind of radar does it carry?"

"None," Boomer told him. He saw the surprise on the older man's face and explained. "We don't need it. The Coyote is a missile truck, not really a recon or dedicated strike bird. All it needs are communications links so the human fighter pilots in the same battle can pass targeting data and firing commands. It uses some short-range area sensors for formation flying with other aircraft, but that's it. It flies in, launches at whatever it's told to attack, and then splits."

"And the payload?"

"Up to ten AIM-120 advanced medium-range air-to-air missiles in an internal weapons bay."

Martindale nodded, absorbing what he was being told. That was more than the number of AIM-120s an F-22 Raptor configured for stealth could carry. And it was two and half times the missile capacity of the F-35 Lightning's internal weapons bays. "Can this Coyote of yours deploy other weapons?"

"The MQ-55's bay is also big enough to hold up to three satellite-guided GBU-32 joint direct-attack munitions or four GBU-53 small-diameter bombs," Boomer said. "We could drop JDAMs using targeting data supplied by other aircraft. But we haven't really tested an air-to-ground strike configuration yet."

"Impressive," Martindale said. He looked at Boomer. "What's your flyaway cost for these birds?"

"Right around twenty million dollars each for the first four Coyotes we've built," Boomer told him. "But I think we can cut that down to about fifteen million per in sustained production, once we iron out all the kinks and streamline our manufacturing processes."

Martindale whistled softly. Those cost estimates were astoundingly low, especially compared to the price of the manned fighter aircraft the MQ-55s were designed to support. "So how many of these Coyotes are you building for the U.S. Air Force?"

"None," Boomer said, not hiding his bitterness. He sighed. "President Barbeau's administration only wants to build existing airframes, preferably ones that require pilots and carry big price tags. New weapons systems are not welcome, especially inexpensive ones involving out-of-the-box thinking."

"Or that have the Sky Masters label on them," Martindale guessed.

"That, too," Boomer admitted. "Ever since Barbeau and her crowd went to town smearing Ken Phoenix and the Starfire Project to win the last presidential election, our corporate name has been mud inside Congress and the Pentagon."

"And so you thought about me and my little company?" Martindale said with a low chuckle.

"The thought that Scion might be interested in this kind of capability did cross my mind," Boomer said warily.

"I'm touched, Dr. Noble," Martindale said, grinning wider now. "Really touched." He moved closer to the parked MQ-55, gently kicked its tires, and then looked back at Boomer. "You say you've built four of these already?"

"Yes, sir."

"How long before you work out the kinks?"

Boomer shrugged. "Not long. We've been working on this design concept for four years, so it's pretty mature technology—we tweak it now and then to keep up with the state of the art."

"Excellent," Martindale said. "I love them. Wrap all four of them up for me, Dr. Noble. If I could, I'd take them home with me right now." Smiling broadly, he came back to Boomer and threw an arm around his shoulders. "Now let's talk about that fleet of XF-111 SuperVarks you've finished refurbishing. I may need them, too."

EAST OF ZAGREB, OVER CROATIA
The next day

"Zagreb Control, Pilatus Six-Eight November on final to Bjelovar Airfield," the pilot of the Swiss-made Pilatus PC-12 turboprop said. "And thank you very much for your assistance."

"Roger, Pilatus," the controller radioed back in lightly accented English. "You are welcome. Switch to common traffic advisory frequency approved. Enjoy your stay in Croatia."

Making sure his mike was switched off, the pilot, a short, broad-shouldered Englishman named Mark Darrow, glanced across the cockpit at Brad McLanahan with a wry grin. "Enjoy our stay in Croatia? Oh, that we will, right? All five dull minutes of it. Then things are likely to get a wee bit exciting."

Watching the long grass landing strip ahead growing larger through the turboprop's windshield, Brad wondered what the other man meant. Bjelovar was a typical small, noncommercial airfield, used mostly by flying clubs and those wealthy enough to own their own planes. A white-painted wood building and an old-fashioned hangar sat off to one side, with a variety of small, single-engine aircraft parked beside the strip. It didn't exactly look like a hotbed of intrigue or action.

Darrow had met him on arrival in Paris, taken him in tow to a hotel to sleep off some of his jet lag, and then driven him out to Le Bourget Airport. Once the center of French flying and the place where Charles Lindbergh had landed in *The Spirit of St. Louis*, Le Bourget was now used only for general aviation traffic. The Pilatus PC-12 was parked there, waiting for them.

According to its registration papers, the sleek turboprop was owned by a man named Jan Beneš.

"He's a rather eccentric Czech multimillionaire," Darrow had explained. "The fellow has homes all over Europe, but he never takes the train or drives. Hence this plane."

"Will I meet him?" Brad had asked.

That was the first time he'd seen the other man's quick, lopsided grin. "I shouldn't think so," Darrow had said. "Our Mr. Beneš is totally fictional. But he pays quite a lot in tax, which is rather a point in his favor as far as the authorities are concerned."

Now, two hours after taking off from Le Bourget, they were landing at Bjelovar, roughly forty miles east of Zagreb, the Croatian capital. The late-afternoon sun cast long shadows across the grass.

Humming to himself, Darrow brought the Pilatus in low and dropped gently onto the soft grass surface. Slowing gradually, they rolled almost all the way to the end of the strip and then swung around, with the prop still turning.

"Now what?" Brad asked.

"Now we head for our real destination," Darrow said. "But first I do this." He reached down to the center instrument panel and turned a series of knobs.

"You're turning off all the transponders?" Brad remarked, not trying to hide his surprise. Darrow gave him a sly wink. Aircraft transponders were a key component in air traffic control and safety. When interrogated by radar, a transponder automatically sent back a code identifying the plane and reported its current altitude. Flying without your transponder on was a definite no-no in civil aviation, because air traffic control then had to rely on radar "skin paint" for aircraft position, which was not very reliable. In some countries, especially in Eastern Europe, an aircraft without a transponder was automatically considered a hostile and was engaged without warning. He looked at Darrow. "Oh, man. We are going to be in *so* much trouble."

The Englishman laughed. "Only if we get caught." He pushed the throttles forward. The Pilatus rolled back down the grass strip, gathering speed fast. "And all it takes to avoid *that* little bit of unpleasantness is keeping right down on the deck for a few hundred kilometers or so. Then we stay off everybody's radar."

"A few hundred kilometers on the deck. At night," Brad said flatly. "In this crate."

"Relax," Darrow told him cheerfully. "I used to fly Tornado fighter-bombers for the RAF before I hired on with Scion. We always said that if you were more than fifty meters above the treetops, you were too bloody high."

Brad looked pointedly around the cockpit. "This isn't exactly a Tornado."

"Quite true," the Englishman admitted. Then he grinned again. "But squadrons in your own U.S. Air Force Special Operations Command use these same aircraft for low-level night infiltration and resupply missions. That's one of the reasons Mr. Martindale likes them so much."

He pulled gently back on the yoke and the Pilatus soared off the runway, heading east into the rapidly darkening sky. "Next stop, the Scrapheap."

"The Scrapheap?"

"Our own private air base," Darrow said. He winked at Brad. "It's a strange little place, full of odd aircraft and rather unusual people. I think you'll like it."

NEAR DONETSK, UKRAINE
That same time

A long line of dingy, rusting yellow dump trucks crawled south along the highway. Piled high with coal, the big KrAZ trucks were headed from nearby mines to factories elsewhere in the Russian separatist-controlled Donbass region. Before the war, railroads moved the coal, but most of the rail lines had been wrecked in the fighting and never fully repaired. Clouds of black coal dust swirled across the road behind the slowly moving convoy.

Men rode in the back of each dump truck, uneasily perched atop the swaying, shifting mounds. From their faded clothing and soot-stained faces, they were miners sent along to help shift the coal once it reached its destination. In war-ravaged eastern Ukraine, men were cheaper than machines.

Near the rear of the convoy, one of the riders kept his eyes fixed on the western sky, squinting against the reddish glare from the setting sun. There, he thought, catching sight of a speck moving so slowly that it almost seemed to be hovering. It was flying low, perhaps less than a thousand meters off the ground. It appeared to be paralleling their course.

After several minutes, though, he saw the glint of sunlight on wings as the object banked back to the north. Moving unhurriedly, he reached inside his jacket and pulled out a short-range tactical radio. It was not much bigger than a cell phone and its signals were far less likely to be intercepted.

"I have a drone in sight," Pavlo Lytvyn reported. "But it's checked us out and seems to be moving away to the north. We should be clear in five minutes."

"Any idea who it belongs to?" Fedir Kravchenko radioed back. "The OSCE or our friends from Moscow?"

"The Russians," Lytvyn said, continuing to follow the drone as it flew slowly away, still heading north. "One of their Israeli-made *Forpost* models, I think." He watched the drone until it disappeared in the distance. "That's it, Fedir," he said. "We are alone."

Below him, riding inside the dump truck's cab, Kravchenko peered out through a coal-dust-coated windshield. In the growing darkness it was difficult to make out much more than the glowing red taillights of the vehicle they were following.

He glanced at the driver, a wizened little man who sat perched behind the wheel, industriously puffing away on a foul-smelling cigarette. "How much further to the turnoff?"

The driver took another drag on his cigarette and then stubbed it out in the overflowing ashtray perched on the seat between them. "About twenty-five kilometers, Major."

Kravchenko summoned up a mental image of the map he had memorized. Given their current speed, it would be fully dark when the time came for this truck and the others driven by his men to break away from the main group. A cold, satisfied smile flitted across his maimed face. It was perfect. They should be completely unobserved when they headed for the scheduled rendezvous with the rest of his partisan group. And by the time the Russians or their traitorous separatist allies realized several dump trucks were missing from the coal convoy, it would be too late for them to do anything about it.

Far, far too late.

THE SCRAPHEAP, FORMERLY SILIŞTEA GUMEŞTI MILITARY AIRFIELD, ROMANIA
Two hours later

"Hang on, McLanahan," Mark Darrow said, banking the Pilatus PC-12 turboprop into a tight turn. Below the night-vision goggles he'd donned shortly after they took off from Bjelovar, the English pilot's mouth twisted into another crooked smile. "This next bit may be just a little rough."

"Gee, thanks for the warning," Brad said drily, tugging his seat belt tighter for what seemed the thousandth time. What the hell did this crazy ex-RAF pilot consider "rough" compared to the last couple of hours when they'd been hedgehopping across a pitch-black rural countryside? He'd spent most of the bumpy, turbulent flight low over Croatia, Hungary, and southern Romania gritting his teeth and staring out into the night sky beyond the cockpit—trying to figure out if he'd have time to see the power pylon, tree-studded hillside, or church steeple that killed them before they were, well, actually dead. At more than two hundred and fifty knots, that seemed unlikely.

Oh, he had to admit that Darrow was a damned good pilot. Even with the benefit of high-quality night-vision goggles, pulling off a stunt like this without terrain-following radar required incredible skill. But part of him kind of wished the Englishman weren't acting as though this was nothing more than a fun-filled jaunt on the world's longest thrill ride. Just a little show of nerves would make him seem more human somehow.

"Ah, there you are, you sneaky little bitch," Darrow said gleefully, rolling the turboprop back level. He chopped the throttles back and dropped the nose. The Pilatus slid down through the night sky, rapidly losing altitude.

"Mind telling me exactly what you're doing?" Brad asked, staring ahead into blackness. Glowing lights off in the distance marked what looked like a small village. He could just make out what looked like a long patch on the ground, a surface that was only slightly paler than the darker fields and wood-lots they were skimming over.

Darrow flashed another wild, madcap grin in his direction. He pushed a lever down and Brad heard and felt the hydraulic whine as the turboprop's landing gear came down. "Oh, didn't I say? We're here."

Abruptly, the Pilatus touched down, bounced back up in the air, and then came down again with a teeth-rattling jolt. Suddenly the plane was rolling along a badly cracked and overgrown runway, lurching, rocking, and shuddering through the clumps of brush and tall grass growing between each slab of old concrete. There were no lights. Everything outside was perfectly dark and still. The ex-RAF pilot applied beta, using the big propeller as a huge speed brake; a few seconds of reverse thrust; then tapped the brakes gently, gradually slowing the turboprop in its madcap, bounding rush.

A ray of light shot onto the unlit runway ahead of them, widening fast as two big hangar doors slid open off to their right.

Sliding the prop lever forward again, Darrow slewed the Pilatus toward the opening door and taxied straight into the hangar. He cut off the engine and turned toward Brad with a faint smile. "Welcome to the Scrapheap, Mr. McLanahan." The hangar doors were already rolling shut behind them.

For the next hour, Brad followed the Englishman on a quick, guided tour through an array of aircraft hangars and other facilities. Everywhere he looked, he saw a bewildering mix of old and new. The pattern, though, was clear. Seen from the outside, the onetime Romanian Air Force base was nothing more than a collection of worn-out buildings surrounding a runway that looked as though it hadn't been used for at least a decade. But seemingly dilapidated hangars were full of sophisticated manned and unmanned aircraft. Garages with peeling paint were crowded with upgraded Humvees, Land Rovers, and other vehicles. And the airfield's tower, warehouses, and other buildings were jam-packed with the latest computers, communications gear, and sensors.

"We try to keep a low profile," Darrow explained,

leading the way through an old barracks that had been extensively renovated, though only on the inside, and partitioned into separate living quarters for the Scion personnel stationed at the Scrapheap. "As far as the locals are concerned, this place belongs to an international holding company with more cash reserves than business sense. From time to time, the nominal owners float various proposals to reactivate the field as an air freight depot, but nothing ever seems to come of them."

"Which is why that runway is left in such crappy shape," Brad realized.

"Exactly," Darrow said, grinning. He shrugged. "It's actually in much better condition than it looks. A number of camouflage experts put rather a lot of work in on it. In daylight, it may look like an overgrown rubbish pile, but quite naturally we don't want any real FOD left lying about."

Brad nodded. FOD, foreign object damage, was a constant menace for any field operating jet aircraft. Small rocks and other bits of solid trash sucked into a jet-engine air intake could seriously mangle turbine blades.

They left the barracks and headed toward what looked like a rusting equipment shed. It was surrounded by mounds of worn-out tires and empty oil barrels. "Well, this is where I leave you," Darrow announced.

"Here?" Brad asked, staring at the ramshackle building in front of them.

"Go on, McLanahan," the other man said matter-of-factly, nodding toward a pair of large doors. "There's someone inside who very much wants to see you." He yawned. "As for me, I'm off to get some kip. All play and no sleep makes Mrs. Darrow's fair-haired lad a very dull flier."

Brad waited until the Englishman was gone and then slowly, almost reluctantly, pushed open one of the big doors to the shed. He stepped inside and closed it behind him.

The interior was brightly lit and clean. Various pieces of electronic gear and a few metal canisters lined the walls. Other than a single, sleek, twelve-foot-plus-tall shape standing motionless facing the door, the center of the shed was completely empty.

Brad stared up at the enormous, humanlike machine. Spindly-looking arms and legs were joined to a long torso, which sloped from broad shoulders to a narrower waist and hips. A six-sided head studded with sensor panels rested atop the robot's shoulders.

It was a Cybernetic Infantry Device—a human-piloted robot first developed by a U.S. Army research lab years ago. Sheathed in highly resistant composite armor, the CID's hydraulically powered exoskeleton was faster, more agile, and stronger than any ten men put together. A special haptic interface translated its pilot's muscle and limb motions into movement by the exoskeleton's limbs, enabling the CID to move with almost unnatural grace and precision, despite its size and power. Sensors of all kinds, coupled with a remarkably advanced computer interface, gave its pilot incredible situational awareness, and the ability to aim and fire a wide array of weapons with astonishing speed and accuracy. Boiled down to the essentials, a single CID could carry heavier firepower and possessed more mobility and recon capability than an entire U.S. Army infantry platoon.

Brad took a deep breath and then let it out. He stepped closer. "Hi, Dad."

"Hello, son," said the electronically synthesized voice of former Air Force Lieutenant General Patrick McLanahan. "Welcome to Romania."

TRAINING AND STORAGE DEPOT, UNITED ARMED FORCES OF NOVOROSSIYA, SOUTH OF DONETSK, UKRAINE
That same time

Sited forty kilometers south of the industrial city of Donetsk, the Russian-allied separatist base served several purposes. Its location, near the junction of several country roads, made it easier for the rebels and their Russian military "advisers" to terrorize, tax, and otherwise dominate the surrounding villages and farms. In addition, the base—set among wheat fields and orchards—made a good training site. Drafts of new recruits, mostly drawn from the urban streets of Donetsk and Luhansk, were taught the basics, discipline, small-arms marksmanship, and open-field combat tactics, before being sent on to active-duty units for more advanced training. Finally, the compound was a storage depot for RPGs, shoulder-launched SAMs, and other heavy weapons, including a battery of the BM-21 Grad launchers whose 122mm rockets had proved so deadly during the 2014 "hot war."

The separatist rebels and their Russian masters felt secure behind a minefield and a barrier made up of long coils of barbed wire. A heavy metal mesh gate offered the only way in or out past the defenses—and it was flanked by solid earth-and-log bunkers bristling with machine guns and antitank weapons.

They were about to learn an old lesson of war. Fortifications were only as effective as the soldiers who manned them. And static defenses were no match for a determined enemy given the time to prepare an assault.

Thirty meters from the western perimeter of the camp, Fedir Kravchenko slithered cautiously through tufts of tall grass growing among brown stalks of dead wheat and tangled weeds. He followed a narrow, winding path marked out by torn pieces of reflective tape. Before the Russians and their lackeys built their base, this fertile patch of ground had been planted in wheat. Now it was sown with antipersonnel mines.

Kravchenko moved slowly, allowing his eyes to pick out the faint glimmer from each piece of tape and then confirming what he saw by touch. It was almost completely dark. The new moon had set hours before and now there were only the stars speckling the night sky. Beyond the barbed wire, a few moving red sparks glowed.

Sentries smoking cigarettes, the Ukrainian decided. His mouth twisted in disgust. Amateurs.

He crawled out into a more open patch of ground,

only a few meters from the wire. The tape-marked path had ended. He moved to the side, clearing the way for the other men coming up behind him.

Pavlo Lytvyn loomed up at his shoulder. Leaning in close, the big man showed him the bayonet he held in his right hand and shook his head emphatically three times. *No more mines*, Kravchenko translated. Lytvyn was one of the men he'd selected to lead the three partisan assault teams through the minefield, probing for mines hidden among the grass and wheat with nothing more sophisticated than their fingers and bayonets.

As more and more dark-clad men came crawling out into the safer ground in front of the wire, he motioned them to deploy to the left and right. He collared the last two, both of whom were hauling heavy packs. Moving carefully and cautiously, they opened their packs and began screwing together threaded sections of explosives-packed pipe—assembling improvised Bangalore torpedoes that should blow holes in the separatist barbed-wire entanglement when they were detonated.

Kravchenko pulled a small, handheld radio out of his equipment vest. He pushed the power on and inserted a tiny earpiece. A soft hiss marked an open channel. He clicked the transmit button three times and then waited.

Two faint clicks came back.

Kravchenko switched the radio off and put it away. Gently, he tapped Lytvyn's shoulder, signaling the bigger man that they were ready.

Off in the distance, they heard the dull growling roar of a heavy truck motor. It was drawing nearer.

* * *

Teeth clenched against constant pain, Hennadiy Vovk reached out with his good hand and shoved the dump truck's gearshift down, slowing its 330-horsepower diesel engine. His prosthetic hook was firmly anchored to the steering wheel. Sweat trickled from under his cap. His last dose of morphine had worn off about an hour ago. He had another ampule, but he couldn't risk fogging his mind with painkillers. Nor slowing his reflexes. Not now.

Cranking the wheel to the right, Vovk turned off the paved road. He drove slowly up a rough dirt track, heading toward the Russian separatist base. There, caught in the dump truck's headlights, he could make out the metal mesh gate closing off the entrance. The hummocky shapes of camouflaged bunkers loomed up in the shadows on either side of the track.

Several uniformed guards were visible near the gate, already unslinging Russian-supplied assault rifles. Another waved a handheld flashlight from side to side, signaling him to stop.

"*Ostanovka!* Halt!" one of the guards yelled, stepping forward with a hand held up palm out.

Vovk braked, stamping down hard on the pedal with his right foot. His left leg ended in a stump just below the knee. More agony flamed through his damaged body. He hissed out through his teeth, fighting off the pain.

"You there!" an angry voice snapped. "What the devil are you doing here?"

The truck driver looked up. Two of the guards had moved right up to the side of the dump truck, peering into the darkened cab. Four or five others, eyes slitted against the glare of his headlights, were aiming their assault rifles at the windshield.

"Hey, easy there, Comrade," Vovk stammered, keeping his good hand in view. "I've got a load of coal for the Vuhlehirska Power Station. But I must have gotten turned around somewhere." He forced a shaky laugh. "It's damned dark out here."

One of the guards scowled. "You are way fucking lost, idiot. Vuhlehirska is at least thirty kilometers from here. Back that way." He gestured off to the north.

The other guard was staring at Vovk's prosthetic hook and missing left leg. "Jesus, what a cripple," he sneered. "How'd you lose them, gimp? In a crash because of your shitty driving?"

Suddenly Vovk felt perfectly calm, perfectly at peace. He smiled broadly at the soldier who'd taunted him. "Oh, no," he said gently. "It wasn't an accident. You bastards took them from me three years ago."

Before they could react, he reached out and tripped a switch rigged up on the dump truck's dashboard. Twenty kilograms of Russian-made PVV-5A plastic explosive planted beneath the left fuel tank detonated. In a blinding flash of searing white light, an enormous blast ripped through the huge KrAZ dump truck, obliterating it in a single split second. The guards, gate, and nearby bunkers vanished in that same instant, torn to shreds by the huge explosion. Hurled outward by the blast, jagged shards of smoking metal rained down across the compound. This deadly hailstorm of shrapnel killed even more Russian-allied separatist soldiers.

OVER EASTERN UKRAINE
That same time

One hundred kilometers to the north, a pair of Russian Sukhoi-24M2 fighter-bombers orbited at ten thousand meters. Assigned to patrol over the separatist-controlled regions of eastern Ukraine, they had already been on station for two hours. None of the four Russian airmen aboard the two planes was particularly happy with their mission. Su-24M2s were high-speed, low-level strike aircraft, modeled on the American-made F-111. Slated for eventual replacement as more of the newer and more capable Su-34s entered Russia's inventory, they were not designed for high-altitude routine surveillance. Besides that, the crews found the routine mind-numbingly dull.

Their protests were ignored. Given the Kremlin's new insistence on maintaining constant armed patrols over Belarus and this part of Ukraine, the commanders of Russia's air force were forced to use every plane in their inventory—whether perfectly suited to the mission or not. It was the only way they could avoid burning through engines and flight crews faster than was wise.

The lead Su-24 was banking, turning onto the next leg of its fuel-conserving racetrack holding pattern, when an enormous flash lit the sky to the south, briefly turning night into day.

"What the hell? Did you see that, Stepan?" the pilot, Captain Leonid Davydov, radioed his wingman.

"See what?"

"Some sort of explosion to the south. A big one," Davydov said.

"Negative," Captain Stepan Nikolayev reported. There was a pause. "Lieutenant Orlov and I both had our heads down, checking some of the engine readouts."

"Do you have trouble?"

"Maybe," Nikolayev admitted. "The second-stage turbine pressures on our number two engine are fluctuating a lot more than I would like."

Davydov swore under his breath. Even with all the upgrades added to this model, Su-24s were forty-plus-year-old airframes and their Lyulka AL-21F3 turbojet engines were even older technology. And no matter how much maintenance their ground crews did, things were bound to go wrong eventually. Engine failures were high up among the leading accident causes for any military aircraft, especially in Russia's aging Su-24 fleet.

He keyed his mike. "Right. Now listen to me, Stepan. Don't screw around with this. Break off and head for the barn. Belinsky and I will fly the rest of the mission on our own. Got it?"

"Understood," Nikolayev said reluctantly. "Heading for home now."

Davydov looked aft out of the canopy and saw the other Su-24M2 curving away, flying east. He glanced back at his weapons officer, Lieutenant Yuri Belinsky. "Well, there goes our foursome for vint."

Belinsky smiled dutifully. The Russian card game *vint*, similar to bridge, was a passion for his commanding officer. "That's a real shame, Captain."

"Now get busy and call in a report on that explosion I just saw," the pilot ordered. "Find out if Vornezh Control knows what on earth is going on down there."

TRAINING AND STORAGE DEPOT
That same time

Before the last shattering echoes of the truck-bomb blast faded, Kravchenko signaled the two partisans carrying their improvised Bangalore torpedoes forward. Bent low, they scuttled up to the edge of the barbed-wire entanglement, thrust the two lengths of pipe in under the wire, and raced back to the others—unreeling lengths of detonator cord as they ran.

"Down!" Kravchencko shouted to his assault teams. "Get your heads down!" He threw himself flat, pressing his face to the ground.

WHUUMMP! WHUUMMP!

Both Bangalores went off—shattering the darkness again. Smoke and dust boiled away along with tiny pieces of blackened and twisted wire.

Kravchenko got up on one knee, peering through the blast-created haze. The breaching charges had worked perfectly, blowing meter-wide gaps through the barbed-wire entanglement.

He jumped up, readying his AKS carbine. "Attack! Attack!" he yelled. *"Nemaye uv'yaznenykh!* No prisoners! *Take no prisoners!"*

"Vbty! Vbty! Kill! Kill!" his partisans roared,

pouring through the gaps and into the heart of the enemy compound. Assault rifles stuttered and grenades went off with earsplitting cracks as they advanced—systematically clearing barracks buildings and huts. There were screams and panicked shouts from the bomb-stunned defenders, but no organized resistance.

Kravchenko and Lytvyn charged in right behind them, followed by ten more men. They skidded to a halt near one of the buildings, checking their bearings.

"Take your sapper team and blow the shit out of those damned Grads, Pavlo," Kravchenko snapped. "You've got five minutes."

Lytvyn nodded once and moved off at a trot, followed by five partisans carrying heavy backpacks stuffed full of satchel charges. Destroying the deadly 122mm rocket launchers so prized by the separatists was one of their chief objectives.

But Kravchenko had other plans, too. With a sharp hand signal, he led the remaining partisans around the corner of the building and deeper into the enemy base. Crumpled bodies littered the ground, many clad only in T-shirts and their underwear. The Ukrainian smiled cruelly. His attack had caught the Russian-loving bastards in their sleep.

A dazed separatist soldier staggered out of the nearest barracks. Blood dripped from a deep gash on his forehead. He was unarmed.

Kravchenko raised his carbine, shot the reeling man twice at point-blank range, and jogged on without pausing. He had once remembered that these men were fellow Ukrainians—they could even be relatives, for all he knew—but the last time he had that thought seemed a very, very long time ago. Now they were just targets to be eliminated. They weren't even collaborators or turncoats to him anymore—they were just targets that had to be put down so he could accomplish his mission.

Another building loomed up out of the darkness. This one had no windows and its door was padlocked. The Ukrainian nodded. This was what he'd been looking for. He dropped to one knee, covering the others while they went to work with bolt cutters.

"We're in, Major!" he heard one of them yell.

And then the whole eastern edge of the compound lit up in a series of dazzling explosions that sent huge orange and red sheets of fire rippling skyward. The ground rocked.

"Nice work, Pavlo," Kravchenko murmured. So much for the Grads.

He ducked through the low door of the building his team had broken into. It was a weapons storage bunker. The Ukrainian already had a flashlight out, waving the beam across wooden racks holding meter-and-a-half-long green tubes. Other racks held white-painted missiles. "Those are what we want," he said. "Take as many as you can carry!"

One by one, his partisans grabbed 9K38 Igla "Needle" shoulder-fired antiaircraft launchers and missiles and hurried back out into the burning compound. The fires set by the detonation of their truck bomb and by the big artillery rocket launchers Lytvyn had destroyed were spreading fast.

Outside the storage bunker, Kravchenko pulled out a whistle and blew three short, shrill blasts. That was the signal for his assault teams to break off their attack and fade back into the pitch-black countryside. Once away from the blazing, ruined base, they would break up into small groups and disperse.

By the time the Russians or their separatist lackeys managed to push an armored or truck-mounted reaction force out from Donetsk, the partisans would be long gone.

The Ukrainian raised his head, eyeing the night sky. No, there was only one enemy threat left that he had worried about.

Then he smiled to himself. And now he didn't really have to fear even that.

OVER EASTERN UKRAINE
That same time

"My God," Captain Leonid Davydov said sharply, staring out through the canopy of his Su-24M2. Far off to the south, multiple explosions went off one after another and then faded out—leaving a flickering red and orange glow. "I don't care what Voronezh Control says, Belinsky. They may not have any reports of trouble, but something damned big is burning down there!"

He rolled the big swept-wing fighter-bomber into a tight turn toward the south, pulled the wings back to sixty-nine degrees sweep, and shoved his throttles forward. Driven by two massive turbojet engines producing almost thirty-four thousand pounds of thrust, the Su-24 accelerated fast.

Settling on course toward the distant fires, Davydov rolled hard left, letting the loss of lift pull the fighter-bomber's nose toward the ground. He felt himself floating up against his harness as the gentle dive produced a zero-G-like condition. Unloaded, with the aircraft's nominal weight reduced almost to nothing, the Su-24 picked up even more speed.

"Inform Voronezh that we are investigating," he told his weapons officer as he rolled wings level.

"Yes, sir," the lieutenant replied.

"And get the Kaira-24 optical system up and running," Davydov ordered. The Kaira-24 was a combined laser designator and infrared television scanner system. Comparable to the Pave Tack target detection and designation pods first used by American F-111F strike planes, it sent thermal images to a TV screen at Belinsky's station. If necessary, the Su-24's weapons officer could use those images to pick out targets for the laser-guided bombs they were carrying.

Five minutes later, Davydov leveled off at about five hundred meters, reduced his throttles, and pushed the fighter-bomber's wings forward to forty-five degrees for the slower-speed ingress. Now that he had a good fix on the fires burning ahead, coming in too hot would only make it more difficult to figure out just what was going on. The airspeed indicator on his HUD dropped steadily.

"Five kilometers out," Belinsky said, peering intently at the grainy infrared images on his monitor. "I see multiple fires burning in what looks like some kind of complex, possibly a military base."

"Christ," Davydov muttered. "That must be one

of ours. Go active on all countermeasures, *now*." He thumbed a button on his stick. "Arming cannon." For strafing runs, the Su-24 carried an internal GSh-6-23 cannon with five hundred rounds.

"There are bodies on the ground in the complex!" Belinsky said suddenly, still staring at his screen. "Many bodies. None moving."

Davydov swallowed hard. "Warn Voronezh! Tell them this is a terrorist—"

Suddenly there were more bright flashes lighting up the dark ground ahead of them. Streaks of flame slashed up into the air at incredible speed, already curving toward the Su-24 as it streaked past overhead.

"*Missile attack!*" Davydov yelled. Desperately, he slammed the defensive countermeasures button on his stick, simultaneously yanking the fighter-bomber into a gut-wrenching, high-G turn to the left. White-hot magnesium flares blossomed behind the rolling Su-24, trying to decoy the heat-seeking missiles homing in on the wildly maneuvering aircraft.

It was no use. Ambushed at low altitude, and without enough maneuvering room or airspeed to evade successfully, the Su-24M2 was easy prey.

Two of the five shoulder-launched SAMs fired by Kravchenko's partisans were spoofed by flares and blew up hundreds of meters behind the fleeing Russian fighter-bomber. One never locked on. It climbed wildly into the night sky before exhausting its solid-rocket propellant and plunging back to earth. But two smashed home and detonated, shredding the Su-24's control surfaces. Still rolling off to the left, the Russian plane slammed into the ground at several hundred kilometers an hour and blew up, strewing burning pieces of itself across Ukrainian wheat fields in a tumbling ball of fire and scorched earth. It happened so fast that neither crewmember had a change to reach their ejection handles.

CHAPTER 5

*Don't be afraid to give up the
good to go for the great.*

—John D. Rockefeller,
American industrialist

**THE SCRAPHEAP,
NEAR SILIŞTEA GUMEŞTI, ROMANIA**
That same time

Brad McLanahan looked up at the Cybernetic Infantry Device piloted by his father, Patrick. No matter how hard you tried, he thought, there were some things you never got used to. This was one of them.

Nearly two years ago, he was sure that he'd seen his father killed—mangled when a 30mm cannon burst from a Chinese J-15 fighter had ripped into the left side of the XB-1 Excalibur bomber they had been flying together. There had even been a funeral service for him, attended by both the sitting president and the vice president of the United States.

Then, last year, during his work on the Starfire Project, he had come face-to-face with this CID, or one just like it, and learned that his father had not died of his terrible wounds after all. Or at least not permanently.

Kevin Martindale had dispatched a Scion team to Guam to collect intelligence data on the Chinese sneak attack that had smashed Andersen Air Force Base. There, in a little clinic outside the base, they found Patrick McLanahan resuscitated from clinical death and still clinging feebly to life. But he was in critical condition and it seemed highly unlikely that he would survive long enough to be evacuated back to the United States. As a desperate emergency measure, the Scion team had placed him inside a CID, hoping the robot's automated life-support systems could help keep him alive long enough to die in a hospital. To their amazement, the CID had not only stabilized Patrick's condition, it had brought him back to full consciousness.

But there was a catch.

Patrick McLanahan could fully function inside the manned robot, piloting it and employing its weapons and sensors effectively. The CID's systems monitored his body and brain and supplied the oxygen, water, and nutrients needed to sustain his life. And its sensor arrays and computers allowed him to see and interact electronically with the world. But the CID could not heal him. Outside its confines, his damaged body, unable to breathe on its own, would gradually slip into a coma.

Faced with a choice between life trapped in a machine and the endless twilight of a permanent vegetative state, he had opted for life . . . at least, life of a sort.

Since then, Brad knew his father had become part of Scion—training with Martindale's direct-action teams and using the CID's computers and sensors to assist in the company's intelligence-gathering, planning, and counterterrorist surveillance operations. From some of the things Patrick had said in their relatively few private conversations, he suspected there was a lot more to it than that.

And it was probably high time that he found out exactly what that was.

"It's really great to see you, Dad," Brad said, working hard to keep his voice from shaking. "But I guess you didn't bring me all the way out here just for a father-son chat."

"No, Brad, I didn't," his father said somberly.

"Have you picked up intel on some new murder plot by the Russians?" Brad asked. Last year, Scion security teams had stopped several attempts by Russian agents to kill him—attempts directly ordered by Russia's president. That was what had first prompted his father to reveal his own unexpected survival to Brad. Another effort by Gennadiy Gryzlov to try wiping out anyone carrying the McLanahan name could explain why he'd been yanked out of Sky Masters and the U.S. so covertly.

"Not precisely," Patrick said.

"Then why am I here?" Brad wondered. He shrugged. "I mean, seeing all this supersecret spy stuff is really cool, but it's not really my forte.

Besides, my junior year at Cal Poly starts in mid-September. And I don't think my professors will buy the 'please excuse my absence, because I was visiting a covert private military base' line—even if you or President Martindale would let me use it."

The CID was silent for several moments. Brad wished again that he could see his father's face or hear his real laugh. It was unnerving to look up and see only the robot's smooth, expressionless armor, even knowing that the older McLanahan was co-cooned inside.

"To some extent, you're here partly *because* we don't have a good fix on Gryzlov's plans or intentions," Patrick said finally.

Brad frowned. "Look, Dad, no offense, but I can take care of myself. Sergeant Major Wohl and his countersurveillance guys taught me pretty well."

"Chris Wohl was a good man," his father agreed. "But that's not the point, son."

Brad took another deep breath. "Okay . . . what is the point?"

"You saw the news about that Russian general who was assassinated and Moscow's revenge attack on that Polish village near the Ukrainian border?"

Brad nodded. "Yeah. It sounded pretty bad, like that crazy son of a bitch Gryzlov's gone off his meds again. But what's that got to do with me?"

"Maybe nothing," his father admitted. "But maybe everything. Intelligence gathering, even with my ability to poke around inside secure computer systems, is an inexact science. We only ever see fragments of the real picture, so we have to do a lot of interpolation and extrapolation from the scraps of hard data we *do* pick up."

"Like figuring out a thousand-piece jigsaw puzzle when you've only got handful of the pieces," Brad realized.

"And when you're not even sure that all the pieces you found belong to the same puzzle," Patrick agreed. "It's a question of learning to recognize certain patterns—patterns of encrypted communications, troop and aircraft movements, leadership rhetoric, weapons procurement decisions, and a lot of other factors."

"And now you're picking warning signs of something bad happening?" Brad asked carefully.

"It's more like seeing the intelligence picture we thought we had a grip on suddenly shift into something we don't yet recognize," his father said. "Which means we're in the dark right now, as far as figuring out what the Russians are up to goes. And being in the dark about what a tyrant like Gennadiy Gryzlov intends is a very dangerous place to be."

"Yeah, I understand that," Brad said. Then he looked up at the CID. "I'm sorry, Dad, but none of what you've just described sounds like a serious reason to blow the kind of money or pull the kind of covert stunts your people just used to fly me here."

"We're convinced the Russians may be planning something big," Patrick said stubbornly. "Something that may be very dangerous. The murder of that general of theirs, Voronov, was a catalyst of some kind. We're picking up signs of heightened readiness in every branch of the Russian armed forces. They're flying more aircraft near Poland and the Baltic states. More tank and motor-rifle brigades are moving from cantonments deep inside Russia to new bases closer to the Ukrainian border. And their tactical missile forces appear to be running repeated firing drills."

Brad whistled softly. "Okay, that doesn't sound good." Then he shook his head. "But that's not evidence of any threat to me personally."

"Except for the fact that the last time Gryzlov decided to take a shot at you, he also started firing missiles at our spaceplanes and Armstrong Space Station," his father reminded him. "He has a track record of trying to settle personal grudges at the same time that he's pursuing strategic military options."

"That's pretty thin, Dad," Brad said slowly.

"Yes, it is," his father agreed. "But you're my son. And I've learned the hard way to trust my instincts. I'm not prepared to risk your life in the hope that Gennadiy Gryzlov or the killers he gives orders to have learned to leave the McLanahans alone. If I'm wrong and there aren't assassins hunting you again, we'll know soon enough, and you can go back to Cal Poly. In the meantime, we really do need you here."

"You need me?" Brad didn't bother hiding his surprise. "Why?"

"You've met Mark Darrow," his father said.

Brad nodded, keeping his expression carefully blank. He still wasn't sure what he thought of the ex-RAF flier.

"Well, we're assembling a cadre of pilots like him, all with similar skills and experience," Patrick said.

"So far, they're mostly from the U.S., the UK, and Canada. They're all ex-military, trained to fly some of the most advanced aircraft in the world."

"Which is interesting, but still it doesn't explain why you've brought me here," Brad said.

"These men and women are great aviators," his father said. "But they're still just a collection of individual pilots. They don't yet form a cohesive unit. What we need them to become is a tough, top-notch flying and fighting squadron. And that's what I want you to build them into."

"*Me?*" Brad exclaimed. "Look, Dad, I'm just a college kid. My total real military leadership experience is just about zero, even if you count my time in the Civil Air Patrol."

"I watched you build your Starfire team, son," Patrick said. "You took a bunch of eccentric, brilliant individualists and turned them into an incredible scientific and engineering group—a group that was able to meet and overcome obstacles that were far bigger than anyone could have predicted. You then built a design and consultation portfolio with the names of hundreds of scientists and engineers all over the world, all of whom volunteered to assist."

"I had Jerry Kim and Jodie Cavendish," Brad said. "They were the marquee names. That's what attracted the technical and money contributions."

"They were superstars, no doubt, but there's also no doubt that the team never would have happened without your leadership," Patrick said. "Jodie had been working on her own for years; Jung-bae Kim was so high in the theoretical-science stratosphere that no one ever thought about recruiting him . . .

except *you*. Then, you made them all work together. That kind of leadership is hard to find."

"Maybe that's true," Brad said. His eyes darkened at the thought of his friend and fourth teammate Casey Huggins, the youngest female and the first paraplegic ever to travel to Earth orbit. She had been killed in the Russian attack on Starfire, awarding her yet another historic first: the youngest woman to die in Earth orbit. "Casey died in the process."

"That wasn't your doing," Patrick said. "Blame Gryzlov and his thugs."

"Even so, Starfire was different," Brad insisted. "Corralling students, scientists, and engineers to design and build and test that microwave laser was one thing. It was an incredibly cool project we all loved. But asking me to do the same thing with a bunch of zipper-suited sun-god fighter pilots and bomber jocks . . ." He shook his head. "That's totally different."

"Maybe not as different as you imagine," Patrick said.

"I don't get that."

"I'd guess Darrow did some showing off on your flight in," his father said carefully.

"Oh, yeah," Brad said sourly. "He's absolutely a shit-hot pilot. And I got the definite impression he wanted me to know it."

Patrick said nothing for a few moments. Then he asked, "Didn't it ever occur to you to wonder why he bothered to do that? I mean, if you're just a college student like you said, right? Why should a top-of-the-line veteran RAF aviator give a damn about what you think of his flying skills?"

"Maybe he was trying to impress you through me," Brad said. "You know, get the word to the boss, former Lieutenant General Patrick S. McLanahan, through his kid."

"He doesn't know who I am, son," his father said. "None of them do. We're still keeping the fact that I'm alive a closely held secret. To Darrow and the other pilots here, I'm just a faceless man in the machine or a call sign on the radio or an identifier tag on a Scion e-mail."

"Oh," Brad said, trying to hide the sorrow he suddenly felt. His father had always insisted that he didn't want anyone's pity—and that he didn't regret the choice he had made.

"You, on the other hand, are not exactly anonymous," Patrick went on doggedly, not giving him the chance to dodge. "You've flown in real combat—both against the Chinese and in space, against the Russians. Maybe that's old news to a lot of people on the outside, but it's not in the military aviation community. And especially not among the kind of people we recruit into Scion. Whether you believe it or not, Brad, the other pilots assembling here at the Scrapheap already know that you are their equal. Of course, they would all rather screw the pooch in front of the rest of the others than admit that."

Not sure of what to say to that, Brad colored in embarrassment. He looked down at his shoes, waiting for the telltale warmth to fade. Then he glanced up at the huge CID standing motionless in front of him. "But what do I do, Dad? I mean, I can't just strut into the ready room, strike a heroic pose, and say, 'Hey, boys and girls, I've got an idea, let's get together and build ourselves an elite combat air squadron!'"

"Just be yourself," his father said. "Trust your instincts about people and about how to motivate them. Get to meet the other pilots first and—"

He broke off suddenly. The CID's six-sided head swiveled away smoothly, as though it were listening to something in the distance.

"Dad?"

"It looks as though you got here just in time, Brad," his father said. "I'm picking up a whole series of emergency signals on frequencies used by the Russian Air Force. One of their Su-24s just went down over eastern Ukraine."

"Was it an accident?" Brad asked grimly.

"Only if someone *accidentally* fired off a number of shoulder-launched SAMs at the same moment that Russian pilot flew overhead."

"Oh, crap."

The CID nodded. "I am glad you're here now, son. Because I suspect we are about to get very, very busy."

THE KREMLIN, MOSCOW
The next morning

"So, once again, it seems that my vaunted military is left with egg all over its foolish face," President

Gennadiy Gryzlov said acidly, staring down the length of the conference table at Gregor Sokolov, the minister of defense.

Sokolov turned pale. "With respect, Mr. President," he said. "The General Staff and the Defense Ministry are not responsible for the tactical errors of the United Armed Forces of Novorossiya! These Ukrainian separatists are an independent militia, one which is not under our direct command and control."

"Bullshit!" Gryzlov growled. "Peddle that lie to someone else, perhaps to some of those idiots in the UN or the EU." He slammed a clenched fist on the table, rattling the teacups and ashtrays placed before the increasingly worried-looking members of his national security team. "We all know who calls the shots in the eastern Ukraine." He swung around on his chief of staff, seated next to him. "Correct, Sergei?"

"Yes, sir," Tarzarov said. "We do."

"Goddamned right." Gryzlov turned back to Sokolov. "So cut the crap, Gregor. Tell me, how many 'volunteers' from our armed forces were inside that compound last night? Before the terrorists blew it all to hell, I mean."

The defense minister looked down at his tablet computer, checking through the notes prepared by his staff. He looked up, even paler now. "Seven officers, Mr. President. A colonel, two majors, and four captains. They were assigned to the separatists to handle training and weapons familiarization."

"And how many of them survived this little debacle?" Gryzlov asked.

"None," Sokolov admitted.

"Perhaps that is just as well," the president said coldly. "Otherwise, I would have been forced to sign orders for their immediate execution for incompetence and cowardice in the face of the enemy—after the obligatory field courts-martial, naturally."

Still scowling, he looked at the powerfully built, white-haired man sitting impassively next to the minister of defense. Colonel General Valentin Maksimov, commander of the Russian Air Force, had taught at the Yuri Gagarin Military Air Academy during Gryzlov's days as a cadet there. Despite the respect he still felt for his old commanding officer, Gryzlov had no intention of allowing any of his subordinates to wriggle off the hook. Coming so soon after the murder of Lieutenant General Voronov, these multiple military fiascos in the eastern Ukraine were inexcusable.

"And you, Maksimov," Gryzlov asked. "How do you explain what happened to your Su-24?"

"The evidence is fairly clear," the older man said calmly. "Captain Davydov's plane was hit by at least one surface-to-air missile. I've dispatched an incident team to the crash site. Once they send me a more detailed report, I'll know more. In the meantime, preliminary data suggests the weapon used had a small warhead, probably something on the order of one of our own 9K38 Iglas or the American-made Stinger missiles."

"I'm *not* talking about Davydov's aircraft!" Gryzlov snapped.

"Sir?" Maksimov looked puzzled.

"I want to know about the *other* Su-24!" Gryzlov said. "The one that turned tail and ran before Davydov's bomber was shot down."

"I am afraid you are misinformed, Mr. President," Maksimov said, frowning. "Captain Nikolayev and his weapons officer returned to base because their aircraft showed clear signs of a potentially hazardous engine failure."

"And you believe their story?" Gryzlov asked skeptically.

"I believe the maintenance report submitted by the Seven Thousandth Aviation Base at Voronezh Malshevo," the other man said stiffly. "Engine failures are always a risk, especially in aircraft with so many years of service."

"I see." Gryzlov smiled. "That is very . . . illuminating." He turned his dark gaze on Viktor Kazyanov.

The minister of state security appeared even more nervous than the others, Gryzlov noted. That was as it should be. Not only had the intelligence agencies nominally under Kazyanov's control completely failed to identify the terrorists responsible for Voronov's assassination, they had also failed to pick up any warning signs of this new terrorist attack in the Ukraine. No doubt Kazyanov expected to be immediately dismissed from his post and perhaps imprisoned or worse. That was tempting, he thought. But poor Viktor made a useful whipping boy. For now.

"Kazyanov!" Gryzlov said sharply, watching with inner glee as the other man swallowed convulsively.

"Yes, Mr. President!"

"I want an immediate investigation of the maintenance staff at the Seven Thousandth Aviation Base," Gryzlov ordered. "Find out if any of its officers or men are saboteurs in league with these terrorists."

"Sir!" Maksimov cut in. "I must protest. There is no evidence of any sabotage against our aircraft!"

"Of course there isn't, General," Gryzlov said coolly. "Then again, we haven't started looking for it yet, have we? Who can say what dirty little secrets Kazyanov's ferrets may uncover?"

He turned back to the rest of his national security advisers, most of whom sat transfixed in their seats, watching him as closely and as fearfully as a flock of sheep might eye a wolf circling ever nearer. "So much for the humiliating failures of the past twenty-four hours," he said. "Now we face a bigger challenge."

His chief of staff was one of the few apparently unfazed by their leader's display of temper. Tarzarov raised an eyebrow. "In what way?"

"It is time to face unpleasant facts," Gryzlov said. "It is time to realize that we face an enemy who is waging a war against us, a secret war. And that this is a war we are losing."

"I am not sure that two separate terrorist attacks— however destructive—can or should be construed as acts of war," Foreign Minister Daria Titeneva said, choosing her words with evident care. "If we do so, we might be tempted to overreact."

Her colleagues, still watching Gryzlov's grim, tight-lipped face, edged perceptibly away from the foreign minister—as if they were subtly and not so subtly disassociating themselves from her cautiously expressed dissent.

"Overreact, Daria?" the Russian president said with deceptive mildness. "You truly believe the risk of *overreacting* is the real danger we face here?"

Titeneva sat rigid, clearly aware that she was treading on dangerous ground. But she forced herself to go on. "It is *one* of them, Mr. President," she said. "We were very fortunate that our last retaliatory strike into Poland did not provoke a larger international crisis."

"I think you are mistaken," Gryzlov told her flatly. "In fact, it is precisely our own demonstrated weakness which now tempts our enemies into carrying out ever-more-deadly attacks against us."

"I do not understand what you mean, Mr. President," Titeneva said, plainly troubled.

"Think about it!" he snapped. "The first terrorist attack cost us twelve dead, including a senior officer. And what was our reaction? A pinprick, nothing more. One tiny village destroyed, along with an old missile radar and a pair of near-obsolete fighter planes. Nothing of significance!"

Gryzlov looked around the conference table. "And what have we done since then? Tell me, what?"

There was silence.

"Exactly," he snarled. "We have been passive. Idle. Locked in a defensive crouch. Certainly, we've had more fighters and bombers circling endlessly on patrol. But to what end?" Angrily, Gryzlov stabbed a finger at the conference room's large flat-screen monitor, which showed gruesome images taken by the first Russian troops rushed in to reinforce the burned-out separatist base. "To that end! More than two hundred dead. A battery of heavy rocket artillery annihilated. And one of our fighter-bombers blown out of the sky."

He turned to the minister of defense. "Tell me, Gregor. How many of the terrorists who attacked that camp have your soldiers killed or captured so far?"

"None," Sokolov said reluctantly. "It appears that the enemy force dispersed well before our reaction force arrived."

"Leaving us looking like fools," Gryzlov said bluntly. "Weak, incompetent, cowardly fools." He shook his head. "That must stop. We must act boldly and decisively against this terrorist threat. And we must do so before it metastasizes into something infinitely more dangerous."

Titeneva stirred herself. "We cannot attack Poland a second time, Mr. President! Not in retaliation for this act of terrorism, which occurred hundreds of kilometers outside its territory. Weak though she may be, you heard the American president's warning. If we strike the Poles again without clear evidence that Warsaw is somehow involved in this atrocity, the United States might be forced to honor its alliance."

"True, Daria," Gryzlov said regretfully. "But I do not intend to punish the Poles again. At least not yet."

"Then what other options do we have, Gennadiy?" Tarzarov asked, keeping his voice low.

In answer, Gryzlov put his own tablet computer on the table and lightly tapped its slick surface. The pictures of dead men and ruined buildings vanished, replaced by a map of Ukraine. Pockets of red centered on eastern industrial cities like Donetsk and Luhansk showed the extent of the territory controlled by separatists acting on Russian orders.

The Russian president let them all stare at the map for a few moments and then, smiling coldly, he touched the tablet's screen again. "You ask what we can do?" he said. "This is what we *will* do."

Abruptly, the area shown in red expanded, growing rapidly to cover the entire eastern half of Ukraine—all the way up to the line of the Dnieper River. Only a small sliver of territory, containing the eastern half of Kiev, Ukraine's capital city, remained untouched. There were muffled gasps around the table.

"Annex virtually all of eastern Ukraine?" Tarzarov said, staring at the sea of red. He shook his head. "No one will stand for that, Gennadiy. It's too much."

"But we are not annexing this territory," Gryzlov told him with a wolfish smile. "We are simply establishing a temporary 'zone of protection' for the innocent ethnic Russians whose lives and property are in danger from these continuing terrorist attacks. After what happened last night, who can blame us for taking such reasonable and measured precautions?"

He stood up and went up to the display, tracing the long line of the Dnieper River with his finger. "This river is the key," he told them. "Once our troops control the bridges and ferries across the Dnieper, we can soon get a grip on these terrorists and then tear them to pieces."

"By cutting their lines of supply and retreat," Sokolov realized. For the first time that morning, the defense minister looked less hunted.

Gryzlov nodded. "If their hiding places and arms caches are on the east side of the Dnieper, our Spetsnaz forces will eventually find and destroy them. They will have nowhere to run and nowhere to hide."

"And if the terrorists are receiving Polish support as you suspect?" Titeneva asked quietly.

"If Warsaw is involved, we will soon find out," he told her. "And it will be much easier to intercept new shipments of Polish-supplied weapons and explosives if they have to cross the Dnieper first."

"The Ukrainian government will resist our invasion," the dark-haired foreign minister warned him. "They cannot stand idly by and watch while we seize most of the rest of their heavy industry and move tanks and soldiers right up to the suburbs of their capital."

"You think not?" Gryzlov wondered. He turned to Sokolov. "How many troops can we move into eastern Ukraine within forty-eight hours?"

"More than forty thousand, Mr. President," the defense minister said, glancing down at his computer. "Including two tank and four motor-rifle brigades. We can also use elements of the Seventh-Sixth Air Assault Division and the Forty-Fifth Special Reconnaissance Regiment to seize the Dnieper crossings by surprise."

"And what is your evaluation of the fascist Ukrainian regime's ability to resist our operation?" Gryzlov asked.

"Negligible," Sokolov replied. "We shattered

their regular army and their so-called volunteer battalions with ease three years ago. Since the Western powers have refused to supply them with arms or ammunition, the Ukrainians are even less able to fight us now. We could destroy their ability to resist in a matter of days at most. Conquering their whole country would be a mere matter of marching!"

"You see?" Gryzlov said to Titeneva. "Kiev's rulers are not idiots. Given a choice to keep half their country or lose it all forever, they will be sensible." He shrugged. "Besides, I will promise them that this is only a short-term move to suppress terrorism. If the Ukrainians peacefully withdraw the remnants of their army to the west side of the Dnieper, our troops will stop at the river line. And once we are satisfied that we have destroyed the terrorists who have been attacking us, our tanks and soldiers will return to Russia."

"Will they?" Tarzarov asked. The older man had a cynical look in his eyes.

"Of course," Gryzlov said, grinning openly. "After all, Sergei, I am a man of my word, am I not?"

FORWARD ELEMENTS, 9TH MOTOR-RIFLE BRIGADE, NEAR KONOTOP, EASTERN UKRAINE
Two days later

Surrounded by his staff and headquarters security troops, Major General Konstantin Zarubin stood on a low hill, watching his brigade's T-90 tanks and BMP-3 infantry fighting vehicles rumble west along the highway. Thick clouds of diesel exhaust hung low above the long column of armored vehicles.

Off to the west, the distant clatter of rotors marked the darting flight of Ka-60 reconnaissance and Mi-28 attack helicopters belonging to the 15th Army Aviation Brigade. The helicopters were probing ahead of his advancing battalions, ready to smash the least sign of Ukrainian resistance with rockets, antitank missiles, and 30mm cannon fire.

Zarubin frowned. So far, of course, there had been no resistance. Confronted with President Gryzlov's ultimatum and sworn pledge that this military venture was purely a defensive and temporary measure, Kiev's government had ordered its forces to withdraw west of the Dnieper without engaging the advancing Russians.

Well and good, Zarubin thought. It was always better to take territory without a fight. But he wasn't sure this relative peace and quiet would last much longer. Already there were reports of mass protests and rioting in Kiev and other western Ukrainian cities. If the current government fell, its successor might feel compelled to wage a hopeless war for honor.

The general contemplated that with some unease. Oh, he knew a conventional war against the Ukraine's outgunned and outnumbered regulars would not last long. One or two sharp battles should finish them off as a coherent force. No, what he worried about was the possibility that open fighting might trigger a bitter guerrilla war here in the east.

Despite what Moscow might say about the ultimate loyalties of the Russian-speaking population of eastern Ukraine, Zarubin had seen few signs of enthusiasm from the locals as his tanks and troops rolled toward the Dnieper. A few Russian flags had fluttered from various public buildings as they drove through towns and cities, but he privately suspected most of those had been planted by Spetsnaz and GRU recon teams sent in ahead of his motor-rifle brigade.

The prospect of facing stony indifference or even cold disapproval from the Ukrainians did not bother him. Unlike the foolish countries of the West, Russia did not train its soldiers to worry excessively about winning the "hearts and minds" of those it conquered. But the general knew that open hostility from even a small fraction of the population in Moscow's newly proclaimed "Zone of Protection" could present a serious challenge.

Once Zarubin's tank and motor-rifle battalions reached the Dnieper line, his brigade's supply lines back to Russia would stretch for more than three hundred and fifty kilometers. That was a lot of territory to guard if partisans began sniping at convoys or planting mines and other improvised explosives. And though Moscow already planned to send additional troops to protect those roads and railroads— both its own border-guard units and groups of Russian-allied separatists brought in from Donetsk and Luhansk—they would still be stretched pretty thinly.

Any protracted guerrilla war would be a big military and diplomatic headache, especially since the whole purposes of this invasion was to isolate and destroy the terrorist bands that had already attacked Russian interests in this region. That was why Zarubin and the other commanders advancing toward the Dnieper were under direct orders to make the painful consequences of any armed resistance or sabotage explicit now, while the local reaction was still in flux.

He turned away from the highway and marched back down the hill toward the gaggle of wheeled and tracked command vehicles that marked his brigade headquarters. A herd of worried-looking civilians waited there, hemmed in by grim-faced Spetsnaz troops in body armor. Most of them were local government officials from the neighboring towns and villages. Others were business owners, Catholic and Orthodox priests, and schoolteachers. They had been rounded up in the early-morning hours and held for his arrival here.

Zarubin clambered up onto the hood of his GAZ Tigr-M 4x4 command car and stood there, looking down at the crowd with his hands on his hips. "Citizens! Since I know that you all want to return to your homes, offices, and places of business, I will make this very short," he said, raising his voice just enough to be heard. He smiled thinly. "If not so sweet."

There were no answering smiles.

Undeterred, he carried on. "This region is now part of the Zone of Protection. During this short campaign against terrorist forces, your own local police and officials will remain charged with maintaining law and order on a day-to-day basis. My soldiers and I are here only to protect you from terrorists, not to subject you to our rule." Zarubin paused for a moment, graciously allowing anyone who felt like it to applaud.

There was only silence.

He shrugged. That was not surprising. Now he hardened his voice. "But make no mistake! The armed forces of the Russian Federation will exercise ultimate authority for as long as is necessary. And interference with our operations will not be tolerated!"

Zarubin eyed the crowd. He had their full attention. Good. Now to ram home today's civics lesson. "The rules are very simple," he said sternly. "Obey the orders we give without question and there will be no trouble. But—"

Moving slowly and deliberately, he unsnapped the flap of the holster at his side and drew his 9mm pistol. The faces of the civilians at the front of the crowd turned pale. The Russian general smiled. He raised his pistol so that everyone could see it. "Attacks of any kind on my soldiers or my vehicles or on those we place in authority will be met with deadly force. I warn you now that our reprisals will not be proportionate or measured. On the contrary, they will be designed to inflict enormous pain on the terrorists who attack us—and on anyone who aids these terrorists or even simply turns a blind eye to their criminal actions. For every Russian who is murdered, ten Ukrainians will die! For every piece of Russian equipment destroyed or damaged, ten homes or shops will be burned to the ground!"

That created a stir in the crowd, a palpable ripple of fear.

Seeing it, Zarubin nodded to himself in satisfaction. The threat of Russian reprisals should turn the populace against itself—significantly increasing the numbers of those who could be tempted to report their neighbors for suspicious activities. The lessons of antipartisan warfare were clear. Networks of local collaborators and informants were the key to crushing any attempted campaign of ambush and sabotage.

He jumped down from the Tigr and then beckoned the Spetsnaz captain who commanded this detachment of commandos. "Good work, Pelevin," he said. "Now get rid of this bunch. Let them walk home. Then send your men out ahead of the column and round up the next batch of local leaders. God help us, but we'll need to do this all over again another thirty kilometers down the road."

THE WHITE HOUSE, WASHINGTON, D.C.
A few hours later

President Stacy Barbeau listened to General Spelling's report on the Russian advance into eastern Ukraine with unconcealed irritation. Less than two weeks ago, she had persuaded Gennadiy Gryzlov to agree to high-level negotiations aimed at defusing tensions in Eastern Europe—and now he pulled this stunt? Was Russia's president as crazy as Ken Phoenix and his crowd had claimed? Sure

somebody, probably fanatical Ukrainian national-
ists, had wiped out a Russian-backed separatist base
and knocked down one of Gryzlov's planes, but how
could anyone sane think that justified moving thousands of troops and tanks into a sovereign country?
Damn it, didn't the Russians realize the risks they
were running? If she couldn't find a way to smooth
this over and fast, hard-liners here at home would
use it to justify their demands that she take a stronger line overseas—at the expense of all her domestic
programs.

"All of our sources confirm that the spearheads
of Russia's invasion force have already pushed more
than eighty miles into Ukrainian territory," the
chairman of the Joint Chiefs said. "We believe—"

Barbeau's temper snapped. "This is decidedly *not*
an invasion, General Spelling! And we will not label
it as such. President Gryzlov may want to provoke a
full-fledged confrontation with this stunt, perhaps
as way to deflect some of the political heat he must
be taking for not stopping the terrorist attacks on
Russian forces. Well, we are *not* going to play that
game with him," she said. "I want everyone in this
room to be very clear on that." She looked around at
the others crowded into the White House Situation
Room. "Is that understood?"

Some of the military and intelligence officers
around the table seemed surprised at her vehemence.
Her political people, led by her chief of staff, Luke
Cohen, were not. The lanky New Yorker nodded
slightly and flashed her a discreet thumbs-up.

She turned back to the chairman of the Joint

Chiefs. "Is there any evidence that the Ukrainians are shooting at these columns of Russian forces in their territory, General?"

Frowning now, Spelling shook his head. "No, Madam President. All the data we have—including signals intercepts and video feeds from OSCE drones monitoring the Russian forces—indicate that the Ukrainian Army and volunteer battalions are withdrawing ahead of them without engaging in combat. Those are the orders their government gave them, and they seem to be obeying."

"That settles it, then," Barbeau said. "You can't have an invasion without combat. If the Ukrainians aren't inclined to fight, we certainly aren't going to embarrass them by using loaded terms that make it look as though they're cowards."

CIA director Thomas Torrey stirred himself. "If moving at least six brigades of combat troops into a neighboring country doesn't count as an invasion, what do we call this Russian action?"

Barbeau made another mental note to find a replacement for Torrey. Along with General Spelling, she'd kept the CIA chief on after her inauguration to reassure foreign allies made nervous by some of the political rhetoric she'd used in the campaign, but the intelligence chief had made it increasingly clear that he wasn't a team player.

"The director has a point," Karen Grayson said reluctantly. The secretary of state shrugged her narrow shoulders. "My public affairs people tell me the press is pushing hard for an official State Department reaction. I imagine it's the same here at the White House and over at Defense. If this isn't an invasion, what is it?"

"An incursion?" someone suggested.

Barbeau frowned. *Incursion* still had a hard edge to it. To many Americans it would seem awfully close to calling what the Russians were doing an invasion. That would scare some people, already made nervous by repeated brinksmanship with Moscow over the past decade. It would anger others, who might start demanding an American response she was unwilling to make.

Luke Cohen leaned forward. "The folks in my speechwriting shop favor 'unfortunate infringement of Ukrainian sovereignty,'" he said. "We think that demonstrates our real lack of support for what Moscow is up to, without getting too inflammatory. It also suggests that we're not going to accept any effort by Gryzlov to grab eastern Ukraine permanently."

Barbeau nodded slowly, mulling over the phrase Cohen had suggested. It sounded a bit wonkish, but maybe that was exactly the right tone to take in this case. Using it could reinforce the message that her administration was not going to allow itself to be sidetracked by unforeseen circumstances—and that she was strong enough to resist the temptation to score cheap political points by engaging in a senseless war of Cold War–like rhetoric with the Russians.

"Have your people focus-grouped it?" she asked.

Cohen nodded. "Yep." He grinned. "It scores pretty well with all the key demographics."

Barbeau caught the chairman of the Joint Chiefs exchanging a disgusted glance with Torrey. She hid a frown. Maybe she would have to find an excuse to get rid of both of them. It was hard enough handling an international crisis without having to deal with two men who were too set in their ways to understand the vital role politics always played in policy. Without political backing from the American people, the best policies in the world were useless. She'd watched too many of her predecessors in the Oval Office fail because they had not grasped that central truth.

Well, she was not going to be one of them.

She rapped sharply on the table. "Okay, ladies and gentlemen. Here's the line we're going to take. We make it clear that we fundamentally disapprove of what the Russians are doing. Say that, while we agree that Ukraine's government must stop these extremist groups attacking Russians, we still find Moscow's eagerness to take inappropriate military measures disturbing. You can also indicate that we intend to raise this issue with President Gryzlov's government during the high-level talks we're planning. But at the same time, I want everyone in this administration to emphasize that Russia's actions do *not* directly threaten American or NATO interests. Got it?"

Heads nodded eagerly.

"Then we're done here," Stacy Anne Barbeau said. "You all have your marching orders. When you talk to the media, remember to stress that America will not be stampeded into hasty and ill-considered reactions to events outside our national borders. As the world's strongest power, we don't need to prove anything to anybody."

OFFICE OF THE PRESIDENT, BELWEDER PALACE, WARSAW, POLAND
Two hours later

"Gentlemen, I have just ordered the mobilization of my country's reservists," President Piotr Wilk told his counterparts from the Baltic states via a secure video teleconference link. "I would strongly urge you to do the same."

He looked closely at the video monitor set on his desk, watching their reactions. Although Poland's electronic counterintelligence specialists assured him this remote conference link was secure, he wished it had been possible to meet in person. Even the best high-definition video "flattened" images, making it far more difficult to read the subtle facial and body language cues that formed so much of diplomacy. Unfortunately, with masses of Russian troops invading Ukraine, none of the others—the prime ministers of Lithuania, Latvia, and Estonia— thought it wise to be away from their own small countries, even for a few hours.

Wilk could not blame them. With Moscow's armored legions on the move against Kiev, no one could really be sure that Gryzlov's ambitions ended at the Dnieper. The leaders of the three Baltic states knew only too well that the Russians regarded the current existence of their independent democracies as an error of history—one that should be "corrected" at the first possible moment.

"Are you sure mobilization is wise, Piotr?" Lukas Tenys, Lithuania's prime minister asked. "Russia may point to your order as evidence of hostile intent. As a provocation."

"Gennadiy Gryzlov is a man willing to seize on anything we do as justification for his own actions," Wilk said bluntly. "But I suspect he finds weakness in others more tempting than strength. If NATO had supplied the Ukrainians with the weapons they begged for years ago, I do not believe we would face this crisis now."

"True," Sven Kalda agreed. Then the solemn-faced prime minister of Estonia shrugged. "However, that is an error of the past. We must focus on the dangers we face now."

Wilk nodded. "I agree. And that is why I have ordered Poland's reservists to join their active-duty units immediately. Even if Russia stops at the Dnieper for now, its forces will have moved several hundred kilometers closer to my country's eastern border. By seizing so much of Ukraine, Gryzlov cuts our strategic and operational warning time to the bone. This means if Moscow decides to up the ante by attacking us again, our armed forces *must* already be on a war footing to have any hope at all."

The other leaders nodded. Pressed up against Russia as they were, their own countries did not have the same luxury of space, but they understood its importance to Poland. Wilk's nation had fewer than fifty thousand active-duty soldiers in its ground forces. Bringing its three divisions and six independent brigades to full combat strength required calling up tens of thousands of reservists and assigning them to their wartime posts. But doing so took time, time measured in days and weeks. Time the Russians had just stolen by advancing their own tank and motor-rifle units so much farther west.

"What do the Americans say?" Kunnar Dukurs, Latvia's leader, asked. "My ambassador in Washington has not yet been able to talk to their secretary of state."

"The Americans do not plan to do anything of significance," Wilk said. "Their president believes this Russian invasion of Ukraine is a matter for diplomacy, not saber-rattling."

"You know this for a fact?"

Wilk nodded grimly. "I still have a few friends in the Pentagon. They passed me this news a few minutes ago. Their political leaders will protest what Moscow has done, but they will not do more than talk."

"Will the Americans at least think again about deploying troops and aircraft to our countries? For training purposes, if for nothing else?" Kalda asked. "Even a token presence would make the Kremlin more cautious."

"They will not," Wilk replied. He shook his head in disbelief. "Apparently President Barbeau doesn't want to give Moscow any excuses to turn this incident into a Cold War–style showdown."

None of the other three leaders bothered to hide their dismay. They knew all too well that without American urging, the rest of the major NATO countries would not act either. Berlin and Paris and

London had their own economic woes and skeletal, downsized militaries. Without pressure from the White House, none of them would risk sending even a single platoon or plane as a pro forma demonstration of allied resolve.

Poland and the three small Baltic states were on their own.

When the secure videoconference ended in disarray a few minutes later, Wilk sighed deeply. He snapped off the power to his desktop monitor. The rippling background image of Poland's red-and-white-striped flag vanished, replaced by a dead black screen that seemed depressingly symbolic of his country's near-term prospects.

He swiveled his chair around to look at Captain Nadia Rozek, who stood waiting patiently near the outer door to his office. He signaled her to come closer. "You see the problem, Captain?"

She nodded. "No one will stop the Russians. Ukraine's government has just surrendered half its national territory without firing a shot. The Baltic states fear them. The rest of the NATO countries are too weak, both economically and militarily. And the Americans are interested only in their own domestic politics."

"Succinctly put," Wilk said with a wry smile. "Which leaves us in the same poor strategic position we were in when I asked you to investigate the private military company called Scion. And to make discreet contact with its owners."

"Yes, sir."

"So, do you have anything to report in this regard?" Wilk asked.

She nodded crisply. "Sir, I do." Unconsciously, she dropped into the parade-rest position, with her hands locked behind her back.

"You may stand at ease, Captain," Wilk told her drily. The hint of a smile flickered across his otherwise troubled face. "As your commander in chief, I promise not to have you charged with insubordination."

Nadia bit down on a grin of her own and re-laxed slightly. "Yes, Mr. President," she said. "My research so far proves that Scion demonstrated re-markable military capabilities during its operations in Iraq seven years ago—capabilities far in advance of those possessed by its competitors and even by governments, including that of the United States."

Wilk raised an eyebrow at that. Her assessment matched the rumors he'd heard, but he'd thought they must be exaggerations. For all of his adult life, America's weapons and military technologies had been regarded as the best in the world. How was it possible for a mere corporation, even a contractor specializing in defense and security technologies, to rank higher? "Go on, Captain. Consider me in-trigued."

"These capabilities included mobile combat machines of a new type, equipped with weapons ranging from conventional grenade launchers and automatic cannon to electromagnetic rail guns. I also found verifiable reports that Scion pilots flew a number of manned and unmanned aircraft armed in a variety of ways, including at least one which mounted a high-powered airborne laser."

Wilk sat up straighter. Weapons-grade lasers and rail guns? In the hands of a private corporation? "Who are these people?" he asked.

"Scion appears to be privately and closely held," Nadia told him. "It was first registered as a corporation in Las Vegas, in the American state of Nevada. But almost none of its other records are publicly accessible. So I ran background checks on the shareholders listed in its registration papers."

"Not officially, I hope," Wilk said. "The last thing we want right now are stories in the American financial press about Polish government interest in this corporation. Or, for that matter, angry accusations of invasion of privacy from some of those shareholders."

This time Nadia didn't bother to hide the amusement in her blue-gray eyes. "My father is a software engineer who specializes in Internet security. When I was a teenager, I wanted to guard my online privacy from prying parental eyes, so I spent a lot of time studying his work. Believe me, I know how to be very careful." Then she shrugged. "Besides, I can guarantee that not a single one of Scion's shareholders will protest."

"Explain that," Wilk demanded.

"None of them are real," Nadia said. "They are all what the Americans call 'false fronts.'"

Wilk stared at her. "All of them?"

"Yes, Mr. President."

"Then who really owns Scion?" Wilk asked.

Nadia hesitated. Even as a child she had hated having to admit failure. Despite all her military training in the importance of prompt and accurate reports, it was a trait she still had to resist. "I do not yet know. Scion's operations are structured in layers of subsidiary companies, private trusts, and holding corporations. Every time I crack one layer of security, I find another beneath it."

Wilk frowned. "Could it be a front for the American government, perhaps for the CIA or one of their other intelligence agencies?"

She shook her head. "I do not think so. There are signs that Scion may have occasionally contracted its services to the CIA, but there is no evidence of any real command-and-control relationship. I believe it to be a genuine private operator."

"Whose owner or owners are completely mysterious," Wilk said flatly.

"Yes, sir," Nadia admitted.

"Then how do we contact them without effectively announcing our interest to the whole wide world?" Wilk asked.

"I sent the company an e-mail inquiring about its services and availability," Nadia told him. Before he could explode, she explained. "I created a false front of my own—a fictitious Swiss-based company interested in hiring Scion to provide security for proposed mining operations in Africa. Any reply to my e-mail will go there first. Then we can establish a more secure channel of direct communication."

"But you haven't received any reply so far, Captain?"

Nadia shook her head. "Not yet."

With an audible hum, the monitor on Wilk's desk powered up. Astonished, the Polish president turned to look at it. He scowled. His computer was operating on its own, without any input from him. How was that possible? It was equipped with top-of-the-line security systems—both software and hardware that should have blocked any intrusion or at least set off alarms in every nook and cranny of Poland's intelligence service.

As he sat watching, three short lines of text flashed onto the screen and sat there, waiting for his response.

Still stunned, Wilk leaned forward, fumbled for his keyboard, and typed in a one-word reply. *Tak.* Yes.

The message vanished instantly, leaving only a blank screen behind. He turned back to Nadia, shaking his head in disbelief.

"Mr. President?" she asked. "Is something wrong?"

"Wrong? No," Wilk said. "Or so I hope." He looked up at her. "But it seems that Scion also includes high-level computer hacking and network intrusion among its capabilities, Captain Rozek. That was the company owner's response to your inquiry about its services."

Watching her eyes widen in surprise, he nodded. "So now the question is, have we made contact with a magician? Or with the Devil himself?"

23RD AIR BASE, MINSK MAZOWIECKI AIRFIELD, POLAND
Later that evening

"This is not wise, sir," Major Dariusz Stepniak said quietly.

Like the rest of Piotr Wilk's security detail, Stepniak wore running shoes, sweatpants, a T-shirt, and a lightweight windbreaker concealing a shoulder holster. Agents of Poland's BOR, the Bureau of Government Protection, its equivalent of the U.S. Secret Service, always accompanied their nation's chief executive in public. That included going with him on his regular evening run—part of a rigorous daily exercise regimen Wilk had maintained since his days as a cadet at the Air Force Academy in Deblin.

Ordinarily, the Polish president took great pleasure in pushing his bodyguards to their physical limits, sometimes running them into the ground. But this evening was different. He had just ordered Stepniak and his three agents to let him run alone.

"The international situation is too unsettled," the major insisted. "You should not take unnecessary risks."

Wilk shook his head. "I don't need you dogging my heels tonight, Major." He waved at their surroundings, the edge of a small forest adjacent to the military airfield's runways and revetments. "We're inside the perimeter fence here. No one who isn't authorized can get in or out past the sensors and security guards." He smiled. "I promise I'll stick to the trails and I'll have my phone ready, just in case. Okay? Look, what I really need right now is some uninterrupted thinking time—some peace and quiet."

The roar of a MiG-29 taking off from a nearby runway punctuated his words.

Major Stepniak raised his voice to be heard. "You call this peace and quiet, sir?"

Wilk grinned. "Dariusz, for an old fighter pilot like me, the sound of a jet engine is like a childhood lullaby." He patted the taller man on the shoulder. "Now don't worry. I'll be careful. Just wait here for me and only come running if I call, right?"

Ten minutes later, Wilk loped along a dirt trail that wound back and forth among tall oaks, ash, and birch trees. Patches of shadow alternated with slashes of red-tinged light cast by the setting sun. He ran easily, not even breaking a sweat yet. But he kept one hand close to the phone clipped to his windbreaker. Despite the confidence he had shown Stepniak, he couldn't deny that this might turn out to be an incredibly stupid move.

He came around a bend and saw a man waiting for him, standing motionless in the shadows.

Wilk stopped.

Smiling politely, the man came forward onto the trail, out into the sunlight. "Thank you for agreeing to meet me like this, Mr. President," he said. "I appreciate your trust."

An American from that accent, Wilk judged. And an educated and sophisticated one, it seemed, wearing a perfectly tailored suit. They were about the same height and build, but the other man was older, with longish gray hair and a carefully trimmed gray beard. Which raised the question of just how someone of that age and dressed so neatly had managed to pass, undetected, through the airfield's security perimeter.

For a moment, the Polish president's hand moved

toward his phone. Maybe he should call for backup after all. Then he saw the flash of amusement in the other man's eyes. "My phone has no signal, does it?" he asked carefully in fair English.

"Probably not," the gray-haired man admitted. He stepped closer. "Captain Rozek's message to my company stressed your desire for absolute discretion. In the circumstances, I consider that very wise. My people tell me the Russians have really ramped up their intelligence operations in your country over the past couple of weeks."

Wilk shook hands with him and then looked more closely . . . and slowly his eyes widened in undisguised surprise. "Martindale," he realized. "You are Kevin Martindale, once the president of the United States."

"I was," the other man said calmly. "But now I run Scion."

"As a private citizen?" Wilk asked.

Martindale nodded. "That's right. Scion takes U.S. government contracts from time to time, but I don't take orders from politicians." He showed his teeth in a quick grin. "Unless I agree with them, of course."

"Then you are a . . ."—Wilk searched for the right words—"a *najemnik*? A mercenary? A hired gun?"

Martindale shook his head. "Not exactly." He looked closely at Wilk. "As president of the United States, I focused most of my energy and attention on its defenses and on the defense of the whole free world."

Wilk nodded. "Of course."

"Well, that's still my focus," Martindale said. "In

some ways, I find it a lot easier now. Operating out of the limelight and without all the fretting about short-term politics means that Scion can be far more effective than any government outfit—even those supposed to act covertly like the CIA."

Wilk frowned. "But acting without government sanction seems—"

"Dangerous?"

Wilk nodded again. "I was going to say 'irresponsible,' Mr. President."

"Irresponsible, no," Martindale said. "Dangerous . . . of course. The world is still a dangerous place, perhaps even more dangerous than it was during the first Cold War," he continued softly. "Men like Gennadiy Gryzlov and other rogue state leaders don't feel constrained by ideology or even caution and common sense the way the old Communist Party hacks often were. They're increasingly aggressive and increasingly willing to use force to achieve their objectives." The American studied Wilk for a few moments. "Then again, you know that better than anyone, don't you?"

The Polish president nodded stiffly. *"Tak, panie prezydencie,"* he said. "Yes, Mr. President."

"Well, that's where Scion comes in," Martindale said. "You've been looking for a means to offset Russia's superior numbers and more advanced weapons. My company has what you need. We can provide Poland with a small but extremely powerful and incredibly effective combined ground and air strike force—one that will be able to conduct deep-penetration raids against the Russians if they attack you again."

"Under whose command?" Wilk demanded. "After all, you've just told me that you don't take orders from politicians. And I, for my sins, am the political leader of my country." He stared hard at the gray-haired American executive. "But first and foremost, I am the commander in chief of Poland's armed forces, Mr. Martindale. I have no interest in employing other military forces beyond my control. Which means I will not hire soldiers or pilots or weapons technicians whom I cannot trust to obey my orders."

"That's a fair point," the other man acknowledged. "What I would propose is this: as Poland's president and commander in chief, you would retain absolute strategic control over any Scion strike forces we provide. That means you pick the targets and you decide whether or not to execute any operations using our people. But you leave the operational and tactical decision making to us. You tell Scion what to hit and when to strike, but you leave the details of how we employ our weapons and systems to accomplish those missions to us."

"In other words, I should not act like another Lyndon Baines Johnson during the Vietnam War, sitting in my office and picking out bomb loads and aircraft routes?" Wilk suggested with a thin smile.

"Precisely," Martindale said with an answering smile. "If you hire us, you're hiring experts who understand all the ins and outs of the advanced weapons we can bring to bear. You fight the war. Let us fight the battles."

"Your offer is tempting," Wilk said slowly. "And

I know how effectively your Scion teams fought against the Turks invading Iraq."

"But?"

"But Russia's ground and air forces are more powerful than the Turkish divisions and fighter squadrons your company faced, perhaps by an order of magnitude." Wilk sighed. "As impressive as your capabilities are said to be, I do not see how they can provide a significant edge against Moscow. No matter how powerful your weapons are individually, the sheer numbers of tanks, artillery, and aircraft Russia can bring to any battle will inevitably over-whelm any small force. No matter how much I fear and despise Gryzlov and his kind, I would be irre-sponsible to stake my country's fate on a confronta-tion we cannot win."

"John F. Kennedy once quoted the Irish states-man Edmund Burke as saying that 'all that is nec-essary for the triumph of evil is that good men do nothing,'" Martindale said. "Burke also wrote that 'when bad men combine, the good must associate; else they will fall one by one, an unpitied sacrifice in a contemptible struggle.'"

He looked closely at Wilk. "Give me access to a secure military area, Mr. President," Scion's chief executive suggested quietly. "And I will show you some of what we can do together against our common enemies."

CHAPTER 6

*What we think, or what we
know, or what we believe is,
in the end, of little consequence.
The only consequence is what we do.*

— JOHN RUSKIN, BRITISH ART
CRITIC, WRITER, AND
PHILANTHROPIST

**DRAWSKO POMORSKIE MILITARY TRAINING AREA,
NORTHWEST POLAND**
Several days later

Set in western Pomerania's patchwork of woods,
rolling hills, swamps, broad clearings, and villages, the military training area was the largest of
its kind in Europe, with more than one hundred
and thirty square miles of territory available for
maneuvers and live fire exercises. Littered with
the burned-out hulks of old Soviet tanks and self-

propelled guns, it had been used by the Polish Army since 1945 and by NATO forces since 1996.

Now Drawsko Pomorskie had been turned over to Scion. For more than seventy-two hours, Sky Masters cargo aircraft had been busy flying in more old military equipment—U.S. Army surplus Humvees, M-60 tanks, M-113 armored personnel carriers, Huey helicopters, and aircraft salvaged from the U.S. Air Force's Boneyard, including F-4 Phantoms and T-38 Talon trainers. Polish Army combat engineers and other technical specialists had dispersed this array of vehicles and aircraft across a sector of the exercise area. At Kevin Martindale's suggestion, they had also liberally seeded the range with barbed-wire entanglements, antitank obstacles, concealed minefields, and hidden machine-gun emplacements set to fire by remote control. None of the minefields or machine-gun nests were marked on the maps given to Scion's demonstration team.

President Piotr Wilk, Defense Minister Gierek, Martindale, and a handful of trusted aides and senior Polish officers crowded inside a secure bunker built into a hillside. Firing slits and observation ports overlooked a valley now filled with dozens of pieces of camouflaged military hardware.

"All monitoring and defense systems ready," Captain Nadia Rozek told them, repeating the radioed message passed along by the training area's exercise control team. She listened to the next transmission as it came through her headset and looked up. "All perimeter security units on full alert. Standing by."

Wilk lowered his binoculars and glanced at Martindale. "I hope that you are sure about this.

Between the minefields we have emplaced and the heavy weapons zeroed in on this sector, it is a potential deathtrap for the personnel in your demonstration unit."

Scion's chief executive smiled. "I think our guy will be okay."

"One man?" Wilk asked in surprise. He nodded toward the exercise area. "Against a simulated force larger than a battalion?"

"That's right," Martindale said. He shrugged. "I told you that Scion could give you an edge against the Russians if the balloon goes up. Well, it's time to show you exactly what I meant."

"I suggest we give Mr. Martindale his chance to dazzle us, Piotr," Janusz Gierek said drily. Since being briefed on Scion's offer, the defense minister had made no secret of his doubts about the company's claims. "Then, after all of his special effects fade away, we can make a sensible and pragmatic decision."

"I hope you will forgive Janusz," Wilk said to the American with a smile. "He is our resident skeptic. If I tell him it is a dark night out, he usually insists on personally verifying that with a light meter."

"No offense taken, Mr. President," Martindale said. He chuckled. "Every good government needs a take-no-prisoners bullshit detector. My own country could probably have saved a few trillion dollars over the past couple of decades if we'd listened more carefully to our own folks like Defense Minister Gierek."

"Very well," Wilk said. "Then you may tell your Scion unit to move into position."

"He's already there," Martindale said, grinning openly now. He glanced at his watch. "By my estimate, he's been in position at the edge of those woods about two kilometers west of here for at least the last half hour."

"That is impossible!" Gierek snapped. "That area has been under constant observation—both visually and with thermal imaging systems—since the sun rose. No one has reported any movement there."

"You asked Mr. Martindale to dazzle us, Janusz," Wilk said carefully, hiding his own amusement. "Perhaps he has already begun." He turned back to the gray-haired American. "You can signal your man to begin the demonstration."

Martindale turned to Nadia Rozek. "Would you do that for me, please, Captain?" he asked, with another broad smile. "Just broadcast, 'You're good to go, CID One,' over that radio of yours."

Nadia arched a finely sculpted eyebrow. "Over which frequency, Mr. Martindale?"

"Oh, you can pick one at random," he told her confidently. "That should do the trick."

Carefully controlling her expression, Nadia turned back to her American-made SINCGARs combat radio set and punched in a new frequency—deliberately choosing one far away from that which she had been using all morning. Then she picked up the handset and said, "This is Drawsko Pomorskie Exercise Control. You are good to go, CID One."

Crouched down in a clump of bushes at the edge of the forest, Patrick McLanahan waited patiently.

It had taken some careful maneuvering to get his twelve-foot-plus-tall Cybernetic Infantry Device so close to the exercise area without being spotted. Those who had never seen one of these humanlike machines in action would not have believed it possible for something so big to move so quietly and agilely, taking advantage of every available piece of cover and fold in the ground. Sometimes he thought Kevin Martindale enjoyed these moments of showmanship a bit too much, but there was no denying that the former president knew how to wow an audience.

A red dot pulsed at the edge of his vision. The CID's sensors, which automatically scanned all radio frequencies, had picked up an incoming transmission at the very edge of the VHF spectrum. He flicked a finger and heard Captain Rozek's voice giving him the "go" signal.

Without waiting any longer, Patrick surged into motion. His CID burst out of the woods, already accelerating toward the exercise area at a speed of more than sixty miles an hour. A shape, an old M-60 main battle tank draped in camouflage netting, was suddenly silhouetted off to his left, more than a thousand yards away. The CID's battle computer evaluated it as a priority target.

"Gotcha," Patrick said under his breath. He detached the electromagnetic rail gun from one of the weapons packs his CID carried and powered it up. Still running, he swung the gun toward the tank and fired once. In a burst of plasma and with a deafening, tree-shaking *CCRRACK!* a small superdense metal projectile hurtled downrange at more than

Mach 5. Slamming into the M-60, it ripped straight through the tank's heavy armor and punched out through the other side. The enormous impact vaporized metal in a dazzling white flash and set the air inside the turret and hull on fire.

More targets appeared, each marked in a different color corresponding to its perceived threat level and the weapon the CID's computer judged most appropriate. In quick succession and while moving at high speed, Patrick switched between firing the rail gun, a 40mm grenade launcher, and a 25mm autocannon—often firing two weapons almost simultaneously at different targets.

Humvees, armored personnel carriers, and parked aircraft were torn apart by explosions or shredded from end to end. A dense cloud of smoke by the burning vehicles drifted across the exercise area.

Patrick plunged ahead, charging directly into one of the fake villages built by the Polish Army for urban combat training. He skidded around the edge of a building and ran down the main street. Suddenly a remotely controlled machine gun opened up on him from a second-floor window; 7.62mm rounds hammered his torso, ricocheting off its composite armor in a shower of sparks.

He swiveled and fired, sending a 40mm high-explosive grenade straight through the window. It went off. The machine gun, wrecked by the blast and fragments, fell silent.

Patrick veered right. His CID smashed through the walls of one of the buildings without slowing and erupted out into open ground again in a cloud of dust, broken concrete, and splintered wood. He angled back to the left, circling around the village while systematically knocking out defensive positions highlighted by his sensors.

Still on the move, he fired the electromagnetic rail gun again, smashing a tank parked hull down near a mocked-up church, complete with a tall steeple. Explosives rigged to simulate stored ammunition inside the M-60 cooked off. A huge explosion sent its massive turret tumbling skyward and turned the church into smoldering pile of shattered rubble.

A tangle of barbed wire loomed up out of the smoke. The computer highlighted a swath of ground twenty meters wide beyond the wire. Its thermal imagers and radar had detected a belt of antipersonnel and antiarmor mines sown to catch anyone breaking through the barbed-wire obstacle. More remotely controlled machine guns were sited to kill anyone trying to clear the mines.

"Nice try, fellas," Patrick murmured, grinning now. "But not today."

Without hesitating, he raced right up to the barbed wire and then jumped—bounding high into the air, soaring across the minefield and well beyond it. While still in the air, he fired again and again, smashing machine-gun nests with grenades and 25mm cannon shells. His CID came down on the run and put on more speed.

Another alert pinged his senses. Audio pickups, filtering out all the battle noise, were picking up the sound of rotors drawing closer. Patrick twisted, seeking the source of the noise. There!

A Scion drone, configured to emulate the noise

and heat signature of a Russian Mi-28 helicopter gunship, popped up over a distant hill and sped toward him. Without pausing, he slid the 40mm grenade launcher back onto its weapons pack mount and detached a Stinger surface-to-air missile. While running across the track of the oncoming drone, he swiveled his CID's torso, letting the handheld missile's infrared seeker scan. A harsh buzz sounded. The Stinger had locked on.

He fired.

The missile tore away in a plume of fire and white exhaust, visibly guiding on its target. Hit just below its rotors, the drone blew up in a cloud of fire, black smoke, and spinning fragments.

"Exercise complete. Repeat, exercise complete!" Patrick heard Captain Rozek radio. Her voice, up to now so calm and businesslike, contained an undercurrent of shock and awe. "Weapons safe, CID One. Halt in place for further instructions."

"My God," Wilk said, peering through his binoculars. The valley below their bunker was a sea of wrecked and burning vehicles and buildings. "It is incredible. Absolutely incredible." He glanced over his shoulder at Martindale. "The reports I read do not come anywhere close to capturing what your weapons systems can do. They certainly do not do justice to the astonishing power of these manned war machines."

"True," the American said. He shrugged. "And we've worked very hard to make sure that they don't. Fortunately, very few political or military decision makers are willing to believe the stories told by those who've survived close contact with the CIDs. So far, we don't think the Russians or the Chinese have the ability to reverse engineer this technology, but we'd rather not give them any more incentives to try than they already have."

Martindale looked toward Janusz Gierek. "Well, Defense Minister? Can I consider you dazzled?"

Slowly, Gierek turned away from the firing slit. His face was pale. He looked down at his watch and then back up at Wilk and the others in amazement. "Twenty minutes!" he said hoarsely. "A whole battalion destroyed in twenty minutes. By *one* piloted robot."

"In fairness, a battle fought against maneuvering armored vehicles and aircraft manned by living, thinking opponents would have been more difficult," Martindale said. "But in the essentials, the outcome would have been the same."

"You say this machine, this Cybernetic Infantry Device, is invincible?" Wilk asked, still studying the large, humanlike machine standing motionless amid the drifting smoke.

"Invincible?" Martindale shook his head. "No. Not invincible. But in the hands of a skilled pilot employing the right tactics, the CID can fight and expect to defeat larger enemy forces with substantially more firepower." He gestured toward the distant war machine. "Together with the other weapons and technologies Scion can put in the mix, the CID's combination of speed, agility, precision targeting, and protection acts as a remarkable force multiplier." Then he chuckled. "That may sound like a hack-written defense-contractor marketing brochure, Mr. President, but now you know it's the God's honest truth."

Wilk nodded slowly. "No one can dispute that." He studied Martindale's face. "I would like to take a closer look at this astonishing machine of yours, if that is allowed."

"Certainly," Martindale agreed. "But let's have him come here. Your combat engineers planted a few too many land mines out there for my taste." He held out his hand to Nadia Rozek. "May I, Captain?"

Still shaking her head in disbelief at what she had just witnessed, she handed him the radio mike.

"CID One, this is Scion Prime," Martindale said, keying the mike. "Pack up your troubles in your old kit bag and report to the observation bunker. It's show-and-tell time."

Five minutes later, the small group of Polish officers and government officials stood blinking in the sunlight outside the bunker, staring up at the Cybernetic Infantry Device towering over them. When it was seen up close, hundreds of small hexagonal tiles covered a significant portion of the robot's "skin."

"This is a Mod III CID," Martindale told them. "We've upgraded some of the sensors and squeezed out better battery and fuel-cell life. But those tiles represent the major improvement we've made to this version."

Furrowing his brow, Gierek looked closer at the hexagons coating the humanlike machine. His eyes widened momentarily in astonishment. "You have added thermal adaptive camouflage!" He turned to Martindale. "No wonder we did not detect this machine moving into position!"

"Bingo," Martindale said smugly. "Those tiles are a special material that can change temperature extremely quickly. Our CIDs are already equipped with a large number of sensors, so the Mod III takes thermal imaging data collected from the local environment and then adjusts the temperature of each tile to mimic its surroundings—displaying the heat signatures of trees or bushes or buildings and the like. Essentially, when moving slowly or at rest, a CID equipped with this system is effectively invisible to thermal sensors."

"Why only then?" Wilk asked.

"For two reasons," Martindale explained. "First, while the thermal adaptive tiles can change temperatures very quickly, there are still limitations. Once the CID is moving fast, it's moving through so many different heat textures that the system can't really keep up. But the chief reason is power consumption. At rest or at low speeds, the amount of power required to adjust the tile temps is relatively low. Trying to do the same thing at higher speeds is just too big a drain on the CID's power supplies."

Gierek had been circling around the manned robot. Now he pointed to several of the camouflage tiles on its torso. They were cracked or showed signs of high-velocity impacts. "Your machine has sustained some damage."

Martindale nodded. "The material in those tiles is tough, but it's not impenetrable. Direct fire from machine guns or other heavy weapons will damage them." He smiled. "Fortunately, the thermal adaptive system is modular and any wrecked hexagons are easy to swap out between missions, or even in the field. Besides, you'll find that the composite armor underneath those damaged pieces is completely intact."

He raised his voice. "CID One, why don't you show these folks your weapons packs? Let's give them a better sense of the kinds of firepower you can bring to any battle."

Safely hidden away inside the pilot's compartment of CID One, Patrick McLanahan followed Martindale's suggestion, smoothly uncoupling the various packs attached to his robot. One by one, he laid out the weapons they contained—the electromagnetic rail gun; a pair of 40mm automatic grenade launchers able to fire a variety of fragmentation, thermobaric, tear-gas, high-explosive, and antiarmor rounds; a 25mm autocannon with a mix of armor-piercing discarding sabot and high-explosive incendiary rounds; and three more Stinger surface-to-air missiles.

"This is the normal weapons load for an ordinary attack mission," Patrick heard Martindale explaining. "Naturally, we can configure each CID with a different package for more specialized assignments—up to and including antitank guided missiles, rocket launchers, 84mm recoilless rifles like the Carl Gustav, and some more specialized nonlethal weapons."

"We have seen this machine destroy older American armored vehicles," a Polish colonel wearing the unit patch of the 10th Armored Brigade said. "But can it defeat more modern Russian tanks like the T-80 and T-90?"

"With some of its weapons, especially the rail guns, absolutely yes," Martindale said. "But the CID's armor is designed primarily to stop small-arms, machine-gun, and heavy autocannon fire. Any hit by an armor-piercing 125mm tank shell will penetrate. So the trick is to avoid stand-up fights against Russian armored units—"

Another red dot pulsed angrily in Patrick's vision, this time centered on another wooded hill about half a mile away down the valley. *Satellite phone link being established*, the computer alerted him. *Link chosen is the Thuraya satellite constellation, but encryption methods are Russian.*

Crap, he thought. They had uninvited guests. Another finger twitch activated the CID's jamming package. The red dot pulsed to yellow. The targeted electronic noise his system was emitting had temporarily blocked the phone out there from connecting to a communications satellite in geosynchronous orbit. *Estimated jamming burn-through in forty-five seconds*, the computer reported.

Caught with his weapons packs off, Patrick knew he didn't have the ability to grab anything and hit a target that far away in time, not without risking harm to Martindale and the fascinated Poles who were busy poking through his gear. Besides, he'd burned through most of his ready-use ammo during the demonstration. And with so many people crowd-

ing around him, he couldn't even safely break away
to chase down these intruders. There was too high a
chance that he might accidentally injure or even kill
one of the high-ranking spectators. Not even Martindale's high-powered salesmanship could paper
over a screw-up like that.

Good thing we had a fallback plan, he thought.
With another flick of his fingers, he activated his
radio and relayed the alert to the second CID still
concealed among the trees he'd left a few minutes
ago.

"Data received," a voice replied.

"Go get 'em, son," Patrick snapped. "Take 'em
alive if you can. Dead if you must."

Piloting the second Cybernetic Infantry Device,
Brad McLanahan lunged out of the woods. He had
to take a deep breath to try to flush away the intense
thrill of excitement he felt as he put the CID into
motion. Piloting this incredible machine was an
experience like nothing else. He remembered the
first time he had done so, while still a senior in high
school, and it was pretty intense to be able to do the
things the CID could do. But in this new version,
somehow the rush of power and awareness was even
more pronounced, more visceral—almost orgasmic.
He felt it as soon as it was activated after climbing
aboard; but now, in motion and on the hunt, the
feeling shot from his brain throughout his entire
body like a bolt of lightning.

Concentrating on his sensors and the task at hand
helped suppress the almost overwhelming electric

sense of power he felt . . . but, he thought ruefully, a guy could really get freakin' hooked on this.

Brad leaped straight over a still-burning M-60 tank and ran across the wreck-strewn exercise area in seconds. Suddenly he was in the trees on the other side of the shallow valley—smashing through undergrowth and low-hanging branches with hurricane-like force.

Two green, roughly man-shaped blotches appeared in the center of his vision. His thermal imaging sensors had picked up two intruders, but their images weren't as bright as he would have expected. They were probably wearing ghillie suits coated with antithermal IR materials, Brad realized.

One of the shapes swung toward his CID as he charged uphill through the forest, rapidly bringing up a rifle. Several shots cracked out. Three rounds smacked into the robot's armor and bounced off.

"Hi there, guys," Brad said, tweaking his electronic voice to full, earsplitting volume. "Is this a private party?"

The gunman, now visible in his twig-, leaf-, and branch-studded sniper's camouflage, tried backing up farther, still shooting.

Casually, Brad leaned down, snatched the rifle away with the CID's powerful hands, and snapped it in half.

"*Presvataya Bogoroditsa!* Holy Mother of God!" the man screamed in panic. He was still screaming when Brad picked him up and tossed him high into the branches of the nearest tree. The screams cut off.

Horrified, the second intruder turned and tried to make a run for it.

Shaking the CID's head in disgust, Brad jumped again—bounding high overhead. He came down ahead of the fleeing man and spun round to meet him head-on. "Going somewhere?"

The second intruder fumbled for something at his waist. A pistol? Or maybe a grenade? Or the detonator for a suicide vest? Not cool either way, Brad decided. He reached out and tapped the man with one of the CID's fingers—sending him tumbling head over heels for several yards, right into the trunk of a gnarled oak tree.

"Ouch," Brad said sympathetically, turning down the volume this time. Sighing, he grabbed the fallen man and then turned to retrieve the intruder he'd tossed into a tree.

Watching the second CID trotting toward them with two bruised and bloodied prisoners held tightly in its arms, Patrick felt a surge of paternal pride. His son had handled what could have been a serious security breach with speed and efficiency. Somewhere out there was a Polish army officer who could not say the same thing. The Drawsko Pomorksie Training Area was supposed to be locked down tight for the duration of this demonstration. No one should have been able to get close enough to see what Scion was doing here.

"Good work, Brad," Patrick radioed, choosing a frequency he knew the Poles were not currently monitoring.

"Thanks, CID One," his son replied, plainly unwilling to risk revealing his father's identity, even inadvertently.

Patrick turned toward Martindale and the waiting Poles, tuning his own electronic voice to conceal its characteristics. "I suspect you'll find these clowns are GRU agents or possibly members of a covert Spetsnaz reconnaissance unit."

Piotr Wilk showed his teeth in a tight, fierce smile. "I suspect you are right," he said, coldly eyeing the unconscious men gripped by the second Scion robot. "In any case, we will make sure our unwanted visitors experience Polish hospitality for a very, very long time."

OFFICE OF THE PRESIDENT, BELWEDER PALACE, WARSAW
A few hours later

"So now we come to what you Americans call the nitty-gritty details," Wilk said. "What we saw this morning proved the potential value of your weapons and other defense technologies. The question remains, what exactly can you provide to our country and how much will it cost us?"

Poland's president had invited the two most important members of his government—Prime Minister Klaudia Rybak and Defense Minister Gierek—to this evening meeting with Martindale. The American had come alone, trusting subordinates back at Drawsko Pomorskie to handle the necessary work of clearing away any evidence of Scion's presence at the Polish military training area. The three men and one woman were alone in Wilk's private office, seated around a small conference table equipped with a computer and flat-screen display.

"My company can provide you with a highly capable special missions force," Martindale told them. Images and graphics flashed onto the display as he spoke, echoing and amplifying his words. "The core of our ground element will be the two Cybernetic Infantry Devices, CIDs, you saw in action earlier today—along with their weapons packs and other equipment—"

"Why do you call those astounding war machines by such a drab, prosaic term?" the prime minister interrupted. "Surely they deserve a more fitting name, one that better captures their tremendous power? They moved with such grace and ferocity, more like wolves, *iron wolves*, than mere 'devices.'"

Martindale smiled politely at her. "CIDs were called that by the folks who first invented and developed the hardware and software. They were part of an Army R-and-D outfit, which means they were engineers, not poets." He shrugged his perfectly tailored shoulders. "I guess the designation they picked just stuck." He turned back to the others. "If I may?"

"Please proceed," Wilk said. A quick smile flashed across his own face. "Though I agree with Klaudia. Perhaps a true warrior should also have the soul of a poet."

Martindale chuckled. "You may be right. Unfortunately, my own inclinations lead me more to questions of business and strategy."

"Perhaps we can discuss literature and philosophy a bit later and stick to cold, hard facts for now," Janusz Gierek said gruffly. The former professor of mathematics looked closely at Martindale. "What else do you offer us?"

"The rest of our Scion ground component would include an expert group of specialists, vehicles, and transport aircraft to support CID operations—with maintenance, field repair, and resupply. It will also include teams trained in deep-penetration covert reconnaissance," Martindale went on. He nodded to Wilk. "I know your country has highly effective Special Forces of its own, Mr. President. But our recon operators are trained to work closely with the CID pilots. They know exactly what these machines can and cannot accomplish. Special Forces units used to fighting with conventional weapons will need extensive training to accustom them to working with our manned robots."

"That makes sense," Wilk agreed. "I would not expect a helicopter pilot, no matter how talented, to fly an F-16 without a lot of study and practice."

"As a gesture of good faith, however," Martindale told them, "we would be willing to train one of your own officers as a CID pilot. That would give you more insight into any missions we propose. It would also ensure closer liaison with your troops."

"That is a generous offer," Wilk said. "And one I would gladly accept. Perhaps I might suggest one of my military aides, Captain Nadia Rozek, as a suitable candidate?"

Martindale nodded. "She would be an excellent choice. In our experience, the best CID pilots are physically tough, mentally agile, and already comfortable with a range of advanced technology. From what I've seen of her thus far, your Captain Rozek possesses all those qualities."

He keyed in another command, bringing up a new series of images on the display. "But the ground component is just one piece of our proposed special missions force. We would also deploy a range of manned and unmanned aircraft—aircraft able to conduct stealthy reconnaissance, electronic warfare, and strike and interdiction operations. The aircraft operators and the specialized equipment on board are designed to fully integrate with the CIDs."

"Drones?"

"Full-scale combat aircraft, refurbished with modern materials and systems and made fully operational," Martindale said. "They compare to drones like a wolf compares to a puppy." Wilk and the other Poles sat rapt, listening while the American laid out the full range of advanced military capabilities Scion could offer their country. When he finished, they sat in silence for a few moments more, each wrapped up in his or her own thoughts.

At last, Wilk ran his gaze around the table, noting the slight nods from his two colleagues. He cleared his throat. "Your offer is impressive, Mr. Martindale. But let me be blunt. One question remains: Can Poland afford to hire Scion's services?"

"That will be your decision," Martindale said quietly. "I can only quote our price, and I will be blunt, too. This is not a price subject to negotiation or haggling. It's the bare minimum my company can charge and remain viable. We're determined to help you stop Gennadiy Gryzlov's aggression, but Scion is fundamentally a business—not a nation-state. We can't simply print money, and we won't beggar ourselves in the process of helping you defend your country."

"So how much will it cost us?" Gierek asked brusquely.

"We'll supply you with all the forces I proposed for the base price of five hundred million dollars a year," Martindale told him. "In addition, you would pay additional compensation for any Scion personnel killed or injured in Polish service, along with extra charges as necessary to replace any of our equipment destroyed in combat."

"Five hundred million dollars? Almost *two billion* zlotys? That is out of the question," Gierek growled. "Such a figure represents more than five percent of our entire national defense budget!"

Martindale nodded. "I realize the price seems high." He brought up the image of a Cybernetic Infantry Device on the screen again. "But you should also consider that these war machines and the other weapons systems we possess will significantly increase Poland's land *and* air combat power—and by far more than five percent. Duplicating this range of capabilities would be impossible for your country, at least not without the expenditure of many tens of billions of zlotys in R and D and procurement. And that would take years."

"Years we do *not* have," Wilk pointed out, frowning.

Martindale nodded. "Exactly."

"Nevertheless, the difficulty remains," Prime Minister Rybak said. She looked at Wilk and

Gierek. "No such sum of money exists in the defense budget already passed by Parliament. Obtaining it would require a new appropriation, which would require a full debate. As would any move to cancel existing defense programs and reallocate their funds."

"A debate the opposition would drag out for weeks," Wilk agreed, not bothering to hide the sour look on his face. Some of Poland's opposition parties still contained men and women who were all too willing and even eager to build closer economic and political ties with Russia. He shook his head. "And even if we could debate the question in closed session, the news of what we were doing would be bound to leak to the press." He snapped his fingers. "Just like that!"

"Which would give Moscow every incentive to attack us now, *before* we can bolster our defenses," Gierek muttered. Gloomily, he shrugged his shoulders. "As I said, this is impossible."

"There may be an alternative," Martindale said carefully.

Gierek narrowed his eyes. "I thought you said you would not bargain on price, Mr. Martindale? Was that not so?"

"What I said earlier was accurate: I won't bargain on price, Defense Minister," the American answered. "But I anticipated that securing a direct appropriation might be too difficult, and perhaps even impossible. No, what I'm referring to is an alternate method of payment—one which would also bind us even more closely to your nation's defense and prosperity."

"Unlike the prime minister, I am not an economic genius," Wilk said, speaking slowly and cautiously. "So I can safely admit confusion about your precise meaning. If you did not expect we could transfer the necessary money from our defense budget, how precisely do you expect to be paid?" He smiled thinly. "Unless you are willing to take an IOU or my personal check."

Martindale grinned suddenly. "Close, but not quite on target, Mr. President. What I propose is a trade, a straight swap," he continued. He tapped another key, bringing up a table of figures showing the government money allocated to Poland's Special Economic Investment Incentive Funds. These funds were used both to lure foreign companies to build manufacturing plants in Poland and to boost innovative private Polish firms by providing them with seed money for expansion and new equipment. "Scion trades you our services for a year. In return, you buy shares in various Polish corporations, using these special incentive funds—shares you then transfer to my company."

He brought up another list on the screen, a list of small but growing businesses and industries that would all profit from an infusion of cash. "Shares in these companies, I think."

Visibly stunned by his suggestion, none of the Poles said anything for several moments.

"*Jesteś szalony?* Are you insane?" Gierek asked finally. "You ask us to use our government's investment money to buy shares in Polish industries to pay for your mercenaries? That is pure madness."

"On the contrary," Martindale said coldly. "It's

pure common sense. The money exists in your budget to make investments for Poland's future. Very well, you use it for the purpose intended. The only added step is that you transfer your government's stake in these private firms to Scion. Doing that without making a fuss should be fairly simple."

Wilk nodded slowly, thinking it through. "Our American friend is right, Janusz." He held up a hand to quiet the defense minister's continuing protest. "What he proposes is doable."

"Nevertheless, Piotr," Klaudia Rybak said. "This proposition is completely irregular. Using our economic incentive funds to purchase military services from a foreign defense contractor? Can you see how that would look?"

"Don't you trust President Wilk?" Martindale asked, with a wry glint in his eyes. "Are you afraid he'll succumb to the temptation to play tin-pot dictator, using our equipment and specialists?"

"Of course not!" the prime minister snapped. Her fierce tone left no doubt that she knew she was being goaded, but it also left no doubt that she was determined to make her point. "But you ask the president to risk handing the opposition a weapon they would gladly use to destroy him!"

"Which is all the more reason to make sure this all stays secret for as long as possible. Both our acquisition of Scion's military services and the means we use to pay for them," Wilk said suddenly. He turned a hard-eyed gaze on Martindale. "You realize that any shares we choose to transfer to you could not be sold to anyone else for several years?"

"Naturally."

"Nor would your ownership of these shares convey *any* rights in the management of those Polish industries and companies."

"I would not expect them to," the gray-haired head of Scion said firmly. "Every company on that list is brilliantly run, held back only by a lack of investment. I learned a long time ago to pick the best people for a given task and then stay the hell out of their way."

The Polish president nodded again. That sounded like the truth, though he was quite sure Martindale had also long ago mastered the difficult political art of sounding sincere at all times and in all places. He eyed the other man. "Earlier, you suggested this *swap*, as you call it, would tie Scion more tightly to Poland's success and survival. What did you mean by that?"

"What value would the shares you give to us have if your country were conquered by the Russians?" Martindale asked in turn. He shrugged. "By giving us a serious financial stake in Poland's future, you give us even more incentive to fight hard for you if war breaks out and to win as quickly, cleanly, and cheaply as possible."

He looked across the table at Gierek. "Your defense minister called us mercenaries. That's become an ugly word. But there is a certain cold-edged accuracy to it. Ultimately, we at Scion *are* selling our services as soldiers to you. I would argue that we're a lot more than that, because we *won't* fight for the highest bidder—but only for those whose cause we consider just." He shrugged his shoulders again. "Still, call us what you will. As our paymasters, that's your privilege. But keep in mind that the arrangement I propose offers you insurance against the real dangers involved in relying on mercenaries—dangers so ably described by Niccolò Machiavelli more than five hundred years ago."

He paused briefly, plainly waiting for an invitation to continue.

"I read *The Prince* in my leadership classes at the Air Force Academy, Mr. Martindale," Wilk said wryly. "But from the puzzled looks on their faces, I suspect the book may not have been in the university curriculum for my colleagues."

"Basically, Machiavelli wrote that anyone who holds his country with hired troops will 'stand neither firm nor safe; for mercenaries are disunited, ambitious and without discipline, unfaithful, valiant before friends, cowardly before enemies,'" Martindale quoted, with a distant look in his eyes, reaching back into his memory. "'They are ready enough to be your soldiers whilst you do not make war, but if war comes, they take themselves off or run from the foe.'" He looked around the table. "But you can see that giving us a stake in your future changes that equation. If the Russians attack you again and we run away or lose, we gain nothing."

"You make a good case," Wilk admitted. Then he smiled, but it was a smile that did not reach his eyes. "But perhaps I should also remember Machiavelli's warning against mercenary captains. 'They are either capable men or they are not; if they are, you cannot trust them, because they always aspire to their own greatness . . . but if the captain is not skillful, you are ruined in the usual way.'"

Martindale matched his tight grin. "As to our skillfulness, you'll have to trust the reputation we've earned the hard way—and at a high cost. As to the dangers of relying on me . . ." He smiled more genuinely. "There you'll have to trust in the good sense of your fellow countrymen. As much as I value my own political skills, I can't quite see myself successfully taking over as president of Poland."

Now Wilk laughed. "A fair point." Then he looked across the table at the American. "Nor do I really believe that a man with your abilities and history would be content to rule my small country."

Martindale's grin turned rueful. "You think I'd always long for a bigger stage?"

Wilk nodded. "I think perhaps that you are a man who would always find it 'better to reign in Hell than serve in Heaven,' Mr. Martindale." He held out a hand. "But that is a matter between you and your own conscience. For my part, we are agreed. I will hire Scion to help defend Poland."

THE SCRAPHEAP, NEAR SILIŞTEA GUMEŞTI, ROMANIA
The next day

Wayne "Whack" Macomber stalked through the living quarters assigned to Scion's CID Operations Team, banging on doors. "Okay, boys and girls! We're a go. So grab your packs and get out of your racks! Next stop Poland. We're wheels up in two hours!"

Macomber, big and powerfully built, was a veteran of the U.S. Air Force's Special Operations Command. After commanding the elite ground troops attached to the 1st Air Battle Force, he had joined Scion—spearheading its efforts to recruit and train CID pilots and commandos equipped with the Tin Man battle armor system. And whenever possible, he personally piloted one of the CIDs in combat. He didn't really prefer the robots so much—he always felt like little more than a slave to the damned gadget—but getting checked out in the unholy thing gave him plenty of the chances he craved to kill bad guys and break things in new and interesting ways.

He grinned broadly at the colorful array of muttered curses and loud grumbling that greeted his door banging. Scion recruited the best special operators in the world—men and women with the right mix of combat, sapper, language, and technical skills needed to pull off incredibly dangerous and demanding missions. Social graces were always welcome, but they weren't on the required skills list.

"Hey, Uncle Wayne! It's good to see you again," a familiar-sounding voice said from behind him.

Whack Macomber spun around. The young man standing in the corridor was an even taller and bigger version of the blond-haired high school kid he last remembered seeing. "Well, well, well, if it isn't Brad McLanahan. Nice to see you, too, kid." He looked the younger McLanahan up and down with a critical eye. "Geez, you look mean as hell and ready to kick some ass. I guess all the fancy martial-arts training Wohl put you through paid off."

Brad nodded. "The training saved my life. Several times. So did the sergeant major." For a moment, his eyes went dark with remembered pain. Former Marine Corps Sergeant Major Chris Wohl had been killed saving him from one of Gryzlov's top assassins.

"Yeah, I heard about that," Macomber said abruptly. He shook his head. "For an old, crabby-ass, Marine son of a bitch, he did good." Then he clapped Brad on the shoulder. "Speaking of good work, I heard about those two Russian goons you nailed for CID One. Nice job. But I sure as hell hope you didn't scratch my ride doing it."

"If I did, I'll wash and wax it for you, Major." Brad forced himself to smile, pushing aside the regret he still felt about Wohl's death.

"You thinking about joining Scion as a rock-'em, sock-'em He-Man robot driver?" Macomber asked. "From what I saw a few years back in Nevada, you've got the chops. And I damned well *know* you wouldn't mind working with at least one of my other pilots." Whack was one of the few people who knew Patrick McLanahan was still alive.

"I'll take a rain check on that," Brad said, grinning more easily now. He shrugged. "I'm still planning to go back to Cal Poly and get my degree—once this all blows over. In the meantime, I've been asked to work with your aviation team, to bring them up to speed on some of the aircraft they'll be using during this assignment. I put in a lot of time in the simulators and on the flight line at Sky Masters this summer learning the ins and outs of a lot of the birds Scion flies." He cleared his throat uncomfortably. "And, well, I'm also supposed to form them into a more cohesive unit."

Macomber nodded. "Yeah, I heard about that, too." He shook his head. "Frankly, better you than me. If they'd put *me* in charge of pulling those sterling young *aviators* into shape, I'd probably just have wound up beating the shit out of a couple of them instead."

"Oh?"

"I'm not saying they're not good pilots. Hell, they're some of the best I've ever seen," Macomber allowed grudgingly. "But that's part of the problem. Every damned one of them thinks he or she is the ace of aces. Or should be, anyway."

Brad nodded, thinking about what he'd seen of the other pilots before being sent to Poland with his father for Martindale's demonstration. Like Mark Darrow, they'd all been friendly enough. But also like the ex-RAF Tornado driver, each of them had gone out of their way, politely to be sure, to let him know that they personally were the hottest pilot flying out of the Scrapheap. "They're all wannabe chiefs and no Indians," he realized.

"Yeah, that's it exactly. So forming them into a solid team is going to be like herding cats." Whack eyed Brad with a sardonic look that was probably as close to showing pity as the big man ever came. "I sure hope you brought your circus whip and ringmaster's top hat, because you're going to need them."

"Swell," Brad said drily. "I appreciate the vote of confidence."

"Oh, I'm confident all right," Macomber said with

a quick laugh. "I'm confident you've got a damned hard job ahead of you." Then he lowered his voice. "But if your old man thinks you're up to it, that's good enough for me. He may be a lot of things, not all of them nice or real pretty, but he's not stupid."

Brad nodded, hoping that both the other man and his father were right. They were putting a lot of trust in him and he would hate to let them down.

"Speaking of circuses," Whack asked. "What's the deal with this new name they're supposed to be slapping on our outfit?"

"It's partly for security," Brad explained. "The Poles don't want the Russians or anyone else to know they've hired Scion. If the situation heats up, they want to retain the element of surprise. And Martindale agrees with them."

"Okay, that makes sense," Macomber said. He narrowed his eyes. "You said 'partly.' What's the other reason?"

Now it was Brad's turn to grin. "Poetry."

"Poetry? You're shitting me," the other man growled.

"As God is my witness," Brad deadpanned, crossing his heart. "I'm telling the truth. Plus there's a pun involved."

"Poetry and a fricking pun, too? Jesus, do I really want to know all this?" Macomber asked sourly.

"Oh, yeah, Whack, you do. You really do," Brad told him cheerfully. "The pun comes from the fact that the Polish president's last name means 'wolf' in English."

"Swell," Macomber said, frowning. "So fucking what?"

"So we're no longer working for Scion," Brad told him. "Now we're part of the *Eskadra Żelazny Wilk*."

"Which means what when it's at home?" Macomber asked.

"The Iron Wolf Squadron," Brad said.

Slowly, almost reluctantly, a crooked smile spread across Whack's hard-edged face. "Iron Wolf Squadron, huh? Hell, I kind of like it."

SS *BALTIC VENTURE*,
PORT OF HOUSTON, TEXAS, UNITED STATES
That same time

U.S. Customs and Border Protection officer Frank Talbot stood on the bridge of the SS *Baltic Venture*, watching a huge crane gently lower a big aircraft, completely shrink-wrapped in white plastic, into the fast freighter's forward cargo hold. A second identical aircraft sat on the front apron near the ship, waiting its turn.

He frowned. That plastic wrap would protect the planes from salt air and sea water during the coming voyage. It was standard overseas shipping practice for all flyable military aircraft.

Which was part of the reason for Talbot's concern.

He glanced at the big, beefy man standing placidly beside him. That was the other thing that worried him. Marcus Cartwright was supposed to be the broker handling this transaction. But the customs officer had the uneasy feeling that Cartwright was a lot more. Something about the guy smelled of "spook." And if there was one thing he had learned in fifteen years of federal service, it was that you wanted to stay far, far away from anyone who used the word *covert* during their normal daily work. Plus, there were a few peccadilloes in his past—usually involving minor amounts of illicit substances coming into the United States—that made the prospect of dealing with anyone connected with intelligence even more disconcerting. Still, this wasn't exactly something he could safely ignore. Not with all the trouble going on overseas.

"Let me get this straight," Talbot said slowly. "You say these old F-111 fighter-bombers are going to Warsaw as 'static display aircraft'?"

"I not only say that, Agent Talbot," Cartwright said, still standing patiently watching the crane lower its cargo. "I've already shown you the papers to prove it." He nodded toward the two shrink-wrapped aircraft. "Two decommissioned F-111s are being shipped to the Museum of the Polish Army in Warsaw. They are going to form part of a special Cold War exhibit. My firm is handling this transaction. I fail to see the difficulty."

"That's the point," Talbot said, nerving himself up. "Nobody puts planes on museum display with working engines. And all four engines on those F-111s are intact. Also, I poked around those aircraft a little while your crews were wrapping them up, and they were in really good shape. A lot better shape than they should be if they'd just spent twenty years sitting outside in the Arizona desert."

"My word, you have been observant," Cartwright

said mildly. "That's an excellent point about the engines. Somebody should have noticed that earlier." He shrugged sadly. "Now it's too late. It's not as though we have time to send these particular planes back to the Boneyard. The exhibit opens in just a few weeks. And as it is, these F-111s will already take more than fifteen days just to reach Gdansk."

"That's not my problem," the customs officer said stiffly. "My problem is your plan to export fully operational military aircraft without the required end-user certificates and licenses."

"Licenses and end-user certificates?" Cartwright asked. "Is that all?" He reached inside his suit coat and pulled out a thick envelope. "If only you'd spoken up sooner. Here you are, Talbot. I think you'll find all the necessary documents in perfect order."

Frowning, Talbot took the envelope. It wasn't sealed. He slid it open and froze—not for long, just long enough to estimate that the envelope contained at least $20,000 in cash. He swallowed hard. If this was a sting and he took the money, he was screwed. But maybe it wasn't a sting, he thought hopefully. Maybe this was part of a CIA black-ops program to ship weapons across the Atlantic without getting the U.S. officially involved. Scuttlebutt around the customs service said that kind of stuff happened, and a lot more often than anyone outside the government imagined.

He looked up to see Cartwright watching him calmly. He breathed out. Maybe it was worth taking a chance. He slipped the envelope into the inner pocket of his blue uniform jacket. "I see what you mean."

"I thought you would," the other man said, smiling. "We did rather a lot of careful research on you, you see."

Talbot felt a shiver run up his spine. The less time he spent with this spook the better. "Well, I guess we're done here, then," he muttered.

"Yes, I believe so. Thank you for your cooperation," Cartwright told him politely, already tuning the customs officer out and turning away to watch the big harbor crane swinging back toward the fighter-bomber still waiting on the front apron.

The Iron Wolf Squadron's first two XF-111 SuperVarks would soon be safely on their way to Poland.

THE CHURCH OF ST. LOUIS OF FRANCE, MOSCOW, RUSSIA
That same time

Wearing a drab overcoat and cap and using a cane, Sergei Tarzarov hobbled slowly up the broad steps to the mustard-colored Church of St. Louis of France. No one seeing him would have recognized the quiet, soft-spoken chief of staff to Russia's flamboyant president. He looked much older and poorer now, like one of the many elderly pensioners who eked out a paltry living doing odd jobs for Moscow's wealthier elites.

This late at night, the normally busy streets of the surrounding shopping district were quiet. A few lights glowed in the windows of the taller neighboring brick buildings. For nearly a century, the buildings had housed the parish rectory, a French school, a small hospital, and a Dominican monastery, but they had been seized by the old Soviet regime and converted into government offices.

The church itself, built by the French in 1830, served as a place of worship for many in Moscow's diplomatic community. That had kept it safe even during the darkest days of Stalinist repression.

Tarzarov slipped into the shadows cast by six massive Doric columns across the front of the church and drew out a key to unlock the main door. The civic ordinances that required that the keys and alarm codes of certain public buildings be deposited with local fire, police, and medical authorities were always useful, he mused. Especially to someone like him who occasionally needed discreet private access to certain places when they were supposed to be closed.

He cracked open the door and went inside.

The interior of the church was mostly dark, lit only by a few flickering candles and dimmed electric lights on a few of the small brass chandeliers between marble columns lining the central aisle. Streetlights gleaming through stained glass windows cast faint patterns of blue, gold, white, and red across the altar.

Tapping along the marble floor with his cane, Tarzarov hobbled toward a plain wood confessional set against the right wall. He entered one of the booths, closed the door, and knelt down. A red light flicked on, illuminating his face.

The grille separating him from the priest's tiny, unlit chamber slid open. A shadowy figure was barely visible through the wood lattice.

"*Otets, prosti menya, ibo ya sogreshil,*" Tarzarov murmured. "Father, forgive me, for I have sinned."

"I am deeply shocked to hear that, Sergei," the man on the other side said drily. "I hope you aren't confessing that you were followed here?"

Tarzarov smiled thinly. "A crow might have followed me. But not a man. I know my business, Igor." He rapped gently on the lattice. "And the Catholic priest whose place you have usurped? What of him?"

"Called away to a hospital on the outskirts of Moscow to administer the last rites to a dying parishioner," the other man said. "We have plenty of time alone here."

"A convenient *accident*?" Tarzarov asked.

"Nothing so melodramatic," the other man said, chuckling. "Merely a matter of fortunate timing, for us at least. Much better that way, eh?"

Tarzarov nodded. He had no moral objection to arranging the death or injury of anyone, not even an innocent bystander, if that proved necessary to his plans. But there were always risks to direct action. Even the best-trained hit team could make mistakes, leaving traces for some honest policeman or clever foreign spy to follow.

"So then, to business," the other man said. "Tell me, what is your assessment of your protégé now? Is he still so consumed by rage and driven by desire for revenge? I know there were moments last year, during the Starfire crisis, when you feared that he might drag us all into absolute disaster."

"Gennadiy is . . . calmer," Tarzarov said slowly. He shrugged. "At least on the surface. No doubt his anger still burns white-hot inside, but he seems better able to control it. Now he uses his fury as a directed weapon against those who fail, rather than unleashing it in some uncontrollable explosion that consumes everything around him."

"Interesting," the other man said. Tarzarov thought he sounded disappointed. "And unexpected."

"Victory may soften many rough edges," Gryzlov's chief of staff pointed out. "Though the price was high, Gennadiy achieved what many of us have sought for so long—the complete destruction of the American military space station. This has given him great confidence in his abilities and in his decisions."

"Do you share this confidence?"

Tarzarov shrugged again. "For the moment." He looked steadily through the lattice. "Certainly, I cannot fault the way he has exploited this most recent terrorist attack against us. Using it to justify occupying the eastern Ukraine was bold, but his maneuver has succeeded beyond my earlier expectations. So far, the Americans have done nothing serious to oppose us, and because of that, NATO stands exposed as a paper tiger."

"True," the other man agreed, again reluctantly.

"As a result, Gennadiy is more popular among the people than ever," Tarzarov continued.

"Popularity!" the other man muttered bitterly. "Now, there's a two-edged sword, as I know only too well. The people back you only as long as you seem to be winning. But they turn on you when things grow difficult. They are untrustworthy."

"All men are untrustworthy," Tarzarov said calmly. "But for now the president's support among the people gives him more power among the bureaucrats and the military. He has achieved almost total control over the Kremlin and the armed forces."

"I see," the other man said. "So you believe Gryzlov has become a man without weaknesses."

"A man of steel?" said Tarzarov, playing off the often-cited meaning of Joseph Stalin's chosen name. He shook his head. "No. Not that. Not yet." He knelt silently for a few moments before going on. "There are still potential weaknesses in his policies and in his passions—weaknesses that greatly trouble me."

"Such as?"

"I worry that his hatred for the Poles may lead us into direct confrontation with them—and through them, with the Americans and the rest of NATO," Tarzarov admitted. "We have been lucky so far. But Gennadiy may push our luck too far."

"I thought Warsaw was at least partly responsible for these terrorist attacks?" the other man said. "If so, our actions are more than justified."

"I very much doubt the Poles have anything to do with these terrorists," Tarzarov replied. "The evidence for their involvement in the murder of General Voronov was never more than circumstantial. And there is no evidence whatsoever that they were responsible for the most recent atrocity. I do not trust or like the Warsaw government, but I do not truly think Piotr Wilk and his gang are that insane."

"And yet . . ." the other man prompted gently.

"The president believes otherwise," Tarzarov said. "He is absolutely convinced that Poland has attacked us, using these terrorist groups in the Ukraine as its proxies. He craves an excuse to punish them for this, to take revenge for the deaths they have caused and the damage they have inflicted. For now, the ease of our occupation of the eastern Ukraine satisfies him, but I worry that an obsessive need to hit back at Warsaw may lead him to take bigger risks."

"This begins to sound alarmingly familiar," the other man observed acidly. "Is it possible that Gryzlov's near mania for revenge on that dead American general, Patrick McLanahan, and his family has transferred itself to the Poles? To a whole country?"

Tarzarov was silent for a time. At last, he said, "I sincerely hope not. After all, there are valid strategic reasons for wanting to see Poland diminished."

"Yes," the other man agreed. "Of all our former possessions, the Poles are the richest, the strongest, and the most stubbornly independent. If it were possible to break Poland without risking all-out war, many of the smaller, weaker nations in Eastern and Central Europe would begin falling back into our orbit."

"That is likely," Tarzarov agreed, though reluctantly. "But others understand that, too. And if we push too hard too soon, we may yet trigger a reaction from those, like the new American president, who might otherwise be willing to turn a blind eye to our growing strength."

"An excellent point," the other man said. "I greatly value your insights on these matters. They are extremely useful. And I appreciate your willingness to convey them to me—despite your obvious loyalty to President Gryzlov."

"I am a loyal servant of the state, Igor," Tarzarov said quietly. "Not of any one man."

"So I have long observed, Sergei," said the man sitting in darkness on the other side of the lattice. "I look forward to our next . . . discussion."

Long after Gennadiy Gryzlov's chief of staff left to make his circuitous way back to the Kremlin, Igor Truznyev, former president of Russia, stayed behind, contemplating the information he had been given—and considering the various uses to which he could put it. Earlier, he had hoped that the Ukrainian maniac Kravchenko's terrorist attacks would show Russia's military and political elites their error in replacing him, Truznyev, with the younger man, by goading Gryzlov into a disastrous overreaction. Well, if Gryzlov was becoming better at controlling his rages, Truznyev would just have to find a way for his unwitting Ukrainian puppets to up the ante.

CHAPTER 7

*Knowing your own darkness is
the best method for dealing with
the darknesses of other people.*

—CARL JUNG,
SWISS PSYCHIATRIST

TRAKHTEMYRIV NATURE AND ARCHAEOLOGICAL RESERVE, WESTERN UKRAINE
The next night

Fedir Kravchenko crouched down in cover, watching the opposite bank of the Dnieper through night-vision binoculars. A few kilometers to the south, the natural flow of the river was obstructed by the Kaniv Hydroelectric Power Plant's massive dam—forming a huge reservoir that was almost two kilometers wide at this point.

To some extent, that made this stretch of the Dnieper more dangerous as a potential crossing point, since any boats would be out on the open water for that much longer. On the other hand, the Trakhtemyriv Reserve's dense belt of woodland ran all the way to the water's edge. The forest canopy made it easier for his partisans to conceal their motorized inflatable rafts and gear from Russian reconnaissance drones and aircraft while they were moving up to the shoreline. As an added plus, the eastern shore was also thickly wooded, offering shelter and ready camouflage for infiltrators right after they landed. The woods there were also cut by a number of small tracks and farm roads—offering his partisans the opportunity to move quickly inland to safe houses and hidden camps farther east.

Kravchenko knew that all military decisions involved calculated risk. You weighed the different options and took the ones that seemed to offer the greatest gain for the least chance of disaster. Making the right call was always a gamble.

Unfortunately, anytime you gambled, you could lose.

And this time, he had lost.

Pop-pop-pop.

Seen through the night-imaging binoculars, three green sparks soared skyward on the other side of the water. They flew high directly over the two motorized rafts speeding eastward across the reservoir. Even this far away, he could see the four men on each inflatable suddenly look up in horror.

"Hell."

Kravchenko lowered the binoculars right before the flares burst into full light over the Dnieper. Sputtering evilly, they drifted slowly downwind— illuminating everything for hundreds of meters.

More flashes stuttered among the trees on the far bank of the Dnieper, casting eerie, dancing shadows that lit up a tangled mosaic of leaves and branches. Fountains of white spray erupted all around the fast-moving inflatables. The Ukrainian partisan leader bit down on another oath as the chatter of Russian heavy machine guns echoed across the water.

He had just sent eight men straight into an ambush.

Through the radio clipped to his body armor, Kravchenko could hear them screaming and pleading for help. "Covering fire! We need covering fire now!" one of them yelled. "We're getting murdered out here!"

Slowly, clenching his teeth so hard that his jaw ached, the Ukrainian looked away. Those enemy machine guns were too far away, out of effective range of the assault rifles carried by the men deployed on this side of the river. Trying to hit the Russians would only give away his own positions, and offer the enemy a juicy target for their artillery and mortars.

No, he decided grimly, the partisans trapped on those rafts were as good as dead. Either the Russians would keep shooting until nothing moved, or they would send out boats of their own to take prisoners for interrogation. Then, once torture and truth drugs had squeezed every morsel of information out of their captives, the Russians would simply murder them.

There was only one thing he could do for his men now.

Kravchenko turned to Pavlo Lytvyn. "Execute code OMEGA."

"Very well, Major," the bigger man agreed, not trying to hide his own regret and anger. He carefully set a frequency on his own radio transmitter and clicked the send button. Then he switched to another frequency and hit the button a second time.

Charges rigged to the inflatables detonated. Two huge explosions rocked the surface of the Dnieper. When the smoke and spray drifted away, there was nothing identifiable left—only bits and pieces of debris left floating in the foaming water.

For a few moments more, Kravchenko stared blindly out across the wide river, aware only of the bitter taste of failure and defeat. Until he could figure out how to move more men and weapons to the east without suffering unacceptable losses, the Russians were out of his reach.

IRON WOLF SQUADRON SECURE COMPOUND, 33RD AIR BASE, NEAR POWIDZ, CENTRAL POLAND

The next morning

"CID Two, stand by for field resupply maneuver. Iron Wolf One-Five coming in hot. Two minutes out."

"Two copies, Wolf One-Five. Ready to rock and rearm."

Captain Nadia Rozek stood near the flight line at the 33rd Air Base, listening closely to the crisp, confident messages crackling through her radio earpiece. She was one of several Polish Special Forces officers newly assigned to the Iron Wolf Squadron. Most of her comrades would serve as translators where needed and as liaisons between the Scion-organized unit and Poland's more conventional air and ground units.

She had other orders. First, she was slated to receive training on one of the squadron's two Cybernetic Infantry Devices—the "Iron Wolves" that gave the unit its new name. Perhaps even more importantly, she was here to act as President Piotr Wilk's personal "eyes and ears," keeping him closely posted on the squadron's plans and operations.

"You will not be a spy, Captain," Wilk had told her with a smile. "But I want you there to help me cut through the regular chain of command if necessary. From what we have seen, if it goes into action, this Iron Wolf force will use tactics far outside the realm of conventional military experience and training. It's vital that I receive firsthand reports from an officer who understands and can thoroughly evaluate how Martindale's people do their fighting."

Which meant she was something of a spy, after all, Nadia decided—though not a hostile or especially covert one. No one in the Iron Wolf Squadron would be surprised to find out that their new employer planned to keep a careful watch on his $500 million investment.

At least this new assignment had brought her back to her old stomping grounds. This air base, halfway between Poznan and Warsaw, was home to Poland's 7th Special Operations Squadron. She'd spent a year here flying Mi-17 helicopters, practicing nap-of-the-earth flying and all the other dangerous maneuvers needed to insert Polish commandos behind enemy lines and retrieve them under fire. Its existing ties to Poland's Special Forces made Powidz the logical place to base this new unit. The 33rd Air Base had a tight security perimeter and the local civilians were already used to hearing unusual aircraft coming and going at odd intervals.

Through her earpiece, Nadia heard another signal from the Iron Wolf Squadron aircraft that was supposed to be approaching the 33rd Air Base. "CID Two, this is Wolf One-Five. Field in sight. Thirty seconds. Out."

"Standing by," the CID pilot said laconically.

Puzzled, she turned around, scanning the horizon in all directions. Nothing was in sight. No airplane. No helicopter. And certainly no huge manned war robot. Were these Americans pulling a practical joke on her?

Abruptly, a large, twin-engine aircraft in mottled dark green, light green, and gray camouflage streaked into view, booming in from the south just over the treetops. As it crossed over the field, it banked into a steep, tight turn, decelerating dramatically, almost impossibly, fast.

Nadia's eyes widened. The huge propellers on each wing were swiveling upward, turning into rotors. Of course, she thought, figuring it out. This mysterious aircraft was a tilt-rotor, designed to take off and land like a helicopter while cruising long distances at high speeds like a conventional turboprop. It looked very much like the V-22 Ospreys flown by the U.S. Marine Corps and U.S. Air Force, but it was somewhat smaller and seemed more agile than the Ospreys she had seen before.

She realized this must be another of the experimental planes built by Sky Masters. The aerospace engineers working for that American firm seemed to have an almost limitless ability to push the boundaries of aircraft design.

Rotors spinning fast, the twin-engine aircraft descended toward the wide grass verge beside the runway and touched down. As soon as it settled, a rear ramp whined open and a small, four-wheel vehicle roared out and onto the grass. Swinging wide around the still-spinning rotors, it drove toward her at high speed. There were three crew—two in front and a top gunner manning a .50-caliber M2 machine gun in the back.

Nadia forced herself to stand absolutely still as the 4x4 sped right past her, racing by at more than sixty kilometers an hour. The gunner, wearing a helmet, body armor, and goggles, gave her a cheerful wave.

Suddenly the driver slammed on his brakes and spun the little vehicle into a tight, hard turn, coming to a dead stop in a spray of gravel and grass just a few meters away. The driver and the other man seated in front were already unbuckling their safety harnesses while the gunner stayed put—swinging his heavy machine gun around to cover the nearby woods.

Nadia caught a flicker of motion out the corner of her eye and then gasped as one of the tall Cybernetic Infantry Devices bounded past her and slid to a halt right beside the 4x4. Its arms were already in motion, shrugging off heavy weapons packs and sliding them onto the small vehicle's cargo deck. As soon as the old packs were stowed, the CID retrieved new weapons and ammunition carriers. At the same time, the two crewmen who'd dismounted were busy popping open panels on the huge robot's legs and torso, disconnecting depleted lithium-ion batteries and hydrogen fuel cells and then replacing them with fully charged batteries and fuel cells. Their coordinated speed and precision was astounding, reminding her of a top-notch Formula One pit crew.

In less than two minutes, they were finished.

"Rearm and recharge complete!" Nadia heard the CID pilot report.

Both vehicle crewmen slapped the torso panels closed and then hopped back aboard their 4x4. As soon as they'd buckled in, the driver sped off back down the runway toward the waiting tilt-rotor. Slowing, he drove straight up the aircraft's rear ramp.

In seconds, the ramp closed and the aircraft lifted off, climbing just high enough to transition its rotors for level flight. Moments later, it streaked away just over the treetops and was gone.

"Iron Wolf One-Five outbound," Nadia heard the tilt-rotor's pilot report. "Field resupply complete. Mission time on ground: approximately five minutes."

Beside her, the CID crouched down, extending one leg and both arms backward. A hatch popped open on its back and a broad-shouldered, blond-haired man wearing a black flight suit climbed out. The name tag over his left breast pocket read BRAD MCLANAHAN. He dropped lightly to the ground and walked over.

"So what did you think, Captain Rozek?" he asked, with a mischievous grin. "Impressive enough for you?"

Nadia eyed him carefully. This American had a nice smile and some of the cocky swagger that marked many young pilots . . . including, she admitted to herself, a certain Nadia Rozek when she was fresh out of flight school. Well, there were ways to deal with that.

"Your resupply maneuver?" she asked. "Is that something your crews practice routinely?"

Brad nodded. "Yep. We can use that Sky Masters XV-40 Sparrowhawk tilt-rotor you saw or a specially modified Chinook helicopter, something along the lines of the MH-47G models used by the U.S. Army's One Hundred and Sixtieth Special Aviation Regiment. Both of them can lift that fast little four-by-four resupply vehicle we use to haul ammo, weapons, batteries, and fuel cells. And by the way, that four-by-four is a version of the Interim Fast Attack Vehicle our Marine Force Recon guys use—a souped-up Mercedes-Benz Wolf 290GDT."

"A Wolf four-by-four?" Nadia said, raising an eyebrow. "Really?"

His grin grew wider. "Yeah, really. I guess this new Iron Wolf name suits us for a lot of reasons."

"So I gather," she said coolly, really hoping this brash McLanahan character could restrain himself before he started pretending to howl at the moon or do something equally childish. "And you are one of those who will pilot these Iron Wolves in combat?" she asked, nodding toward the CID.

To her relief, he looked slightly abashed. "Me? No, probably not." He shrugged his shoulders. "I've driven CIDs a few times. But my real passion is flying, which is why I'm assigned to the squadron's aviation team. We'll be handling the unit's drone aircraft and the remote-piloted XF-111 SuperVarks once they get here."

"McLanahan! You are related to General McLanahan?" Nadia said, suddenly realizing why this young man's name had seemed so familiar. Among her peers in Poland's air force, the missions flown by Patrick McLanahan and the men and women under his command were legendary.

"He's . . . I mean, he *was* . . . my father," Brad said quietly.

"I am very sorry," Nadia told him, fumbling slightly for the proper English phrases. "He was a great man. Please accept my condolences on your loss."

She looked even more closely at the younger McLanahan. Now that her memory was working at full speed, it reminded her that this boyish-looking American had flown on the daredevil bombing mission in which his father was killed. And that, later, he had also gone on to fly in outer space as part of the ill-fated Starfire Project. She colored slightly, abruptly aware that she might have come across as just a bit patronizing to someone whose real-world experience easily exceeded hers by a factor of ten.

Fortunately, Nadia decided, seeing the equally embarrassed look on his face, he seemed unaware of that.

"Thanks, Captain Rozek," Brad said, clearing his throat uncomfortably. "I really appreciate it." He looked down at his shoes and then resolutely back up at her. "I hope you don't think I was just showing off or anything earlier. President Martindale and Whack Macomber suggested I take this practice run to keep my CID piloting skills sharp. Just in case."

On impulse, she smiled at him. "If we are going to be flying and fighting together, Mr. Brad McLanahan, I think you can call me Nadia."

"Really? That's great, Captain . . . I mean, Nadia," Brad said, looking more cheerful again. He straightened up, squaring his shoulders. "Then how about I get started familiarizing you with old Robo Lobo there?"

"Robo Lobo?" Nadia asked, confused again. Then she got it. "Oh, no! Not more of your American 'wolf' humor?"

"Yes, ma'am," Brad said jauntily. Then he relented, looking slightly contrite. "Sorry, Nadia. But it was just hanging out there, waiting to be said, and I couldn't stop myself."

Almost against her will, she laughed. "Never mind. I will forgive you." She held up a single finger. "Once. But you will resist the temptation from now on, is that understood?"

"Or else?" he asked, intrigued.

"Exactly," Nadia said, with great satisfaction. "Or else."

THE KREMLIN, MOSCOW
A few hours later

The phone on President Gennadiy Gryzlov's desk beeped suddenly, interrupting him at the worst possible moment. "*Sukin syn!* Son of a bitch," he muttered, trying to ignore the sound. But it was no use. His concentration was broken. Still swearing under his breath, he fumbled for the phone. "Yes! What the hell is it? I said, no calls!"

"It's Minister of State Security Kazyanov, Mr. President," his private secretary said apologetically. "He is here in the outer office, asking to see you immediately. He says it is urgent."

"It had damned well better be, Ulanov!" Gryzlov snapped. "I'm right in the middle of a serious foreign policy discussion, you know."

"Yes, Mr. President."

Gryzlov sighed. "Very well. Give me a couple of minutes." He slammed the phone down and turned to the attractive, full-figured woman who was still bent across his desk. "Get your clothes back on, Daria. It seems I have other work to do."

Foreign Minister Daria Titeneva looked back over her naked shoulder with a slightly provocative smile. "That is unfortunate, Mr. President."

"Yes, it is," he agreed glumly. He zipped his fly and then moved around to sit behind his desk. When she had finished slipping back into her businesslike jacket, blouse, and skirt, he picked up the phone. "I'll see Minister Kazyanov now." He looked up at Titeneva. "There's no point in your waiting for me. If poor little Viktor's actually managed to nerve himself up to come over here in person, he must really believe he's got something important."

She simply nodded and went out by the side door.

Kazyanov hurried in moments later, a file folder clutched in his hands. As usual, the intelligence director looked nervous, with sweat already beading his high forehead.

"Well?" Gryzlov barked. "What's so damned urgent?"

"Two of our top GRU agents have gone missing," Kazyanov said quickly. "They failed to make a scheduled contact yesterday and we have been completely unable to get in touch with them since then."

"So?" Gryzlov said dismissively. "Agents go quiet all the time—for any number of reasons, some good and some bad. For all you know, these spies of yours might just be lazing around a swimming pool somewhere, taking an unauthorized vacation. Or maybe they got spooked by something and are simply lying low for a bit."

Kazyanov shook his head. "With respect, Mr. President, not these two men. Colonel Lermontov and Major Rodchenko are both extraordinarily reliable, competent, and experienced field operatives. They would not abandon an important mission so easily."

"All right," Gryzlov said, shrugging. "I'll bite. Where were these missing paragons of espionage stationed?"

"Poland."

The Russian president started paying attention. "Go on."

"Their last message indicated that they were planning to penetrate a Polish military training area, at Drawsko Pomorskie in western Poland," Kazyanov reported, sliding a map out of the folder and showing it to Gryzlov. "They'd picked up rumors of an important military exercise planned there—an unscheduled exercise."

"Oh, really," the president said, frowning. That *was* highly unusual. To avoid accidents and the risk of unintended escalation, it was common practice for both the NATO powers and for Russia to announce their important military drills, exercises, and war games in advance. "Was this a NATO maneuver of some sort?"

"No, sir," Kazyanov said. "Before they disappeared, Lermontov and Rodchenko said the rumors they picked up indicated this secret exercise was supposed to be a strictly Polish affair."

"But you don't believe the rumors?" Gryzlov asked, hearing the uncertainty in the other man's voice.

"There are . . . incongruities," Kazyanov admitted. "When we could not regain contact with our operatives, I asked my best analysts to examine our most recent Persona reconnaissance satellite images of the Drawsko Pomorskie region." He handed the president a series of photos from his folder. "These enlarged images were taken during a pass over the area three days ago. As you can see, they show a significant number of pieces of military hardware scattered around the training area—vehicles, tanks, guns, and even fighter aircraft."

Gryzlov flipped through the photos. His mouth

tightened. "These are all old American tanks and planes. Look at this one, an F-4 Phantom! They're not even in the Polish inventory! Hell, almost no one flies them anymore!"

"Yes, sir," Kazyanov confirmed. "My analysts say that all of this equipment appears to be surplus. Which begins to explain what we picked up during a satellite pass twenty-four hours ago." He slid another set of images across the desk.

The Russian president stared down them in silence. Each showed a collection of burned-out armored vehicles and wrecked aircraft. He looked up at his minister of state security. "Astounding."

Kazyanov nodded. "It appears that every single piece of surplus military equipment was destroyed during this war game. Without exception."

"Which Polish units did all this?" Gryzlov asked, still looking at the photos. "We may have to reassess their combat effectiveness."

"That is one of the incongruities," Kazyanov told him carefully. "We believe a Polish mechanized infantry battalion *was* assigned to secure the training area, but it does not seem to have been involved in the maneuvers themselves. In fact, we cannot find evidence that *any* unit of the Polish armed forces participated in this exercise."

Gryzlov stared at him. "What?"

"Every piece of intelligence we can assemble—signals intercepts, agent reports, satellite photos, and the like—shows the rest of the Polish Army, including its Special Forces, posted at their ordinary duty stations," Kazyanov said.

"My God, Viktor," Gryzlov said, piecing it together as he stared at the pictures. "Do you realize what this means?"

"Sir?"

"You may just have uncovered the evidence we've been looking for!" Gryzlov said sharply, irritated by the other man's inability to see what should be obvious to anyone with even a fraction of average intelligence. "Are you blind?"

"Mr. President, I'm afraid that I'm not following—"

"The terrorists, you idiot!" Gryzlov snapped excitedly. "The terrorists who've been attacking us! Who else could the Poles be training in such secrecy?"

KIEV, UKRAINE
The next day

Fedir Kravchenko studied the faded signs on the buildings they were driving past. This section of western Kiev was a mix of drab Soviet-era apartment blocks, run-down shops, and old warehouses. Cars parked along the streets were mostly older models, some so covered in rust and graffiti that it was clear that they'd been abandoned for years. At least there were enough trees along the sidewalks and streets to soften the harsher edges of this impoverished neighborhood.

He spotted the bleached-out red, white, and blue tobacco kiosk he'd been told to look for and tapped

Pavlo Lytvyn on the shoulder. "There, pull in and park. Then wait for me."

Nodding unhappily, the big man obeyed. He found an empty spot just large enough for the ZAZ Forza subcompact he was driving.

"I don't like this, Major," Lytvyn growled, hunched over the steering wheel. "I don't trust this *prykhyl'nyk*, this backer, of ours. If he's really an ally, why hide himself from us—working only through faceless intermediaries?"

Kravchenko shrugged. "We're operating outside the law, my friend. It's no great surprise that our anonymous patron wants to keep us at arm's length." He sighed. "But we have no choice. We need this man's cash and connections to buy weapons and equipment."

He popped open the car door and climbed out onto the sidewalk.

"I still don't like it," Lytvyn said stubbornly, leaning over to talk through the little car's rolled-down passenger window. "For all we know, this guy could be a boss in the *Mafiya*, nothing but a criminal. We might be waging our war with dirty money—drug money, even."

"All money is dirty, Pavlo," Kravchenko said. "As is war, if it comes to that. Besides, what choice do we have?" He hawked and spat. "Go hat in hand to the government again, begging for their help? The cowards in Kiev turned us down years ago and now they crawl before the Russians, pleading only to be left alone."

He shook his head. "You might be right about our

patron. He could be a criminal. But I think it's more likely that he is one of the big oligarchs, the billionaires, who raised and equipped our volunteer battalions during the 2014 war. Why else would anyone but a patriot back our cause now?"

Lytvyn scowled. "Oligarch. Crime boss. What's the real difference?"

Kravchenko grinned crookedly. "Weapons and explosives for us, instead of cocaine and heroin shipments for him."

The big man looked unconvinced. "I say this meeting is too risky. Why do they forbid you to bring your own people? That's new and it stinks. This could be a trap."

Kravchenko looked into Lytvyn's eyes. "Yes, that is possible. But if this is a trap, what can they really do to me?"

"They can kill you," the other man snapped.

"Kill me?" Kravchenko repeated mildly. Then his maimed face contorted into a terrible, twisted smile that sent a cold shiver of fear down Lytvyn's spine. "No, they can't. Not really. After all, Pavlo, we both know that I truly died with the rest of our battalion three years ago, back on that cursed road between the trees." He turned away. "Wait for me."

"And if I'm right and this is a trap?" Lytvyn called after him.

"Then avenge me," Kravchenko said over his shoulder, already heading toward the warehouse chosen for this clandestine rendezvous. It was set back from the street, down an alley littered with uncollected garbage and old crates. Boarded-up or broken windows looked down on the alley from both sides.

A sign in dirty, peeling white letters hung over a rusting metal roll-up door identified this as *URVAD TSENTR POTACHANNYA 20*—Government Supply Center 20. He scowled. This had probably once been one of the storehouses where the old Soviet-era bosses hoarded fresh food and luxury goods for the *nomenklatura*, the governing elite. Now it was nothing but a ruin.

He dialed a number on his cell phone. It was answered on the first ring. "I'm here," he said flatly, and broke the connection.

The metal door squealed and rattled open, grinding upward.

It slid down behind Kravchenko as soon as he walked into the abandoned warehouse, banging down with a hollow echo on the cracked and pitted concrete floor. Lights came on, revealing a big black Mercedes sedan parked in the center of the empty building.

A man in jeans and a brown leather jacket moved in behind the Ukrainian. He must have been waiting in the shadows beside the door. "Your phone," he said coldly. "You'll get it back when we're done here."

Shrugging, Kravchenko handed him the cell phone and then held his arms out wide, waiting patiently while the sentry frisked him for weapons or hidden recording devices.

Satisfied that Kravchenko was clean, the other man stepped back and waved him toward the waiting car. "Go on."

The rear passenger door of the Mercedes opened when he got within a few meters. A second man, this one wearing an elegant business suit and sunglasses, got out and stood facing Kravchenko. He was taller than the Ukrainian partisan leader, with gray, short-cropped hair and a square jaw. The business suit fit him perfectly, but he would probably have looked equally at home in a uniform.

"My employer is . . . unhappy, Major," he said quietly.

"So am I," Kravchenko retorted.

"You were given substantial resources to accomplish a specific objective—the liberation of the Russian-controlled areas of our motherland. To achieve this, you assured my employer that your actions would bring Moscow into direct collision with the United States, Poland, and the other NATO powers. Instead, the Russians now control half of our country, including most of our energy resources and heavy industry!"

"The West has proved more cowardly than I imagined," Kravchenko admitted.

"Your lack of imagination has cost us dearly," the man in sunglasses sneered.

"My plans were approved at every stage," Kravchenko pointed out coldly. "Your boss saw nothing improbable in the supposition that our attacks would lure Russia's leaders into repeated military action against Poland, action that would trigger direct NATO involvement in this region to our ultimate benefit. If *my* imagination failed, so did that of your employer."

"It would be safer for you to avoid insulting him," the other man said. His mouth tightened. "He is not a man inclined to forgive affronts—or failure."

"I don't give a damn about my personal safety," Kravchenko said bluntly. "I only care about winning. And killing as many Russians as possible." He stared hard at the man in sunglasses. "My question is: Can your boss say the same? Or is he ready to quit now that things have gotten tough? Is he just a summer soldier? A patriot only when the sun is shining?"

"My employer is equally interested in victory," the other man replied. "He only questions your ability to achieve it."

"Then your boss needs to learn more patience," Kravchenko said flatly. He shook his head in disgust. "For God's sake, we've lost a single battle, not the whole damned war! And even in losing, we've picked up a crucial insight into what makes this Russian leader, Gryzlov, tick."

"Now you claim to see profit in defeat?" the other man asked skeptically.

"The Russians reacted exactly as we had hoped to Voronov's murder, lunging headlong into Polish territory like a maddened bull," Kravchenko pointed out. "Our mistake was in assuming that Gryzlov and his generals would react the same way to our next attack. But we were too subtle for them."

"Subtle?!" The man in sunglasses seemed amused. "There are many words I would use to describe the slaughter you inflicted on that separatist base. *Subtle* would not have been among them."

"Think about it," Kravchenko persisted. "The key difference between our two attacks was their distance from the Polish border."

The other man snorted. "Maybe so, but having successfully occupied our country up to the Dnieper, Moscow is not likely to send more soldiers and generals for you to shoot near the frontier. Not unless they were already invading the rest of Ukraine, which is not something we want!"

"True," Kravchenko said. "But you miss my point. If the mountain will not come to Mohammed, then Mohammed must go to the mountain. If our Russian targets will not venture close to Poland, then . . ." He sketched out his new plan, which was far more ruthless than anything he had proposed before.

When he was finished, the man in sunglasses stood silent for several long moments, pondering what he had heard. At last, he nodded. "What you propose does have a certain brutal elegance, Major. It may even succeed. But you ask much of my employer—in time and in money and in other, less easily replaceable, resources."

"Yes," Kravchenko agreed. "I do."

"Very well," the other man said. "I will present your plan to him. I will even recommend that we proceed."

"Thank you."

"But you must understand something very important, Major," the man in sunglasses warned. "My employer will not tolerate another failure. If your plan does not work, the consequences to you will be severe. Fatal, even."

"If I fail, I would not wish to live anyway," Kravchenko said simply.

* * *

Once the Ukrainian partisan leader was gone, the man in sunglasses slid back into the rear seat of the Mercedes. He took out his phone and began composing a short text message to his real employer, Igor Truznyev, in Moscow: MEETING WITH GULL ONE SUCCESSFUL. NEW SALES PROPOSAL WILL FOLLOW. WILL REQUIRE CLOSE COOPERATION WITH WARSAW OFFICE. PROSPECTS GOOD.

DONEGAL AIRPORT, COUNTY DONEGAL, IRELAND
That same time

Descending on its final approach, the lead Scion-owned XF-111 SuperVark flew low over the long, rolling North Atlantic waves. Wings swept forward, it crossed over the rugged, cliff-lined Irish coast and banked back south. It touched down on the black asphalt runway and braked, rolling past the wide white sandy expanse of Carrickfinn Beach—followed a few minutes later by its counterpart.

One after the other, the two fighter-bombers taxied toward a fuel pit not far from a small, blue-roofed terminal building. There were no other planes in sight. This quiet regional airport was used mostly by small turboprops making commuter hops to Dublin or Glasgow, or by oil-company helicopters servicing offshore installations out in the newly developed Corrib natural gas field.

For the Scion XF-111s, this was just a refueling stop—their second since departing the North American coast. Their first stop had been at Greenland, two and half hours ago. According to their export licenses, both refurbished planes were supposedly being sold to a private Polish corporation for use as "flight and technology demonstrators." Accordingly, they could not be transferred with drop tanks or with active air refueling systems, which limited their range to about two thousand nautical miles.

In the lead XF-111's left seat, Mark Darrow pulled off his flying helmet and rubbed at his eyes. "Tell the stewardess to bring me a coffee, will you, Jack?" the Englishman asked. "Black, no sugar."

Jack Hollenbeck, the American assigned as his copilot and systems operator for this flight, grinned. He rattled their empty thermos apologetically. "Sorry, boss. We're fresh out. Want me to head on over to the terminal and pick you up a shot of Irish whiskey, though?"

"Christ, no!" Darrow said. "Not unless you want to see if this big beast really can be remote-piloted from Powidz. One good dram of Bushmills and I'll be out like a light."

"I reckon I'll pass on that for now," Hollenbeck said, pushing his Texas drawl up just a notch. "If God had really meant man to fly from a console, he'd have given him a built-in video monitor and a high-speed data link instead of eyes."

Chuckling, Darrow glanced out the canopy, eyeing the little terminal building. He sat up straighter. "Look over there, Jack. We've got company."

Hollenbeck leaned forward to get a better look. Two men in hats and overcoats stood outside the Donegal Airport terminal. Both were busy taking pictures of the parked XF-111s.

"Plane spotters?" he wondered. "Lots of folks like to collect photos of big bad old warbirds."

"This early in the morning?" Darrow shook his head. "Not bloody likely." He chewed his lower lip. "Warm up the sensors and let's get a few pictures of our own, eh? Run what we get through that image-matching software the technical boys at Scion boast about all the time."

"Gotcha." Hollenbeck busied himself with the SuperVark's sensor systems for few minutes, humming to himself while he snapped a series of close-ups of the two men still watching them from outside the airport terminal. Then he sent them via satellite link to Scion's powerful and highly capable computers back in the United States.

Almost to his surprise, the software was able to identify both men.

"Oh, man," he murmured.

"What?" Darrow asked.

"That fat guy on the left is listed as an assistant commercial attaché at the U.S. embassy in London," Hollenbeck said.

"Which means he's CIA," Darrow said, disgusted.

"Yep."

"And the skinny fellow on the right?"

"Oleg Azarov, supposedly a perfume salesman for Novaya Zarya, in Moscow." Hollenbeck shook his head. "But the computer says he's really a captain in the GRU." He reached for his keyboard again. "I'd better call this in and let Mr. Martindale know we've been tagged."

THE KREMLIN, MOSCOW
The next day

Sergei Tarzarov studied the satellite photos intently, moving slowly from one to another with care and precision. He made sure his face revealed nothing more than casual interest. The years he had spent as Gennadiy Gryzlov's chief of staff had taught him the dangers of inadvertently triggering the younger man's turbulent emotions. Opposition might send Russia's president into a towering rage, but too-hasty agreement with some of his irrational leaps of intuition were equally likely to send Gryzlov into fits of soaring overconfidence. The psychological improvements he had covertly described to former president Igor Truznyev were real—but they were thinly rooted. No, Tarzarov decided, the wild man still lurked inside Gryzlov. And it was his unenviable job to help keep that beast of unreason chained by logic, evidence, and Russia's true national interests.

He looked up. "These photographs are, indeed, suggestive, Mr. President." He tapped his chin reflectively. "They definitely prove that the Poles are developing some new military capability in secret. Unfortunately, that is *all* they will prove to others in the international community."

"You disagree that this is evidence that the Poles

are training terrorists?" Gryzlov asked. His voice was dangerously calm.

"The Poles may very well be arming those who have attacked us," Tarzarov countered. "But from the purely technical standpoint of persuading other powers—the Americans, the other Europeans, the Chinese—these images by themselves are insufficient. If they were taken *before* we were attacked, that would be a very different matter. As it is, the Poles could easily pass this secret military exercise off as a response to our retaliatory strike against them after General Voronov's assassination."

"You suggest that we ignore this evidence, Sergei? That we shred these photos and go skipping merrily on our way like idiot children?" Gryzlov said, even more icily than before.

"On the contrary," Tarzarov said patiently. "We should use this information, but as effectively as possible." He shuffled the satellite photos together and slid them back across the desk to the president. "Foreign Minister Titeneva will meet with the American secretary of state in Geneva soon, yes?"

Gryzlov nodded. His eyes narrowed. "You think Daria should confront the Americans with this information—and what it could mean?"

"Yes, Mr. President," Tarzarov agreed. "If the Americans know what the Poles are up to, they may tell us themselves, in order to calm our darker suspicions. And if Warsaw has kept whatever was going on at Drawsko Pomorskie *secret* from the Americans—"

"We sow distrust between the Poles and their strongest ally!" Gryzlov realized. Glowing with enthusiasm, he smiled broadly at the older man. "Well done, Sergei! That is a chess move worthy of a true grandmaster. Without support from Washington, Poland would stand virtually naked."

OFFICE OF THE CHAIRMAN OF THE JOINT CHIEFS OF STAFF,
THE PENTAGON, WASHINGTON, D.C.
The next day

Air Force General Timothy Spelling, chairman of the Joint Chiefs of Staff, stood up from behind his desk and came over to greet his visitor, CIA director Thomas Torrey. "Nice to see you, Tom."

He led the other man over to a small round conference table with a view of the Potomac and invited him to sit down.

"I'm guessing this isn't exactly a social call?" Spelling asked. It was rare for Torrey to come all the way over to the Pentagon in person. Coordination between the higher echelons of the CIA and the Defense Department was usually handled by secure e-mail or a conference call.

"You guess correctly," Torrey acknowledged. He flipped open his laptop and turned it on. "It's about the President's Daily Brief for tomorrow. I need your help in evaluating some new intel and figuring out how to present it to President Barbeau."

Spelling raised an eyebrow. The whole U.S. intelligence community—the Defense Intelligence Agency, the State Department's Bureau of Intelligence and Research, the NSA, and the FBI, plus a host of others—helped coordinate the process of preparing the PDB, which fused intelligence from a variety of sources, but the CIA was solely responsible for the final product. And the Agency jealously guarded its prerogatives, especially in these days of constrained budgets. Having Torrey ask for his input at this stage of the process was a little bit like hearing the pope consulting a Buddhist monk about a tricky theological question.

"Here's what's got me flummoxed." The CIA director tapped through to a file and opened a series of digital images. He spun the laptop toward Spelling.

The chairman of the Joint Chiefs took a close look. "F-111s? Two of them?" He glanced at Torrey. "Where were these pictures taken? And when?"

"In Ireland, a couple of days ago."

"Who took them?" Spelling asked. "If you don't mind telling me, of course." Like all good intelligence officers, the CIA's chief had a natural reluctance to reveal too much about sources and methods.

"One of my junior people based in London," Torrey said. "The station chief there got a tip that Sky Masters wanted to do some hush-hush refueling at a little airport in Donegal and decided to take a closer look."

Spelling leaned back in his chair, his eyes hooded. "Sky Masters, huh? Well, that makes sense. We retired our last F-111s almost twenty years ago. These two must be some of the old Boneyard aircraft Sky Masters refurbished on spec a couple of years ago. As the planned second stage of that interim XB-1

Excalibur bomber program Patrick McLanahan sold to President Phoenix and Vice President Page before the Chinese hit Guam."

"Which was one of the very first DoD programs canceled by President Barbeau," the CIA director remembered.

"Yeah." There was no emotion in Spelling's voice, but that was a matter of long training and practice. The easiest way to shake off senators and representatives trying to make names for themselves during congressional hearings by savaging the military was to sound as dull and dry as possible. "Helen Kaddiri and her people kept after us to allow them to sell the remaining aircraft overseas. But the Defense Security Cooperation Agency put so many restrictions on any proposed uses that I thought the company had given up. It looks like I was wrong."

"So it seems," Torrey agreed.

"Did your guys pick up any word on where those two refurbished F-111s were headed?" Spelling asked.

"Poland."

"Color me not surprised," Spelling said. He nodded. "I knew Piotr Wilk back before he got into politics. He's always been air-minded, and one of the weapons systems Poland lacks is a dedicated long-range strike bomber."

"Will those planes make a difference?" Torrey asked seriously.

"Against the Russians? Just two of them?" Spelling said. He shook his head decisively. "Not a chance in hell. McLanahan talked a lot about how much more effective the F-111s could be with all the modifications and upgrades his people were adding. But no two old warbirds like that, no matter how souped-up they might be, could tip the strategic balance in Poland's favor."

"What if the Poles got their hands on more of them?" the CIA director asked.

"Do you have any evidence of that?"

Torrey shook his head. "Nope. It's just a hunch so far."

"Well, my guess is that your hunch is pretty good," Spelling said seriously. "President Wilk isn't an idiot. He has to know that he'd need a hell of a lot more of those planes to make any difference at all."

"And if he got them?"

The chairman of the Joint Chiefs of Staff shook his head again. "It still wouldn't matter. You can't just buy an effective bomber force off the shelf. Without trained and experienced crews to fly them and top-notch technicians to maintain them, the best planes in the world are just expensive toys. Even if the Poles could somehow afford to buy thirty or forty of those old birds from Sky Masters, it would take them years to train up a decent force."

"Then why are they doing this?" Torrey asked.

Spelling looked grim. "Wilk and his people must be completely desperate, Tom. Hell, if I were in their shoes, I would be. They counted on our support if the Russians got frisky, and now they're finding out that they're pretty much on their own."

"Which raises the question of whether or not this information should be in the President's Daily Brief," Torrey said slowly.

The Air Force general didn't try to hide his surprise. "Come again?"

"How do you suppose Madam President Barbeau will react to the news that Poland is trying to build up a long-range bomber wing?" Torrey asked.

"Not well," Spelling said slowly, thinking it over. He grimaced. "If she doesn't understand what it takes to stand up a useful bomber force, it'll be another excuse for her to figure the Poles don't need our help after all."

"And if President Barbeau *does* understand how useless those planes are by themselves? Without the crews and infrastructure?"

The chairman of the Joint Chiefs looked even more worried. "Then she'll be pissed because she'll think Warsaw is provoking the Russians for no good reason."

"You see my problem," Torrey said.

"Yeah, I do." Spelling studied the pictures of the two F-111s refueling again. "Do the Russians know the Poles are buying these planes?"

The CIA director nodded. "My guy says there was a GRU-type dogging his heels the whole time—taking his own set of pictures."

"Then you have to include this intelligence in the PDB," Spelling said firmly, still frowning. "You can bet Gryzlov will blow his top when he finds a private American company is selling upgraded F-111s to Warsaw. If he goes screaming to Barbeau and you didn't tell her about this, your head will be on the chopping block before she even gets off the hotline phone."

"I suspect there are plenty of staffers in the White

House who've already picked out an ax and looked up my collar size," Torrey said drily.

"Maybe so," Spelling agreed. He shrugged his shoulders. "And I bet that I'm on the same hit list. Still, why make it easier for the bastards? Every day you're on the job at Langley is one more day you can use to try to tapping a little more sense into Barbeau and her crowd of sycophants."

The CIA director snorted. "I'm not sure I'm cut out to go tilting at windmills much longer. Don Quixote came to a sad end, you know." He closed his laptop. "No, you're right. I can't keep this data out of the Brief." He shook his head wearily. "But God help the Poles when Stacy Anne Barbeau finds out what they're doing. Because nobody else will."

**REMOTE OPERATIONS CONTROL CENTER,
IRON WOLF SQUADRON,
33RD AIR BASE, POWIDZ, POLAND**
A few days later

Brad McLanahan opened the door into the large building and stepped aside, allowing Nadia Rozek to go in first. "Welcome to the Rock," he intoned dramatically. "The Remote Operations Control Center—the nerve center for the Iron Wolf Squadron's aviation component."

She walked inside and stopped, fascinated and slightly daunted all at the same time.

Less than a week ago, this part of Powidz Air Base had been just an empty clearing in the woods behind the control tower. Then Scion's site engineering team swept in, rapidly assembling sections of this modular building as they were ferried in by Sky Masters cargo planes. In little more than twenty-four hours, they had the basic shell up, slotting together sections of prefabricated exterior wall, flooring, and finally, a roof. Once that was done, other teams went to work on the interior—rapidly installing piping and electrical wiring, putting in partitions, and then rigging and connecting fiber-optic cables and computers. More flights brought in generators to provide clean, reliable power for all the electronics crammed into this new building. A maze of satellite dishes and antennas now crowded its flat roof.

Nadia swung around in a complete circle, transfixed. It was almost as though some sorcerer had waved his wand, summoning an army of magical creatures to build an entire palace overnight. Everywhere she looked, she had the impression of clean, cool, perfectly lit modernity—without any of the clutter or jumble of equipment she would have expected in any ordinary military structure erected so quickly. Wide corridors led to separate sections of the building, all carefully laid out with an eye to efficiency and ease of movement. Muted pastels quickly and easily identified the different functions assigned to each part of the building.

"Let me give you the fifty-cent tour," Brad said with a grin.

She followed him through the building, more and more impressed by Scion's organizational and logistical skills. The new Iron Wolf Squadron already had a ready room, with comfortable chairs for the aircraft crews and a large built-in video display for mission planning and briefing. A small canteen offered a selection of drinks and packaged meals for anyone on duty at odd hours. A maintenance office included stocks of computer and electronic components, along with workbenches and tools for on-site repairs.

Most impressive of all, though, were the dozen or so remote-piloting stations. Set in separate, sound-proofed bays, each resembled an aircraft cockpit—complete with seats for the pilot and systems operators, screens to show real-time images transmitted from the drones and other remotely piloted aircraft, joysticks, throttle controls, systems readouts, and multifunction displays.

"We can't give our pilots the sense of motion they'd get in an actual XF-111, say, or in a full-up simulator," Brad explained. "But we've compensated some for that by making sure that the control layouts in each remote station track the real cockpits as closely as possible."

"So each piloting station can only control a single specific type of drone or plane?" Nadia asked.

Brad shook his head. "Nope. Everything's basically modular and plug-and-play. Working all-out, we can reconfigure any station to control a new aircraft or drone in about thirty to forty-five minutes. In a pinch, we can just do a software swap-out so that you could fly an MQ-55 Coyote from a station configured like an XF-111 cockpit, but it's easier and safer and more efficient to remotely fly an aircraft if all the controls and readouts are right where a crew expects them to be."

"This is incredible," Nadia said, still drinking it all in.

"The equipment sure is," Brad agreed. A quick frown flitted across his face and then vanished, almost before she noticed it.

"And when will you put this operations center to its first test?" she asked, wondering what was bothering the young American.

He checked his watch. "In about an hour. We're going to be running the squadron's first simulated deep-penetration raid against a hypothetical Russian target."

"Flying those first XF-111s you have received?" Nadia asked.

"For real?" Brad shook his head. "Not this time. This will be strictly a computer simulation." He looked at her. "Want to ride along—virtually, anyway? I'll be controlling and monitoring the raid from a workstation that should give you a really good bird's-eye view of the whole mission as it unfolds."

Nadia nodded eagerly. "Absolutely." She gestured at the nearest remote-control cockpit. "I will look forward to seeing your fellow pilots show what they can do, even if it is only against make-believe Russians. I'm sure it will be most impressive."

Again, Brad got that odd, worried look in his eyes. Then he forced a smile, a crooked one this time. "Impressive? Well, maybe. We can hope so, anyway." His smile turned a little more genuine.

"But one thing's for sure, I expect this mission to be educational as hell."

An hour later, Brad walked straight to the front of the ready room and took his place at the lectern. One quick glance at the laptop on the lectern showed that the text and visuals for his full mission brief were keyed in and ready to be projected on the big wall display. Somehow, though, he had the not-so-funny feeling that he wasn't going to need much of it.

The other XF-111 pilots, along with their as-signed weapons systems officers, lounged carelessly in their seats. A couple of them sat up straighter, at least trying to seem interested in what he was going to say. But most seemed to have decided to go for an air of casual detachment, shading on outright boredom. They all wore a mix of civilian clothing—jeans, khaki slacks, polo and button-down shirts, and even a few leather flight jackets with their old squadron patches still displayed.

For about the thousandth time, Brad wondered if his father really knew what he was doing in pitching him straight into the middle of this bunch. The other Iron Wolf aviators might respect what they'd heard about his experience in the air and in Earth orbit, but there was no hiding the fact that he was at least ten years younger and several hundred flight hours short compared to the rest of them. From his time as a teenage cadet in the Civil Air Patrol, he knew enough about squadron dynamics to realize he was still the FNG, the fucking new guy, here.

Nadia Rozek knocked on the open door of the ready room. She wore camouflage battle dress with her dark green Special Forces beret clipped to her shoulder. "May I come in?" she asked. "I hope I am not too late?"

"Not at all," Brad told her, inwardly regretting not having suggested that she go straight to the simulator control station. What was likely to be embarrassing was only going to be worse when it happened in front of her. He glanced around the room. "I think most of you have already met Captain Nadia Rozek, one of the squadron's Polish liaison officers, right?"

Heads nodded and most of the pilots murmured greetings as she made her way to a chair near the front. She drew a number of closer looks, even from some of the other women. Suddenly Brad realized it wasn't exactly Nadia's slender, wiry figure they were admiring—delightful though it was. No, it was her uniform that caught their attention and even their envy.

Interesting. He filed that thought away for further consideration later.

Right now, though, he'd better start the briefing before the other members of the squadron got even more bored or more restless than they were already pretending to be.

"The target for today's exercise has been carefully selected," Brad said. He hit the enter key to bring up his first graphic.

That drew a laugh.

He glanced at the display and grinned. It was the picture of a bottle of Talisker Single Malt Scotch.

"Oh, geez, sorry about that. I must have picked up Mark's Christmas wish list by accident."

Darrow grinned back. The ex-RAF officer's ability to consume large quantities of hard liquor without apparent ill effect was already the stuff of which nightmares were made for those who'd agreed to go bar-hopping with him.

"Now, here's your real simulated target," Brad said. He brought up a satellite image, showing two large runway complexes joined together. "Lipetsk Air Base, roughly fifty nautical miles north of Voronezh. This is the Russian equivalent of Nellis Air Force Base, back in the States. Lipetsk is home to more fighter and fighter-bomber squadrons than any other single airfield complex in Russia. It's also the headquarters of the Fourth Center of Combat Application and Conversion of Frontline Aviation— Russia's Top Gun air combat school. We have several fixed targets at the base, primarily their command center, fuel depot, and radar complex."

There were murmurs from the Iron Wolf pilots.

"Jesus, kid, getting a little ambitious, aren't you?" Bill Sievert asked. Sievert was a hard-nosed former F-15E Strike Eagle driver and high up on the list of those Brad mentally cataloged as "not especially in awe of General McLanahan's fair-haired boy." "Hell, why don't you pick something more doable, like say . . . some supersecret Russkie missile complex buried a bazillion meters deep in reinforced concrete way out in the back of East Bumfuckistan."

That drew more laughs.

Brad waited them out and then shook his head. "Sorry, Bill. But if the balloon really goes up, Poland's national command authority picks the targets—whether we like them or not. That's part of the process we're simulating today."

"Swell," Sievert growled. He sat back, glowering, in his chair.

"There's no denying this is a tough target," Brad went on, starting a mental countdown. Thirty. Twenty-nine. Twenty-eight. "But, given the right mix of weapon load-outs and specific mission assignments, I think our XF-111 force can take Lipetsk's command and control and fighters out of action, at a reasonable cost in downed and damaged aircraft."

Twenty. Nineteen. Eighteen.

He tapped through to another graphic. This one showed line drawings of nine XF-111s in top-down plan view. The nine aircraft were assigned to three flights labeled IRON HOWL, IRON CLAW, and IRON FANG—and the aircraft in each flight were shown carrying a mix of different weapons. The three SuperVarks in HOWL flight mostly carried special decoys and drones designed to blind and confuse enemy radars and knock out radio and cell-phone communication. The three XF-111s in the CLAW flight were heavily loaded with antiradiation missiles and AIM-120 medium-range air-to-air missiles. And the final three, flying in FANG flight, were shown equipped largely with AGM-158 Joint Air-to-Surface Standoff guided missiles.

"As large as the payload capacity is on the Super-Vark, it can never carry enough weapons to do the job," Brad said. "So we'll form three strike packages of three aircraft, each with defensive, antiradar, and attack load-outs. You go in on different tracks, but form up just before you go tactical and make your attack runs together."

Ten. Nine. Eight.

"This is a bunch of crap, McLanahan," Sievert exploded. "Three aircraft going in together? What if the guy with the bombs goes down? What are the other two going to do? What if the guy carrying the MALDs goes down? The rest of the package can't do shit."

"Why didn't you ask us to help you plan this, Brad?" Mark Darrow asked. "We could have given you some good advice and saved you a lot of work."

"This is just a training mission," Brad said. "I want to see how well you guys can fly the Super-Varks and run the systems. My plan was to switch crews in each aircraft to give everyone an opportunity to employ each weapon and practice the tactics. Later we can—"

"Oh, for God's sake," Sievert exploded. "Cut the cutesy Boy Scout and Civil Air Patrol crap! You train like you'll fight, McLanahan, ever hear of that idea? Each plane should carry its own mix of attack and defensive weapons. And what do you need AM-RAAMS for? We're going up against MiG-29s, Sukhoi-35s, and maybe even the Su-50. What do you expect us to do—dogfight with them? If we're jumped, we go low, go fast, and hopefully SPEAR does its thing."

"The SuperVark has an air-to-air capability—we should use it," Brad said. "A beyond-visual-range shot could be the thing to get close enough to the target to—"

"Now you're a fighter expert as well as an attack

expert, eh?" Sievert said. "McLanahan, as far as I'm concerned, your job is to get us the stuff we need— you let us do the planning and we'll kick some ass. We'll go after Lipetsk Air Base, but spare us all the overelaborate plans, okay? Every crew in this room knows what it takes to go in and hit a heavily defended target. You say the 'simulated' Poles want us to hit this 'simulated' Russian field and its hardened aircraft shelters? Fine. All you gotta do is give us the weapons and intel we ask for, point us in the right direction, and then get the hell out of the way! We'll take it from there."

Brad fought very hard to keep his face from showing any anger. This was what he'd expected to happen, after all—and this was probably the right time and the right place and the right way. He ran his eyes across the rest of the Iron Wolf crews. "Anybody else agree with Bill?"

A majority of the pilots and weapons officers in the room nodded, though not quite as large a majority as he had privately expected and feared. To his surprise, Mark Darrow was not among them. Instead, the former RAF pilot simply looked thoughtful.

"Okay," Brad said simply, shrugging. "Let's see how it goes. You can all pick your own ordnance loads and flight plans."

"You're not going to fuck around with the sims, are you?" Sievert asked suspiciously. "Just to screw us over?"

"Nope," Brad said virtuously, fighting against the temptation to make the three-fingered Boy Scout sign. "The computer's already loaded with everything we know about likely Russian defenses and re-action times. And Captain Rozek will stay with me throughout the mission. She can make sure there's no cheating. Does that satisfy you, Bill?" Sievert did not reply but stayed quiet and glared at him.

"Right, then," Brad said. "Crews, man your virtual planes. You've got thirty minutes to pick your armaments loads and input your own terrain-following flight plans. After that, you're on your own." He grinned evilly. "And the best of luck to you all!"

Now Darrow looked even more thoughtful.

After the pilots had filed out, Nadia came up. She seemed worried. "I had not expected these people to be so . . . *niezdyscyplinowani*. So undisciplined. Are you sure this is a good idea, Brad?"

"I sure hope so, Nadia," Brad answered. He smiled thinly again, remembering what he'd read about the Russian defenses in and around Lipetsk. "Some people learn the easy way. But I guess most of us really only learn the hard way. And unfortunately for them, it looks like the Iron Wolf Squadron is full of hard-learning folks."

Enlightenment dawned on her face. "Ah, that is what you meant when you said this simulation would be *educational*."

"The guy is a total waste of my time," Bill Sievert grumbled. He was in the pilot's seat in one of the XF-111 control cabs. The systems inside the cab had been reset from remote-control mode to sim-ulation mode in order to run their individual attack plans. Beside him was his weapons officer, George "Smooth" Herres, an ex-B-1B Lancer offensive systems officer from Kentucky, several years older than Sievert but still pretty sharp in everyone's estimation. "I wonder how the little punk got the job? Who's he trying to impress with that screwed-up complicated mess he called an ingress and attack plan?"

"Rookie mistake," Herres said. "He might be a good stick—at least, that's the dope I get from the others—but he doesn't know dick about planning."

"'Kiss' it: 'Keep It Simple, Stupid,'" Sievert said. "Who doesn't know about that? Well, we'll show his punk ass how the pros do it."

The plan he and Herres had devised was indeed simple: emulating a civil business jet, they would cruise single-ship at high altitude through Poland at 360 knots, cross into Ukrainian airspace near Lviv, and follow the commercial airways to Kiev, under radar contact and with an international flight plan filed to Kharkiv Airport on Ukraine's eastern border. Once on an instrument approach to Kharkiv, they would simply keep on descending to two hundred feet with the XF-111's digital terrain-following system, push the airspeed up, and begin the attack run. They planned to fly south and east of Lipetsk then attack from the southeast. It was less than two hundred miles from Kharkiv to Lipetsk, so the run would take just twenty-two minutes at 540 knots. The egress would be much shorter, since they would dodge south around Belgorod and come back into Ukraine near the town of Markivka. Once safely out of Russia and away from the Russian-occupied provinces of Luhansk and Donestsk, they could climb back up to cruise altitude, pick up a flight plan, and head home.

The catch: the airspace within five hundred miles around Moscow had always been one of the most heavily defended in the world, and with the conflict in Ukraine it was doubly so along the border. Russian air traffic control procedures required all flights in Ukraine to check in with Belgorod Approach Control when within fifty miles of the border or risk being engaged by fighters or surface-to-air missile batteries, and Russian controllers would assign a transponder code and carefully monitor the flight—any violation of their directives or deviation from the flight plan would trigger an air defense alert. The terrain would not help the inevitable pursuit—except for moraine ridges, it was flat, rolling, and featureless all the way to the Ural Mountains.

The answer: extreme low altitude, fast attack speed—supersonic if necessary—and the incredible ALQ-293 SPEAR, or Self-Protection Electronically Agile Reaction system. More than just a jammer and threat-warning system, SPEAR was a "netrusion" device: it could insert malicious code into certain digital radars to create false targets, feed erroneous flight and tracking data into targeting computers, and even cause computers to shut themselves down or reboot. Both crewmembers had seen the videos and attended the briefings on SPEAR and agreed it was worth ten times more than all the jamming pods and antiradiation missiles back at base.

Their stores load-out was simple as well: an auxiliary fuel tank in the bomb bay, giving them an additional five hundred gallons of fuel; two AGM-154D JSOWs, or Joint Standoff Weapons, one on each inboard pylon; and two clusters of two ADM-160 MALD-Js, or Miniature Air-Launched Decoys, also one on each wing. The JSOWs were a stealthy glide weapon with GPS and inertial navigation with imaging infrared terminal guidance, carrying a breaching warhead designed to penetrate buildings. They were older weapons, produced in the 1990s, and Herres would have preferred to carry the longer-range and more powerful AGM-158 JASSM, or Joint Air-to-Surface Standoff Missile, but Poland currently had a very limited number of JASSMs for their own F-16 attack planes, so even for this simulated mission they chose not to use them, assuming they would not be available to the Iron Wolf Squadron. The MALDs were small cruise missiles with jammers and decoy features that could make the tiny missiles appear to be as large as a B-52 Stratofortress bomber to an enemy radar.

They knew that Sky Masters had a bunch of other very cool air-launched weapons as well back home that the SuperVark could employ, but they couldn't play with those either.

Sievert and Herres followed the computerized air traffic controller's instructions as they cruised across Poland, entered Ukrainian airspace, and proceeded to Kiev. The flight was quiet and uneventful . . . until about a hundred miles east of Kiev when they heard, *"Dynamics One-One-Seven Alpha, contact Belgorod Approach on frequency three-two-zero-point-seven-two."*

"What?" Herres remarked. "We're still a hundred fifty miles from Kharkiv. What gives?"

"Probably a bunch of nonsense from McLanahan," Sievert said. "Doesn't matter. We'll play his game—then shove it back in his face." On the radio: "Kiev Approach, Dynamics One-Seven Alpha, verify you want us to switch to Belgorod Approach *now?*"

"*Affirmative, One-Seven Alpha,*" the computerized controller's voice replied. "*You are clear to leave my frequency. Have a nice night.*"

"One-Seven Alpha, roger." Sievert shook his head in exasperation as he switched to the new frequency. "Belgorod Approach, this is Dynamics One-One-Seven Alpha, level at flight level two-niner zero, direct Kharkiv. We will be requesting the ILS approach to runway one-two, full stop."

"*Dynamics One-One-Seven Alpha, this is Belgorod Approach, understand you are at flight level two-niner zero direct Kharkiv,*" the new computerized controller's voice responded. "*Please say type aircraft.*"

"It's on our flight plan," Herres said. "I assumed the Russians would have a copy of it. Maybe they don't."

"Part of McLanahan's ploy to distract us," Sievert said. On the radio: "Dynamics One-Seven Alpha is a Gulfstream Four slant Lima." The Gulfstream Four was very similar to the XF-111A in cruise performance and would look very similar to air traffic controllers on radar . . . until the combat started, and then the SuperVark was in a world all its own. The slant-Lina suffix meant that the aircraft had the latest GPS-guided Reduced Vertical Separation equipment, which meant it could send air traffic controllers enough data to keep it separated from other traffic, independent of ground-based radar.

"*Understand*," the computer said. "*Say souls and remaining fuel on board.*"

More distractions. Sievert checked around the cockpit to see if McLanahan had put in any malfunctions that he needed to catch . . . but everything looked fine. He didn't trust the little prick one bit, but so far McLanahan wasn't pulling any funnies. "Two souls on board," Sievert responded, "and three hours' fuel on board."

"*Understand*," the computer responded. "*Fly heading one-five-zero for sixty seconds, then proceed direct Kharkiv.*"

"Heading one-five-zero for sixty seconds, then direct Kharkiv, Dynamics One-Seven Alpha, wilco," Sievert acknowledged. That was a typical air traffic command, although unusual for flights in complete radar contact and with full transponder codes and flight plans in the system. On intercom he said, "That bastard is just fucking screwing with us. He just wants to—"

"*Caution, unidentified L-band search radar detected*," the SPEAR threat-warning system announced.

"Identify!" Herres ordered.

"*Negative identification*," SPEAR replied. "*Possible agile active frequency signal. Stand by.*"

"What the fuck is going on, Smooth?" Sievert thundered. "What is that?"

"L-band active frequency signal is probably a Russian AWACS," Herres said. "The Russkies have an AESA AWACS up over eastern Ukraine." The Russian AWACS, or Airborne Warning and Control System, was an AESA, or active electronically scanned array radar, that sent pulses of radar energy through a mass of emitters that changed L-band frequencies several times a second—SPEAR sensors could detect the emitter, but because the frequency changed several times a second it was impossible to get a range, bearing, or even a positive identification of the emitter. "They don't have us locked up, but we can't lock them up either."

"This is bullshit," Sievert exclaimed hotly. "The Russians can't detect us this far inside Ukraine. The simulation is bogus. This is—"

"*Warning, warning, X-band target search radar, MiG-29, two o'clock high, forty-three miles, six hundred knots,*" the computer announced. "*Possible flight of two.*"

"Countermeasures active," Herres ordered.

"*Countermeasures are active,*" the computer responded. "*MiG-29 flight of two now thirty-eight miles and closing . . . warning, MiG-29s not detected.*"

"Not detected?" Sievert exclaimed. "Launch a MALD!"

"*MALD away,*" the computer responded.

"Engage DTF, two hundred hard ride!"

"*Warning, DTF overridden.*"

"Overridden? *Why?*"

"It gives the MALD time to get away," Herres said. "Should only be a few seconds."

Sure enough, seconds later: "*DTF engaged, two hundred feet hard ride,*" the computer announced. The SuperVark started a steep twelve-thousand-feet-per-minute descent. The DTF, or Digital Terrain Following system, used a digital global terrain and obstacle database coupled with the flight control system to fly as low to the earth as possible, without having to use terrain-following radar that was imprecise and could give away their position. Sievert pulled the wings back to their full seventy-two-degree wing sweep to pick up speed in the rapid descent.

"What happened with that MiG?" Sievert thundered. "Why did SPEAR lose the contact? What the hell . . . ?"

"IRSTS attack," Herres said. "If the Russian radar plane has a lock on us, they can shoot with just a target bearing from their infrared tracker."

"Shit," Sievert swore. "Can SPEAR shut down that AWACS?"

"No indication yet," Herres said. "All countermeasures are—"

"Warning, warning, missile launch detection," the computer suddenly announced in the same maddeningly relaxed, matter-of-fact tone.

"Shit!" Sievert swore. He threw the XF-111 into a hard right turn at ninety degrees of bank, and SPEAR automatically responded by ejecting chaff and flares from the left side, opposite of the break.

"Search radar, L-band phased array, Russian Beriev-100, ten o'clock, seventy-five miles," the threat computer reported.

"Engage Beriev-100," Herres commanded. But he saw that SPEAR had already sent spoofing signals to the Russian radar plane, not jamming the radar signal but electronically moving the return in a different direction while making the Russian fighter believe he was still locked on to his target. "SPEAR is active. SPEAR is . . ." And at that instant they saw a bright flash of light off to the left of the nose. "Good miss," he said.

"Warning, warning, X-band search radar, MiG-29, nine o'clock high, forty-seven miles, not locked on," the threat-warning computer announced.

"Passing ten thousand feet," Herres said. He checked a digital chart on his left multifunction display. On the left side of that display in stunning detail was a digitally produced drawing of the terrain ahead, with "signposts" pointing out towns, airports, and high obstructions. "Terrain is about seven hundred feet." The right multifunction display on Herres's side had a status readout of their weapons and a depiction of the threats around them and how SPEAR was reacting to them. The Russian fighter was well above them and continuing to cruise westbound, quickly passing behind them. "SPEAR is not engaging the MiG. It's moving off to our seven o'clock."

Sievert pulled the throttles back as the SuperVark began to decrease its rapid descent. "I think we'll be okay on fuel even with the early descent," he said. "Better double-check, though, and find out what kind of reserves we'll—"

"Warning, warning, India-band search radar, S-300 missile system, twelve o'clock, eighty miles, not locked on," the threat-warning computer said. *"Warning, warning, Lima-band search radar, Beriev-100, nine o'clock,*

forty-two miles . . . warning, warning, Lima-band radar in narrow-beam mode, locked on . . . warning, warning, India-band search radar in narrow-beam mode . . . !"

"Pushing it up to six hundred knots," Sievert said. "Go target direct."

"We're target direct," Herres said. "Slightly higher terrain left, big city off to the right. Give me weapons."

"Weapons permission Sievert," he said.

"Weapons permission Sievert, acknowledged," the computer responded.

"You got weapons."

"Weapons permission Herres."

"Weapons permission Herres acknowledged. Warning, weapons are ready."

"We're going in hot," Sievert said. "Let's get the—"

"Warning, warning, infrared threat, three o'clock," the computer said. *"Warning, warning, India-Julia band target tracking radar, nine o'clock, thirty miles . . . warning, India-Julia band missile guidance radar . . . warning, warning, second infrared target, three o'clock . . . warning, third infrared target detected, nine o'clock . . . !"*

"MALDs! MALDs!" Herres shouted. "They got us between two SAMs!"

"MALDs deployed."

"Coming left," Sievert said. He threw the Super-Vark into a tight left turn. The terrain was higher in this direction, but not by very much. SPEAR punched out decoy chaff and flares out of the right-side ejectors.

"Warning, warning!" the threat computer said

in the same monotone, even, unhurried female voice, as if nothing at all were happening anywhere in the world. *"Warning, warning . . . !"* The warnings were almost continuous now. As he thrust his aircraft into another tight right turn, Sievert wished he could meet the woman who recorded that voice . . .

. . . so he could punch her right in the damned mouth.

Four hours later, the last disheveled XF-111 crews dragged themselves back to the ready room, joining others who'd been sitting slumped wearily in their chairs for a lot longer. This time there was no banter, no laid-back swapping of worn-out jokes and good-natured teasing. There was just silence, a heavy, embarrassed silence.

Brad waited for the last of Iron Wolf pilots and weapons officers to get settled before taking his place at the front. He stood there for a few moments longer, eyeing them closely. Very few of them seemed able to meet his cool, ironic gaze. Most seemed content to study the floor or the ceiling or their folded hands. They were certainly a far cry from the cocky, arrogant bunch who'd sauntered out to take a whack at a computer-simulated Lipetsk Air Base.

"Well, that was . . . *interesting*," Brad said, carefully choosing the most neutral word he could think of. Total freaking disaster was probably the most accurate description, but, hey, why pile on any harder than he already planned to? "Before I run through the full after-action brief, I'll just summarize the results. Unless anyone has any objections?"

No one spoke up.

"Okay, here it is," Brad said. "It's short. But it sure as hell isn't very sweet. Total number of XF-111 SuperVarks departing Powidz: nine. Number of XF-111s shot down over Russian territory: six. And a seventh plane crash-landed in Belarus as a total write-off. Number of XF-111s returning safely to Poland: two. Just two. And both of them landed with significant battle damage." He let those horrifying statistics hang sourly in the air for a bit before going on. "Getting more than a billion dollars' worth of advanced aircraft shot to shit is bad enough. What makes it even worse is the total number of bombs on target at Lipetsk. Which was precisely none. As in zero. Nada. Nil."

As he expected, that drew return fire from Bill Sievert. The former F-15E Strike Eagle pilot had been one of those shot down on the way to the target.

"Sure we got clobbered!" Sievert snarled. "Crap, anybody would have gotten the snot beat out of them. Between the SAM belt on the way in, a bunch of fucking MiGs fighters already in the air looking for us—over Ukraine, for Christ's sake!—and an even bigger shitload of SAMs ringing that freaking airfield, we never stood a chance. The damned target was completely impossible. Just like I said right from the get-go!"

"Wrong," Brad replied, no longer bothering to hide the disgust he felt. These men and women were supposed to be highly capable and aggressive aviators, not a bunch of whiny, argumentative, undisciplined brats. "Was Lipetsk a tough nut to crack? Absolutely. Would we have lost some XF-111s going after Lipetsk no matter what we did? Possibly. Was the mission target impossible? Absolutely not. What made it impossible was the half-assed, fly-by-the-seat-of-your-goddamned-pants way you all went after it!"

"Maybe you'd better explain that somewhat more thoroughly, Brad," Mark Darrow said, sitting up straighter. There might have been just the barest hint of a smile hovering on the Englishman's face. "For those of us like me who are a bit slow, I mean."

"Glad to," Brad agreed. He brought up some of the data captured by the simulation program during their mission. The first image showed a schematic of the ordnance loads each XF-111 crew had selected. "Anybody see the problem?"

Slowly, hesitantly, several of the Iron Wolf pilots and weapons officers nodded. "We screwed up our load-outs," murmured one of them, Karen Tanabe. Before joining Scion, she'd been a B-52 pilot for the U.S. Air Force.

"That's right," Brad went on. "I let a couple of you load JASSMs, and the ones that did got them off, but we can't count on Poland letting us have any. The rest loaded up on JSOWs and MALDs. A couple loaded AIM-120s and took out some MiGs, and they made it out of Russia, but no one took a shot at the Beriev-100. No one brought antiradar missiles . . . *no one*. You had Belgorod's radar in your face almost all the way after passing Kiev but no one could take it out. You eventually had to fly close enough to Belgorod so it could get a tight lock on you, and that together with the Beriev-100 and the S-300 was enough to get good missile guidance on you. And why did you all make that mistake? Because everybody focused on grabbing the big prize—dropping bombs on Lipetsk—and nobody wanted second place."

Still scowling, he brought up his next exhibit, this one an animated illustration of the flight paths selected by each crew. It showed a set of nine blue-colored lines arrowing out from Powidz and then curving through different arcs to enter Russian territory at multiple points and widely separated times.

Brad let them look at the damning sequence in silence while it played through once. Then he set the animation on autoplay, looping through over and over while he spoke. "The most charitable thing I can say about your *total* failure to coordinate your flight plans is that the spaghetti mess you see on the screen might have confused the Russian air defense controllers. Maybe. *If* they were already drunk. Of course, as it turned out, all you did was give their early-warning radars the maximum bite at the detection apple, along with exposing your aircraft to fire from multiple SAM battalions."

He sighed. "Look, I will try to get this across one more time slowly. The XF-111 SuperVark is *not* a stealth bomber. All the improvements Sky Masters worked in *do* reduce its radar cross section significantly, and the ALQ-293 SPEAR gives it a remarkable ability to jam and spoof a wide range of enemy radars. *But* the hard reality is that single XF-111s *cannot* successfully carry out long-range penetration missions—not against a swarm of advanced Russian radars, S-300 and S-400 SAMs, and advanced fighter interceptors. If you guys try to fly a mission all on your own, like the Lone Ranger, you're just going to wind up as dead as George Armstrong Custer at the Little Bighorn. Which is exactly what happened today."

This time Brad noticed others besides Mark Darrow looking thoughtful. Maybe he was getting through to them—though it still felt a little weird lecturing the rest of the Iron Wolf crews. Then again, it was pretty clear that all the flight-line and simulator hours he'd put in at Sky Masters, along the special tactics classes he'd taken, *did* give him an edge over them . . . at least as far as knowing how XF-111 missions should be put together and flown.

"We have *got* to learn to fight and fly as a coordinated strike force," he said. "No more of this stupid 'I'm Batman!' crap."

"But I *am* Batman," Jack Hollenbeck whispered sotto voce to Darrow, pretending to be offended. That broke everybody up, including Brad.

When the laughter died down, he went on in a slightly more relaxed tone. "Look, this squadron needs to develop tactics and mission plans that will let us tear right through Russian air defenses and then rip out the throat of any target we're assigned. The only way we're going to do that is if we fly as a team, not a bunch of lone wolves." Again, for several long moments, there was only silence.

At last, Bill Sievert, of all the Iron Wolf pilots the one Brad would least have expected to side with him, said, "Okay, McLanahan. I get it. We screwed the pooch big-time. But do you really think your mission plan, the one we bailed out on this morning, was a step in the right direction?"

"There's only one way to find out, isn't there?" Brad said levelly. "We can run the mission again, this time according to my plan. And if I've screwed up somehow, there's more than enough brainpower and flying experience in this room to take the scenario apart and figure out a new approach."

Sievert climbed to his feet and looked around at his fellow pilots. "The kid's right. We need to try that frigging Lipetsk raid again."

"I can set up the sim for another run-through tomorrow," Brad told them. "But don't expect all the defenses to play out the same way. The computer throws in different random elements every time. We get 'intel' from the computer as if we're getting it from real recon sources, but like the real world it may be up-to-date and accurate, or it may be bogus."

Now it was Darrow's turn to speak. "We should get started on this today, Brad. Not tomorrow," the Englishman said seriously, looking around the room. "Those bloody fools in Moscow could push this situation over the edge at any moment. Tomorrow may be too late." There were more murmurs of agreement from the assembled Iron Wolf crews.

Brad nodded slowly, taking it all in. "Okay. Go grab something to eat. While you're doing that I'll reconfigure the sim. And this time I'll fly it with you. Captain Rozek can act as my copilot and weapons officer. That'll give her a better look at what these planes can do, and it'll give us ten aircraft on the raid. We'll meet back here at 1530 for a full briefing."

One by one, the pilots and weapons officers levered themselves out of their seats, heading for the canteen next door. And once again, Brad noticed their eyes resting enviously, almost longingly, on Captain Nadia Rozek's neat, trim uniform. Ah, he thought, piecing it together at last. Morale and unit cohesion were made up of more than just common purpose and professional respect. What was it that Napoleon had said when handing out medals? Something like, "It is with such baubles that men are led." Napoleon might have been a cynical son of a bitch, but there was an elemental truth there. One worth considering.

He'd learned a lot about these men and women over the past couple of weeks—listening to their stories over meals or while working together to get the ROCC stations up and running. None of these Americans, Canadians, or Brits had quit their respective militaries because they were misfits. If anything, they'd left because their air forces were changing for the worse—cutting flying hours that would keep pilots alive in combat, skimping on maintenance, and scrapping good planes without acquiring better ones. These pilots weren't careerists. They were dedicated professionals who couldn't stand watching the squadrons they loved fade away into pale shadows of what they had once been. Maybe the Iron Wolf pilots were hungrier for a renewed sense of shared purpose than he had first thought.

After the room emptied out and they were alone,

Nadia rushed over to him and kissed him soundly on both cheeks. "That was *fantastyczny*, Brad! Fantastic!"

He blushed. "Really?" He hemmed and hawed a little and then rushed on. "I was kind of afraid that I was coming across like a know-it-all prick."

"Oh, you were," she said, laughing softly. "But I think you were just the kind of 'know-it-all prick' they needed to hear."

"Gee, thanks," Brad said wryly.

"It was nothing," Nadia told him, still laughing.

"Now that you've popped my little bubble of pride," he said, "I sure could use some more help."

"You may ask anything of me," Nadia said, quickly sobering up. "I am at your service."

With a tremendous effort, Brad forced down the immediate impulse to ask her out to dinner, focusing instead on what he needed—instead of what he wanted. "I need the telephone number of a good, superfast military tailor."

CHAPTER 8

*Discussion is an exchange
of knowledge; argument an
exchange of ignorance.*

— ROBERT QUILLEN,
AMERICAN JOURNALIST

**ZEDNIA FOREST SUPERINTENDENCY, POLAND,
NEAR THE POLISH-LITHUANIAN BORDER**
The next day

The Polish countryside due east of Bialystok was mostly woodland, with farms and small villages nestled among the patches of forest. About sixteen kilometers from the city, a narrow two-lane road ran north and south through stands of tall trees and small clearings. A few hundred meters from the State Forest Service's local headquarters, an even narrower dirt track intersected the paved road, heading east, deeper into the woods.

Two men lolled near a dark blue panel van parked at this junction. They were smoking cigarettes, apparently enjoying the afternoon sunshine. Both were dressed like ordinary rural laborers, in dirty jeans, drab work shirts, and dark, often-patched coats. Something about their watchful eyes and tight-lipped mouths, though, suggested they would be more at home in the tougher, grittier neighborhoods of a big city.

One of them straightened up slowly, watching a battered Fiat Panda heading toward them. He flicked his cigarette away. "There's Górski," he muttered.

"About fucking time," his comrade growled. Both men were speaking in Ukrainian.

The Fiat pulled up just behind the panel van. The driver, a plump, middle-aged man, squeezed awkwardly out from behind the wheel and walked over to them.

"Sorry I'm late," the newcomer said nervously, in Polish. "Our goddamned officers wanted to run another combat resupply readiness drill. Right before the weekend, for Christ's sake!"

"All officers are bastards," one of the two Ukrainians agreed in perfectly colloquial Polish, rolling his eyes at his companion. "It's almost like there's a war on." He hardened his voice. "Look, did you bring the stuff we asked for, or not?"

"Oh, yes. Definitely. No problem," Staff Sergeant Teodor Górski stammered. "It's all in the back."

"Show us," the second man snapped.

Sweating now, the Polish noncom popped open the rear hatch on his Fiat. Blankets covered an assortment of lumpy shapes piled in the cargo area.

He flipped them away—revealing a collection of weapons, ammunition, and communications gear.

The first Ukrainian leaned in past him and picked up one of the weapons, an American-made Colt M4A1 carbine. It was the assault rifle of choice for Poland's GROM "Thunder" Special Forces unit. Quickly, with practiced hands, he checked it over, nodding in satisfaction. He put the rifle back and hauled out an even bigger piece of hardware, a Swedish-made Carl Gustav 84mm recoilless rifle. Like the M4, this antitank weapon was used exclusively by Poland's Special Forces, not by its regular troops. It was in perfect condition. Pleased, he turned back to Górski. "Is any of this going to be missed?"

The Pole shook his head, visibly gaining confidence as he explained. "Not a chance. All of this gear and ammo is marked as 'unrepairable and junked' or 'expended' in our logbooks and computer files. I've had it all stashed away in my apartment for months. Nobody's going to come looking for this stuff, no matter how many times they check the supply depot's inventory."

"What about the serial numbers on the weapons?" the second Ukrainian asked.

"They're still there," Górski told him. He shrugged. "You'll file 'em off, right?" He smiled weakly. "I mean, you wouldn't want anyone tracing them back to your best supplier, would you?"

"No," the first man agreed flatly. "We certainly would not want that. Your services have been extremely useful to us."

"So we have a deal?" the Pole asked.

"We have a deal," the second Ukrainian confirmed. He tossed the Pole a packet containing more than thirty thousand zlotys, the equivalent of $10,000, in a mix of currencies—euros, zlotys, American dollars, and British pounds. "Unfortunately, once again I seem to have mislaid the tax forms for this transaction. I assume you will handle the necessary paperwork yourself?"

"Naturally." Górski smirked. He went back to avidly counting his money.

"And take this as a bonus," the first man said, handing over a business card. The card bore the picture of a very attractive nude redhead and a Warsaw telephone number. "Her name is Franciszka. She's expecting your call this evening, around midnight. It's our treat."

The plump, middle-aged Pole stared down at the business card. He swallowed hard, staring down at the young woman's incredible body, her moist lips, and her bright, open, inviting eyes. He usually made do with the services of aging prostitutes working out of the sleazier brothels on the left bank of the river. This Franciszka must be one of the high-end escorts who were the favorites of rich businessmen and tourists. "That is . . . very gracious of you," Górski murmured, eyes greedily drinking in every line and curve. "Most appreciated."

"You deserve it," the second Ukrainian told him. He smiled. "Nothing but the best for one of our friends, eh? She'll take very good care of you. She knows lots of"—he winked—"*special* tricks."

Once they transferred the weapons and other military hardware to the blue panel van, the Polish supply sergeant was almost pathetically eager to get on his way. With a jaunty wave, he pulled back out onto the little country road and drove off at high speed.

"There goes one fat little jumped-up puddle of piss we won't have to see again," one of the Ukrainians muttered. "Thank God."

"God will have nothing to do with it," his comrade said with a cruel, ice-cold grin. "We'll owe Franciszka for that one."

WARSAW, POLAND
That night

"*Na zdrowie!* Cheers!" Teodor Górski slurred, knocking back another shot of the faintly yellow-tinged Żubrówka vodka. He smacked his lips, savoring the faint overtones of almond and vanilla. And then smacked them again. "'S damn good," he forced out. "And strong. Feels way more than eighty proof. Can't hardly feel my mouth . . ."

The beautiful redhead sitting across from him on the bed smiled slyly. "Careful there, tiger. You don't want to wind up with a limp noodle, do you?"

Grinning foolishly, Górski fell back on the pillows. God, Franciszka was an eye-opener. Not only was she stunning and going to be his for the whole night, but she'd even come with a gift—a wonderful, delicious, expensive bottle of vodka. Imagine that, he thought. A whore bringing him a present! The other sergeants and corporals at the base who were always teasing him because he'd put on a few extra kilos over the past few years should see him now! None of *them* could say they were about to enjoy the favors of such a gorgeous piece of ass.

For free, too.

That was the best part of this deal. He'd just made almost thirty-four thousand zlotys and he wasn't even going to have part with one thin groszy for hours and hours of screwing. All she'd asked for was one of his cigarettes. The opened pack lay on the nightstand table.

He frowned, or rather tried to, since his face felt so numb now that he wasn't sure his mouth was moving the way he wanted it to. Why *had* Franciszka asked him for a cigarette? She wasn't smoking it. The cigarette was just lying there on the nightstand by her purse, along with a book of matches.

She sat quietly, watching him through amused eyes. "You seem to be having some trouble, Teodor. Too much to drink?" She shook her head. Her smile changed somehow—transforming into an odd, warped, mean little expression that sent shivers down his spine. "That would be foolish, wouldn't it? How can we have our fun if you're too soused to see straight or even paw at me? For shame."

Górski tried to lift his head. Then his arms. Then his fingers. Nothing worked. He couldn't move! His eyes widened. My God. Oh my God, he thought, starting to panic.

Franciszka nodded calmly, leaning forward to study his pupils. "The drug usually takes full effect in about ten minutes, Sergeant." She checked the watch on her thin, elegant wrist. "In your case, it took almost fifteen. I guess that's because you have so much fat piled up around your ugly belly."

Casually, she leaned across him to reach into the nightstand drawer. Her full breasts brushed across his sweating, immobile face. "Nothing? No twitch in your little *chuj*, your dick? How sad."

She showed him the packetful of cash she'd pulled out of the drawer, the packet the two Ukrainians had given to him. "Did you think this was for you?" Still smiling nastily, she shook her head, slipping the packet into her gold lamé purse. "Well, you were wrong. The money was always going to be mine, Sergeant. As a fee for my *special* talents. But don't worry, you can have *all* of the vodka. Every *last* drop."

Turning back to Górski, she picked up the half-full bottle and upended it above him. Vodka splashed over his frozen, horrified face, unshaven chin, and chest, soaking his unbuttoned shirt and the grubby T-shirt he wore underneath. Rivulets of the high-proof alcohol dripped off onto the bedclothes.

"There now, see the mess you've made?" she said in disgust. "You have *so* many bad habits, Sergeant," she told him, picking up the cigarette and lighting it. "Including smoking."

Holding the lit cigarette between her fingers, she stood up off the bed, turned gracefully, and placed it between his frozen lips. "In fact, I think smoking is what's going to kill you."

The cigarette fell out of his mouth and onto his chest. With a soft, devilish *whoosh*, Teodor Górski's alcohol-soaked clothing went up in flames. In seconds, the whole bed was engulfed in a rippling, dancing sea of fire.

The woman who called herself Franciszka left his apartment without looking back, pausing only to wipe her fingerprints off the door handle. By the time she reached the sidewalk outside the building, the curtains pulled across his windows were already smoldering.

IRON WOLF SQUADRON, POWIDZ, POLAND
Several days later

Wayne Macomber waited impatiently for the solid black executive jet to finish taxiing off the rain-drenched main runway and into the camouflaged aircraft shelter. As soon as the jet's twin engines spooled down, he was in motion—striding toward the forward cabin door, which was already opening.

Kevin Martindale trotted down the air stairs, pre-ceded, as usual, by his two stern-faced bodyguards. "Good morning, Major Macomber," the former president said cheerily. "I hope you don't mind my dropping in unannounced on you like this."

"It's your dime, sir," Whack said, grinning back. "But if you expected to catch us with our drawers down, you missed a bet. CID One had your super-secret itinerary pegged as soon as you hit the send key on that fancy, high-security laptop of yours."

"He did, did he?" Martindale replied. He shook

his head ruefully. "I really must talk seriously to our mutual friend about that obsessive computer-hacking habit of his. Breaking into classified Russian systems is one thing. Breaking into sensitive Scion databases so easily is another."

"Oh, you can talk to him," Whack agreed. "For all the good it'll do you. When have you ever known that guy to let the rules get in the way of accomplishing his mission?"

Martindale chuckled, acknowledging the hit. In all the years he'd known Patrick McLanahan, he'd never seen the other man buffaloed by formal protocol or conventional wisdom. If the former Air Force officer had wanted to get something he thought was important done, he'd always bulldozed right through any opposition—no matter what it cost him personally or how it affected his military career. Which, of course, was what had made him perfect for Martindale's various secret weapons projects when he was in government and now for Scion's private ventures.

"Now that you're here, what can I do for you?" Macomber asked. "Or are you bringing us some news? Like about when all this training stops and all the fun stuff starts."

"As in an action alert?" Martindale shook his head. "Sorry, Major. We're still in a holding pattern—which suits our Polish employers just fine. And frankly, I don't blame them one bit. Besides, we're still short of most of the aircraft we need. Let's not rush into a war we're not ready for, and let's hope Gennadiy Gryzlov gives us the time we need to get ready."

"You think he will?"

Martindale shrugged. "Possibly. The Russians are pretty quiet right now. They've killed a number of armed insurgents trying to cross the Dnieper and no one has laid a real glove on their occupation forces yet. It could be that Gryzlov and his commanders are satisfied with the half of Ukraine they've got and they're not hungry for anything more."

"Yeah, right," Whack said, with a skeptical look in his eyes. "That'd be a first."

"It would," Martindale agreed, with equal skepticism. "My personal belief is that it's only a matter of time before the Russians see what else they can grab while the grabbing's good."

"Well, if things go south, I can tell you that the Iron Wolf ground component is up and running pretty damned well," Macomber said.

"I'd like to see that for myself if you don't mind, Major," the former president said, softening his insistence with a practiced, self-deprecating smile. "Those of us who sit and serve behind desks sometimes need reassuring that the men at the tip of the spear aren't as soft as we are."

"No problem," Macomber said, leading the way to the Polish-manufactured Tarpan Honker 4x4 he'd commandeered to drive around the sprawling Powidz compound. As soon as Martindale had settled himself in the passenger seat, Whack Macomber took off at high speed, careening out of the shelter and onto a muddy side road heading deeper into the woods around the airfield proper.

It had been raining all night, but the big masses

of dark clouds scudding overhead looked as though they were finally starting to break up.

"You won't see General McLanahan on this visit," he said, peering through the mud-splashed windshield. "I've got CID One out on a field recon prowl about thirty klicks north of here. I wanna see just how effective that fancy-ass thermal camouflage is in real life."

Martindale looked worried by that news. "You sent a Cybernetic Infantry Device roaming around outside the security perimeter?"

"Yeah."

"Isn't that unnecessarily risky?" Martindale asked, frowning. "What if the CID is spotted by people who aren't cleared to know about them? Like Polish civilians, for example?"

Macomber glanced at him. "Well, that *would* suck, wouldn't it?" He shrugged. "But it would suck a lot less than finding out that thermal adaptive shit doesn't work the way it's supposed to when it's too late—like say when we're ass-deep in Russian troops and tanks."

"I certainly hope you have a cover story ready if anything goes wrong," Martindale said stiffly. "I assured President Wilk and his cabinet that the Iron Wolf Squadron would operate covertly as long as possible."

"Relax," Whack said, grinning again. "If some Polish farmer starts screaming about a giant robot running loose in his crops, we'll just say it's a special-effects prop from a science-fiction movie we're filming."

"That might work," Martindale allowed, though

with evident reluctance. He grimaced. "You certainly like to push your luck, though, Major."

"Yep, I sure as hell do," Whack admitted placidly. He showed his teeth. "Then again, Mr. President, that's exactly why you pay me the big bucks, right?"

"There you have me," the older man agreed slowly, again with a rueful shake of his head.

The dirt road curved around a bend and entered a thicker belt of woods. The trees grew so close on both sides of the track that it was as if they were driving into a leafy green tunnel.

Suddenly Macomber slammed on the brakes. They jerked to a stop just short of a fallen tree blocking most of the narrow road. It looked as though it had blown down during last night's storm.

Growling under his breath, Whack started to back up. And stopped just as quickly. They were surrounded by grim-faced soldiers who seemed to have risen up right out of the ground in the blink of an eye. Masked in mud and camouflage, they were all aiming M4 carbines at the two men in the 4x4.

Before Martindale or Macomber could say or do anything, one of the camouflaged soldiers stepped closer. "Bang," he said simply, sighting down his rifle at them. "You're both dead."

"That we are, Ian," Whack said, grinning now. "Dead as a doornail or any other part of the goddamned door you care to name. Nice doing business with you and your boys."

"A pleasure, sir," the other man told him, matching his grin—with white teeth that gleamed oddly bright against the drab veil of brown mud and green and black camouflage stripes covering his face. He sketched a quick salute and nodded to his team.

Moving rapidly, they hauled the fallen tree out of the road, clearing the way for Macomber's Tarpan to drive on.

"Who the devil was that?" Martindale demanded when they were out of sight.

"Captain Ian Schofield," Whack told him. "I snagged him out of the Canadian Special Operations Regiment last year. He was busy going crazy doing nothing interesting—in the usual peacetime army kind of way."

"And what does he do now?"

"I made Schofield the commander of my deep-penetration recon and ambush teams," Macomber said. He grinned. "And as you can see, he's very, very good at it."

"Did you know he was going to pull that ambush on us?" Martindale demanded.

"Nope," Whack said fervently. He shook his head in wonderment. "Last I heard, Ian and his guys were way north of here, running cover for CID One." He glanced at the gray-haired chief executive of Scion. "When I said my Iron Wolf troops were good, I meant it."

"They're certainly . . . surprising," Martindale agreed sourly. Then he forced a thin smile. "I'm just glad their little stunt didn't give me a heart attack."

"Yeah, I guess so," Macomber said slowly.

"You guess so?" Martindale asked, raising an eyebrow.

Whack nodded, holding in another grin. "Well,

sure. With General McLanahan riding CID One practically full-time, I've only got one spare robot. If I had to sling you in CID Two to keep you alive, my combat power would be cut in half. And that would be bad."

"You know something, Major?" Martindale said, plainly exasperated. "You are one amazingly insubordinate son of a bitch."

"Yes, sir," Macomber agreed happily. "That's why—"

"I pay you the big bucks," the former president finished for him. Slowly, almost against his will, he snorted a short laugh. "All right, I give up, Major. Just try to get me through the rest of this show-and-tell you've obviously got planned in one piece, okay?"

"I'll do my damnedest," Macomber assured him cheerfully. He spun the wheel to the left, turning onto another dirt track that ran west. "Next stop, the Rock."

"The Rock?"

"The Remote Operations Control Center," Macomber explained. "The high-tech playground for Brad McLanahan and his Flying Circus of Merry Young Aviators. They've been real busy lately figuring out how to get shot down in computer-simulated XF-111s and other aircraft in a number of different, interesting, and expensive ways. Along with some other things that might surprise you, especially once the tailoring receipts come through from corporate accounting."

"Am I going to like this, Whack?" Martindale said, obviously trying to figure out if he should sound angry, irritated, or just plain confused. Macomber only smiled.

When they arrived outside the large, antenna-studded control center, he led the way inside and went straight toward the ready room. He stopped short of the open door and silently motioned Martindale forward to get a good look at what was going on.

None of the pilots or weapons officers crowding the room noticed them. They were too busy taking down mission briefing notes using tablet computers. All of them wore dark, rifle-green uniform jackets, collared shirts, and black ties of a design that looked something like World War II–era RAF battle dress. Their squadron patch showed a metal gray robotic wolf's head with glowing red eyes on a bright green background.

Martindale shook his head in disbelief.

Brad McLanahan was up at the front, running through the details of their next exercise. "We're going to be practicing a pretty tricky air defense plan this morning. It's something Captain Rozek and I have worked out in consultation with Colonel Paweł Kasperek, the commanding officer of Third Tactical Squadron. Colonel Kasperek and his guys fly F-16 Falcons. Our plan is designed to coordinate their fighters with a mix of our unmanned and remote-piloted aircraft. We'll be testing it against a simulated heavy, full-spectrum Russian air attack—an attack that will include Su-34 fighter-bombers armed with top-of-the-line air-to-ground and antiradiation missiles, backed by Su-35 fighters flying cover. And there may be a few other unpleasant surprises, depending on which variant the computer picks to throw at us."

"You trying to get us all virtually killed again, Brad?" one of the pilots asked plaintively.

The younger McLanahan grinned. "Not everyone, Bill. Just you. See, you're not being paranoid, because I really *am* out to get you." The Iron Wolf pilots, including the one who'd spoken up, laughed easily at that.

"Nominal mission time will be 0200 hours," Brad went on. "Once the program starts running, we'll get a better fix on the weather, but it'll probably be crappy."

"So, basically, a dark and stormy night," another of the Iron Wolf weapons officers chimed in.

"Right on the nose, Jack," Brad agreed. He turned more serious. "You can expect that we'll be operating in a high electronic-noise environment, one where the Russians are trying to jam the hell out of Polish air defense radars—"

Figuring this was a good time to break away before they inadvertently interrupted the briefing, Macomber jerked his head back down the hall. Martindale nodded, without any readable expression on his face.

Outside the Remote Operations Control Center, Martindale let his breath out in a rush. "Uniforms?" he said slowly, shaking his head again. "Brad McLanahan has my Scion air crews wearing military *uniforms*?"

"Yep." Whack shrugged his massive shoulders. "He claims the uniforms are helping him build unit cohesion—along with kicking their sorry asses in computer-simulated air battles. Besides, they're not just Scion employees anymore. They're part of the Iron Wolf Squadron now."

"Would your other special operators wear uniforms like that?" Martindale asked dubiously.

"Outside of a combat environment where camouflage and coordination make sense, you mean?" Macomber said. "Hell, no. But then again, my people are used to wearing anything they need to blend in with the locals. Up to and including turbans, full beards, and tennis shoes . . . you name it. Dressing up all nice and pretty like the kid's elite aviators back there wouldn't be their first choice."

"But is it working the way Brad claims?"

"Yeah. Yeah, it is." Macomber nodded. "I thought it was a lot of crap at first, that the kid had gone loco. Or maybe just power-crazed. But I've gotta admit that bunch of prima donnas you saddled him with are starting to shape up into the kind of fighting squadron you and General McLanahan wanted. Those guys and gals were getting their heads handed to them by the computer a few days ago. Now they're actually starting to win some of the crazy-ass battle scenarios the kid tosses at them."

Martindale took that in silently, chewing what he seen and heard over mentally for several moments. At last, he looked up at the bigger man with a very serious expression on his face. "Something occurs to me, Major."

"Sir?"

"If what you've told me about Brad McLanahan's

accomplishments with the Iron Wolf Squadron's air crews is true, maybe it's about time you stopped calling him just a *kid*."

Now it was Whack Macomber's turn to think. Finally, he nodded solemnly. "You know, Mr. President, I think you're absolutely right."

U FUKIERA RESTAURANT, OLD TOWN MARKETPLACE, WARSAW, POLAND
Several days later

Discreet waiters circulated behind the elegantly uniformed officers seated at the long, white-tablecloth-covered table dominating the private dining room. Deftly, they removed plates with the scattered leftovers from a traditional feast—potato pancakes slathered in red caviar, boiled eggs, and onions; prawns swimming in olive oil, garlic, and sweet peppers; salmon steamed with spices and vegetables; veal cutlets served with quail eggs and cucumber salad; and beef tenderloin in a wine-and-wild-mushroom sauce atop potato noodles. Behind them came beaming waitresses carrying trays piled high with desserts, including parfaits with pistachio meringues and orange sauce, mouth-watering cheese cakes, and piping-hot slices of fresh-baked apple pie topped with ice cream and cinnamon. And finally, still more servers trooped in, bringing in armloads of bottles of fine wine, craft beer, and vodka.

Seated at the head of the table, with Brad McLanahan on her right, Captain Nadia Rozek waited until the restaurant staff finished their work and withdrew, closing the door behind them. Then, smiling, she pushed back her chair and rose, only slightly unsteadily, to her feet. She raised her wineglass. "Comrades, fellow soldiers, and friends! A toast! *Do Eskadry Żelazny Wilk!* To the Iron Wolf Squadron!"

With dazzling grins, the assembled officers—men and women of the Polish Special Forces assigned to liaison duty and members of the Iron Wolf Squadron itself—jumped to their own feet. The Poles wore their regulation dress uniforms, while the Iron Wolf pilots were clad in their rifle-green jackets, shirts, and ties, though without the give-away robotic wolf's-head squadron patch.

"The Iron Wolf Squadron!" they murmured, echoing her toast. They drained their glasses and refilled them. This celebratory dinner and its associated weekend leave in Warsaw was the payoff for the past weeks of hard work, long hours of study, and rigorous training and practice. It marked their transition to operational status.

Through the warm haze created by great food, plentiful liquor, and budding camaraderie, Brad McLanahan turned to Nadia, raising his own glass. "To Poland!" He searched back through his memory of the various articles he'd been reading about this country. The Poles were a proud people and it was essential that he get this right. And then, almost without effort, the phrase he needed leaped into his mind. "*Za wolność naszą i waszą!*" he said, making sure he pronounced the words properly. "For our freedom and yours!"

It was the traditional slogan of Polish exiles, driven from their homeland, when they fought as soldiers to help liberate others around the world.

With an approving roar, the Poles and their new Iron Wolf allies repeated the toast and drank deep.

Nadia glowed with delight. "That was perfect," she murmured, leaning over to kiss him on both cheeks. And then, to Brad's surprise and pleasure, she kissed him again, this time full on the lips. Her blue-gray eyes sparkled impishly.

His breath caught in his throat.

More toasts followed, one after another in a freely flowing river of wine, beer, vodka, and sentiment. The Poles, it seemed, were determined to send their new Iron Wolf Squadron comrades back to the base at Powidz with memories—and hangovers—they would long remember.

Brad, after studying the playful expression on Nadia's lovely face, fought hard to stay in control. He confined himself to sips, rather than knocking back a fresh glass with each new tribute to the squadron and its Polish comrades. If her innermost thoughts and feelings were really moving in the direction he hoped they were, he decided that he definitely did not want the phrase "drunk and incapable" attached to his name tonight.

The party went on until well after midnight, ending only when the exhausted restaurant staff finally coaxed their mostly inebriated and entirely cheerful guests out into the cool night air. Even then the songs and boisterous laughter continued for a while longer, echoing off the cobblestones and Baroque-style buildings of the marketplace square. Then, almost reluctantly, the group of officers broke up with loud good-byes, handshakes, and embraces—with groups and pairs and individuals drifting slowly apart as they made their separate ways through the darkened streets of Warsaw's historic Old Town.

To his great delight, Brad found himself walking with his arm snugly around Nadia Rozek's trim waist as they parted from the others. Smiling to herself, she leaned in against his shoulder.

"*Dobranoc!* Good night, Nadia! And you, too, Mr. American!" they heard a slightly slurred voice say happily. Still clinging to each other, they turned around to see one of the other Polish Special Forces officers, Captain Kazimierz Janik, beaming at them.

"Where you off to, Kazimierz?" Nadia asked.

"My girlfriend's place," Janik murmured happily. "Her roommate is a flight attendant and away in New York or London or somewhere. For hours and hours. Or maybe days! Which is good luck for me, eh?"

"Indeed," Nadia agreed, suppressing her own grin. "Well, good hunting, Kazimierz."

"Thanks!" The young Polish officer eyed them owlishly. "And yourselves on this fine night? Where are you headed?"

"I thought I would take Mr. McLanahan on a walking tour of the Old Town," Nadia said blandly. "To show him the sights."

"That is a great idea!" Janik agreed equably. "Good night, again!" With a final wave, he turned and walked off across the square, humming to himself.

"So, where exactly are you really leading me?" Brad asked quietly, feeling greatly daring.

"Well, I *do* have a flat here in the Old Town," Nadia said, with an enchanting smile that set his pulse racing. "So we will have to walk there."

"And what about *your* roommate?" Brad asked, through lips that were suddenly dry. "Is she still in town or away, too?"

Nadia laughed softly. "Fortunately for you," she said with another impish look in her bright eyes, "I do not have a roommate."

Neither of them noticed the dark blue panel van idling across the square. Or the two men sitting inside its darkened interior.

"There," one of them said, nudging his companion and pointing through the dirty windshield. "That's the one we want."

The other man leaned forward to get a better look, squinting slightly. He flashed a penlight down at the sheaf of black-and-white surveillance photos in his lap and then nodded. "You're right. That's our target for sure." He grinned nastily, slipping a syringe out of his coat pocket. "Talk about easy. I almost feel guilty getting paid for this job."

The first man snorted. "Sure you do." Then, reaching down, he put the van in gear. "Just make sure there's no fuss or bother. The boss wants this one delivered specially gift-wrapped to the customer."

**NEAR KONOTOP,
RUSSIAN-OCCUPIED EASTERN UKRAINE**
The next night

Captain Kazimierz Janik swam slowly up out of what seemed to be a very dark, bottomless pit. Unseen waves sloshed against him, bouncing him against its stony sides in an odd, jerky rhythm. A low, dull roar filled his ears, growing louder every second. His head ached abominably.

With an effort, he pried his eyes open. He was not swimming in a dark, lightless pit, he realized groggily. Instead, he was sitting on a rough bench in the back of a canvas-roofed truck, crowded in among a number of other men. It was pitch-dark outside and pouring rain, but he could see just enough out the open back to guess the truck was bumping and swaying along a rough, rutted country road. There were no signs of streetlights or houses.

What the hell was going on? he wondered. His last conscious memory was saying good night to Nadia Rozek and that tall, broad-shouldered American. Had he been so drunk that he'd climbed up into the back of this truck and then passed out? Or had someone scooped him off the pavement after he lost consciousness? Was this all part of a practical joke being played on him by the other guys in his unit?

Janik looked down at the clothes he was wearing. Irregular blotches of darker and lighter shapes swam and rippled in his fogged eyesight. Camouflage battle dress, he realized stupidly—finding it difficult to focus. What had happened to his other clothes, to the dress uniform he'd been wearing at the restaurant? Just how long *had* he been wandering around in a drunken stupor?

Fighting against the mind-numbing drowsiness that still clouded his thoughts, the young Polish Special Forces captain looked up at the six other men crammed in the back of the truck with him. Most of them were wearing camouflage uniforms, too. But unlike him, they were all armed, cradling M4 carbines and other weapons. Their watchful eyes met his puzzled gaze without any discernible expression. Worse yet, he didn't recognize any of them.

Christ, Janik thought wildly, what was this? Who were these men? He opened his mouth to ask.

And then closed it abruptly when the grim-faced man sitting across from him swung the muzzle of his rifle around to aim straight at his chest. The other man nodded coldly. *No talking*, he mouthed silently.

With a jolt, the truck veered off the rutted country road and turned onto a city street. They were passing between blacked-out buildings now, lit only sporadically by flickering streetlamps.

Brakes squealed softly as the truck slowed and then stopped.

"Out," the man pointing the rifle at him growled.

Awkwardly, Janik obeyed, clambering out over the tailgate of the truck. The others did the same, forming up in a loose huddle. Driving rain slanted down out of the sky, pelting the cracked and broken pavement. A door creaked open on one of the neigh-

boring buildings and several more men poured out
onto the street.

These new arrivals wore dark-hued civilian clothing, and they were also armed to the teeth—most
with Russian-made small arms. Their leader, a lean,
wiry man with a gruesomely scarred face, carried an
AK-74M assault rifle gripped in his capable-looking
hands. Still struggling against the gray haze cloud-
ing his mind, Janik stared at the scarred man. There
was nothing in the man's eyes, he thought, beginning to be even more afraid. No emotion, no fear,
no anger . . . nothing human at all. Just a look of
cold, ruthless calculation.

Death, Kazimierez Janik realized with horror. I
am looking on Death.

Through the darkness and pouring rain, Fedir
Kravchenko saw the young Polish Special Forces
officer turn white. He nodded once to the men
grouped behind their captive. Silently, they spread a
tarp across the wet pavement and backed away.

Kravchenko lifted his AK-74. He saw their prisoner's eyes widen and nodded again. "You have my
apologies, Captain," he said quietly, in Polish. "But
your unfortunate fate will serve a greater purpose,
both for your country and for mine."

"No, wait—" Janik stammered, raising his hands.

Kravchenko shot him twice, once in the stomach
and a second time in the chest.

The young Pole went down in a heap. He was
dead in seconds.

"Wrap him up in the tarp," the Ukrainian told

his men calmly. "And bring him with us." He checked his watch. They had half an hour to drive the ten kilometers to the rendezvous point where Lytvyn and the rest of his command waited. Plenty of time, he decided, especially since this miserable weather seemed to be persuading the Russians to stick close to their existing checkpoints and fortified compounds.

KONOTOP AIRFIELD PERIMETER
A short time later

Pavlo Lyvtyn crouched next to the rusting chain-link fence. Topped by newer rolls of razor wire, the barrier stretched away into the rain-drenched countryside on either side, finally disappearing into the darkness. When the Russians had seized this old Ukrainian airfield as a base for their own planes, they must have strengthened its defenses. But if so, the additions weren't immediately obvious. The big man frowned.

"Trouble?" Kravchenko murmured.

Lytvyn shrugged. "Those Russian bastards aren't stupid. They've probably wired this fence into a sensor net. Which means they'll know we're coming as soon as we make our first cut."

"Yes, they will," Kravchenko agreed. He eyed the bigger man. "You know the plan."

"I know the plan," the big man growled. He shook his head. "It just seems like a hell of a lot of trouble to go through in order to fail in the end."

A thin, humorless smile flashed across Kravchenko's maimed face. "Ah, but Pavlo, in this case, failure *is* the plan." He tapped Lytvyn on the shoulder. "So cut the damned fence and let's get on with it!"

Grumbling under his breath, the big man set to work with a pair of bolt cutters, quickly slicing a wide opening in the rusting airfield perimeter fence. There were no audible alarms, but lights began flicking on across the distant compound, illuminating hangars, aircraft shelters, and sandbagged guard posts.

Kravchenko whirled to the partisans kneeling behind him. "Go! Go!"

Silently, they scrambled to their feet and poured through the opening. The Ukrainian major and his bigger subordinate came right behind them, followed by another four-man party hauling the tarp-wrapped corpse of the Polish Special Forces captain.

Beyond the fence, hand signals sent the attackers fanning out through the tall, rain-soaked grass. Pavlo Lytvyn led one group off to the right. The men carrying Janik's body went with him.

Kravchenko led the rest to the left. Besides riflemen, his group included a two-man team equipped with an 84mm Carl Gustav recoilless rifle. One partisan carried the launcher. The other lugged a haversack filled with two high-explosive and two antitank rounds.

The staccato rattle of automatic weapons fire echoed across the airfield. Lytvyn's men were engaging Russian sentries outside the control tower and hangars at long range—firing short bursts and then dashing to new positions before the outgunned and outnumbered sentries could zero in on them.

Kravchenko's group dropped prone in the wet grass beside a long concrete runway. They were about three hundred meters away from two newly constructed aircraft shelters. He wriggled forward to get a better look through his night-vision binoculars. These temporary Russian shelters weren't hardened against air attack. Built out of lightweight metal and Kevlar fabric, they offered some protection against fragments and small-caliber rounds. Really, though, they were mostly designed to let mechanics and technicians to perform maintenance work on aircraft in all weather conditions.

Like this hard, drenching rain, the Ukrainian thought, baring his teeth in a fierce predatory grin. From the amount of light leaking out of both shelters, the Russian ground crews were busy tonight—readying two Su-25SM ground-attack aircraft for tomorrow's scheduled patrols over the so-called Zone of Protection.

He glanced over at the Carl Gustav team. "Load with high explosive, antitank. Your target is the shelter on the right."

The loader nodded, tugging one of the two HEAT rounds out of his haversack. He slid the round into the recoilless rifle's breech and dogged it shut. The gunner went prone, aiming across the tarmac. "Ready!"

"Shoot!" Kravchenko hissed.

KA-WHUUMMP!

The Carl Gustav fired with a blinding flash and

backblast—hurling the antitank round downrange at nearly three hundred meters per second. It hit the Russian aircraft shelter squarely, tore through the Kevlar fabric like a white-hot knife through butter, and exploded inside. Bits and pieces of the Su-25's shattered fuselage pinwheeled out of the burning, collapsing structure. Moments later, stored fuel, 30mm cannon rounds, and ground-to-air rockets went up, cooking off in a rippling series of explosions that strobed across the surrounding tarmac.

"Let's go!" Kravchenko yelled to the men closest to him. They jumped up and followed him toward the hole in the perimeter fence. He dragged his whistle out and blew a series of short, sharp blasts, relaying the same withdrawal order to Lytvyn's group.

Abruptly, clumps of dirt and torn grass sprayed up across the ground behind the running partisans, traversing from right to left as the guards near the control tower brought a light machine gun into action. The Russians were finally waking up, Kravchenko thought. And about time, too. But given the range and the driving rain, it would be almost impossible for them to hit anything.

Still, those machine-gun rounds were coming close enough to make the next part of his plan plausible. "Drop the Carl Gustav launcher," he snapped to the recoilless rifle crew. "Keep the rounds."

The gunner nodded reluctantly, tossing the heavy tube aside into the long grass for the Russians to find later.

When they regrouped outside the fence,

Kravchenko looked for Lytvyn. As usual, the big man was the last man out. "Anybody hit, Pavlo?" he demanded.

"No one," Lyvtyn replied.

"Except for poor Captain Janik, you mean," Kravchenko corrected him with a crooked smile.

"Except for him," the big man acknowledged drily. "We dumped his body back near where we opened fire on the sentries."

Kravchenko's smile turned more genuine. "Very good. I'm sure the Russians will find what their prize has in his pockets very . . . clarifying."

NORTHERN OUTSKIRTS OF KONOTOP
Later that night

Using his rain poncho as an improvised tent to hide the beam of his flashlight, Spetsnaz Captain Timur Pelevin peered down at the bloodstained scrap of paper found on the terrorist killed at Konotop Airfield a few hours ago. Besides an abandoned Swedish-made recoilless rifle, it was the one piece of evidence the rattled garrison had recovered from the battlefield. The dead man's comrades had apparently stripped him of everything else before escaping. His lips moved as he haltingly converted the Roman characters of the street address to more familiar Cyrillic letters. "Zelena Street, number seven," he murmured.

He switched off the flashlight, waited several

seconds for his eyes to readjust to darkness, and flipped the poncho back up. His two senior lieutenants were crouched nearby, waiting for his orders. "Looks like those air-force intelligence pricks got it right, for once," he told them, pointing up the darkened street. "Our target is that fourth house on the right."

They turned to follow his gesture. Even through the rain, they could make out the shape of a small, low-roofed detached building. Like the rest of the houses on this little street, it had a tiny garden plot out back and a separate, bedraggled-looking tool and storage shed.

"We need to hit that terrorist safe house hard and fast," Pelevin stressed. "If they don't realize what their dead guy had on him, we could still take them by surprise."

One of the lieutenants raised an eyebrow. "And if the terrorists have booby-trapped the place?"

"Then it will be a very bad day for Mama Pelevin," the Spetsnaz captain grunted. "But just for that, you go first, Yury."

The lieutenant grinned tightly. "In that case, I withdraw my suggestion."

"Too late," Pelevin told him. "But don't worry, I'll be right behind you." He studied the faint, glowing numbers on his watch. "Get your men in position, gentlemen. You have five minutes."

Silently, carefully, the highly trained Russian commandos fanned out around the darkened house—ghosting across little fields and backyards and wriggling through gaps in run-down fences.

They advanced in pairs, with one soldier always providing cover while his partner moved.

Before Pelevin's stipulated five minutes were up, he and his men were ready, with assault teams positioned at the front and rear doors and snipers covering the windows.

The captain took a deep breath and let it out softly, slowing his racing pulse. He keyed his radio. "One. Two. Three. *Vkhodi!* Go in!" he ordered.

Troopers wielding sledgehammers smashed in the doors and then spun away, allowing others to toss in flashbang grenades. Even before the ear-shattering noise and dizzying, kaleidoscopic bursts of light faded away, more Russian commandos poured in, with their weapons ready.

The house was empty.

Scowling, Pelevin waited while his soldiers rummaged through drawers and cupboards and closets. Everywhere they looked, they saw signs that whoever had been living here had left in a tearing hurry. There were plates tossed in the sink with food still on them. Suitcases that had been left half packed. Unmade beds, with dirty sheets trailing on the floor. But there were no weapons. And worse yet, no papers or documents that might identify the terrorists.

"Captain!" one of his men suddenly shouted from outside. "Come and take a look at this!"

Within minutes, Pelevin found himself poking around inside a dimly lit chamber dug right under the house. Cinder blocks lined the walls, but the floor was dirt. When it was first built, it must have been meant to serve as a root cellar, he decided. But now it was something else entirely.

It was an armory.

Several assault rifles leaned against the far wall. He pulled one out and looked it over. It was an American-made M4A1 carbine. So were the others. An open crate held boxes of 5.56mm ammunition and magazines. Others were full of grenades of various types, including Polish-manufactured RGZ-89 antipersonnel grenades. Stashed in the corner and loosely concealed by camouflage netting, he found a U.S.-built SINCGARS combat radio.

Frowning deeply, Pelevin turned back toward the ladder. This was above his level of expertise. It was time to call in a GRU investigative unit. Maybe they could figure out where the terrorists had acquired all this advanced military hardware.

Something gleaming on the dirt floor caught his eye. He knelt down. Someone's muddy boot had tromped down on a plastic card, half burying it in the dirt.

Gingerly, the Spetsnaz officer pried the card out of the loose-packed earth. He studied it carefully in his flashlight beam. It was a photo identity card of some kind. And the face was familiar somehow. He took a short, sharp breath, surprised despite himself as he remembered where he had last seen this man's image.

Sweating now, Pelevin haltingly read off the name and rank embossed on the ID.

JANIK, KAZIMIERZ
KAPITAN, JEDNOSTKA WOJSKOWA GROM

Mother of God, he thought, turning pale. The terrorist who had been killed in tonight's raid on a Russian-occupied airfield was a captain in Poland's most elite Special Forces unit.

Still in shock, Pelevin scrambled up the ladder and grabbed his radioman. "Patch me through to General Zarubin! Now! Tell him this is urgent!"

CHAPTER 9

*Progress begins with the belief
that what is necessary is possible.*

—Norman Cousins,
American journalist

THE KREMLIN, MOSCOW
Early the next morning

Sergei Tarzarov walked toward President Gennadiy
Gryzlov's private office with the same unhurried
stride that had served him well through decades of
service at the highest levels of the Russian government. Long experience had taught him the value of a
reputation for remaining eerily composed in the face
of any crisis. His steady, almost unnaturally calm demeanor was famous for boosting the morale of trusted
subordinates, soothing rattled political masters, and
unnerving would-be internal enemies.

Inside his weary mind, though, where no one

else could pry, Tarzarov felt as anxious as a plump, well-fed rabbit unexpectedly invited to a meal by a hungry tiger. News of the terrorist attack on the air base at Konotop seemed all too likely to send Gennadiy Gryzlov into yet another of those towering, destructive rages that Tarzarov found alternately terrifying and tiresome. For all the younger man's admitted brilliance and charisma, his occasional temper tantrums that were worthy of a spoiled two-year-old brat were maddening. Certainly, they tested his chief of staff's prized patience to the breaking point.

He paused outside the door. Ivan Ulanov, the president's private secretary, looked haggard and bleary-eyed, but otherwise unmarked. That was one small positive sign, Tarzarov thought. In the not-so-distant past, Gryzlov had been known to physically take out his fury on defenseless underlings—sometimes to the point of sending them to discreet private medical clinics for emergency treatment.

"You are to go in at once, sir," Ulanov told him tiredly. "The president has just been briefed by General Zarubin over a secure line."

Tarzarov nodded. He had already seen a summary of the evidence unearthed by the Spetsnaz troops attached to Zarubin's motor-rifle brigade. He still found it astounding that the Poles had been stupid enough to attack Russia directly, let alone stupid enough to get caught red-handed doing so. And yet the incriminating facts on the ground seemed to admit no other realistic possibility. Perhaps Piotr Wilk was not as smart as he had seemed—or more panicked by Russia's occupation of eastern Ukraine than anyone had guessed. He raised an eyebrow. "And what is the state of the president's office furniture this morning?"

"As yet intact," Ulanov said, with a wan smile.

Tarzarov clamped down on a sudden, wholly out-of-character urge to whistle in surprise. For a moment, he didn't know whether to be more worried by Gennadiy Gryzlov's atypical demonstration of self-control or by the possibility that the younger man was just waiting for a bigger audience before he exploded.

Still puzzled, he went in.

Gryzlov looked up from his desk and nodded curtly. "Good morning, Sergei. You may sit."

Tarzarov did as he was ordered, lowering himself cautiously into the chair directly opposite the president. "Mr. President?"

"You will arrange a meeting of the full security council," Gryzlov told him. "We will convene at noon."

"To discuss the significance of the discoveries made by our forces at Konotop?" Tarzarov asked.

"Don't you ever get tired of resorting to such bloodless bureaucratic euphemisms, Sergei?" Russia's president asked, with a thin, humorless smile. "Let us speak bluntly and to the point. Our national security council will be meeting to approve my planned response to the clear, direct, and irrefutable evidence of Poland's treacherous aggression against our motherland and its citizens. No other discussion will be necessary. Or welcome."

Tarzarov nodded, acknowledging the other man's point. "Yes, Mr. President." He glanced at the digital clock on Gryzlov's desk. "That will give me time to have these captured weapons and that Polish Special Forces ID card flown here for closer forensic examination."

Gryzlov shook his head. "That also will not be necessary." He shrugged. "Or possible, for that matter. I have already disposed of this evidence."

Caught completely by surprise, Tarzarov sat bolt upright. "What?"

Gryzlov grinned. "Ah, the iceman cracks at last." He chuckled. "Do not worry, Sergei. I haven't flushed those rifles down the toilet or burned the ID card. What I mean is that I have sent the evidence where it can do the most harm to our enemies."

Tarzarov breathed out slowly. Was it possible that Russia's president had discovered that he could terrorize his staff as effectively with ham-fisted attempts at crude humor as with near-demented fits of wrath? Perhaps so, he thought wearily. He sat back, forcing himself to appear more relaxed. "May I ask where exactly that would be, Mr. President?"

"Geneva," Gryzlov said simply.

COUNCIL CHAMBER, UNITED NATIONS OFFICE, PALAIS DES NATIONS, GENEVA, SWITZERLAND
Later that day

The UN office in Geneva, the Palace of Nations, was supposed to be famous for its views of Lake Geneva and the snowcapped peaks of the French

Alps, Foreign Minister Daria Titeneva thought caustically. Unfortunately, it seemed those breathtaking vistas were only for tourists. Working diplomats found themselves confined to a succession of stuffy meeting rooms.

This morning's session, with the diminutive American secretary of state, Karen Grayson, was no different. Together with their respective staffs, and with observers from Poland and the other NATO countries, they were gathered in the palace's council chamber. Gold-colored drapes blocked the floor-to-ceiling windows, enclosing them in a room whose green carpet, green leather seats, and white marble walls struck her as more appropriate for an oversized funeral director's office than for genuine international negotiations. The gold and sepia murals supposedly showing human progress through technology, health, freedom, and peace did nothing to change her unfavorable opinion. It was yet another wonderful irony of history that the murals—painted by the Catalan artist José María Sert—had been given by the Spanish government to the UN's predecessor, the ill-fated League of Nations, in May 1936, only weeks before the Spanish Civil War ripped Spain apart.

Perhaps, she thought icily, there was truth in the old saying that diplomatic meetings were where genuine peace and justice went to die.

For the moment, at least, Titeneva and her American counterpart were busy murdering them in relative private. The semicircular visitors' gallery overlooking the council chamber had been sealed off. None of the parties involved in these talks were ready for the details to become public knowledge.

Up until now, that is, she thought after reading the brief cryptic text that popped up on her tablet. Turning to her closest aide, she murmured, "It's time, Misha."

He nodded, rose discreetly, and quietly left the chamber.

Titeneva sat back, pretending to listen carefully to the American secretary of state as the petite woman launched into yet another fusillade of pathetic disclaimers of any involvement by her country or NATO in the terrorist attacks aimed at Russia and its interests. From the pained expression on the face of Poland's top diplomat, Foreign Minister Andrzej Waniek, he found Grayson's speech equally embarrassing in its naïveté.

As well he should, Titeneva thought icily.

"As you know, I have been instructed by President Barbeau to convey her deepest personal regret over any loss of Russian life or property," the American secretary of state said. "Such acts of terrorism are, and must always be, wholeheartedly condemned by any civilized nation."

My God, Titeneva realized. This so-called American diplomat was *actually* trying to convey her sincerity by stressing every separate word slowly and distinctly, as if her audience were all either deaf or simpleminded children. Was she really that stupid? Or that inexperienced?

"For this reason, my government again offers its absolute assurance that neither we nor any allied government would *ever* support those who have attacked your armed forces," Grayson went on. "We offer this firm commitment despite our equally firm and consistent disapproval of Russia's unlawful occupation of eastern Ukraine—"

A sudden flurry of motion and babble of noise from the visitors' gallery above them brought Karen Grayson to an abrupt and embarrassed halt in full rhetorical tide. She turned around, clearly stunned to see a flood of print journalists and TV news crews pouring into the chamber. "What on earth?" she began, then hurriedly turned off her microphone, and leaned over to whisper frantically to one of her aides.

With a supreme effort, Daria Titeneva kept herself from smiling in open triumph. She rose to her feet and turned on her own microphone.

"I am very sorry, Madam Secretary of State," she said smoothly. "I very much regret this necessary disruption of ordinary protocol, but I have just received news from Moscow that *cannot* and *must* not be kept secret from those truly interested in peace!" She gestured toward the gallery. "It is for this reason and this reason alone that Russia has invited members of the international media to witness these proceedings."

As TV camera lights clicked on, bathing the chamber in their glare, Titeneva waved a hand toward the large bronze doors, which were already opening. She raised her voice, riding over the American woman's attempt to object. "For days now, our American friends and their Polish . . . puppets . . . have denied playing a part in these evil attacks on my country and its people. For days, they have pleaded their innocence and assured us all of their goodwill toward Russia." Her expression hardened. "For days, they have been lying to us all."

Shocked, Karen Grayson jumped to her feet, startled out of the meek obsequiousness she obviously thought appropriate to her new role as a diplomat. "That is not accurate, Madam Foreign Secretary," she snapped. "My government has told the truth. And nothing but the truth!"

Titeneva smiled thinly. She shrugged her shoulders, as if generously willing to be persuaded. "Perhaps that is so." Then she drove the dagger home. "But then you Americans have also been deceived. And deceived by those who proclaimed themselves to be your friends and your dear allies. By Poland and its foolish and aggressive government!"

Several staff members from the Russian embassy entered the chamber, carrying open-lidded crates full of rifles and other military equipment. The buzz from the gallery grew exponentially as reporters and camera crews leaned over the railings to get a better look, all the while earnestly babbling to audiences around the world about what they were seeing.

"Last night, terrorists attacked Russian soldiers and air crews at a base in the Ukraine," Titeneva went on. "These criminals hoped to disrupt routine flight operations which have proved essential to providing peace and security for those in our Zone of Protection. But their vicious attack was defeated! And in the aftermath of this defeat, the men and women of our brave armed forces were able, for the

first time, to obtain evidence linking these murderers, these terrorists, to a foreign power."

Again, the American secretary of state attempted
to interject, and again Daria Titeneva cut her off.
"There can be no doubt of this! No denials that
anyone will believe! The crates you see before you
contain American-manufactured weapons and military hardware. Weapons and equipment which we
can *prove* were sold to Poland's army—supposedly
for use by its so-called Special Forces. Instead, these
weapons were handed over to terrorists, who used
them to kill innocents, both Russians and Ukrainians of Russian heritage."

The clamor from the excited reporters crowding
the visitors' gallery soared to an even higher level,
drowning out all ordinary speech.

Titeneva waited patiently for the noise to subside
a bit before continuing. "If that were all Warsaw's
insane leaders had done, it would be bad enough,"
she said harshly. "Supplying terrorists with arms
and equipment is an act of war." She shook her head.
"But that is *not* the end of the evils worked against
Russia by these foolish and deluded men."

Silence spread gradually through the large room
as her words struck home.

"Last night, our heroic soldiers were also able
to kill one of the men leading these brutal and evil
terrorists," she said coldly and calmly. "He was *not*
a Ukrainian. He was *not* a Chechen." Deliberately
and slowly, she half turned, directly facing the sea of
TV cameras now trained on her. They were hanging on her every word. It was . . . perfect. "The man

they killed was Captain Kazimierz Janik, an officer
in Poland's most elite commando unit—a unit which
boasts of its ability to conduct deadly raids far beyond
Poland's own borders. This fact can have only one
meaning. It is undeniable. The Polish government
is conducting a secret war, a covert war, against my
country—a war of aggression in violation of all international law and all accepted norms."

This brutally frank assertion drove the crowd
of reporters beyond any bounds of decorum. They
began yelling out questions at the top of their lungs,
making it impossible for anyone to hear them, let
alone attempt to answer them.

Daria Titeneva only smiled, waiting patiently for
the appalling din to diminish so that she could continue.

To her surprise, the Polish foreign minister
looked genuinely shocked by her revelations. She
had not thought Andrzej Waniek was that skilled an
actor. Perhaps, Titeneva thought, his own government had kept him in the dark about what it was
doing in Ukraine. Certainly, she was quite sure that
Gennadiy Gryzlov would hide many of Moscow's
own darker covert actions from her, if he judged it
prudent.

Which raised questions that were perhaps better
left unasked, she realized suddenly. Wondering just
how so much conclusive evidence had suddenly
dropped into the laps of the Russian intelligence
services was probably not the safest or most sensible
line of inquiry.

Again, the Russian foreign minister stood straight
and tall, waiting for her moment. When she judged

that she could be heard plainly without straining her voice, she went on. "By any standard of international law, my country would be fully justified in issuing an immediate declaration of war against Poland." She smiled into the abruptly stunned and fearful hush that followed her pronouncement. "But we shall not do so. Russia is interested only in peace. Unlike those who have so ruthlessly and viciously attacked us, we do not embrace violence for the sake of violence. Nevertheless, we are not weaklings or simpletons. Crimes have been committed against us—crimes which cry out for justice and for retribution."

She turned to face the Polish foreign minister directly, acting as though the Americans and the diplomats from the other NATO countries were of no importance. "Accordingly, my government instructs me to issue the following ultimatum to Poland's president, Piotr Wilk, and the members of his cabinet. *First*, Poland must immediately cease all its covert attacks on Russian troops and Russian interests—whether in the Zone of Protection or in Russia itself. *Second*, Poland must hand over all of the terrorists and their Polish advisers and commanders for trial in my country, under Russian law. *Third*, all combat aircraft belonging to the Polish Air Force must immediately stand down, and remain grounded until this crisis is resolved to my government's satisfaction. To ensure this, we shall require that vital engine and weapons systems components be removed from each warplane and stored under strict international supervision. *Fourth*, we make the same demand for all elements of Poland's air defense systems—including its radars and surface-to-air missile batteries. *Fifth*, all units of Poland's land forces must be restricted to their existing bases, again under international supervision. All mobilization measures, including President Wilk's ill-considered call-up of reserves, must also be completely reversed. And *sixth*, Poland must pay substantial reparations for every Russian soldier and civilian killed by its terrorist attacks. It must also compensate my country fully for all military equipment damaged or destroyed in these attacks."

For long moments after she finished speaking, a painful, almost breathless silence hung over the council chamber.

At last, Andrzej Waniek, his long, lean lawyer's face gone bone-white, rose to his feet. "I will not dignify these vile fabrications and outright slanders by even attempting to refute them at this moment," he said hoarsely. "Nevertheless, in duty to my government and to the people of my beloved and honorable country, I am bound to ask: How long are we being given to consider the outrageous demands contained in this absurd ultimatum?"

"You have five days," Titeneva told him. "Five days to fully comply with every demand."

"And if we refuse?" Waniek asked grimly.

"Then Russia will be forced to use harsher measures," she said, with equal grimness. "Measures that will impose a lasting peace on the entire region—a peace which will fully secure Russia's safety and security for decades to come."

THE WHITE HOUSE, WASHINGTON, D.C.
A short time later

"You cannot be serious in making these demands," President Stacy Anne Barbeau said in exasperation to the image of her Russian counterpart via a secure video link. "You're asking the Poles to drop all their weapons and then trust you not to take advantage of their weakness. No sovereign government in the world could accept those conditions." She leaned forward in her chair. "Look, Mr. President, I completely understand your anger at what seems to have been going on in the Ukraine, but I'm sure we can figure out a more realistic set of preconditions for negotiations to resolve this mess. All I ask is that your people and mine sit down together with the Poles to sort this out without further violence."

"You misunderstand the purpose of my call," Gennadiy Gryzlov retorted. "I am informing you, purely as a gesture of diplomatic courtesy, of my government's intentions. Nothing more." His expression was icy. "For the moment, I am willing to entertain the possibility that you Americans were truly unaware of this Polish conspiracy against us—that you were simply unwitting dupes in a diabolical scheme run entirely by the fascist clique in Warsaw. But if you wish me to continue accepting this theory, whether it is fact or merely a polite fiction, you *will* stand aside."

Barbeau blinked, but finally her eyes narrowed

in perplexed anger. "President Gryzlov, I'm telling you—"

"There is nothing to discuss," Gryzlov said flatly. "Poland will be punished for its aggression against my country. If you choose to side with Poland, you admit your own guilt in supporting terrorism—guilt that all the world will see and understand. Think about *that*, Madam President. Think very hard." He flicked a single finger to someone off-camera. The Situation Room display went dark as the Russians cut the videoconference link.

"Well, *that* went well," Edward Rauch, her national security adviser, muttered.

"*Fuck*," Barbeau snarled. "What the hell did that son of a bitch Wilk think he was doing? Orchestrating a terror campaign against the Russians? And using his own soldiers to conduct it? Jesus Christ! Did he really think he could swipe at someone as batshit crazy as Gryzlov and get away with it?"

"President Wilk has assured us that his government is not doing anything of the kind," Thomas Torrey pointed out. The CIA director looked troubled. "The Poles are still investigating exactly how those weapons and this Captain Janik ended up in the Ukraine, but they're pretty sure the weapons were planted—probably by the Russians themselves. And that Janik was kidnapped off the street in Warsaw and then murdered."

"Oh, for God's sake! What a bunch of crap!" Stacy Anne Barbeau looked ready to explode. "*Of course* that's the story Wilk and his morons are peddling . . . as if anyone but the dumbest bunch of troglodyte right-wingers would buy it." She swung around in her chair to face General Spelling. "So how do they explain those satellite pictures the Russians shared with us? The ones showing some kind of hush-hush military exercise at this Pomo-place?"

The chairman of the Joint Chiefs of Staff frowned. "I talked to Defense Minister Gierek about that, Madam President. He insists that the maneuvers at Drawsko Pomorskie were purely local and defensive in nature."

"Involving which units of the Polish armed forces?" Rauch asked. He shook his head. "I've studied those images and I wouldn't have said the Poles had anything in their arsenal that could inflict that much damage with such precision."

"Gierek claimed the exercise involved elements of the Polish Special Forces," Spelling admitted, though with some hesitation.

"Which elements? Does that include the units based at Powidz?" Rauch wondered. His eyes narrowed. "Is that why they've locked that base down so tight?"

"What?" Barbeau sat up straighter. "What are you talking about?"

"We've had a few reports of much higher security restrictions at a Polish Air Force base outside Powidz, which is in central Poland," Torrey told her.

"Which is the duty station for Poland's Seventh Special Operations Squadron," Rauch pointed out.

"So?"

Rauch's mouth turned down. "Well, that's the helicopter outfit trained to infiltrate Polish Special Forces teams behind enemy lines . . ."

Barbeau shook her head in disgust. "Jesus. Gryzlov was right. Those bastards in Warsaw have been lying to us, right from the get-go. There's no other way to figure it. Between those secret commando exercises and buying up those long-range XF-111 bombers on the sly, the Poles have been preparing for a war with Russia. But maybe it was a war they planned to start themselves!"

"I don't think we should jump to conclusions yet, Madam President," Spelling urged. "I've known Piotr Wilk for a long time. He's not crazy. And he's not suicidal." He looked around the table. "The most important thing right now is to find some way to slow Gryzlov down—to stop this situation from blowing up into a full-scale conflict and buy time for more investigation and diplomacy."

"Just what are you proposing, General?" Barbeau asked.

"That we send troops and aircraft to Poland," the chairman of the Joint Chiefs said. "Even a token force might persuade the Russians to back off their ultimatum, at least temporarily."

"We could couple that with the promise of a serious international investigation into these terrorist attacks," Thomas Torrey agreed. "Agreeing to a joint CIA-SVR probe would throw Gryzlov a bone he might need to save face at home while still making sure we got to the bottom of what's been happening in Ukraine."

"Absolutely not!" Barbeau snapped. "You heard President Gryzlov. He is not bluffing and I will *not* try to rescue the Poles from a mess of their own making at the cost of American lives. NATO ally or not, this is not a case where the Article Five mutual defense clause applies." She scowled. "And even if I were inclined to believe Poland's story, which I'm *not*, there's no realistic chance we could send enough help to win any conventional war. Right?"

Slowly, reluctantly, her top military and intelligence advisers nodded. Earlier drawdowns had removed almost all U.S. ground troops from Europe. At the height of the Cold War, almost four hundred thousand American soldiers had been stationed in Germany to deter Soviet aggression. Now there were just two light brigades there, neither of them equipped with heavy armor. The U.S. Air Force was in even worse shape. It still had not come close to recovering from the losses sustained in earlier conflicts or from recession-induced budget cuts. Neither service was currently prepared to go head-to-head with the Russians in their own backyard.

"Which means the only way we could stop the Russians—if they really hit Poland—would be to threaten an escalation to nuclear war. And mean it," Stacy Anne Barbeau said coldly. She shook her head decisively. "Well, screw that, ladies and gentlemen. I will not drag the United States to the brink of thermonuclear destruction. Not for the Poles. Not for anyone. And certainly not for such a bad cause."

THE KREMLIN, MOSCOW
That same time

Defense Minister Gregor Sokolov entered the conference room, trailed by a small cadre of senior officers and junior aides. He stopped just beyond the door, surprised to find only three men waiting for him—Gennadiy Gryzlov, Sergei Tarzarov, the president's chief of staff, and the president's private secretary, Ulanov. Given the importance of this meeting, he had expected to find the other members of the security council there, except, of course, for the foreign minister who was scheduled to fly home to Moscow from Geneva later that night.

Russia's president swung away from the large display, now showing a detailed map of Ukraine, Belarus, and Poland. "Ah, there you are, Gregor," he said, smiling broadly. "It is good to see you." He nodded to the group of military officers, including them in his greeting. "Please, gentlemen, be seated."

Sokolov and the others obeyed, arranging themselves around the long conference table.

"You are here to receive my orders for the coming war," Gryzlov told them, ignoring the startled looks on the faces of several junior aides who had evidently missed recent developments. "You will then translate these orders into the operational plans necessary to achieve victory—as swiftly, decisively, and cost-effectively as possible. Is this understood?"

"Yes, Mr. President," Sokolov said, not daring to give any other answer. "So the Poles have rejected our ultimatum?"

"Not yet," Gryzlov said with a shrug. "But they will. Even the American president, not one of nature's brighter intellects, understands as much. Our demands have backed Wilk and his gang into a corner. Oh, they will squirm and wriggle for as long as possible, desperately seeking some safe escape from the snare, some means of survival." His smile turned more wolflike. "In fact, I am counting on Warsaw to use every hour we have given them before finally rejecting our ultimatum."

"The Poles may use those five days to strengthen their defenses, sir," General Mikhail Khristenko warned. Khristenko was the chief of the General Staff. "Their reserves are only partially mobilized at this moment, but every hour we wait gives the enemy more time to integrate these men into active-duty brigades and battalions."

"That is true, General," Gryzlov agreed. He swung back toward the map and used a control to highlight the current concentration areas of Russia's own ground and air forces in the Ukraine, along Russia's border with Belarus, and within Russia itself. In every case, they were at least several hundred kilometers from the Polish border. "But who really benefits *more* from five uninterrupted days of preparation—and maneuver?"

"You mean for us to conduct our prewar marches while the Poles dither," Sokolov realized suddenly.

"Exactly!" the president said, nodding. He grinned at them. "While Wilk and his government ministers scuttle about, looking for any possible alternative to war, our tank, artillery, and motor-rifle formations will mass on the Polish frontier. And when all of Poland's futile efforts fail, as they must, our soldiers will be ready to strike with overwhelming force—backed by our most advanced combat aircraft and missile units."

"What if the Poles attack us on the march, before the ultimatum expires?" Khristenko asked quietly. "In war, the enemy always has a vote."

Gryzlov shrugged again. "With what? A few companies of commandos flown on aging Mi-17 helicopters? A handful of near-obsolete F-16s and MiG-29s? Our Su-27, Su-30, and Su-35 interceptors and our mobile SAM battalions would swat them all out of the sky!"

There were murmurs of agreement from the officers gathered around the table. Up to now, the Polish-backed terrorists—attacking covertly and at times and places of their own choosing—had been able to evade the overwhelming numerical and qualitative superiority of Russia's armed forces. In any open engagement, however, they were doomed to defeat.

"Besides," Gryzlov went on, with an even colder smile on his face, "if the Poles attack *us* before our ultimatum expires, they will be marked even more plainly as aggressors in the eyes of the world."

Sokolov noticed even cynical Sergei Tarzarov's head nodding at that. The minister of defense suspected there was little else about this situation that made the president's chief of staff happy. The older man had long been a proponent of watchful caution in international affairs, and nothing about what was happening now smacked of either watchfulness or caution.

"My orders are simple and straightforward," Gryzlov told them. "I want two full armies—the Twentieth Guards Army and the Sixth Army—in position on the Polish border within five days. The

Sixth Army will advance through Belarus. Its government, so closely linked with ours, has already given its consent. The Twentieth will move through the northern sectors of the western Ukraine. Foreign Minister Titeneva has already received my instructions to secure Kiev's full cooperation for the peaceful transit of our troops." He showed his teeth. "Since the Ukrainians face certain destruction if they thwart us, I think we can count on their acquiescence."

"Let us hope so, sir," Tarzarov said drily. "Two foreign wars at one time might be considered overly ambitious by some."

Rather than turning red with fury as Sokolov half expected, the president only gently waved a finger at his chief of staff. "Now, now, Sergei. There'll be time enough for your perpetual naysaying later, if things go wrong, eh?"

"As you wish, Mr. President," Tarzarov murmured.

Sokolov and Khristenko exchanged discreet, worried glances. Stripped down to the essentials, their president's plan required moving more than one hundred thousand soldiers and several thousand artillery pieces, rocket launchers, tanks, and infantry fighting vehicles over huge distances within a very short period of time. It was doable, but it would be difficult—even without possible opposition from the Poles or the Ukrainians. Between the limited number of trucks available and the relatively low capacity of the road and rail net in those regions, their first-echelon troops would probably only be able to bring stocks of fuel and ammunition augmented slightly above peacetime levels. While those supplies might suffice for a short, sharp campaign, heavier fighting would require huge resupply convoys moving regularly between depots in Russia and the battlefront. Without protection against air or missile attack, those columns of supply trucks and fuel tankers would be incredibly vulnerable.

Satisfied, Gryzlov went back to issuing orders. "Both field armies will be supported by strong detachments of our most advanced combat aircraft—including fighters and Su-24 and Su-34 fighter-bombers. These air-force units should be based as far forward as possible. I want guaranteed full air superiority over the Poles as soon as the war begins!"

Sokolov breathed a little easier. Maintaining air superiority was vital to moving and supplying such large ground forces so far from Russia's current borders. He should have realized that Gryzlov, well schooled in air tactics and strategy by virtue of his earlier military training, would understand that.

"Finally, as an operational attack force of last resort, I want a brigade of Iskander R-500 cruise missiles and Iskander-M tactical ballistic missiles deployed within range of Warsaw, other industrial centers, and key Polish air bases." Gryzlov tapped one of the computer-driven display controls, bringing up a new graphic overlay on the map. It showed several positions east of the city of Kaliningrad, a small enclave situated on the Baltic Sea between Poland and Lithuania. "I suggest this site. These woods offer good camouflage against satellite detection and we can ring the Iskander launchers with mobile SAM battalions."

Khristenko studied that for a moment and then nodded. "An excellent choice, Mr. President. New solid-rocket propellants give our Iskander-M rockets much greater range, but the Western powers do not yet fully realize this. Even if they detect the movement of our missile brigades, they will not see a deployment there as an effective offensive threat."

"Indeed," Gryzlov said smugly. "And yet, from this area, our missiles can strike most of northern and central Poland with little more than six minutes of warning time—hitting any targets we select with incredible accuracy and force. So, if Poland's defenses prove stronger than we expect, we will pound them into burning heaps of rubble!"

The assembled generals and staff officers nodded again. Iskander-M missiles carried warheads with almost a ton of conventional high explosives; plus, their inertial and optical homing guidance systems gave them high precision, a circular error probability rating of just five to seven meters. The newer R-500 cruise missiles, fired from the same launchers, had even longer range and better accuracy. Left unspoken, but front and center in all of their minds, was the fact that both versions of the Iskander could also be fitted with nuclear warheads—should their president opt in the end to annihilate the Poles rather than simply conquer them.

"Excuse me, sir," Tarzarov said, "but may I remind you that we have agreed not to station Iskander units in Kaliningrad Oblast? Moving these missiles into Kaliningrad, no matter our level of secrecy, will surely be detected."

"I'm not concerned with that, Sergei," Gryzlov said with a dismissive wave of a hand. "We have been forced to mobilize for war, and I intend to use every weapon at my disposal. The Iskander missiles are our most accurate and survivable battlefield weapon, and I will not keep them out of the fight because of a political concession made years ago. If NATO doesn't like it, they can tell the Poles to back off, or they can declare war on Russia." He smiled and nodded. "I would welcome either."

SECURE HANGAR, IRON WOLF
SQUADRON COMPOUND,
POWIDZ, POLAND
A short time later

The big hangar doors were already sliding closed behind the two-seater F-16D Falcon as it taxied to a stop and shut down its Pratt & Whitney turbofan engine. Even before the fighter's clear canopy whined open, ground crew hurried toward the plane with ladders for the Polish Air Force pilot and his VIP passenger.

President Piotr Wilk climbed out of the rear seat and dropped lightly onto the hangar's concrete floor. He stripped off the flight helmet he'd been loaned and handed it back to the F-16's pilot, a lieutenant colonel. "Wait for me here, Waldemar. And thank you for the ride." He forced a smile. "Maybe you will let me fly your bird on the way back to Warsaw, eh? I promise not to try too many crazy stunts on the way."

"Sir!" The lieutenant colonel snapped to attention.

A tall, powerfully built man stepped forward. Wilk recognized him from earlier visits as Wayne Macomber, commander of the Iron Wolf Squadron's ground troops. "We're all set, Mr. President," Macomber said. "If you'll follow me?"

The big American led him through a pair of large doors at the rear of the hangar and into an adjoining room with a remarkably high ceiling. The reason for the tall ceiling was apparent when Wilk saw the twelve-foot-tall Cybernetic Infantry Device standing absolutely still, facing the doors. It was plugged into an array of cables.

Two men stood next to the huge robot. One was Kevin Martindale. The other was much younger, with bright blue eyes and short-cropped blond hair. Dressed in the dark green uniform adopted by the Iron Wolf Squadron's air crews, he was almost as tall and broad-shouldered as Macomber.

He recognized Brad McLanahan from Captain Rozek's confidential reports. In them, she credited the only son of the legendary General McLahanan with remarkable leadership and tactical skills. Apparently, he had won the loyalty of a hard-nosed group of elite pilots with astonishing swiftness. Then again, Wilk thought with hidden amusement, judging from some of the other rumors he'd heard, that was not all Brad had won recently.

Privately, he hoped the young American knew

what he was getting into. Nadia Rozek was a highly capable, highly trained Special Forces officer. If Brad McLanahan broke her heart, she was perfectly capable of breaking his neck—or any other part of his body that caught her fancy.

Quickly, Wilk shook hands with everyone except the CID, which seemed frozen, utterly inanimate. Was there a pilot in there? he wondered. Or was it only an empty shell right now, brought out of storage for use as a visual aid at this urgent meeting?

Kevin Martindale motioned him toward a conference table surrounded by chairs. "I hope you don't mind if we skip all the usual pleasantries, Mr. President. But time is damned short all of sudden."

"Not at all," Wilk said, sitting down. The others did the same. "I am well aware that we are, as you Americans would say, neck-deep in the shit." His foray into American slang drew quick, slashing grins from both Macomber and Brad, and a pained nod of grudging agreement from Martindale.

"Can you tell us anything more about how those rifles and other gear—not to mention Captain Janik's corpse—wound up in Russian hands?" the head of Scion asked.

Regretfully, Wilk shook his head. "Not yet." He frowned. "But the serial numbers provided by Moscow do match equipment we purchased from the United States. We have traced these weapons as far as we can, but all of them are listed in our records as either scrapped or discarded."

"Who maintains those records?" Brad asked. "Somebody must have fiddled with them."

"In this case, the 'fiddling' seems to have been

done by a staff sergeant in one of our supply units," Wilk said. "Unfortunately, we cannot confirm that through direct interrogation. Sergeant Górski died more than a week ago—burned alive in what the police thought was an accidental fire."

"How very fucking . . . *convenient*," Macomber growled.

Wilk nodded grimly. "True. Though not for us, it seems."

"What about Kazimierz?" Brad looked even more troubled. "Nadia . . . I mean, Captain Rozek and I, must have been just about the last people to set eyes on him. He was drunk as a skunk, so he sure as hell wasn't getting ready to fly off on some solo covert mission to the Ukraine!"

"We believe Captain Janik must have been kidnapped that same night," Wilk told them, not bothering to hide his own anger. "But we have no proof of this beyond the fact that he did not visit his girlfriend. There is no evidence that he ever crossed our borders. It is as if he simply vanished off the streets in Warsaw and then reappeared—quite dead—at that Russian-occupied air base."

"Your whole country's been well and truly set up," Macomber said through gritted teeth. "And then staked out like a kid goat for Gryzlov and company to gnaw on."

"So I believe," Wilk agreed bitterly. "My investigators will keep digging, but I have little hope they will uncover the truth. At least not in time to matter."

"I wish I could argue against that," Martindale said, looking down at his hands. "But you're right.

The damage has already been done. My sources tell me that President Barbeau has ruled out any American help against the Russians."

"So I have been informed." Wilk's shoulders slumped slightly. "The American ambassador telephoned this news to me—on his way to the airport. Washington, it seems, has recalled him for 'urgent consultations.'"

"Jesus," Macomber swore. His face was dark. "Why didn't that bitch Barbeau just hand him a nice sharp dagger to plant in your back while she was at it?"

"Now, now, Major," Martindale said reprovingly, though his expression was equally angry. "Stacy Anne Barbeau would never do anything as aboveboard and honest as that. She prefers making her kills with words, not actions."

"If the U.S. is cutting and running, I suppose the other NATO powers will do the same thing," Brad said.

"Yes," Wilk agreed heavily. "The Germans, the French, and the British will not offer us military or even diplomatic support without American backing. Even the leaders of the Baltic states—who know they will be next in Gryzlov's cross hairs—are frozen in fear and uncertainty. They offer me moral support, but little more."

"So we're on our own," Brad said grimly.

Surprised at his choice of words, Wilk shook his head. "No, Mr. McLanahan. We *Poles* are on our own. With the whole world believing these lies about us, I cannot ask you and the rest of your squadron to share our fate."

"You don't *have* to ask us, Piotr. We already have a contract," Kevin Martindale interjected. The gray-haired former American president looked around the table with a wry smile. "No one had to twist our arms to get us to sign it either. I told you earlier that Scion honors its agreements. Well, now we're going to prove it."

Brad and Macomber nodded solemnly, although Macomber spoiled the moment a bit by muttering, "Hell, yes. There's nothing I like better than a death-defying battle against hopeless odds. Just so long as it's not too early in the goddamned morning."

"You see?" Martindale told Wilk, with just the slightest hint of a thin smile on his own face. "The Iron Wolf Squadron is at your command, Mr. President." He looked squarely at the Polish president. "Which raises the rather pertinent question of exactly how you plan to respond to this Russian ultimatum."

"Poland will not comply with the ultimatum," Wilk said bluntly. "To do so would be national suicide."

"So we fight," Brad said, glancing over at the Cybernetic Infantry Device standing motionless near the conference table.

"Yes, we will fight," Wilk said. "And if Poland must die again, she will die with honor."

Suddenly the CID swiveled its head toward him. "My suggestion, Mr. President, would be to win the war that's coming instead," the machine said in a deep but electronically synthesized voice. "Let the Russians do the dying."

Startled, Wilk stared up at the huge manned war robot. Despite its strange electronic overtones, that voice was . . . familiar, somehow. "Just who the devil are you?" he demanded. "And why are you hiding in that . . . *device* . . . rather than having the courage to confer with us face-to-face?"

"We've met before," the CID told him. "Though only briefly and a long time ago." It dipped its head slightly. "My name is Patrick McLanahan."

Wilk listened in fascinated, and then somewhat horrified, silence while Martindale and the others told the story behind the former Air Force general's apparently fatal wounds, unexpected resuscitation, and now seemingly perpetual imprisonment inside these human-piloted robots. When they were finished, he shook his head in amazement. "And no one else knows about this?"

"Only a handful of others," Patrick said. "And most of them are back in the United States." His voice was hushed. "It seemed better to live on quietly in the shadows, rather than becoming another short-lived, freak-show media sensation. Or worse yet, becoming some sort of circus exhibit for conspiracy theorists."

"And a target," his son reminded him sharply. "If that whacked-out son of a bitch Gryzlov knew you were still alive, you'd have GRU assassins dogging your metal heels no matter how many security guards Scion assigned to your detail."

"Probably so. As you should know better than anyone, Brad," Patrick agreed. And this time Wilk could swear he heard just the hint of amused exasperation in that synthetic voice.

With an effort, the Polish president shook himself out of his bewilderment. Like many other air force officers around the world, he had respected the American general's accomplishments, so it was heartening to learn that the man was still alive, in whatever strange and eerie way, and willing to fight for Poland. But the odds against them still seemed insurmountable. "What did you mean when you suggested we win this war?" he asked.

"If war is inevitable," the older McLanahan argued. "Let's fight it on our terms. On our schedule. And on the enemy's turf—not on Polish soil." The CID leaned down, looming over the table. "Commit the Iron Wolf Squadron to an unconventional campaign against the Russian invasion forces as soon as they start moving toward your frontier."

"Before the ultimatum expires?" Wilk asked skeptically, pondering the possible international repercussions if Poland struck first.

The large war robot shrugged its armored shoulders. "Gryzlov isn't going to stop, no matter what you do. And now we all know the U.S. cavalry isn't going to come riding to the rescue. Nor is anyone else. So if we're going to be hanged by international public opinion anyway, it might as well be for a sheep as a lamb."

Slowly, almost against his will, Wilk nodded. What the American said made sense. Waiting until the last possible moment to reject Moscow's ultimatum would not gain them any more allies; nor would the extra time be of much real help in shoring up Poland's defenses. No, he thought grimly, if the Russians really planned to invade his country, they were the ones who had the most to gain from the five-day ultimatum period.

Then a thought struck him. He turned to Brad McLanahan. "But the Iron Wolf Squadron is not yet completely ready, is it? You still have only four of your XF-111s based here at Powidz. The others are still held back in the United States, are they not?"

Brad nodded. "That's true, Mr. President." He smiled slightly, plainly glad to have some good news to report. "But I've already sent crews back home to fly in the rest ASAP. They left very early this morning on several of Mr. Martindale's private jets. And Sky Masters is already making the fuel system modifications necessary to get the XF-111s here without intermediate stops."

Martindale nodded. "Which means there will be some nasty legal and bureaucratic red tape to unravel—or mostly likely rip to shreds—but we'll get those SuperVarks here. You can count on that."

These Americans, Wilk thought wryly. They seemed almost frighteningly eager to throw themselves into a battle that still seemed impossible to win. Well, Piotr, he told himself, then perhaps it is best that they are on your side. "So be it," he said quietly. "As soon as the Russians begin moving west against us, I will unleash the Iron Wolf Squadron."

SOKOLNIKI PARK, MOSCOW
Several hours later

Igor Truznyev, former president of the Russian Federation, sat on a park bench sheltered from the rain by a black umbrella. He enjoyed the sight of younger couples scurrying past along the path, hurrying to seek shelter somewhere else until this brief storm passed. They paid no attention to the older man sitting so placidly and so alone. The park, once a falconry preserve for the Czar Alexei Mikhailovich, Peter the Great's father, was emptying out fast. Without any crowds to use as cover, watchers would stand out against the backdrop of birches, pines, oaks, and maples.

He also enjoyed the sound of the raindrops pitter-pattering through the leaves of the trees, dripping onto the grass and flower beds, and splashing into nearby ponds. All this ambient noise would make it very difficult for anyone but the most dedicated eavesdropper, using the most sophisticated surveillance gear.

Truznyev restrained the urge to check his watch again. The man who had requested this covert rendezvous would either keep it, or not. Amid all the militaristic furor spreading through the Kremlin and the Defense and Intelligence Ministries, it might be difficult for the other to slip away unnoticed.

Another middle-aged man in a fashionable raincoat and carrying a smaller umbrella came up the rain-soaked path, walking fast. He looked like a businessman, perhaps a banker, out for a bit of doctor-ordered afternoon exercise before going back to the humdrum routine of his daily work.

"May I join you?" Truznyev heard the other man ask politely.

He looked up, unsurprised to see Sergei Tarzarov's brown eyes staring back at him out of a face that looked, for now at least, a couple of decades younger. "*Da, konechno.* Yes, of course," he said, sliding down the park bench a bit to make room. "I was a bit surprised to get your message. Usually, I contact you, not the other way around."

"That is because this time, I need *your* assistance, Igor," Tarzarov said.

"Oh?"

Tarzarov nodded. "I worry that we are being manipulated—lured into a clash with the Poles we might have avoided. I need your help to evaluate this possibility." He frowned. "The evidence our Spetsnaz troops found at Konotop troubles me. It is too . . . perfect. Too closely tailored to fit Gennadiy's beliefs and prejudices."

The former president raised an eyebrow. "Are you sure that you aren't more bothered by the possibility that this hard evidence of Polish involvement proves your earlier skepticism was wrong?"

A thin, wintry smile crossed Tarzarov's face, subtly aging him despite his disguise. "I do not claim to be an entirely disinterested saint," he said drily. "But I am far too old to believe in my own infallibility." He shrugged. "Nevertheless, I think it is important to uncover the truth. If we are being led by the nose to war, I want to know who holds the string."

"That makes good sense," Truznyev agreed. He glanced more closely at the other man. "But isn't it already too late? From what I've heard, the line's been crossed. President Gryzlov is hell-bent on toppling the Polish government—and he has the generals and the people in his pocket. Besides, even if he wanted to withdraw this ultimatum, there is no way he can reverse course now. It would make Russia, and him, a laughingstock around the whole world!"

"True," Tarzarov said. He frowned. "But there will be other crises, other decisions of equal or greater importance down the road. If some unknown party planted that evidence for its own purposes, we must find out who they are and stop them before that next crisis arises. Otherwise we risk ceding control over our policy, over our country, to others—to those who might lead us into disaster for their own mysterious ends."

Slowly, Truznyev nodded his understanding. He looked grim. "I take your point, Sergei. You are right, as always." He sighed. "Though it might help if we had a leader who was less . . . *volatile*. And more level-headed."

The older man snorted politely. "And did you have someone else in mind for the job, Igor? Someone we both know well?"

Truznyev smiled. "Not me, my friend. My time in the Kremlin is long gone—as is my hunger for the trappings of power." He spread his hands. "Now I wish only to serve the interests of the state in my own private and discreet way."

"And to make money while doing so," Tarzarov said pointedly.

The other man smiled. "That, too." He shrugged his expensively clad shoulders. "You know as well as I do, Sergei, that money is a valuable tool. And a useful weapon. Without it, of what use could I be to you now, eh?"

Tarzarov laughed softly, conceding the point.

"Still, why ask me to investigate this for you?" Truznyev asked. "Why not drop the matter in Viktor Kazyanov's lap? He runs the intelligence services now. Have him set his GRU and SVR hounds to work. If someone's been playing games with us, have them sniff out the scent."

"Because Kazyanov is a moral coward," Tarzarov said, his lip curling in disgust. "He pisses himself in fear if Gennadiy so much as raises his voice. Does he seem like the sort of man who would be interested in discovering that his master has been so easily misled?"

Now it was Truznyev's turn to snort. "No," he agreed. "I remember him well from my days in intelligence, as head of the FSB. Viktor would be the last person to tell Gryzlov he's been gulled. And if he did, I doubt the president would believe him."

"So, then, Igor, will you help me?" the older man asked. "If it is a question of money, well, I can tap the secret funds without great difficulty."

After only a brief pause, Truznyev nodded. "Of course I'll help you. But it may be difficult. And it will be expensive." He pulled at his chin, thinking aloud. "As you know, I still have . . . *contacts*, shall we say . . . in some of the most promising possibilities."

"Which are? In your view, I mean?"

Truznyev shrugged. "Beijing ranks high, I think. The Chinese are subtle and, despite the interest we share in seeing the Americans humbled, they still see us as potential rivals for world power. And certainly, their president, Zhou, must resent how ruthlessly Gryzlov bullied him during the Starfire affair."

"Gennadiy was, perhaps, too . . . forceful," Tarzarov admitted sourly.

"That's certainly one word to describe demanding complete control over China's entire antisatellite weapons arsenal in order to destroy the American's space battle station," the other man said, smiling.

"Gennadiy's plan worked, though."

"It did," Truznyev agreed easily. "But now the Chinese may be interested in regaining some of their pride by turning the tables on him—setting Gennadiy dancing to a tune of their choice."

"Perhaps, though I cannot see what strategic or geopolitical interest Beijing would have in seeing us crush Poland," Tarzarov said doubtfully.

"This war will inevitably draw our eyes westward, away from what the Chinese consider their own sphere of influence," Truznyev pointed out.

"True."

"But there are *other* places to look," Truznyev continued. "Kiev is obviously one of them, though I cannot see how even the fascists there could believe they would benefit from tricking us into conquering half their own country, and then marching armies through the rest!" He shrugged. "We should also consider digging beneath the surface in Warsaw itself."

Tarzarov shook his head in disbelief. "Of all your hypotheses, that seems least likely, Igor. Why would any sane Pole drag us into war against his own country?"

"Piotr Wilk has political opponents," the other man said. "Some of them remember the days of the Warsaw Pact more fondly than most Poles. Perhaps they believe a lost war could be the quickest route to ousting Wilk's government and achieving real political power?" He laughed, though without any humor. "Certainly, I know how *that* equation works, if only from the wrong end of the stick!"

Reluctantly, Tarzarov nodded. "It is possible." He sighed. "Very well, Igor. See what you can learn. But discreetly, yes?"

"As always," the other man assured him.

After the older man left, Truznyev sat quietly, waiting for a few minutes before making his own way out of the park. No matter how well disguised Gryzlov's chief of staff might be, it was safest to keep some distance between them.

The rain had stopped, and streaks of sunlight were beginning to break through the clouds. Truznyev furled his umbrella and walked on, smiling to himself—already contemplating the complicated web he would have to weave to carry out Tarzarov's request. It was annoying that the older man's instincts had led him so close to the truth, just as it was annoying that Gryzlov's luck still seemed to be holding.

He shrugged. If this plan to humiliate Russia's new president failed, there would be other opportunities later—especially since Tarzarov still trusted him. As a child, he had always enjoyed playing *priatki*, hide-and-seek, and this covert venture was only another version of that old favorite. In this case, of course, there was one crucial difference. After all, though he did not know it, Tarzarov was asking him to find himself. He began to laugh.

OVER THE NORTH ATLANTIC OCEAN
That night

Twenty thousand feet over the ocean, four XF-111s flew eastward in close formation. Two more Super-Varks were about a mile ahead and a few thousand feet higher, performing the intricate maneuvers required to take on fuel from a Sky Masters KC-10 Extender aerial tanker.

"Wolf Three-One, this is Masters One-Four, pressure disconnect," the boom operator aboard the tanker radioed. "You're topped off and good to go."

"Thanks, One-Four. Clearing away now," the pilot of the XF-111 that had just finished refueling replied, sliding down and away from the KC-10.

"Wolf Three-Two, you're up next," the tanker said. "Cleared to precontact position."

"Roger that, One-Four. Three-Two moving to precontact."

From the cockpit of the lead XF-111, Wolf One-One, one mile back, Mark Darrow could see all the director lights on the KC-10's belly flash twice, followed by a pair of blinking green lights. He could see the last of the six aircraft in his formation slowly moving up into position, getting set to guide in on the KC-10's boom nozzle. Once Karen Tanabe's Wolf Three-Two topped up with fuel, they could break away from the Sky Masters tanker and fly on to Poland.

"You know, Jack," he said to his copilot and weapons systems operator. "This daft little scheme of Mr. Martindale's might actually work."

Over on the right side of the crowded cockpit, Jack Hollenbeck grinned back under his oxygen mask. "My mama always thought I'd end up on the wrong side of the law. But I figure she was thinking more about little old-fashioned crimes like bank robbery or car theft. Airplane smuggling seems like a mighty big step up. More high-class, somehow."

Darrow laughed. The Texan's description of what they were doing was apt. Caught without enough time to move the remaining XF-111s legally—or at least discreetly—to Poland, Scion and its partners at Sky Masters had been forced to improvise. First, technicians had hurriedly installed temporary auxiliary fuel tanks in each refurbished aircraft's bomb bay, significantly increasing the amount of fuel they could carry. Next, Sky Masters reactivated their air refueling systems—technically illegal according to U.S. export laws. Once that was done, contract pilots had flown the planes to different civilian airports along the eastern seaboard, ready for the Iron Wolf crews coming in from Poland take over.

Roughly four hours ago, every one of those six Iron Wolf Squadron XF-111s had taken off—flying east using commercial air and civilian transponder codes that identified them as chartered cargo flights bound for different destinations in Africa and Europe and filing all the necessary Customs and Border Protection electronic forms for crossing the

U.S. border. Nearly three thousand separate flights crossed the Atlantic in both directions every day—six more planes added to that traffic flow should rate less than a blip on anybody's radar, or so Martindale had hoped. Once they left radar air traffic coverage, the XF-111s had switched off their transponders, increased speed, and converged at this planned midocean air refueling rendezvous.

So far, so good, Darrow thought. And one thing was already clear. The other Iron Wolf crews were bloody good at their jobs. Every plane had made it to this difficult rendezvous on time and without trouble.

"Warning, warning, unidentified X-band target search radar detected," the SPEARS threat-warning system announced. *"Four o'clock. Range undetermined."*

"Ruh-roh," Hollenbeck muttered, glancing down at his threat-warning display. "Identify."

"Negative identification," the computer. *"Agile active frequency signal. Stand by."*

"Hell." Hollenbeck stared down at his display. "The frequencies that goddamned radar is using are jumping around like a jackrabbit being chased by a coyote. My best guess is that it's an AN/APG-79."

"Blast," Darrow said. That was almost as good as the AN/APG-81 active electronically scanned array radar carried by their SuperVarks. Besides the refurbished XB-1 Excalibur bombers produced by Sky Masters, the only other aircraft fitted with the AN/APG-79s were the U.S. Navy's F/A-18F Super Hornets . . . which meant they were in big trouble. Quickly, he switched their primary radio to GUARD, the international emergency frequency.

A tense voice crackled through their headsets. "Unknown aircraft heading one-zero-five degrees at angels twenty and angels twenty-three, this is Navy flight Lion Four. Identify yourselves immediately!"

Darrow glanced down at the information fed to one of his multifunction displays by Hollenbeck. Lion Four was a U.S. Navy F/A-18 all right, part of Strike Fighter Squadron 213, the "Blacklions." VFA-213 was currently shown as flying off the *Nimitz*-class carrier *George H. W. Bush*. The Super Hornet's crew must have been on a routine training flight when it picked them up, probably using ATFLIR, its Advanced Targeting Forward-Looking Infrared system. If the Navy fighter had been on station as part of the carrier group's CAP, its combat air patrol, the XF-111 group's warning receivers would have picked up emissions from a wide range of naval radars at long range. And that would have given them plenty of time to hightail it out of this area before being spotted.

So this was just bad luck.

Really bad luck.

If a report of "unidentified F-111s" making a mid-Atlantic refueling maneuver flashed up the Navy chain of command to the Pentagon or, worse yet, President Barbeau's White House, all hell would undoubtedly break loose. At best, the six Iron Wolf Squadron planes and their crews would be ordered back to the States for further investigation—an investigation that was bound to go on for a very long time and lead to a lot of awkward, unanswerable questions. As unpleasant as that would be for him, Jack Hollenbeck, Karen Tanabe, and the others, Darrow realized, it would be a lot worse for the rest of the squadron back at Powidz. Without these reinforcements, they would be forced to go in against the Russians desperately short of aircraft and trained crews.

Well, then, Darrow thought, his six XF-111s were going to have to bluff their way past this Super Hornet pilot and his backseater, at least long enough to break contact and zoom out of detection range. "You'd better do the talking, Jack," the ex-RAF pilot said, frowning. "My accent might prove a bit . . . disconcerting . . . to our friend out there."

Hollenbeck nodded. "Time to find out if our 'get out of jail free' card really works, I guess." He keyed his mike. "Lion Four, this is Blackbird One. My code phrase is EIGHTBALL HIGH. Repeat, EIGHTBALL HIGH. Suggest you run that through your computer, pronto."

COMBAT DIRECTION CENTER, CVN-77
USS *GEORGE H. W. BUSH*,
IN THE NORTH ATLANTIC
That same time

"Say again, Lion Four," Commander Russ Gerhardt, air operations officer for the *Bush*, said into his mike. In the dim, blue-tinted light of the CDC, he leaned forward, studying the radar and infrared images sent via data link from the F/A-18F Super Hornet. They showed a formation of seven separate aircraft, one large plane evaluated as a KC-10 refueling tanker and six smaller, sweptwing F-111-type aircraft. Every single F-111 had long since been retired to the Boneyard, so that was weird. None of them were squawking on any transponders, and that was even weirder.

"These bozos gave us a code phrase to check," the backseater aboard Lion Four radioed. "EIGHT-BALL HIGH, whatever that is."

Gerhardt frowned. Code phrases? Crap. Who the hell were these guys? He turned to the specialist manning the nearest computer station. "Run that through the system, Cappellini."

"Aye, aye, sir," she said, her fingers already dancing over the keyboard. And then stopped as a warning flashed on her screen. "Commander?" the young Navy technician said, in a worried tone. "I can't access that information. I'm not cleared for it."

Bush's air operations officer moved over to get a better look. Her display showed lines of text in bright red: TOP SECRET//OS-SPECIAL ACCESS REQUIRED-EIGHTBALL HIGH. DO NOT REPORT. DO NOT RECORD.

His frown grew deeper. The OS tag on this EIGHTBALL HIGH crap meant this was a Defense Department–approved military operation of some kind. But the Special Access bit meant it was so highly classified that all information about it was restricted to those few with a "need to know." And apparently nobody on CVN-77 or in her assigned air wing met that criterion.

Well, Gerhardt thought, it didn't take a rocket scientist to figure out this was somehow connected to all the shit going down between Russia and Poland. The Pentagon brass and the White House must be running a "black ops" mission to help the Poles. Which explained the DO NOTs attached to the code phrase. After President Barbeau had made such a big deal out of staying neutral, anything the United States did to aid Warsaw would have to be totally deniable.

"Wipe that entry, Specialist Cappellini," he ordered. "It never happened. Understand?"

"Aye, aye, sir."

Gerhardt keyed his mike again. "Lion Four, this is Avenger. Break away from those unknowns and deactivate your radar. Head back home. That's an order."

"Avenger, this is Lion Four. Falcon one-zero-one?!"

Gerhardt grinned, hearing the Navy pilot code for "You've got to be shitting me." "No fecal matter is involved, Lion Four. Back off those guys and shut it down."

OVER THE ATLANTIC
That same time

"I'll be damned," Hollenbeck said slowly, staring at his MFDs. "It actually worked. That Hornet's radar just went off-line. He's turning away."

Mark Darrow breathed out in relief. Scion's computer wizards had claimed they'd done a bit of tweaking inside the U.S. Defense Department's databases to cover this little jaunt. It looked as though they'd done their hacking job properly. He switched back to the frequency they'd been using earlier. "Masters One-Four, many thanks for your assistance."

"Wolf One-One, you're more than welcome. Fly safe," the tanker radioed. "We're heading for home."

Darrow watched the big KC-10 bank away, turning back to the west. Its director lights winked out. Within minutes, even the navigation lights on the aerial tanker's wing tips and tail vanished in the darkness. He keyed his mike again. "All Wolf flights, this is Wolf One-One. Now that we're finally all alone out here, let's pick up the pace, shall we? We'll go to full cruise and take it down to ten thousand feet. Follow my lead, understood?" A succession of clicks and acknowledgments came through his headset as the five other Iron Wolf crews signaled they understood his orders.

"Right, then, Wolf flights. Here we go," Darrow said, sweeping the XF-111's wings back to fifty-six degrees while simultaneously pushing the throttles forward. The big fighter-bomber accelerated smoothly toward its full cruise speed of nearly six hundred knots. He pitched the SuperVark's nose down, watching the altitude indicator on his HUD slide down toward ten thousand feet. One after another, the five other planes followed him down— staying on the course that would bring them to the Strait of Gibraltar, the entrance to the Mediterranean, in a little over two hours.

COMBAT INFORMATION CENTER,
RUSSIAN AIRCRAFT CARRIER
ADMIRAL KUZNETSOV,
IN THE WESTERN MEDITERRANEAN
That same time

Rear Admiral Anatoly Varennikov studied the short transcript of the GUARD channel radio transmission picked up by his aircraft carrier's signals intelligence detachment. He arched an eyebrow, silently translating the English-language phrases into their Russian equivalents. He made it a point to always see the raw data first, but he never pretended to be a first-rate linguist. At last he looked up, meeting the interested gaze of his chief intelligence officer, Captain Yakunin. "EIGHTBALL HIGH? I've never seen that before. What does it mean, Leonid?"

"Based on what they said, it's an operational code of some kind, sir," Yakunin said. He shrugged. "But it's not one we have listed in our files."

"And there was nothing more?" Varennikov asked. "Just a request from the American Navy F/A-18 for identification from these unidentified aircraft? And then this strange code in response?"

"There were no more messages between the mysterious aircraft and the Hornet," Yakunin said. "But when the pilot passed this code back to his carrier, the *Bush,* his commanders told him to abort the intercept. In fact, they told him to turn off his radar immediately and return to the ship. Interesting, eh?"

"Extremely interesting," Varennikov agreed. "It suggests the movement of American military or intelligence aircraft, but a movement so secret that not even its own naval commanders were briefed about it in advance."

He turned to the map plot showing the present position of *Admiral Kuznetsov* and its escorting destroyers and frigates. They were about one hundred and sixty kilometers east-northeast of Gibraltar, steaming almost due east under Moscow's most recent orders to return to the Black Sea. If the Ukrainians chose to impede the Russian troops scheduled to advance toward Poland, President Gryzlov wanted the carrier group in position to help punish them. Then he studied the estimated position, course, and speed of the unidentified group of aircraft out over the Atlantic. They might be heading his way.

Varennikov chewed his lower lip, deep in thought. Was it worth delaying his task force's transit to the Black Sea to investigate further? Yes, he decided. If the Americans really were up to something sneaky, it was important to try to find out exactly what that was. He moved to the command phone connecting him to the bridge. "Captain Bogdanov, signal the task force to reverse course. And ready two Su-33 fighters for launch. I want them to go hunting."

OVER THE ATLANTIC,
NEAR THE STRAIT OF GIBRALTAR
A couple of hours later

"*Warning, warning, X-band target search radar, Su-33, eleven o'clock high, one hundred miles, seven hundred knots,*" the computer said suddenly.

"Signal strength?" Hollenbeck asked.

"*Weak, but increasing,*" the SPEAR system told him. "*Detection probability minimal, but increasing.*"

Darrow frowned. "It's getting awfully crowded in my sky, these days." He clicked his mike. "Wolf flights, this is One-One. Stand by to go to DTF on my mark. Set for two hundred, hard ride. Let's get down in the waves and blow past these Russian buggers before they know we're here."

More clicks acknowledged his order.

"Those Su-33 radars have a decent look-down capability," Hollenbeck warned. "If they get close enough, they'll still detect us."

Darrow nodded. "We'll jink to stay out of their way, if we have to, and hope SPEAR can take care of the rest. Engage DTF, clearance plane two hundred hard ride."

"*Digital terrain following engaged, clearance plane two hundred hard ride,*" the computer responded.

The XF-111 plunged down through night sky, diving toward the ocean at six hundred knots. The digital terrain-following system included occasional bursts of its radar altimeter, which measured the exact distance from its belly to the ocean. The SuperVarks leveled out at two hundred feet above the surface and streaked onward.

Darrow tweaked his stick slightly right, following the navigation cues on his HUD. Soon some distinctive rock formations began to become visible on the digital artificial terrain display. Minutes later, they zipped past a massive wall of rock on the left side of the canopy, glowing faintly white in the moonlight. Lights twinkled at its base.

"Cool," Hollenbeck muttered, craning his head to look aft at the huge headland rising more than a thousand feet above their XF-111. "Was that—?"

"The Rock of Gibraltar," the Englishman replied tersely. "We're over the Med now."

Hollenbeck looked back at his displays. "Those Su-33 radars are at our ten o'clock and moving toward our nine o'clock. Signal strength is still weak and now diminishing." He nodded in satisfaction. "I think we dodged them."

"Let's hope so," Darrow said, tweaking the stick back to the left. "But there still has to be a Russian carrier task force out there somewhere, so stay sharp." He breathed out. "Give me a read on the distance to the Scrapheap on our preset course."

"Eighteen hundred nautical miles, give or take a few," Hollenbeck reported.

Darrow glanced at their fuel state. Between those Su-33s prowling around off to their north and the chance of bumping into the Russian carrier the fighters belonged to, his XF-111s were going to have to stay low all the way to southern Romania. And terrain-following flight burned a lot more fuel than flying higher. His mouth tightened as he ran through the calculations. Thanks to the auxiliary fuel tanks fitted by Sky Masters, it was doable—but just barely. They wouldn't exactly be arriving at the Scrapheap flying on fumes, but it would be a lot more nip and tuck than he had originally planned. Still, after a refueling stop in Romania, the final leg to Poland should be relatively easy.

"*Caution, new Echo-band search radar at eleven*

o'clock, one hundred ten miles," the computer said, breaking into his thoughts.

"Identify radar," Hollenbeck ordered.

"*Fregat MAE-5 ship-based system,*" the computer replied. "*Signal characteristics match radar for Russian aircraft carrier* Admiral Kuznetsov."

"Can it spot us?" Darrow asked, feeling his pulse speeding up again.

"Negative," Hollenbeck said, studying his displays. "Max range for that system against a target our size at altitude is about one hundred forty miles, but we're so far down in the waves they won't even see a flicker on their scopes."

They flew on in silence for another fifteen minutes or so. The radar emissions from *Admiral Kuznetsov* faded in the distance. Occasional chirps in their headsets marked civilian air traffic control and maritime surface-scanning radars sweeping all around them. Hollenbeck strained to look at something ahead. "I think we have surface traffic ahead," he said. "Big sucker."

"I'll go around it to the north," Darrow said. "Five miles should be enough to avoid them getting an eyeball on us."

But as they deviated, it was obvious that the surface traffic was getting busier. "More ship traffic," Hollenbeck said. "I'm going to have to use the radar to snake around them."

"Do it," Darrow said. "If we need to fly nearer somebody, pick the smallest ones."

"Rog." Hollenbeck activated the AN/APG-81 digital radar and set it for surface-scanning mode . . .

. . . and the display came alive with targets, easily two dozen ships of varying size within three minutes' flight time! "Crap," Hollenbeck exclaimed. "This is one busy pond!"

"The Med has some of the busiest shipping routes on the planet, old boy," Darrow said, with a wry grin.

"Some of those bastards are huge," Hollenbeck said. "Come twenty degrees right, large surface traffic at twelve o'clock, ten miles. Looks bigger than an aircraft carrier!"

"Aircraft carriers are some of the *smallest* large surface vessels on these waters," Darrow said as he made the heading correction. "Even a typical cruise ship is bigger than a carrier."

"Ten more right, and we should be clear," Hollenbeck said. Darrow made the correction. "There must be some common traffic route along here running from Algeria to Spain or southern France."

"Ah, I love traveling to Majorca on vacation," Darrow said. "Ever been there?"

"Is that anywhere near Disney World?" Hollenbeck asked. "Because that's where I usually take the kids for . . . *holy shit! Climb!*" Darrow didn't hesitate, but hit the DTF disconnect paddle switch and pulled the bomber skyward. A huge white shape, studded with bright lights, appeared just ahead and barely below them out of the darkness, growing even bigger as they hurtled toward it. It was an enormous ship, at least ten stories high and more than a thousand feet long.

"What the *hell*—" Darrow growled. They streaked just over the ship's massive superstructure at high speed. After a second or two he released the paddle switch and allowed the flight control computer to put them back on course and altitude.

"Right at the edge of the radar scan, close in, we turned right into it . . . I never saw it on radar," Hollenbeck said, his voice still a little shaky even minutes later. "I think we just scared the crap out of a bunch of tourists on a cruise ship."

"Not to mention ourselves," Darrow said, taking a few deep breaths to get his racing pulse back under control. "Time to get our heads back in the game. Plenty of time to talk about vacations later."

ADMIRAL KUZNETSOV, IN THE WESTERN MEDITERRANEAN
That same time

Inside the dimly lit CIC, a phone beeped. Captain Leonid Yakunin snatched it. "Yes?" He listened intently for a few moments, frowning. "I see. And the location of this ship? Very well. Keep me informed." He hung up.

Rear Admiral Varennikov raised an eyebrow. "Well, Leonid?"

"We picked up another signal reporting unidentified aircraft," the naval intelligence officer told him. "The Norwegian captain of the Royal Caribbean cruise liner *Independence of the Seas* is screaming his head off at the Spanish Navy about being overflown at masthead height. He claims several large, twin-engine military aircraft just buzzed his ship at high speed. They came from the west and vanished to the east."

"Where?" Varennikov demanded. Yakunin pointed to a point on the map plot, about three hundred kilometers due east of Gibraltar.

"Our Su-33s missed them," Varennikov muttered.

"I'm afraid so," Yakunin agreed. "And so did our own radar."

The Russian carrier group commander scowled, staring down at the map. "Even if we turn our fighters around now, we can't catch them. Whoever and whatever they are."

"We could launch more Su-33s," Yakunin pointed out.

"No, Leonid," Varennikov said heavily. "The geometry's not right for a successful intercept. To have any chance at overtaking those mystery American planes, our fighters would have to fly all out, at full power. And even then they would run out of fuel before they caught up."

"Then what do we do, sir?" Yakunin asked.

"We make a full and immediate report to Moscow," the admiral said. He shook his head. "Perhaps they have other intelligence that will let them figure out what the Americans are up to. Or maybe our diplomats can somehow pry the information loose from Washington."

VYSHHOROD, UKRAINE
The next morning

The small suburb of Vyshhorod occupied the western bank of the Dnieper River just seven kilome-

ters north of Kiev. The river here was blocked by
the Kiev Hydroelectric Station, a nearly three-
hundred-meter-long dam. Atop the dam, a two-lane
road, Naberezhna Street, crossed the river. Ordinarily, this bridge was used only by locals or by a
few tourists heading north to see the pinewoods and
swamps of the Mizhrichynski Regional Park.

Now the bridge was full of Russian military
traffic—all of it heading west at a slow but steady
speed. Dozens of eight-wheeled BTR-80 armored
personnel carriers were interspersed with BMP-3
infantry fighting vehicles, 2S19 Msta-S 152mm self-
propelled howitzers, and huge KamAZ transporters
loaded with T-90 and T-72 tanks.

Next to the narrow, vehicle-packed bridge, Russian combat engineers were already hard at work,
widening the crossing by building two new pon-
toon bridges and bulldozing new roads down to the
water's edge. Two batteries of 9K22 Tunguska armored antiaircraft vehicles lined the riverbanks—
offering short-range protection against enemy
air or cruise missile attack with their two 30mm
cannons and eight 9M311-M1 surface-to-air missiles. Longer-ranged S-300 SAM battalions were
deployed farther back in eastern Ukraine, await-
ing orders to leap forward to extend the advancing
army's air defenses.

Specks orbited high overhead in the bright blue,
almost cloudless sky. The Russian Air Force's MiG-
29, Su-27, and Su-35 fighters were keeping their own
watch over the kilometers-long military columns
snaking slowly westward.

There were bigger bridges and wider roads to the

south, but they all fed into the crowded city streets of Kiev itself. Thousands of troops would have been needed to secure those urban routes against the possibility of ambush by Ukrainian terrorists or Polish commandos. Instead, Lieutenant General Mikhail Polivanov, the new commander of the 20th Guards Army, had opted to bypass the Ukrainian capital. Threading his army through the narrow Vyshhorod gap would take more time, but it also allowed him to conserve more of his combat power for the coming war with Poland.

Three miles northeast of the hydroelectric dam and Vyshhorod Bridge, a small wooded headland jutted out into the Kiev Reservoir. Two men wearing camouflage ghillie suits lay prone among the ferns and fallen trees lining the water's edge.

"By my count, that's at least four motor-rifle and tank brigades on the move," Captain Ian Schofield murmured to the noncom next to him. The commander of the Iron Wolf Squadron's deep-penetration recon teams focused his binoculars on the bridge approaches to the east. Rows of armored vehicles and guns were lined up there, barely visible through the haze and diesel exhaust. "With a hell of a lot more on the way."

"So we report in?" Sergeant Davis asked, checking the display on a handheld satellite phone. "We've got a good low-Earth-orbit satellite window for the next five minutes. And another one ten minutes after that."

The Canadian nodded. Mentally, he ran through the prearranged code words he'd set up with Wayne

Macomber before infiltrating into the Russian-occupied zone. He and the Iron Wolf Squadron ground component leader had created a whole list of easily memorized words they could use to exchange vital information disguised as otherwise innocuous-seeming messages. VANYA, for example, stood for Vyshhorod. "Text *DYADYA VANYA POSYL-AYE LYUBOV ANASTASIYI.* UNCLE VANYA SENDS LOVE TO ANASTASIA."

"Yes, sir," Davis said, quickly punching keys on the phone. "Text sent," he reported. "And received." Letters streamed across the phone's small display. "Reply coming in: *BABUSYA KATERNYA KHOTIV NOVYY SYNYE PAL'TO.*"

"Grandma Katherine would like a new blue coat," Schofield translated. He whistled softly. "Well, Sergeant, that's it. You may consider yourself at war. Try not to let it unnerve you, eh?"

Davis, a grizzled veteran of at least a dozen covert operations, both while serving the U.S. Special Forces and working for Scion, snorted. "Hell, Captain. I'm always at war. It's peacetime I find scary."

Schofield grinned. "Good point." He jerked his head away from the shoreline. "We need to round up the rest of the team. Major Macomber wants us well east of here by nightfall."

"To do what, exactly?" Davis asked, turning off the satellite phone. He slid it into one of the concealed pockets of his camouflage suit.

"Our orders are to secure a landing zone," Schofield said calmly. "The Iron Wolves are going to come calling on a few of our Russian friends tonight."

CHAPTER 10

*It's fine to celebrate success,
but it is more important to
heed the lessons of failure.*

— BILL GATES,
AMERICAN BUSINESSMAN
AND PHILANTHROPIST

**OUTSIDE KONOTOP AIRFIELD,
RUSSIAN-OCCUPIED UKRAINE**
That night

The Cybernetic Infantry Device piloted by Patrick McLanahan lay prone in a shallow drainage ditch a few hundred meters outside the perimeter of Konotop Airfield. Like pondering a complex problem and imagining possibilities, images and data flashed through his consciousness as his passive and narrow-beam active sensors scanned the Russian-occupied base. The enormous amount of work the

Russians had done to improve their defenses since the last reported "terrorist" raid was clear.

Minefields densely sown with antipersonnel and antivehicle mines paralleled the chain-link perimeter fence. Remotely run, IR-capable cameras mounted on the fence swiveled back and forth, hunting for signs of intruders trying to breach the minefields. Low background tones at different pitches marked the multiple radar emissions picked up by the CID. There were Big Bird radars from the long-range S-300 SAM batteries deployed around the airfield's approaches. Patrick could also "hear" the 3D F-band pulsed Doppler target acquisition radars used by the shorter-ranged Tor SAM units parked around the runway itself. Not only was the Tor system, known to NATO as the SA-15 "Gauntlet," highly effective against aircraft and helicopters, it could also achieve decent kill percentages against precision-guided munitions, including laser-guided bombs.

Thick three-sided earthen revetments now surrounded rows of Kevlar aircraft shelters, offering protection against direct fire from antitank weapons like the Carl Gustav recoilless rifle used in the earlier "terrorist" attack. Other berms shielded pits dug for 122mm mortars and howitzers. Earth-and-log bunkers sited around the perimeter offered hard cover for machine-gun, RPG, and antitank missile teams. Four-wheeled BRDM-2 armored scout cars made periodic patrol sweeps through the surrounding farm fields, woodlots, small villages, and built-up areas.

All in all, Patrick thought, Konotop's base commander had done a superb job of setting up defenses that would stop a conventional ground or air attack cold. He smiled crookedly. That Russian general and his subordinates were about to learn a very expensive lesson.

"CID Two, this is One," he said over his radio. "Give me a status check."

The robot's computer simultaneously encrypted and compressed his signal before transmitting it as a several-millisecond-long burst. Coordinating this mission required secure tactical communication. The combination of encryption, compression, and frequency hopping should make it almost impossible for any Russian monitoring stations to intercept his transmissions, let alone understand them.

"CID One, this is Two," Patrick heard Captain Nadia Rozek reply. "I am in position six hundred meters north of you and ready to proceed on your order."

The same microburst transmission included biometric data showing the Polish Special Forces captain's heart rate was slightly elevated, but all her other vital signs were pegged solidly in the normal spectrum. He shook his head admiringly. That young woman was one cool customer. Sure she'd had a lot of intensive combat training, both inside and outside the CIDs, but very few people could manage to stay so calm and collected this close to real action.

Wayne Macomber wasn't very happy about giving up his ringside seat to Captain Rozek, but President Wilk had insisted that a Polish officer be included at the sharp end in this first Iron Wolf mission. "If you are willing to risk your lives for Poland and its people, then you must also allow some of us to share the risks *with* you," the Polish president had told them firmly.

Privately, Patrick wished Piotr Wilk hadn't been so insistent. He knew how Brad felt about Nadia Rozek. He also knew, only too well, that CIDs were not invulnerable—not up against the kind of firepower assembled at the Russian air base. If she were killed or badly wounded in this raid, his son might never forgive him. For that matter, he wasn't too sure that he would be able to forgive himself. Depressing memories of his wife's horrific death at the hands of Libyan terrorists many years ago crowded into his mind.

Impatiently, he shook his head. Get on with it, Muck, he told himself. Stay focused. Hell, maybe Whack Macomber was right and he was getting too old for this shit. "Coyotes One and Two, say your status," he radioed.

"We're holding at Point Charlie, just outside predicted Big Bird detection range," Brad replied. "All flight and navigation systems are go. JDAM GEM-III GPS receivers are initialized. Ready to move in and data-link on your order."

Inside the CID's pilot compartment, Patrick nodded, seeing their estimated position displayed on a map put up by his computer. The two MQ-55 Coyotes, remotely piloted by Brad and Mark Darrow back at Powidz, were orbiting low about thirty miles away. Even with their stealth characteristics and special radar-absorbent paint, that was as close as they dared come . . . for now. But once he ordered them in, the two drones could be overhead in three minutes or so—and within striking range a lot quicker.

Swiftly, he made contact with the rest of the Iron Wolf Squadron strike force, making sure they were ready, too. The three-man CID rearmament and recharge unit, with their speedy little Mercedes Wolf 4x4, was securely hidden in a belt of forest about ten miles outside Konotop. Not far away, Captain Schofield's deep-penetration recon team guarded the patch of open ground marked out as their extraction point. And the squadron's XV-40 Sparrowhawk tilt-rotor aircraft and its MH-47 Chinook helicopter were standing by at interim fields in western Ukraine, ready to come and get them if things went well—or to rescue any survivors if the mission cratered.

Satisfied, Patrick focused again on the data flowing into his brain from his sensors. Two BRDMs were driving out of the base's vehicle park. Radio chatter picked up by his CID indicated they were starting a scheduled patrol of the inner perimeter. The fingers of his left hand twitched slightly as if typing revised targeting priorities into the robot's attack software—no need to type, of course: he thought about where the data needed to go and they went there—and then sending the altered list to CID Two.

"Targets received," Nadia confirmed, still sounding as cool as if she were only out on another training maneuver.

"Commence blackout in ten seconds," Patrick ordered. His right hand flexed, bringing the war machine's netrusion capabilities online. The CID's active radars could be reconfigured to transmit malicious code to enemy digital electronic systems—radars, targeting computers, and communications networks—creating false images or even commanding them to shut down. Since netrusion had been used several times before against the Russians, they were likely to have developed some countermeasures that would ferret out the inserted codes and regain control over any affected electronics and computer systems. But doing that would take time . . . and time was what the Iron Wolf Squadron needed most right now. "Five . . . four . . . three . . . two . . . one . . . Go!"

His CID jumped to its feet, already swiveling from side to side as it streamed a sequence of new commands into a preplanned series of Russian radars, sensors, and computer systems. Off to the north, CID Two, piloted by Nadia Rozek, moved out into the open, taking down its own list of netrusion targets.

Along the perimeter fence, the remotely controlled IR cameras suddenly froze. Everywhere across the base, phones went dead as the local telecommunications network went down. The high-powered radio transmitter used to communicate directly with the Russian high command went off the air in midsignal, a victim of the linked computer it used to encrypt and decrypt secure messages. Suddenly dozens of panicked-sounding Russian voices crackled across the airwaves—drowning each other out in a babbling, shouting blur of static and noise. With so many separate tactical radio sets in use, there was no way a netrusion attack could knock them all out. But the chaos and confusion caused among the base's defenders by the unexpected loss of their other computer and electronic systems was the next best thing.

And then Patrick heard what he'd been waiting for. The constant, warbling hum of multiple Russian SAM radars abruptly faded to silence. "Coyotes, this is CID One," he said. "Their eyes are blinded for now! Come in fast and link up with me."

"Understood, One," Brad said. "On the way."

"CID Two, let's go!" Patrick radioed, already sprinting at high speed toward the perimeter fence.

Riding snugly in the cockpit of CID Two, Nadia Rozek leaped high into the air—soaring over the Russian minefield in one long bound. Her Iron Wolf robot crashed straight through the perimeter fence without slowing. Moving at more than eighty kilometers an hour, she detached a 25mm autocannon from her right weapons pack and opened fire on the closest Russian bunkers. Hammered by multiple armor-piercing rounds, the bunkers were smashed in seconds. Jagged shards of wood and bullet-shredded sandbags cartwheeled away into the darkness.

Still running forward onto the concrete runway, she fired again and again, systematically knocking out every Russian weapons emplacement within range. Return fire whipcracked past her war machine's armored head. A BRDM scout car wheeled toward her. Muzzle flashes erupted from its conical turret. The gunner manning its 14.5mm heavy machine gun was trying desperately to bring his

weapon to bear, but she was too fast, too agile—
effortlessly dodging away from the stream of tracer
rounds chasing after her. Another quick burst from
her autocannon ripped the BRDM open from front
to back. It skidded off to the side and flipped over,
already starting to burn.

Nadia laughed aloud, suddenly intoxicated by the
power the CID gave her. This was beyond anything
she had experienced in training. For an instant, she
was tempted to hurl herself headlong straight into
the midst of the nearest clump of panicked defenders. Her pulse started to spike as adrenaline flooded
her system.

"Keep it under control, Two," she heard the
other CID pilot snap. "Stay focused and stick to
the plan!"

Startled, Nadia shook her head, pushing back
against the wave of mad exhilaration that had
threatened to swamp her rational mind. "Will
comply, CID One," she radioed. She breathed out
slowly, feeling her heart rate slowing in time with
her breathing. Calmer now, she noticed that the robot's attack computer was highlighting new targets
in her field of view—large, gray-painted metal tanks
full of aviation fuel. She moved right to get a better
shot while simultaneously reloading her autocannon with incendiary rounds.

Another series of short bursts punctured the
tanks and set off thousands of gallons of fuel. Huge
sheets of flame roared high into the air, bright
enough to turn night into day.

Backlit now by the fires burning all along the

flight line, Nadia Rozek's Iron Wolf robot loped deeper into the Russian air base, hunting new prey.

Four hundred yards south, Patrick swiveled his CID's torso. More targets appeared, a dispersed group of four Tor-M1 surface-to-air missile launch vehicles and their mobile command post. With one robotic hand, he slung the 40mm grenade launcher he'd been using to blow holes in the terminal buildings the Russians were using as barracks for their garrison, pilots, and ground crews. With the other hand, he uncoupled his electromagnetic rail gun and powered it up.

CCRRRAACK!

He fired five times, pausing only briefly to center the rail gun on a new target. Brief, blinding flashes of superheated plasma from the rail gun were eclipsed by larger and even brighter explosions as small dense projectiles moving at Mach 5 tore the Russian missile launchers and their command vehicle apart.

Movement alert, the CID's computer warned. *Two enemy aircraft taxiing for takeoff.*

Patrick swung back to the left, accelerating to get clear of the thick columns of smoke boiling away from burning vehicles and buildings. Even his superb thermal sensors were being degraded by all the heat billowing off wreckage strewn across the airfield.

He bounded over an overturned BRDM and came down right in the middle of a group of stunned Russian soldiers. Mouths and eyes widened in horror as they took in the huge, lethal machine suddenly in their midst. One of them shook off his fear fast enough to bring his AK-74 up and start shooting. Bullets smacked into the CID's torso and ricocheted away.

Growling, Patrick spun around—blurring into motion while seizing panicked, screaming enemy soldiers with his open robotic hand. One after another, he tossed them toward the nearest building. Their screams ended in dull, wet thuds as they slammed into metal and concrete walls and slid dead to the ground.

Su-27s on takeoff, the computer reported.

He swung back to the right, following the cues provided by his CID's navigation system. Suddenly he came out of the smoke and haze and into clearer air.

A couple of hundred yards away, two twin-tailed gray-, white-, and black-camouflaged Russian fighters were rolling down the runway—picking up speed fast as their pilots went to afterburner to get into the air as quickly as possible. The two Su-27s must have been on ready alert, prepped to take off at the first sign of any attack. Those were brave airmen, Patrick thought with a brief touch of sadness, but foolish. Still, he couldn't blame them for trying. It was the duty of any pilot to get his plane off the ground under enemy fire.

And it was his job to stop them.

He swung his rail gun toward the lead Su-27 as it lifted off the runway.

CCRRAACK!

The tungsten-steel alloy slug ripped through the Russian fighter's fuselage and blew out the other end in a spray of burning metal and wiring. Knocked out of control, the Su-27 rolled off to the right, slammed back onto the runway, and blew up in a massive orange fireball. The second fighter, moving too fast to steer and too slow to take off, raced straight into the flaming, tangled remains of the first Su-27. Its undercarriage ripped away with an enormous screech and it slid on down the runway in a dazzling cloud of pinwheeling sparks and burning fuel. Suddenly it exploded. Twisted bits of debris pattered down across the airfield.

Two green dots pulsed at the edge of Patrick's vision.

"CID One, this is Coyote One and Two. Good data links established," he heard Brad radio. "We're inbound at four hundred and fifty knots. Altitude one thousand. Range twelve miles. Ready for your targets."

Patrick could hear a low background hum building in his ears. *Warning. Big Bird radars reenergizing*, the computer reported. He nodded. The Russian SAM crews must have finally managed to flush the malicious code he and Captain Rozek had loaded into their systems. He turned and ran toward the rows of earthen revetments holding the remaining Russian aircraft based at Konotop. At the same time, he keyed in and sent a series of GPS coordinates via data link to the incoming MQ-55 drones.

"Target sets received, CID One," Brad told him. "And downloaded into our weapons."

"Then take 'em out, Coyotes," Patrick ordered.

* * *

Remote piloting was a damned odd experience, Brad thought. Most of him felt as though he were flying inside Coyote One—streaking at high speed toward the burning Russian air base. But at the same time, he also knew he was actually seated in a darkened control station more than six hundred miles to the west, watching screens that showed views and data gathered from the cameras and limited sensors mounted on the MQ-55 drone.

"Coyote One to Two," he said. "Execute toss attack."

"Two copies," Mark Darrow replied from the station next door. "Attacking now."

Brad double-checked the attack computer settings as he closed in to the target. Through his headset, he heard the bomb doors whine open as directed by the computer. He saw the flight-director bars suddenly skitter to the left and upward and he held his breath as the MQ-55 banked hard left and roared skyward at a steep angle, climbing fast through five thousand feet.

He saw three "GBU32" indications on his computer screen flash, then blink, then extinguish in rapid succession. One after another, three one-thousand-pound GBU-32 JDAMs, Joint Direct Attack Munitions, released, fell out of the bay, and flew onward, arcing up through the sky. The toss maneuver gave the bombs more range from low altitude than a conventional level bomb run, and the turn allowed the Coyote to escape while the bombs were still in the air. As the bombs hurtled through the air, receivers aboard each bomb were already picking up position data from the GPS satellite constellations high above in Earth orbit.

Inside each JDAM, a Honeywell HG1700 Ring Laser Gyro inertial unit constantly measured velocity, position, and acceleration, feeding this data through a microprocessor in its guidance and control unit. Together with the GPS signals it picked up, the GCU gave the bomb a continuous and highly accurate fix on its current position. Control surfaces in its tail flexed and swiveled, making the tiny adjustments necessary to "fine-tune" the bomb's trajectory as it flew—screaming down from the top of its "toss" to strike within two meters of its programmed coordinates.

Brad's Coyote rolled away, closed its bay doors, and dove back to low altitude. In the screens, he could see the light and dark patchwork of the fields and small towns surrounding the city of Konotop and its airfield rising up to meet him. He leveled off at just over five hundred feet, high enough to clear any buildings and low enough to be more difficult to detect on radar.

"JDAMs away," he heard Darrow say. "Returning to base."

Brad frowned. That was the plan. Once their bombs were gone, the Coyotes were useless and defenseless—dependent for survival entirely on their limited stealth capabilities. By any measure of common sense, he should follow Mark and slide out of the Konotop area while the getting was good. But he couldn't shake the knowledge that Nadia was still in combat and in danger there below him. No matter what the plan said, it felt wrong to fly off to safety, leaving her behind.

Six huge explosions lit the sky, each set at a different point in a complete circle around the airfield. As the biggest flashes faded, he could see small bursts of orange and white fire—secondary detonations as missile propellant and warheads cooked off.

"Those Big Bird radars are down!" his father said. "Good hits on all JDAMs. Nice work, Coyotes. Many thanks."

"Wolf Ferry One taking off," the pilot of the XV-40 Sparrowhawk tilt-rotor transport reported from its hidden position in western Ukraine. "ETA to extraction point is roughly thirty minutes."

"Ferry Two also in the air," said another voice, this one belonging to the pilot flying the Iron Wolf Squadron's MH-47 helicopter. Since the huge Chinook was much slower than the XV-40, it had been concealed even closer to the Dnieper River.

Still undecided, Brad tweaked his joystick slightly to the right, starting a gentle turn that would keep him close to Konotop for just a few more minutes.

Piloting CID Two, Nadia Rozek ran straight up the sloping side of one of the aircraft revetments. Hard-packed dirt and netting tore away beneath the weight of her armored feet, but she was moving so fast that it didn't matter. At the top of the revetment, she jumped again, bounding high over the Kevlar tent sheltering a Russian plane. She came down hard on the other side, right in the middle of a taxiway. She swung around, seeing the long,

pointed nose of a Su-24M fighter-bomber poking
out of the shelter.

She fired a short burst from her autocannon into
the Su-24 at point-blank range. Pieces spiraled away
as the shells hit home, gutting its avionics and controls. The autocannon whirred and fell silent. *Ammunition expended*, her computer reported.

Nadia snapped it back into place in her weapons
pack and drew her rail gun. It whined shrilly, powering up.

Something big thudded down to her left, only
meters away. Startled, she swung toward it—raising
her weapon. And lowered it, just as fast. It was CID
One, piloted by the nameless stranger who commanded this mission. Of all the peculiar experiences
she'd had since joining the Iron Wolf Squadron, realizing that one of their only two war robots was
manned by someone no one ever saw was surely one
of the oddest.

"Easy there, Captain," the other pilot said, somehow sounding amused even through an encrypted
and compressed radio transmission. "You take the
aircraft shelters on the right. I'll go left. Make your
shots count. We're both running low on ammo and
power."

"Understood, One," Nadia said stiffly, aware
that her face was reddening with embarrassment.
She turned right and loped down the row of parked
Russian aircraft, destroying them with single shots
from her rail gun. Behind her, she could hear the
other CID doing the same thing. Caught on the
ground inside their shelters, Su-24 fighter-bombers,
Su-25 ground-attack planes, and MiG-29 and Su-27

fighters all went up in flames or were torn apart by high-velocity impacts.

OVER KURSK, IN WESTERN RUSSIA
That same time

The two Russian Su-35 single-seat fighters were flying east at ten thousand meters, heading for the barn at Voronezh Malshevo airfield after finishing another routine patrol over eastern Ukraine. The lead pilot, Major Vladimir Cherkashin, yawned under his oxygen mask and then fought down the urge to go on yawning. These night flights were deadly dull. Pilots assigned to provide air cover over the armies advancing on Poland during the day at least got to see the seemingly endless columns of tanks, self-propelled guns, and infantry fighting vehicles on the move. At night, there was nothing to see but the occasional pattern of lights from some drab little Ukrainian farm village and the vast sea of stars blinking overhead. And in the absence of any opposition from the Poles or the Ukrainians, there was nothing to do.

"*Drobovik* Lead, this is Voronezh Control. Stand by for new orders," a tense voice crackled through his headphones.

"Control, this is Shotgun Lead. Standing by," Cherkashin said, jolted to full awareness. "Did you hear that, Oleg?" he asked his wingman, flying about two kilometers off his right wing.

"*Da*, Major," the other pilot, Captain Oleg

Bessonov, replied. "It's nice to know that we're not the only ones awake this late."

"Shotgun Lead, Voronezh Control," a new voice said urgently. To his surprise, Cherkashin recognized it as the voice of Major General Kornilov, commander of the 7000th Air Base at Malshevo. His eyebrows rose. Whatever new orders were coming were *not* routine. "Proceed immediately to Konotop. Repeat, *immediately*. Exercise caution! We've just lost all radio and telephone communication with the airfield there, including the S-300 battalion. Orbit over the airfield at five thousand meters and await target vectors. Say state and estimated time en route."

Shit, Cherkashin thought, that didn't sound good. Five thousand meters put them high enough to protect them from shoulder-fired antiaircraft missiles. Was this another terrorist attack? Or something much bigger? "Understood, Control, stand by," he said, quickly bringing up a digital map on his left multifunction display. His two Su-35s were about two hundred kilometers due east of Konotop. Another key press switched the MFD back to a view of his fighter's systems and fuel state. They still had plenty of gas. "ETE less than eight minutes."

"Acknowledged," Kornilov said. "The airspace is clear of all friendly aircraft. If you detect hostiles, you are cleared to engage without further orders. Repeat: weapons hot. Acknowledge."

"Yes, sir, understood, weapons hot," Cherkashin acknowledged. His jaw tightened. Letting them off the command and control leash like this meant the brass was definitely spooked. He keyed his mike, signaling Bessonov. "Shotgun Two, this is Lead. Follow me!"

Cherkashin tugged his stick hard left, yanking the Su-35 into a tight, high-G turn back to the west. At the same time, he shoved his throttle forward, feeding more power to the fighter's big Saturn 117S turbofans. As he rolled out of the turn on a course toward Konotop, the aircraft accelerated smoothly. A quick finger press on his stick powered up his Irbis-E multimode electronically scanned array radar. Whatever the hell was going on up ahead, he and Bessonov were not going to be flying in blind.

KONOTOP AIRFIELD
That same time

Patrick reached the end of the row of parked aircraft and bounded back over the revetment. Between them, he and Nadia Rozek had just wrecked more than twenty Russian fighter and attack planes. Everywhere he looked, there were ruined, burning buildings, trucks, and armored cars . . . and dead soldiers. Lots of dead Russian soldiers and airmen. He winced. There were probably a few terrified survivors hiding in the debris, but he was willing to bet that none of them had ever gotten a real look at the two robots who had just smashed Konotop Airfield. They'd killed any Russian who'd come close enough to see them clearly.

Still moving, he checked his ammunition and

power status. He was out of ammunition for his autocannon and down to just a few shots with the 40mm grenade launcher. Even his electromagnetic rail gun was on its last clip, with just two shots remaining. His CID was down to about 40 percent power, more than enough to make it back to the Iron Wolf recharge and rearmament team, but not enough for another prolonged engagement. *Query CID Two status*, he thought.

The information relayed from the other robot's automated systems appeared almost instantly in his consciousness, as if he was reading the information in his mind's eye. He frowned. The Polish Special Forces captain's machine was in much the same state, although her rail gun was completely empty. She did have a couple of mini-Stinger antiaircraft missiles left in one weapons pack, but not much else that would be of real use in ground combat.

He nodded. They'd done what they came to do. Now it was time to break off, before the Russians were able to react. "CID Two, this is One," he signaled. "Rally and recover as planned. Repeat, rally and recover."

"Acknowledged," Nadia replied.

The two Iron Wolf CIDs turned and sprinted away through the thickening clouds of oily, black smoke rolling across the ravaged Russian air base. They jumped over the still-active perimeter mine-fields and bounded northeast, moving toward the distant extraction point at a steady forty miles an hour.

Warning, Patrick's computer suddenly pulsed in

his consciousness. *Two Su-35s east of your position. Range sixty miles. Closing at seven hundred knots. Altitude fifteen thousand feet. One X-band radar active.*

"Well, that's torn it," he muttered. Those Russian fighters would have a difficult time locking on to the CIDs, but the other Iron Wolf units—especially the XV-40 tilt-rotor and Chinook helicopter coming in to pick them up—would be sitting ducks. And once their robots ran out of battery and fuel-cell power, he and Captain Rozek would be just as dead.

"CID One, this is Two," Nadia said crisply, seeing the same alert. "Suggest we move east and deploy for antiair ambush. Here." She highlighted a group of several drab, six-story-tall, Stalinist-era apartment buildings on the northern outskirts of Konotop.

Patrick nodded, seeing her suggested ambush site mirrored on his own display. Despite the pressure on her, Captain Rozek was thinking clearly, calmly, and showing superb tactical sense. The buildings there would give them good cover from radars and IRSTs, infrared search and tracking systems, on those incoming Su-35s. "Agreed, CID Two. Let's go!"

Brad listened to their quick, terse transmissions with mounting despair. His MQ-55 Coyote was still orbiting at low altitude just five miles west of the city. Stealth design or not, the powerful Irbis-E phased-array radars on those fast-approaching Russian fighters were sure to pick his defenseless drone up in the next couple of minutes. Should he bolt to the west right now, hoping to draw the Su-35s away from Nadia and his father? No, he thought bitterly, that would accomplish nothing. Once those Su-35 pilots locked him up, they could easily knock him out of the sky with a single long-range missile shot. He wouldn't buy the CIDs and the other Iron Wolf ground teams more than a minute or two. At most. Worse yet, breaking west would only lead the Russians that much closer to the even more visible and vulnerable friendly aircraft heading for the planned extraction point.

He bit his lip. There had to be something else he could try. Somewhere else he could fly. He pushed the joystick forward a bit, sliding down to within a couple of hundred feet of the ground. Flying really low and really slow might buy him a few extra seconds to think.

Quickly, Brad brought up a digitized satellite map of Konotop on his secondary display. The two CIDs were going to try hiding among the "clutter" of the city's buildings. Could he try the same thing? A four-lane avenue cutting northeast right through the heart of Konotop caught his eye. Streetlights, telephone poles, and trees lined both sides of the road, but that street looked as though it might barely be wide enough. Maybe. If there weren't any cars or trucks blocking the stretch he picked. Jesus, he thought, what a crazy stunt. He must be nuts. Then he smiled and shrugged. Since every other option was a literal dead end, what choice did he really have?

Still smiling, Brad tweaked the stick right, rolling the MQ-55 into a gentle turn. The television cameras mounted on the Coyote showed him a flickering picture of the terrain sliding past the small turbojet. There, he thought, spotting a set of train tracks running almost due east. That was his way into the city. He took the Coyote lower still and flew along the tracks at one hundred knots, not much above its rated stall speed.

Houses, streets, trees, and light poles flashed past his virtual cockpit, looming up with startling swiftness out of the darkness. He gritted his teeth, flying on pure nerve and instinct now. One tiny twitch at the wrong time and he'd smack the MQ-55 into the ground or a building, turning it into a mangled heap of debris. And all for nothing.

Ahead, the railroad tracks split, with some lines veering off to sidings, huge brick warehouses, and other large buildings set up for locomotive repair and maintenance. That had to be Konotop's main rail yard. Which meant he was roughly twelve hundred feet from his turn point. Twelve hundred feet at one hundred knots per hour. He peered intently at the screen, counting down silently. Four. Three. Two. One.

Now.

He rolled the Coyote sharply left, powering up to keep the drone from falling right out of the sky. And then back sharply right. A wide avenue, blessedly empty of traffic at this time of night, appeared straight ahead of him.

Gently, gently, Brad thought. He tapped a key and heard the MQ-55's landing gear whir down and lock. Down a bit. Down a bit more. The buildings, trees, and streetlights flashing past the screen grew much bigger in a hurry. His digital altitude readout wound down. Fifty feet. Thirty feet. Ten feet.

He chopped the throttles suddenly and the Coyote touched down, rolling fast right down a street in the heart of Konotop. He braked, bringing the small aircraft to a full stop within fifteen hundred feet. The avenue stretched on ahead for another mile or so.

Now to wait, Brad decided. But not for very long.

OVER UKRAINE
That same time

Thirty kilometers out from Konotop, the images captured by the Su-35's OLS-35 electro-optical search-and-track system came up with appalling clarity on Major Vladimir Cherkashin's large right-hand MFD. Stunned by what he was seeing, he keyed his radio mike. "Voronezh Control, this is Shotgun Lead. Konotop Airfield is *burning*. Repeat, the whole damned base is on fire! I see multiple wrecked aircraft and vehicles."

"Are there any signs of hostile air or ground forces?" the controller asked.

"Negative!" Cherkashin snapped. "I have no unidentified radar or IR contacts yet." He thumbed a switch on his joystick, activating his fighter's automated defensive suite. "Shotgun Two. Go active on all countermeasures *now!*"

"Two," his wingman reported.

"Arm weapons," Cherkashin ordered, pushing another switch on the joystick.

"Two," the other Su-35 pilot said. "Standing by."

"We're going to make a quick, hard pass over the field at two thousand meters," Cherkashin said. "Whoever hit our guys can't be far away. Keep your eyes open and be ready to nail them."

"You don't think Konotop was hit by a long-range missile or artillery barrage?" his wingman asked.

Cherkashin shook his head. "No, Oleg. Look at your screen. There are no craters. None. What kind of missile or artillery attack is that accurate? Konotop must have been attacked by an infantry or armor force using direct-fire heavy weapons. So we find those bastards and then we blow the shit out of them."

"Copy that," the other pilot, Captain Bessonov, said grimly.

The two Su-35s dove lower, racing west toward the ruined airfield at high speed.

KONOTOP
That same time

Patrick stood with the armored back of his CID squarely against the dirty brick wall of the apartment building. Row after row of rusting metal balconies draped with laundry rose high above his head. He aimed the electromagnetic rail gun skyward, waiting.

Twenty yards to his left, Nadia Rozek's Iron

Wolf robot copied him, except that she held a mini-Stinger missile ready to fire. The mini-Stinger missiles employed by the CIDs were not designed to take down fast-moving, high-flying aircraft, but it was all she had, and she was hoping for one more bit of good luck tonight. "Standing by," she said softly. "I will take the lead plane, CID One."

"Understood," Patrick said. "I have the wingman." Based on its last sensor reading from the incoming Russian fighters, his computer was running a continuous prediction program—estimating where and when the enemy aircraft would come back into view. Following the visual cues it presented, he swung the rail gun just a couple of degrees to the right.

And suddenly a huge twin-tailed aircraft howled low overhead, racing toward the airfield. Off to the right, another Su-35 appeared, not far behind the lead plane.

"Tone!" Nadia shouted. She fired the Stinger. It flashed skyward in a bright plume of exhaust. Reacting with lightning speed, she loaded the second Stinger and fired again.

The two missiles streaked after the speeding Russian fighter. But its pilot was already reacting, strewing dozens of decoy flares across the sky as he banked hard, breaking away from the Stingers in a high-G turn. The first missile homed in on one of the flares and exploded too far behind the Su-35 to do any damage. The second Stinger flew straight through the expanding cloud of IR decoys but couldn't reacquire the wildly maneuvering enemy plane. It raced on through the night sky and vanished.

Patrick shifted his rail gun slightly, barely leading the second Su-35. He fired. *CCRRAACK!* Plasma flared and then vanished. A miss. One round remaining. He leaned forward slightly, forcing himself to relax, following the cue set by his targeting computer. The distant image of the Russian aircraft pulsed green. Now! He squeezed the trigger again.

Hit with enormous force at supersonic speed, the Su-35 broke in half. Trailing debris, the two pieces tumbled out of the air and smashed into the ground at nearly a thousand miles an hour.

Patrick felt something akin to hunger, but he knew what it really meant: all rail-gun ammunition was expended.

One down, Patrick thought grimly. But that left one Russian fighter plane still in the fight—and neither CID had any weapons left that could touch it. Far off in the sky, he could see the Su-35 curving back toward their position, clearly intent on avenging its downed comrade. "Any ideas, Captain Rozek?" he asked.

"We might be able to hide for a time among the city buildings," she said. "But my power levels are dropping fast."

"Coyote One to CIDs," Patrick heard Brad radio suddenly. "Don't hide! There's a big avenue a couple of blocks away. Head southeast on it at high speed. And make it obvious! Get that pilot to chase you."

"And then what?" Nadia asked, puzzled.

"Leave that to me," Brad told her quietly.

Major Vladimir Cherkashin rolled out of his tight turn and came wings level—slashing back toward

Konotop at full military power. His defensive systems were fully automatic now, continuously launching flares and chaff to decoy any new enemy heat-seeking or radar-guided missiles. A pillar of fire off to his right marked the funeral pyre of Bessonov's Su-35.

Cherkashin swore viciously. He and Oleg Bessonov had been friends and flying comrades since their days as cadets at the Air Academy. And now the other man had been swatted out of the sky without even seeing who had killed him.

Small flashes lit the jumble of buildings and streets ahead. Grenades exploding? Or mortar rounds? Were the Poles or Ukrainian terrorists who had attacked the airfield fighting their way into Konotop itself?

Cherkashin turned slightly to the left, closing in on those repeated flashes. He glanced down at images shown on his right-hand display. Whether they were out in the open or taking cover in buildings, his IRST system should be able to spot the missile teams who had ambushed him and killed Bessonov. He chopped his throttles, dumping airspeed to give himself more time to find and engage the enemy.

A glimmer of movement far down a wide street caught his eye. The Su-35's cameras had picked up two flickering shapes moving southeast at more than eighty kilometers an hour, but his IRST system couldn't lock on to them. They were just a jumble of seemingly unconnected hot spots racing down the middle of the avenue. He frowned. What the hell were those things?

He rolled right and then left to line up on the street. Still no lock.

Fuck it, Cherkashin thought coldly. Throw enough 30mm shells into the middle of those weird thermal images and he'd hit something. He thumbed the guns switch on his stick and felt the Su-35 judder slightly as the GSh-301 cannon in its starboard wing root fired a short burst.

A fusillade of armor-piercing incendiary rounds lashed the street just behind the fast-moving targets—blowing huge smoking holes in the pavement and ripping parked cars to shreds. Damnation, the Russian pilot thought. He was undershooting—they were much faster than he thought. He lowered his aircraft's nose slightly to gain a bit more speed. The glowing guns pipper on his heads-up display slewed toward the two weird, skittering vehicles.

Any second now.

"Warning! Air target at three o'clock low! Range close!" the Su-35's automated system said urgently. *"Collision aler—"*

Horrified, Cherkashin flicked his eyes right. He just had time to see a strange, batwinged aircraft streaking off the ground—heading straight for his fighter at high speed. He yanked the stick hard left, desperately trying to evade.

And failed.

The MQ-55 Coyote hit the Su-35's port wing squarely and tore it off in a hailstorm of shredded metal and carbon fiber. Razor-edged fragments slashed through both mangled aircraft. Trailing fire and smoke, the Russian fighter and the Iron

Wolf drone fell out of the sky, slammed into a row of homes and shops, and blew up.

EXTRACTION POINT, NORTHEAST OF KONOTOP
A short time later

Two Iron Wolf aircraft—their Sparrowhawk tiltrotor and their MH-47 Chinook helicopter—nearly filled the darkened forest clearing. Several recon troopers in camouflage were busy rolling up the electroluminescent panels they'd used to warn the flight crews away from tree stumps and boggy ground. The little Mercedes-Benz Wolf 4x4 was already safely stowed in the tilt-rotor. The two Cybernetic Infantry Devices, fully rearmed and recharged, stood motionless, ready to walk aboard the two aircraft.

Wearily, Nadia Rozek crawled out through the hatch in the back of CID Two and slowly swung herself down to the ground. She felt drained and shaky, almost as though she had aged twenty years in the past hour.

"Nice work, Captain," a tall, broad-shouldered man in a black flight suit said. She recognized the American CID Operations commander, Major Wayne Macomber. "You guys did a real number on Konotop." He grinned evilly. "A bunch of Russians just learned they picked the wrong people to screw around with."

Nadia nodded somberly. "Perhaps. But most of them are now dead."

"That's the way it usually works," Macomber agreed. He climbed up the CID's leg and paused near the open hatch. "Better them than us is the way I always figure it." He looked down at her. "Anyway, grab some food and shut-eye once you're aboard the Chinook." He slapped the armored side of the war machine. "It's my turn next to take this goddamned bundle of gears and circuits out for a little spin."

She nodded again. The squadron's operational plan called for another rapid-fire attack on a second Russian forward operating airfield—this one five hundred kilometers to the northwest, in Belarus. By striking two widely separated targets in quick succession, they hoped to knock the Russians off balance, and to fool them into believing they were facing a much larger force.

Fighting off another wave of fatigue, Nadia turned toward the waiting helicopter. But then she swung back as a sudden thought struck her. "What about the pilot for CID One, Major?" she asked. "Where is his replacement?"

Whack was staring inside the CID at the gray, gelatinous membrane that made up the system that literally sucked up central-nervous-system signals from the body, processed them, and translated the signals into movement, and at the same time transmitted signals from the CID's several hundred haptic and sensor systems directly into the body's central nervous system.

It always made him feel a little queasy lying on that oozy surface, like swimming in warm mud. He also had to remember to hold his breath for about thirty seconds until the hatch behind him closed, the CID locked on to his central nervous system, matched it to his preprogrammed patterns, activated, and then started its life-support systems. "What about him?" he asked distractedly.

"Who replaces him for this next mission?" Nadia wondered.

"No one," the big American said quietly, lowering his voice. "That Iron Wolf machine is a one-man show."

She frowned. "Surely, that is impossible. When will he eat? Or sleep?"

Macomber sighed. "Captain, I wish I could give you a straight answer for that. Because I have the feeling our armored friend over there only plans to sleep when he's dead." With that, he sketched her a quick salute, steeled himself, and slid inside the CID. The hatch sealed behind him.

Still frowning, Nadia moved past the silent, motionless shape of CID One and climbed into the waiting helicopter. There was a mystery here that troubled her. Even with her limited experience inside these powerful and deadly Cybernetic Infantry Devices, she knew that no ordinary human could pilot one without the chance to rest and recover. Not and stay sane. So what did that say about the mysterious man hidden away inside that other Iron Wolf?

THE WHITE HOUSE, WASHINGTON, D.C.

That same time

President Stacy Anne Barbeau worked very hard to keep her face an expressionless mask as Luke Cohen ushered General Timothy Spelling, the chairman of the Joint Chiefs, Thomas Torrey, the director of the CIA, and Admiral Kevin Caldwell, the director of the National Security Agency, into the Oval Office. Usually she kept a flock of tame reporters hanging around just outside, ready to file flattering little stories about her meetings with foreign dignitaries, film stars, and other celebrities, but the corridor was empty this afternoon. There was *no* way she wanted any pictures or news of this particular meeting appearing in the press.

Still stone-faced, she remained seated, not bothering to get up for the usual round of phony "we're all friends and coworkers here" glad-handing. Cohen showed the three men to a row of straight-backed chairs set out in front of her desk. Once they were seated, he dropped casually onto a comfortable couch positioned off to the side.

"I hope I don't need to tell you *gentlemen* how goddamned tired I am of being blindsided by the Russians," Barbeau said scathingly, without any preamble. She nodded to the secure phone on her desk. "I just had another call from Foreign Minister Titeneva. She is demanding immediate information about these mystery aircraft we're supposedly flying secretly across the Atlantic and Mediterranean. And frankly, I want some straight answers myself!"

Spelling cleared his throat. "Madam President, we've been investigating those Russian charges ever since Moscow first made them public."

"Well?" Barbeau demanded.

"One of our F/A-18F crews flying off the *Bush* did intercept a group of six aircraft, identified as F-111s, refueling from a KC-10 Extender aerial tanker at the time in question," Spelling said.

"An F-111?" Barbeau exclaimed. She knew her Cold War–era aircraft—she was an Air Force brat and loved every minute of her time on air bases all over the world. "That was an old Strategic Air Command and Tactical Air Command bomber from the eighties. I thought they were all mothballed."

"These were very much flyable, ma'am," Spelling said. "They were flying without transponder codes and not on an international flight plan. The Hornet crew reported this contact to the carrier, but their report never went any further up the chain of command."

Barbeau's eyes flashed angrily. "Why the hell not, General? Are you telling me that officers of my Navy are conspiring to withhold information from their lawful superiors?"

"No, Madam President," Spelling said. He looked acutely uncomfortable. "The pilots flying those unidentified F-111s gave the carrier's air operations officer a special code phrase to check. When he ran that through *Bush*'s computer, it confirmed they were part of a DoD-authorized Top Secret, operations and support Special Access Program—one with instructions specifically requiring him to avoid logging or reporting the contact. That's why it took a direct query from Admiral Fowler, the chief of naval operations, to confirm this incident."

"You're talking about this EIGHTBALL-whatever code the Russians picked up?" Luke Cohen asked, sitting up a little straighter on the couch.

The chairman of the Joint Chiefs nodded. "That's right, Mr. Cohen."

"That code is dead after right now," Barbeau snapped. "No one else gets to use it."

"Yes, ma'am."

"And those F-111s were probably planes refurbished by Sky Masters and sent on their way to Poland, right?" Cohen asked.

No one in the Oval Office saw it, but Stacy Anne Barbeau's face turned a sickening shade of pale when she heard the name "Sky Masters"—she had not had favorable encounters with that company or some of their people and products over the years.

Again, Spelling nodded, as Thomas Torrey, the CIA director, said, "That's the most logical conclusion. Sky Masters claims they sold the planes to a number of different customers, but it's fairly clear these other companies were acting as intermediaries for the Polish government. Or they might be shell corporations created by Warsaw itself. We're still digging into that."

"Let's cut to the chase, gentlemen," Barbeau snarled. "What all of this proves is somebody in the Pentagon *is* running a covert operation to help the Poles—against my direct orders! And I want that

insubordinate son of a bitch's head on a platter.
Now! Understand?"

There was a moment of strained, embarrassed silence before General Spelling spoke up. "With all
due respect, Madam President, that is not accurate.
We've run a complete internal cross-check on the
EIGHTBALL HIGH code phrase. And what is
very clear is that *no one*—not a single uniformed officer or civilian in the Defense Department, or anywhere else in the federal government—is cleared for
access to this so-called Top Secret program."

"Which means what, exactly?" Cohen asked.
Barbeau nodded slightly to him, signaling her approval. Everyone knew her chief of staff focused
almost entirely on politics, not on the details of national security policy. That meant he could ask the
kinds of basic-sounding questions she couldn't—at
least not without the risk of revealing weakness or
seeming ignorant to these military men.

The head of the NSA, Admiral Caldwell, fielded
Cohen's question. The admiral's almost painfully
ordinary features concealed a brain of remarkable
power. He'd worked his way up through the National Security Agency's ranks on pure merit and
sheer technical brilliance. "What it means, Mr.
Cohen, is that EIGHTBALL HIGH is a fake—a
phrase entirely without a real-world reference.
There is no EIGHTBALL HIGH program. It's
just a designation deliberately created to conceal the
activities of anyone who can parrot the code in response to questions from U.S. government officials
or members of the military." He shrugged. "Or at

least questions from anyone with access to a secure Defense Department computer system."

Cohen raised an eyebrow. "So how did this phony piece of code get into our computers in the first place?"

"*That* is the sixty-four-thousand-dollar question," Caldwell said grimly. He frowned. "At General Spelling's request, I've put my best analysts from the Information Assurance Directorate to work on the problem. But so far, they've drawn a blank. The EIGHTBALL HIGH code phrase doesn't appear in the system's most recent backups, so we know it wasn't there a week ago. Which means this is a very recent intrusion—one probably intended specifically to cover this secret transfer of aircraft."

"Do you seriously expect me to tell Gennadiy Gryzlov that the Poles have *hacked* our most secure national security computer systems?" Barbeau snapped. "If he doesn't believe me, he'll be sure we're secretly backing Poland. And if he does believe me, that Russian lunatic will know that our so-called cybersecurity is a freaking joke!"

Before Caldwell could respond, Cohen said, "Nope." He shrugged. "We lie to him." He looked around the room. "We tell Gryzlov that we did send a few aircraft to one of our bases in Europe, maybe to Italy or somewhere like that. Don't we still have a NATO air base at Aviano, or somewhere else, like Romania? But that we only did it as a limited precaution in case the war Gryzlov is planning spreads out of control. And we stress that we're definitely *not* taking sides as long as this crisis is confined to Poland."

Barbeau nodded slowly, thinking it through. "That could work, Luke." Her fingers drummed lightly on her desk. "But the Russians will want to know more details—what kinds of aircraft did we send and where are they based, for example? Damn it, I can't just make up something out of whole cloth or Gryzlov will smell a rat as soon as his spooks don't find the planes."

"Then we send some aircraft," Cohen said, smiling slightly. "Maybe some of those fancy new F-35 stealth fighters General Spelling is so proud of. Once they're safely on the ground overseas, we leak the deployment to the press. We just have to make sure anyone who talks to the media stays tight-lipped about just *when* they flew in."

The chairman of the Joint Chiefs shook his head. "Our first squadron of F-35s isn't fully operational, Mr. Cohen. I don't think we could send more than six fighters to Europe at this point." He grimaced. "The F-35 is a very capable aircraft, but one flight is too weak a force to have any real impact."

"Which is perfect for our purpose, General," Barbeau said pointedly. "If you know that, so will Gryzlov and his advisers. They won't feel threatened—and we cover our asses while Admiral Caldwell and his NSA whiz kids figure out just who the *fuck* is screwing around in our secure computer systems."

Spelling started to protest. "Madam President, I still don't believe—"

"Can it, General!" Stacy Anne Barbeau snapped, not bothering to conceal her irritation and contempt. Maybe she couldn't fire the Air Force general now, not with a major international crisis brewing. But she could sure as hell make it crystal clear that he'd better start planning his retirement soon. "I'm giving you a direct order as your commander in chief. You will covertly transfer six F-35s to Aviano or somewhere else, I don't care, as soon as possible. Is that understood?"

Stiffly, the chairman of the Joint Chiefs nodded. His eyes were equally cold. "Yes, Madam President."

A cell phone beeped loudly, breaking the awkward, thoroughly uncomfortable hush that had fallen across the Oval Office.

"Excuse me, ma'am," Admiral Caldwell said. Barbeau and Cohen looked angry enough to chew nails at the interruption, so he added, "Only the most urgent call would ring through. Excuse me." He stood, crossed toward the door away from the president's desk, and took his secure cell phone of his jacket pocket. "Yes? What is it?" What little color he had drained out of his face as he listened intently. "Good Lord, Lydia, are you sure? When was this? Have you passed the intelligence on to the NRO so they can check the images from their most recent satellite pass? Very well, keep on it and keep me posted."

He ended the connection and turned to Barbeau. "That was the head of our National Security Operations Center, Madam President. Our satellites and other SIGINT collection stations report that the Russian-occupied air base at Konotop has just been completely destroyed. From the available evidence, it looks like a massive air- or ground-attack caught the Russians by surprise."

Barbeau stared back at him, caught completely off guard. "Destroyed? But that's impossible! The Russian ultimatum doesn't even expire for another three and a half days!"

"It seems that President Wilk and Poland's armed forces decided not to wait that long," Caldwell said drily. "They have opted to strike the first blow. This war just turned hot."

OVER BELARUS
Several hours later

Secure inside CID Two's pilot compartment, Wayne Macomber had the large Iron Wolf robot lie prone on the deck of the big MH-47 Chinook. It was the only way a manned Cybernetic Infantry Device would fit inside the helicopter's cargo area. He tapped his fingers twice, tying his machine into the other visual, radar, and electronic sensors aboard the Chinook.

They were flying west at low altitude to evade radar detection, practically hugging the dirt. Behind them, the night sky was growing paler, the first sign of the approaching dawn. Far off in the distance, pillars of black smoke and flickering fires marked the site of Baranovichi's 61st Assault Air Base—the Iron Wolf Squadron's second target.

Macomber smiled grimly. With the Russians rattled by the earlier attack on Konotop, the Iron Wolf raiding force hadn't achieved complete surprise. Some elements of the garrison had been on alert, prowling around their outer perimeter on the lookout for trouble. But it really hadn't mattered in the end. Lightly armored scout cars and fixed defenses were no match for the faster, more agile, and better-equipped CIDs. A defense built around main battle tanks like the T-90 or the T-72 might have offered stiffer resistance—but the bulk of the Russian heavy armor was grinding toward Poland as part of their two invasion armies. The Russians had never imagined anyone could hit their forward operating air bases so hard and so soon.

Well, he thought, now they knew differently.

He switched his attention to the cramped interior of the MH-47. Captain Nadia Rozek sat slumped in one of the fold-down seats. She looked deeply asleep, crowded in beside the rest of Ian Schofield's exhausted recon troopers and the second three-man CID resupply team. He frowned, seeing them. It was time for a little after-action chat with the commander of CID One.

Macomber lifted another finger, bringing up a secure radio link to the other Iron Wolf robot. CID One was flying far ahead of him, crammed into the fuselage of the Sparrowhawk tilt-rotor, along with the other half of the ground strike force.

"Go ahead, Major," Patrick McLanahan said.

"Want to tell me why you almost fucked up so badly at Konotop, General?" Macomber asked. He kept his tone conversational.

"Captain Rozek and I blew Konotop to pieces, Whack," Patrick said coolly. "I don't see that as a problem."

Macomber set his jaw. "Cut the crap, General.

You helped write the battle drill for these gadgets, remember? Including all the warnings about the need to maintain minimum ammunition and power levels, right? All that shit about CID pilots remembering the importance of firepower and speed in successfully breaking off an action?"

The other man was silent.

"Which makes me wonder how you let yourself and Rozek expend practically every frickin' round of ammo before bailing out of that base," Macomber went on. "You put this whole operation and this whole outfit at risk. If your kid hadn't had the brains and balls to kamikaze that Su-35, we wouldn't even be having this conversation. We'd probably both be dead."

"We still had targets to hit, Whack," Patrick said stubbornly.

"Hell, General," Macomber said in disgust, "there will *always* be more targets to hit. We're going up against half of the goddamned Russian Army and Air Force, for Christ's sake! Which means we have to fight smart, not brave and stupid. Save the Charge of the Light Brigade shit for some day when nobody else is relying on you, okay?"

There was another long silence.

"Do you hear me, General?" Macomber growled.

Patrick sighed. "I hear you, Major." He forced a laugh. "I guess I got a little too fixated in that first raid."

"Yeah, you did," Macomber agreed. He hesitated slightly and then went on. "Look, I need you to know where I'm coming from, boss. If I think that metal suit you're strapped into is starting to drive you kill-crazy, I'll yank you out of it before you can say Jack Robinson. You hear me?"

"You know that would kill me, Wayne," Patrick said quietly.

"Yeah, I know," Macomber said. His voice rasped. "And I would hate like hell to have to do it. But I can't allow any one man—not even you—to jeopardize this whole squadron and its mission. Too much is riding on this, General. Too many other lives. Too many other people's freedoms. Do you read me?"

"Loud and clear, Major," Patrick said. "You're absolutely right. About the stakes and about the dangers. I'll keep a tight grip on this Iron Wolf I'm riding. I promise. And, Whack?"

"Yeah?"

"Thank you," Patrick said simply.

Whack smiled despite himself. That was Patrick fucking McLanahan, he thought. The guy was a retired three-star general and ex-president of one of the most successful high-tech firms in the world . . . but you could always talk to him like any other grunt. If you had something to say to him you could always do so. Rank or status didn't matter. They rarely saw eye to eye on stuff, especially ground or special ops tactics and procedures, but he had his respect. He was a good guy . . .

. . . living one hell of a nightmarish existence. He, Whack thought, wouldn't trade lives with him for all the silver stars in the Pentagon—or all the sausage in Poland.

THE KREMLIN, MOSCOW
Later that day

During his years as an instructor at the Yuri Gagarin Military Air Academy, Colonel General Valentin
Maksimov had earned a nickname from the cadets.
They had called him "the Old Roman" because
nothing—neither personal triumph nor tragedy—
seemed able to shake his stoic, taciturn demeanor.

Well, thought Gennadiy Gryzlov disdainfully,
his fellow cadets should see their revered former
instructor now. Overnight, the so-called Old
Roman, currently the commander of Russia's air
force, seemed to have collapsed in on himself, becoming almost visibly smaller and older. He sat
hunched over in his seat at the conference table.
Beneath his short-cropped mane of white hair,
Maksimov's once-ruddy, square-jawed face was
now gray and lined.

"Well, Colonel General?" Gryzlov snapped. "Are
your losses as serious as first reported?"

"Mr. President, I am afraid they are . . . worse . . .
than we initially believed," the old man admitted.

Murmurs of shock and dismay raced around the
table. For many of Russia's top-ranking political
and military leaders, this emergency session was
their first real news of the twin disasters at Konotop
and Baranovichi. Officially, according to the state-
controlled media, Poland's treacherous decision to
strike first, before Moscow's ultimatum expired,
had inflicted only minor losses in futile, small-scale

attacks. Confirmation that both Russian forward air bases had actually been completely destroyed was an ugly surprise for men and women who been assured that any real war against the Poles would inevitably result in a swift and easy victory.

Gryzlov quelled the murmuring with an icy look. He turned back to Maksimov. "Worse? How much worse?"

Dry-mouthed, the air-force commander took a deep gulp from a water glass handed him by a worried-looking aide and then, reluctantly, made his report. "Our losses at both air bases total fifty-three aircraft completely destroyed. Plus another handful that we deem damaged but repairable. Of those planes wrecked beyond repair, roughly half were fighters, mostly Su-27s and MiG-29s, while the rest were Su-24 and Su-25 strike aircraft."

Gryzlov stared at him. "You've lost more than fifty planes? And you let most of them get blown to hell on the damned ground?"

"Several of our pilots based at Baranovichi made attempts to sortie," Maksimov said, in feeble protest. "As did both the alert fighters at Konotop."

"And succeeded only in getting themselves shot down while they were taking off!" Gryzlov snarled. "Wonderful, Maksimov. Just grand. Perhaps we should name them posthumous Heroes of the Russian Federation, eh?"

Greatly daring, Foreign Minister Daria Titeneva intervened. "Excuse me, Mr. President, but this news seems absolutely incredible. I thought Poland had fewer than fifty modern combat aircraft? And that most of those planes were air superiority fighters, not bombers?" She shook her head in disbelief. "How was it possible for the Polish Air Force to destroy our bases without even being detected? Or without suffering any losses of their own?"

"These were not primarily air attacks, Daria," Gryzlov said flatly. "They were commando operations of some kind, using advanced weapons of types we did not know the Poles possessed."

"Advanced weapons?" Titeneva asked. "Of what kind, precisely?"

"That is unclear, Madam Foreign Minister," Maksimov said heavily. "Many of our aircraft, armored vehicles, and missile batteries were clearly destroyed by conventional rapid-fire cannons, grenades, and explosives. But many others show massive impact damage, damage that could only be achieved by nonexplosive rounds traveling at enormous speeds."

"What about the data collected by our sensors?"

"In both attacks, all of our radars, communications, and cameras were knocked off-line first," Masksimov told her.

"But surely the survivors can tell you what happened? What they saw?" Titeneva pressed.

"Those who survived saw nothing," the aged colonel general admitted. His face sagged. "Our personnel casualties were severe, with more than a thousand dead or seriously wounded. Only those who sought shelter immediately survived unscathed." He shook his head. "All we do know is that both raids were carried out with ferocity and astounding precision and speed."

Gennadiy scowled, looking at Viktor Kazyanov,

the minister of state security. "So now we know what Warsaw was hiding from us at Drawsko Pomorskie."

Kazyanov nodded gravely. "*Da*, Mr. President. My people are still studying the reports, but there seems to be a clear correlation between what we saw on the satellite photos from that Polish training ground and the new weapons and tactics employed against us last night at Konotop and Baranovichi."

"But do we really know who used these mysterious weapons?" Tarzarov asked quietly.

Gryzlov eyed his chief of staff. "What are you suggesting, Sergei?"

The older man shrugged. "I am not suggesting anything. I simply wonder *whom* we are really fighting now. Poland? Employing strange new devices and weapons that do not appear in any intelligence assessment I have ever seen? Or the United States—either indirectly, using the Poles as surrogates . . . or directly, with its own Special Forces?"

"The American President Barbeau has assured me repeatedly that her country is neutral in our dispute with Poland," Gryzlov said slowly. His jaw tightened. "And she has promised that she is abandoning the aggressive policies of her predecessors, especially those two madmen, Martindale and Phoenix."

"Do you think President Barbeau is lying to us?" Daria Titeneva asked Tarzarov, watching him closely.

Again, the older man shrugged. "Deliberately lying? Perhaps not. But can we be sure that she herself is not being misled or lied to by her own military? Or even by some small secret faction inside the Pentagon?" He turned back to Gryzlov. "Such lies have been told to American presidents in the past—as *we* all know only too well. And to our sorrow."

The Russian president flushed, easily catching Tarzarov's oblique reference to the repeated and unauthorized American air raids that had finally pushed his father over the edge. The massive revenge attack ordered by the older Gryzlov had led directly to his own death in yet another bombing raid led by the same renegade American who had hit Russia earlier. He grimaced. "Patrick McLanahan is *dead*, Sergei! Dead, with even his stinking ashes pissed away into a sewer somewhere!"

"Yes, he is," Tarzarov agreed calmly. "But then we must hope that no other American military commander is ruthless enough and criminal enough to adopt McLanahan's illegal, but highly effective methods." He spread his hands. "Until we know more about what really happened last night, however, it might be wise to slow the advance of our armies toward the Polish frontier. At least temporarily."

"You want me to respond to this sneak attack against our air bases by showing fear? By cowering in a corner?" Gryzlov demanded. He glared at his chief of staff. "Let me be very clear, Sergei. *Extremely* clear. *I* will not show such weakness! *Russia* will not show such weakness! Not while I am the president, you understand?"

Calmly, Tarzarov nodded. "I understand, sir."

Plainly fighting to regain control over his temper,

Gryzlov looked around the table, meeting the troubled eyes of his senior advisers with a challenging stare. "Whether we are fighting the Poles alone or the Poles in combination with some secret ally is immaterial. If anything, now we *know* Poland is too dangerous to be left alone—at least not under its current leaders. Between Warsaw's earlier terrorist attacks and now these sneak raids, no one can doubt they are the real aggressors in this conflict, not us!"

Slowly, tentatively, the others around the conference table nodded.

"Then we go forward, as planned," Gryzlov said. New thoughts were beginning to percolate in his mind.

"But these new enemy commando forces do pose a serious threat to our armies—a threat we must address, Mr. President," General Mikhail Khristenko pointed out.

"You think so?" Gryzlov asked, smiling thinly now. Now that he'd had a little more time to think through the implications of last night's disasters, he was beginning to see a range of alternative plans to retrieve the situation. He regretted more than ever having shown any uncertainty or concern in front of these sycophants.

Surprised, Khristenko stared back at him. "You don't? Even after what happened to our air bases last night?"

"We made a mistake—a mistake the Poles took full advantage of," Gryzlov told him drily. "Basing so many of our aircraft so far forward only allowed our enemies the luxury of planning and carrying out a meticulous and coordinated surprise attack on fixed positions. But they will find trying the same sort of raid against our field armies a much more difficult proposition. No matter how well equipped and trained they may be, no small band of commandos can hope to go head-to-head and win against tens of thousands of alert and mobile troops with heavy armor and artillery."

Khristenko nodded. "True, Mr. President. But they may continue attacking our forward air bases, instead."

Gryzlov shook his head. "The Poles will find no such easy targets for their secret forces."

Colonel General Maksimov raised his haggard face from the tabletop. "What?"

"Effective immediately, I order you to withdraw all our aviation regiments and their ground components to secure bases deep inside Russian territory," Gryzlov said. "The only other way to secure our forward bases would require ringing them with the tanks and troops and artillery we need for our field armies."

Defense Minister Sokolov cleared his throat nervously. "Pulling our air units back to Russia itself will significantly reduce their effectiveness, sir. Many of our aircraft will be operating near the edge of their combat radius. Either they'll need to carry external fuel tanks, greatly reducing their weapons loads, or we'll have to accept the serious risks involved in air-to-air refueling in a battle zone."

"That is so," Gryzlov agreed. "But it doesn't really matter."

"It doesn't, Mr. President?" Sokolov asked uncertainly.

"How far will the effectiveness of our aircraft be reduced by basing them farther back?" Gryzlov asked Maksimov, in turn. "By as much as fifty percent?"

The elderly air-force commander frowned. "Possibly. But I would think less—with good planning and sound tactics."

Russia's young president smiled, more genially this time. "And how many capable aircraft can you commit to this war, even after last night's losses?"

"Perhaps as many as five hundred fighter and strike planes," Maksimov said.

Gryzlov smiled even more broadly. "So . . . the Poles have, at best, fifty modern combat aircraft and we can still oppose them with the equivalent of two hundred and fifty. Tell me, Colonel General, all other factors being equal, who wins an air battle where the odds are five to one?"

For the first time in hours, Maksimov looked a little more alive. He sat up a bit straighter in his chair. "We do, Mr. President."

"Exactly," Gryzlov said. He snorted. "Let the Poles and their hidden allies, if they truly exist, savor this first, fleeting success. If we all do our jobs right, it will be their last."

Maksimov sat up even straighter. His face seemed to be recovering some of its normal tone. "Well said, Gennadiy!"

Gryzlov let that bit of unwanted informality pass. After all, the old man had once been his teacher.

"And in that vein, let me strike back at the Poles," Maksimov went on, even more enthusiastically. "Even harder than they hit us!"

Gryzlov raised an eyebrow. "Oh?"

"Our Su-34 fighter-bomber squadrons can launch a deep-penetration raid on Warsaw itself," Maksimov told him. "We can hit this Polish bastard Wilk and his fellow fascists right where they live and work."

"The Polish Air Force will fight to defend its capital, Valentin," Gryzlov pointed out. "Your bomber force will bring every flyable Polish F-16 and MiG-29 down on its head."

The older man nodded vigorously. "Of course, Gennadiy! And that's when our own Su-35s and Su-27s will pounce! If the Poles really do rise to the bait, we'll wipe their whole effective air force out of the sky in one battle!"

Gryzlov smiled again, as much in admiration of Maksimov's astonishing powers of recuperation—or self-deception—as in approval of his plan. "Put your staff to work on the operational orders for such a strike, Colonel General. Then, once they're ready, bring them to me for my consideration."

Later, after the rest of the generals and cabinet ministers had filed out, Sergei Tarzarov looked across the table. The older man had a skeptical look in his eyes. "Do you really believe that a single bombing raid on Warsaw can accomplish what Maksimov claims it will? Destroy Poland's airpower in one fell swoop?"

Gryzlov shrugged. "It might." He smiled crookedly. "But even if it does not, a serious air strike aimed at the heart of Poland's military and political leadership should be . . . *clarifying.*"

His chief of staff looked puzzled. "I do not pretend to be a trained military strategist, Mr. President, so the illustrative effects of a failure, or even a partial success, escape me."

"This is not a purely military matter," Gryzlov told the other man, savoring the pleasure of being able to lecture Tarzarov—of all people!—on international politics. "A serious air strike on Warsaw may not achieve all of the good colonel general's admittedly grandiose objectives. But one thing is certain, Sergei," he said, with a smug smile. "It will force the Americans to tip their hand. If they *are* secretly backing the Poles with advanced weaponry or commandos, the Americans will have to come out into the open to protect their ally's capital from a devastating attack, and then we can destroy them. But if the Americans do nothing, we destroy Poland while NATO and the Americans watch. That will be the end of their alliance."

OFFICE OF THE PRESIDENT, BELWEDER PALACE, WARSAW
That same time

Polish President Piotr Wilk sat alone in his private office. Conferring with the representatives of the Iron Wolf Squadron and some of his senior military commanders via video links imposed some additional security risk in these days of widespread hack-

ing, but it was still safer than gathering in person.
Now that the battle had been joined, a roomful
of high-ranking military and political leaders was
nothing more than a juicy target for Russian bombs
or cruise missiles.

He looked across the array of five serious faces
displayed on his monitor—the two Americans, Brad
McLanahan and President Kevin Martindale, and
three Poles, two of them major generals, Tadeusz
Stasiak and Milosz Domanski, and the last a colonel in the air force, Paweł Kasperek. Stasiak and
Domanski commanded the two Polish task forces
assembling to meet the oncoming Russian 6th and
20th Guards Armies. Kasperek, the commander
of Poland's 3rd Tactical Squadron, was the young
officer he'd tasked with coordinating the country's
F-16s with the Iron Wolf Squadron's XF-111s and
drones.

"I congratulate you on the success of your first
raids, gentlemen," Wilk said to Brad and Martindale. "The results achieved by your forces surpassed
anything I imagined possible."

"Thank you, Mr. President," Martindale replied.
"I think we batted the Russian bear across the back
of the head rather nicely." He smiled wryly. "Of
course, now we've really pissed him off."

Wilk matched the gray-haired American's
crooked grin with one of his own. "That much
was inevitable. What matters more is how this first
defeat affects Moscow's strategy. I assume it is unlikely to make our friend Gryzlov more cautious."

"Probably not on the ground," Martindale
agreed. "As far as he's concerned, his armies out-

number yours so heavily that the sooner they move into contact, the sooner he wins."

"And in the air?"

"If Gryzlov is dumb enough to keep basing aircraft within our striking range, we'll keep clobbering them on the ground," Brad McLanahan said confidently. "But I don't think he's that dumb. Now that we've given him a bloody nose, he's likely to pull his aviation regiments back out of our reach."

"Which would still leave us heavily outnumbered in the sky," Wilk commented.

Brad nodded. "Yes, sir." Then he shrugged. "But we'll still have significantly degraded Russia's air capability—especially its air-to-ground strike capability, which was our primary objective. For example, pushing those Su-25 Frogfoots back to Russian bases makes them a lot less effective. Their unrefueled combat radius is only three hundred and seventy-five kilometers. If Grzylov pulls them back to safety, they'll have to fly three times that far just to reach the battlefield." He inclined his head toward the two Polish Army officers. "Which will make life a heck of a lot easier for your armor formations."

Wilk nodded. Russia's Su-25 Frogfoots were aging, but still effective, close air support planes. Roughly equivalent to the American A-10 Thunderbolt, they were designed to smash tank forces using 30mm cannons, rockets, missiles, and laser-guided bombs. Reducing the threat of attack from the Su-25s would allow his field commanders to use their Leopard 2, T-72, and Polish-manufactured PT-91 main battle tanks more aggressively.

"Anyway, if the Russians do abandon their forward air bases, the Iron Wolf Squadron is ready to move to Phases Two and Three of our plan," Brad continued. "But obviously we won't initiate any serious action until everybody else is set."

"Excellent," Wilk said.

"There is one further consideration, sir," Colonel Kasperek said, speaking up plainly. "Neither Brad nor I believe Gryzlov or his air commanders will stay passive—even if they do pull their air units back to better-defended bases."

"You think they will launch a retaliatory strike?" Wilk asked. He'd known Paweł Kasperek since the other man had flown MiG-29s under his command as a young lieutenant. Kasperek was a very good pilot, and an even better tactician.

"We do," the colonel said bluntly. "And soon. Perhaps within the next several hours."

"And are your F-16s ready to meet such an attack?"

"Yes, sir," Kasperek said. "We have prepared a number of different plans, depending on what the Russians throw at us." He hesitated, looking somber. "But our losses may be high. Very high, if we are unlucky, or if we have miscalculated."

"That is likely," Wilk agreed quietly. "Look, Paweł, chance and error are always a part of war. You can try to minimize their effects, but you cannot erase them. Not entirely."

"Yes, Mr. President," the younger man said. His expression was still very grave.

Wilk studied him for one more moment. "Listen carefully, Colonel. If you are forced to choose between losing your entire squadron and allowing the Russians through to bomb some of our cities, even Warsaw itself, you *must* preserve as many of your planes and pilots as possible. We have been bombed before. Many times. If necessary, we can rebuild. But we need an intact air force to have any chance of surviving this war. So, no death and glory flights, eh? You understand?"

Briefly, the younger air-force officer looked stubborn, prepared to argue against this order. After all, no one joined Poland's military to allow an enemy to kill their fellow Poles without a fight. But faced by his commander in chief's steady gaze, he grudgingly nodded.

"Very good," Wilk said. He switched his gaze to the two Polish Army officers. "Well, gentlemen? General Stasiak? Are your troops ready?"

Major General Tadeusz Stasiak, older and heavier-set than his counterpart, Milosz Domanski, nodded confidently. "My units are moving into position on schedule, Mr. President." Stasiak commanded the vast majority of Poland's hastily mobilized ground forces—the 11th Armored Cavalry Division, the 12th Mechanized Division, and two-thirds of the 16th Mechanized Division. These troops were rapidly deploying along the Polish border with Belarus and digging in. Their job was to stop the Russian 6th Army cold, blocking one prong of Gryzlov's two-pronged invasion force. Given their numbers, which were close to those of the Russians advancing on them, and the advantages of fighting defensively on their own home ground, Stasiak's men had a good chance of success.

"And you, Milosz?" Wilk asked. "Are your officers and men prepared? Do they understand their mission?"

Domanski, as tall and wiry as Stasiak was short and stout, didn't hesitate. "Yes, sir." He grinned at the two Americans. "Though after seeing what these Iron Wolves can do, my boys are a lot less likely to see our role as a form of noble and patriotic suicide."

Wilk snorted. "Let us hope so!"

By training and temperament, Milosz Domanski was a cavalryman—though one thoroughly schooled in the tactics of modern armored warfare. He had a well-earned reputation as a bold, intelligent, and innovative military thinker and leader. That was good, because the mission assigned to him by Poland's war plan would demand every ounce of skill, dash, and daring.

To confront Russia's 20th Guards Army—a formation with more than fifty thousand troops and hundreds of heavy tanks and artillery pieces— Domanski had been given one armored brigade and one independent rifle brigade. Which meant he and his soldiers faced odds of more than ten to one. According to conventional military thinking, that kind of disparity was a recipe for inevitable defeat and destruction. But Domanski's mission was not conventional.

Stasiak's much larger force had no choice but to accept a head-on defensive battle with the invading

Russians. Advancing against them into Belarus was politically impossible, since Poland wanted to avoid giving Moscow's puppet government in Minsk any more reasons to join the war openly.

Domanski's soldiers, though, had the freedom to maneuver beyond the frontier. Military weakness forced Ukraine's pro-Western government to allow the Russians free passage through its remaining territory, but that same weakness gave them every excuse to let the Poles do the same. And that, in turn, meant the general's troops and tanks could wage a fast-moving war of hit and run against the advancing 20th Guards Army—working in tandem with the Iron Wolf Squadron's cybernetic war machines and aircraft.

With luck and skill, they could buy Poland time she would not otherwise have. Though, Wilk admitted grimly to himself, he still wasn't able to see a good outcome, no matter how much delay they were able to impose on the Russians. If he could have counted on NATO and American reinforcements, prolonging the war would make good sense. But could he justify the likely cost in blood and treasure only to delay the inevitable?

"Cheer up, Mr. President," Martindale said, obviously reading his dour mood. "We're in the position of that thief condemned to death by the king. The one who begged for a year of life so that he could teach the king's horse to sing."

Wilk raised an eyebrow. "Oh?"

Martindale smiled. "When someone told him he was crazy, the thief laughed and said: Who knows what will happen in a year? Perhaps I will die. Or maybe the king will die—"

"Or perhaps the horse will learn to sing," Brad finished for him. The tall, young American showed his teeth in a defiant grin. "Well, that's our job, Mr. President. That's why you hired the Iron Wolf Squadron. We're here to teach that stubborn, damned nag to sit up and sing."

CHAPTER 11

Great things are not done by impulse, but by a series of small things brought together.

—Vincent van Gogh,
Dutch artist

EAST OF KALININGRAD, RUSSIA
Later that day

Dozens of huge, mobile Iskander-M and R-500 missile launchers, transporters, command vehicles, and maintenance trucks rumbled slowly along the rutted logging trails and narrow backcountry roads ninety kilometers east of the city of Kaliningrad, moving bumper-to-bumper under the direction of heavily armed Russian military policemen. As the convoys rolled through the dense pine forest, staff officers waved individual groups of vehicles off into clearings already covered by layers of camouflage netting. The Iskander brigade contained twelve forty-ton missile vehicles, each able to fire two missiles in rapid succession. One by one, the launcher units, each accompanied by other trucks carrying extra missiles and support and command vehicles, rolled into precisely calculated positions and halted.

More vehicles, launchers, and command trucks belonging to long-range S-300 and S-400 SAM battalions were already deployed in a wide ring around these new tactical ballistic missile and cruise missile sites. Close-in protection was provided by detachments of Tor-M1 30mm gun and short-range SAM units.

Another convoy of large armored trucks, this one even more heavily guarded by grim-faced Spetsnaz troops, followed the Iskander brigade. These trucks turned off onto a side road and drove deep into the heart of the newly created missile complex. There, in another camouflaged clearing, specialist crews waited to off-load their cargoes of tactical nuclear warheads into a new bunker dug deep into the Russian soil.

Gennadiy Gryzlov was keeping all of his options open. If his conventional forces failed to defeat the Poles, he would still possess the power to turn Poland into a ravaged, radioactive wasteland with a brutal, lightning-fast tactical ballistic and cruise missile strike.

OVER BELARUS
That night

Twenty Su-34 fighter bombers streaked low over the fields and forests of eastern Belarus, flying just high enough to clear trees and power lines. Three big KAB-1500L laser-guided bombs hung from the center-line and inner-wing hardpoints on each aircraft. Two of the fifteen-hundred-kilogram bombs were bunker-busters, designed to penetrate up to two meters of reinforced concrete and then explode with devastating power. The third KAB-1500L carried by each Su-34 was a highly lethal thermobaric bomb. It contained two small explosive charges and a large container of highly toxic and flammable fuel. Once the bomb was dropped, its first charge would detonate at a preset height, splitting the fuel container. As a mist of dispersed fuel drifted down, the weapon's second charge would go off, igniting the fuel cloud in a massive explosion. The KAB-1500's thermobaric warhead was designed to create a searing fireball with a radius of one hundred and fifty meters, while its powerful, lung-rupturing shock wave would kill anyone caught within five hundred meters of the blast.

In effect, the two squadrons of Su-34s were carrying enough precision-guided explosives to turn much of the historic city center of Warsaw into a sea of shattered, burned-out ruins. Two Kh-31 antiradiation missiles and a pair of long-range, radar-guided R-77E antiair missiles on the outer-wing pylons completed their armament load.

Strapped into the darkened cockpit of one of the lead fighter-bombers, Major Viktor Zelin firmly held the Su-34 on course as it bounced and juddered through turbulent pockets of warmer and colder air. He blinked away a droplet of sweat trickling down from under his helmet. Without the terrain-avoidance and terrain-following capabilities ordinarily provided by his aircraft's Leninets B-004 phased-array radar, flying this low seemed like madness. But their orders were to go in without radar until they were almost right on top of their planned targets.

The brass said flying without active radars would help ensure surprise. Maybe so, he thought gloomily. Then again, the generals and politicians who'd ordered this stunt were sitting around knocking back vodka in cushy operations rooms back in Voronezh and Moscow. They weren't the ones who would pay the price for any nasty surprises.

Abruptly, Zelin pulled back on the stick, climbing just high enough to clear the onion-domed top of a little village church that suddenly appeared right in front of them. *"Eto piz`dets!"* he grumbled. "This is fucked up! First, Voronezh wants us to go in practically blind. And then we're not even carrying enough air-to-air missiles to scare off one Polish F-16, let alone tangle with their whole damned air force."

Beside him, his navigation and weapons officer, Captain Nikolai Starikov, smiled tightly. The major was a superb pilot, but he was never really happy until he found something to bitch about. "Mixing it up with the Poles is what those Su-35s out ahead of us are for," he said calmly. "And the boys on the

Beriev have *their* eyes open. They'll let us know if anyone's heading our way."

"They'd better," Zelin said darkly.

Another twenty Su-35 fighters were flying about twenty kilometers ahead of them, ready to zoom farther ahead and bounce any Polish planes that tried to intercept the raid. Technically, Russia could have committed many more combat aircraft to this mission, but not without significantly reducing its ability to effectively command the attack force. The big, four-engine Beriev A-100 Airborne Early Warning and Control plane flying at medium altitude was a huge improvement on the old A-50 "Mainstay," which had been limited to controlling just ten to twelve fighters or strike planes at a time. But there were still limits on how many planes the fifteen systems operators aboard the A-100 could handle.

In this case, the calculation was that the Poles would have trouble getting more than a handful of their best fighters off the ground before the Russian strike force was already on its way home—leaving Warsaw ablaze behind them. But even if they reacted faster than predicted, their F-16s and even older MiG-29s were no match for Russia's Su-35s, at least not in a beyond-visual-range missile shootout.

"Beriev reports no airborne contacts yet," Starikov said, listening intently to information radioed by the controllers aboard the AWACS plane. He glanced down at the digital map on his MFD. It used data from their inertial navigation and GPS receivers to show their current position. "Thirty minutes to beginning of attack run."

REMOTE OPERATIONS CONTROL CENTER, IRON WOLF SQUADRON COMPOUND, POWIDZ, POLAND
That same time

"Search radar, L-band phased-array, Beriev-100 detected. Eleven o'clock. Seventy miles from Vedette Two and closing," Brad McLanahan heard the XF-111's SPEAR threat-warning system report. Although his XF-111 was still parked inside its camouflaged shelter at Powidz, it was receiving and evaluating information collected by some of Sky Masters' newest toys—a series of experimental unmanned aircraft leased out to Scion for testing in real-world combat conditions.

This particular type of drone, designated by Hunter Noble's aerospace engineering team as the RQ-20 Vedette, was about as simple, stealthy, and cheap as could be imagined. Designed around a single lightweight Pratt & Whitney 610F turbofan engine, the Vedette carried only the basic avionics and flight controls it needed for remote piloting and a small package of radar-warning receivers. Rather than using radar to detect other aircraft, Vedettes "heard" the signals emitted by their radars instead. Theoretically, a chain of datalinked Vedettes, all of them orbiting far forward of friendly bases, could use triangulation to get a pretty good read on bearings, ranges, speeds, and radar types—even against agile, frequency-hopping radars like the AESA system carried by that Beriev-100 AWACS aircraft.

Tonight, the Iron Wolf Squadron was putting this theory to the test.

Brad checked the map displayed on his monitor. Vedette Two was currently circling low near a little town called Kuliki in central Belarus. That put the Russian AWACS plane about eighty nautical miles east of Minsk—way too far forward for it to be operating in a defensive role. Unless this was just a feint designed to test Polish air defense reaction times and measures, the Beriev and its crew must be providing early warning and control for an approaching Russian strike force.

Briefly, he pondered that possibility. Like all good chess players, the Russians could be subtle, if they felt the need. Then he dismissed it. Although the destruction of Konotop and Baranovichi must have come as a nasty shock, Gryzlov and his air commanders were probably still confident that their fighter and bomber regiments could steamroll right over Poland's much smaller air force and its relatively weak SAM units. As far as they were concerned, he suspected, subtlety was something important only to the outnumbered and the outgunned.

No, Brad thought, the radar emissions from that Beriev-100 meant the Russians really *were* coming this time. He tapped a series of commands, linking the information from his system to the other remote-piloting consoles and to a whole series of Polish airfields and air defense command centers. Then he picked up a secure phone. "Iron Wolf Ops to Thirty-Second Air Base. I need to speak to Colonel Kasperek. Right away!"

"He is in his aircraft, sir. Out on the flight line.

I will connect you," the air-base operations officer said quickly. Transferring most of his F-16s from Poznan in western Poland to the more central 32nd Air Base at Łask had been one of President Wilk's first responses to Russia's ultimatum.

There was an incredibly short delay and then, "Kasperek here."

Brad grinned to himself. Trust Paweł Kasperek to be on top of things. The Polish Air Force colonel must have been waiting for this call ever since their conference with President Wilk earlier in the day. "It's on, Paweł," he said. "We've got a Beriev-100 radiating east of Minsk and heading our way."

"Any sign of other bandits?" Kasperek asked.

"Not yet," Brad told him. "My bet is their strike aircraft are coming in behind the AWACS a little ways, flying right down in the dirt. They'll have fighters out in front." He tapped a few keys, indicating guesstimated positions and vectors for the as-yet-undetected Russian strike aircraft and their escorts. "And, as we expected, they're all coming in dark."

"I concur," the Polish Air Force colonel said, obviously studying the map images sent to him via data link. "So, which air defense plan do you recommend?"

For a fleeting moment, Brad was struck by the wild incongruity of this situation. He hadn't even finished college, and yet the highly trained and experienced squadron commander chosen to lead Poland's best pilots and planes into combat wanted him to select a battle plan. Then again, weird as it might seem to an outsider, he probably knew the capabilities of Scion's stable of unmanned aircraft better than anyone except Hunter Noble. In fact, he'd spent a good part of his interrupted internship at Sky Masters studying different ways to employ them in action.

Thinking fast, he called up the position of Coyote Four. The MQ-55 was currently on station over the region where Ukraine, Poland, and Belarus all came together. Given the Beriev's present course and speed, the plotted intercept time was around twenty minutes. More quick calculations allowed him to discard several of the options crafted earlier by the Iron Wolf Squadron and Kasperek and his staff. None of their prepared plans was perfect, but, given the geometry and timing, one stood out as a close fit. "I recommend we go with *CIOS Z MAŃKI CHARLIE*, SUCKER PUNCH CHARLIE."

"Very well," the colonel said. "But the timing will be very tight."

"True," Brad agreed. "Still, it's our best shot at them."

"I concur," Kasperek said again. Still holding the secure phone in one hand, he snapped an order in Polish over his radio mike. Within seconds, the sound of multiple jet engines spooling up echoed over the connection. "My alert fighters are taking off now."

"*Pomyślnych łowów!* Good hunting!" Brad told him, using some of his acquired Polish. He hung up and hit another key, instantly connecting him to all the other Iron Wolf pilots on duty in the operations center. "This is McLanahan. This is not an exercise. Execute SUCKER PUNCH CHARLIE immediately."

Responses from Mark Darrow, Bill Sievert, and Karen Tanabe rippled through his headset. They'd pretty obviously been waiting to go as soon as that first report from the chain of Vedettes flashed across their screens.

"Get your birds off the ground pronto and launch as soon as you've got good altitude," Brad ordered. "Bill, you and George are the designated missile-target controllers for Coyotes Two and Three once SUCKER PUNCH goes active. I'm flying Coyote Four myself."

"Copy that," Sievert said. "Smooth and I are gonna have some fun tonight."

Brad grinned. "Just don't get cocky, old man."

Sievert chuckled. "Yes, Mr. McLanahan, sir. We'll be good."

Minutes later, three remotely piloted XF-111s taxied out onto the runway at Powidz, swung into line one after the other, and roared off into the night sky on afterburner—climbing through five thousand feet in seconds. At ten thousand feet, the SuperVarks leveled off and turned east toward Warsaw.

In the right-hand seat of the XF-111 control cab he shared with Sievert, George "Smooth" Herres said, "Configure MALDs to Foxtrot One Six mode." He knew that the weapons officers for Darrow and Tanabe were issuing the same commands at the same time to their own XF-111s.

"*MALDs configured*," the SuperVark's computer reported.

"Set navigation package Sierra Papa Charlie."

"*Navigation package Sierra Papa Charlie set,*" the computer said.

"Countdown to MALD launch?" Herres inquired. Once a strike package was in place, SPEAR would interface with the attack computers and determine the best time to launch the autonomous MALD aircraft.

"*Forty seconds,*" SPEAR responded, followed by, "*MALDs away.*"

Four ADM-160B decoys dropped out from under their XF-111's wings, joining the flock of eight more launched simultaneously by the other two Iron Wolf fighter-bombers. Each MALD's small wings unfolded at launch. Propelled by ultralight turbojet engines, the twelve tiny decoys headed straight toward Warsaw at three hundred knots, followed closely by the SuperVark controlled by Sievert and Herres. Behind them, the other two XF-111s circled back toward Powidz.

At the same time, sixty-plus nautical miles southeast of the Iron Wolf Squadron, the last of twelve F-16s took off from Łask and sped onward, flying very low along a route that would take them well south of Warsaw and then back northeast toward a preplanned point north of Lublin. Ground crews and pilots began frantically prepping the remaining fighters.

Back at Powidz itself, two MQ-55 drones lifted off the runway and flew east-northeast at five hundred knots, on a course that would take them north of Warsaw. Coyotes Two and Three were on the hunt. And two hundred and sixty nautical miles east, deeper in Belarus and still guided by the data coming from the little RQ-20 Vedettes, Coyote

Four arrowed onward—steadily closing the gap with the oncoming Russian Beriev-100.

It was all an incredibly intricate aerial ballet, with more than thirty Iron Wolf and Polish Air Force aircraft, drones, and decoys moving in groups and singly toward the positions laid out in SUCKER PUNCH CHARLIE.

Twelve minutes after launch, the flock of AGM-160 MALDs reached Warsaw. Acting on their programmed instructions, they went active, mimicking the radar signatures and flight profiles of F-16 fighters, and began orbiting the Polish capital. The XF-111 remotely piloted by Bill Sievert flew with them.

"*Caution, L-band search radar detected, Beriev-100, eleven o'clock high, range two hundred miles,*" the SPEAR threat-warning system reported.

"Think they see us, Smooth?" Sievert asked his partner.

"Oh, yeah, those guys on that Beriev should be picking up a bunch of targets on their screens right about *now*," Herres replied. He relayed the information to another operations-center control cab, where Brad sat hunched over his screens, joystick, and keyboard, carefully flying Coyote Four northeast over Belarus on a course to intercept the incoming Russian AWACS plane. "We're over Warsaw and wriggling, boss."

"Copy that, Smooth," Brad said. Based on data supplied by the Vedette radar-warning drones and now from the XF-111 circling over Warsaw, he estimated that his MQ-55 drone was within sixty nautical miles of the Beriev. He took a deep breath. It was time. "Light it up, guys!"

"Activate AN/APG-81 radar," Herres told their XF-111.

"APG-81 active," the computer said.

Herres's display filled with air targets, mostly their decoy flock masquerading as Polish F-16s. But there was one big sucker out about two hundred nautical miles to the east. The computer identified it as the Beriev. The rest of the Russian strike force was still effectively invisible. Even as powerful at the APG-81 was, their radar wouldn't be able to pick up Su-35s or Su-34s until they came within eighty to eighty-five nautical miles. "Designate Beriev-100 as target and relay data to Coyote Four," he ordered.

"Target designated. Data relayed," the XF-111's computer replied.

"That Russian AWACS is all yours, Brad," Herres said.

"Copy that," Brad said, seeing the Coyote feeding the target data to six of the ten AIM-120C air-to-air missiles in its weapons bay. He heard the bay doors whine open and saw six "AMRAAM" indicators blink and then vanish on his display. "Attacking now."

One by one, six advanced medium-range air-to-air missiles released, fell out of the bay, and ignited—accelerating to Mach 4 as they raced up into the night sky toward the distant Russian Beriev-100. For now, their own radar seekers were inactive, ready to energize only when the missiles reached close range.

The Coyote's bay door whined shut again.

ABOARD THE BERIEV-100, OVER BELARUS
That same time

Seven thousand meters above the darkened Belarusian countryside, the converted four-engine IL-476 flew westward at three hundred and fifty knots. A large circular dome mounted on two struts above its fuselage contained the Vega Premier active electronically scanned radar. The dome rotated fast, once every five seconds, giving it high capability against fast-moving targets. Two sleek Su-27 fighters flew lazy circles around the much larger AWACS plane, ready to intervene against any enemy attack.

Staring intently at his radar display, the Beriev's senior air controller, Colonel Vitaliy Samsonov, keyed his mike. "*Groza* and *Okhotnik* Flights, this is Strike Controller One. We detect thirteen bandits over Warsaw. Twelve are F-16s. One is a larger aircraft, as yet unidentified. None of them are radiating at this time."

"Thunderstorm Lead copies," the voice of the lead pilot for the Su-34 fighter-bombers replied.

"Hunter Lead copies," the Su-35 fighter commander said. "Standing by to fly ahead and engage at your order."

Samsonov nodded to himself. Now that they knew the Poles had a strong combat air patrol over Warsaw, it was almost time to unleash the fighters—sending them streaking out in front to knock those F-16s out of the sky before the bombers came within reach.

"Search radar detected!" one of his junior officers

said suddenly. "It's coming from that larger aircraft over Warsaw. Strong signal! I can't identify it, Colonel, the frequencies are switching too fast! It has a lock on us, though!"

Frowning, Samsonov switched his display so that it repeated the information reaching the younger officer's station. He studied it intently. What the hell was that radar? It had to be an AESA type, and the Poles weren't supposed to have any radar systems like that in their inventory. Quickly, he ran the data through another program, looking for some match. He stared intently, watching while the Beriev's computers sorted through some of the known signal characteristics associated with a host of different AESA-type airborne radars.

"Sir?" another systems operator said uncertainly. "I picked up a very small bogey in our front left quadrant. The range was around ninety kilometers. But it's gone now. It was just there for a second or two."

"Then look harder, Captain Yanayev!" Samsonov growled, still focused on his own computer. "And make sure it wasn't just another damned systems glitch." Fielded operationally for the first time a year ago, the Beriev-100 was still a new aircraft, operating with a new radar and new, incredibly complex software. Occasional bugs and blips were a fact of life.

As more signals from that unknown radar accumulated, the computer steadily narrowed down the possibilities—and then, quite suddenly, it offered an identification: *Radar is an AN/APG-81*. For a second, Samsonov stared at the glowing text in shock. That was the type of radar carried by the new American F-35 Lightning II. What the devil was an American stealth fighter, the newest in their arsenal, doing orbiting over Warsaw?

A stealth fighter! Abruptly, he remembered Captain Yanayev's earlier report of a bogey that blipped onto the screen and disappeared. He spun around in his seat to look down the crowded compartment. "Yanayev! Find that—"

Alarms shrieked suddenly and the huge aircraft banked hard to the right, rolling over almost onto its side. Unsecured manuals, coffee cups, and clipboards flew wildly through the Beriev's radar compartment, whacking into bulkheads, crewmen, computer screens, and lights.

"Missile attack!" Samsonov heard the pilot scream over the intercom. "We're under missile—"

Three of the AIM-120Cs slashing up at them out of the darkness missed—jammed or decoyed away by the Beriev's automated defenses. One slammed into the aircraft's starboard wing and exploded. Another blew a massive hole in its fuselage. The third missile smashed into big plane's tail and tore it away. Spinning out of control, the rapidly disintegrating Beriev-100 plummeted earthward, wreathed in flame.

Leading two squadrons of Su-35s spread in fighting pairs across a twenty-kilometer-wide front, Colonel Alexei Filippov listened in horror to the report from one of the two Su-27s that had been escorting their

AWACS plane. "A shitload of missiles just came out of fucking nowhere, Hunter Lead," the lead Su-27 pilot said tersely. "They blew the hell out of the Beriev. And now we've got nothing on our radars. Absolutely nothing."

Forcing himself to speak more calmly than he felt, Filippov said, "Understood, Guard Dog Lead. Did you get a vector on those missiles?"

"We think they came from the southwest," the other pilot said, not sounding calm at all. "But that's only a guess. It was all so damned fast!"

"Head in that direction," Filippov ordered. "See what you can pick up!" He scowled. Without guidance from the Beriev, the bomber strike force and its escorts were on their own. Which meant he was in effective command. Should he abort the raid? It was obvious that the Poles knew they were coming. Otherwise, there was no way they could have ambushed the AWACS so effectively.

No, the colonel thought coldly. Turning and running now would be cowardice. Even without the Beriev, his Su-35s still had a significant edge over those enemy F-16s. They had better radars and carried more long-range missiles. And Moscow would not thank him for handing the Poles another propaganda victory. He switched back to the frequency for his own fighters. "Hunter Flights, this is Hunter Lead. Activate your radars and go to full military power! We'll climb to five thousand meters so we can get a better look at what's in the sky ahead of us. Then we'll go kill some Poles!"

"Warning, warning, multiple X-band target search radars, Su-35s, twelve o'clock high, range one hundred fifty miles and closing, seven hundred knots," the XF-111's computer reported to its control cab at Powidz.

"Looks like we've got their attention, Smooth," Sievert muttered. He kept the SuperVark in a slight bank to the right, still circling over the Polish capital city at five thousand feet.

Herres nodded. "Oh, yeah. That we do." He studied his displays. "We should get a good solid paint on them in about five minutes."

Sievert winked at him. "Hell, that seems like an awful long time to wait. Maybe we should mosey out to go meet those Rooskies in a toe-to-toe *missile* confrontation."

"Now, guys," they both heard Brad say through their headsets, "let's stick to the plan, okay?"

"Only joking, Mr. McLanahan, sir," Sievert said, chuckling. "Just passing the time!"

Beside him, Herres rolled his eyes. He clicked off his mike long enough to say, "Bet the kid's never even seen *Dr. Strangelove.*"

"Ah, the young people these days," Sievert agreed with a grin. "Missing out on all the real classics. It's a crying shame, Smooth. A crying shame."

Two small green dots blinked repeatedly on their map displays. Fifty nautical miles to the northeast, Coyotes Two and Three had reached their preset position and were orbiting low over the little Polish village of Grodzisk Duźy. The two northernmost flank units for SUCKER PUNCH CHARLIE, each loaded with ten AMRAAMs, were on station. A couple of minutes later, more green dots appeared roughly seventy nautical miles southeast of Warsaw. The southern flank—Colonel Kasperek's twelve F-16s—was also in place, loitering silently not far north of Lublin.

OVER POLAND
A few minutes later

Colonel Alexei Filippov glared at the multifunction display showing his Su-35's evaluation of the radar data it was picking up. This was crazy, he thought. Based on size and radar type, his computer was claiming that the target was the new American F-35 stealth fighter-bomber. But obviously the thing wasn't as stealthy as they claimed, since he was picking it up at maximum range. Could it be another aircraft with an F-35 radar on board? What the hell were they facing?

"Hunter Two," he radioed his wingman. "Do you see what I see? A big fat target with an APG-81 radar?"

"*Da*, Colonel," his wingman replied. "And I show a signal strength high enough so that it must have a lock on us."

"Probably," Filippov agreed. "Fortunately, we're well out of their range." Then, still shaking his head in disbelief, he spoke to the rest of his aircraft. "Hunter Flights, this is Hunter Lead. I will take that big bastard at maximum range. The rest of you stand by to engage those Polish F-16s as soon as you get a good lock-on." Acknowledgments flooded through his earphones.

Filippov designated the strangers as the target for his first salvo of four R-77E radar-guided missiles. His thumb hovered over the missile switch on his stick, but he held off. They were still about fifty kilometers outside the reach of his weapons. Firing now would just waste missiles to no effect.

BEEP-BEEP-BEEP.

My God, he thought, horrified. They were under attack—by missiles streaking in from the northwest. But how? There were no radars active in that quadrant, and no reports of any enemy aircraft at all.

Instinctively, Filippov yanked his stick hard left, breaking away from the attack in a high-G turn. Straining against nine times the force of gravity, he thumbed another switch, activating the Su-35's defensive systems. Bundles of chaff and sunburst flares streamed out behind the violently maneuvering Russian fighter, corkscrewing across the sky. At the same time, his wingtip ECM pods poured energy into an array of radar frequencies, trying to jam the seeker heads on any missiles that might be homing in on his aircraft.

Something flashed past his canopy and vanished in the night. Not far away, an explosion lit the sky. A cloud of debris, smoke, and fire marked the end of a warhead-shattered Su-35.

Swearing under his breath, Filippov rolled inverted and dove, hoping to lose any remaining enemy missiles in the ground clutter. A cacophony of desperate voices poured into his ears as other pilots radioed frantic warnings or sought orders. Grimly, the Russian colonel rolled out of his dive at one thousand meters and tried to make some sense out of the information flooding through his data link. He had to regain control over his squadrons.

Second by second, a clearer picture emerged. Six of his twenty fighters were gone—blown to pieces by a salvo of missiles his computer said were American-made AIM-120s. Two pilots had successfully ejected. They were now drifting downwind into Poland and captivity. But the other four were undoubtedly dead. And the rest of his Su-35s were scattered across a wide swath of sky, the inevitable result of each pilot's individual maneuvers to evade attack.

Filippov thought fast. The stealth aircraft that had surprised them had to be somewhere north of Warsaw. Very well, he would swing his fighters away from them fast, fly south of the Polish capital, and then turn back hard to come in straight over the city. Whoever was out there hiding would have to engage the Su-35s head-on, or abandon Warsaw's civilians to the massed strike Su-34 strike force coming in several minutes behind him.

He set a rally point on his digital map display and then sent it to the other pilots via data link. "Form up here," he ordered. "And then we get back into the fight!"

Circling just two hundred meters above the ground, Colonel Paweł Kasperek kept one eye on the plot relayed from Sievert's Iron Wolf XF-111 over Warsaw.

Those Russian fighters were turning south. They were coming right at him. He shrugged. Part of him had hoped the Russian commander would be foolish enough to chase after the undetected Iron Wolf drones that had just savaged his formation. That would have allowed Kasperek's F-16s to hit them from behind.

Instead, things were going to get harder. The Russian Irbis-E radars were better than the AN/APG-68 sets equipping his fighters. With all other things being equal, those Su-35s would lock on to his F-16s sooner and fire first.

Kasperek smiled coldly. Fortunately, thanks to the radar data being relayed by their comrades in the Iron Wolf Squadron, all things were not *quite* equal. He clicked his mike. "Talon Lead to all Talon Flights. Stand by to engage." Quickly, he keyed in separate targets for each of his twelve F-16s. Confirmations rippled across his display as their computers accepted the designations.

He rolled out of his turn and headed north at full power while climbing toward two thousand meters—a move echoed by the rest of the Polish fighters. Glowing visual cues on his HUD gave him a running estimate of the range to the oncoming Russian Su-35s. The two groups of aircraft were closing on each other at incredible combined speed, more than 2,600 kilometers per hour. This, the colonel thought tightly, was going to require almost perfect timing.

The range marker slid down to one hundred and sixty kilometers. Shrill tones pulsed in his headset. The Russian radars had detected them. "Talon

Lead, to Talon Flights. Activate your radars," Kasperek ordered, pressing a switch to light up his own set. Although they couldn't yet "see" the Su-35s, going in totally blind would only make the Russians more suspicious.

One hundred thirty kilometers. Their own radars still hadn't locked on to the Su-35s. But that didn't matter. Not with the data supplied by the XF-111 over Warsaw. And they would be in range of the Russian R-77 missiles in less than thirty seconds. Close enough, the Polish colonel decided. "Talon Flights, *shoot*! And then execute tactical withdrawal!"

Kasperek toggled the weapons release on his stick. "Fox Three!" he snapped, a call echoed almost simultaneously by the other eleven F-16 pilots. Twenty-four AMRAAMs, two from each Polish fighter, streaked north toward the fast-closing Russian Su-35 formation. And as soon as their missiles were away, the Polish pilots broke hard left, pulling high g's as they went to full afterburner, and turned away from the Russians.

"They're running!" one of the Russian fighter pilots shouted. "The Poles are running away!"

Colonel Filippov scowled at the images on his radar display. The F-16s were definitely turning away and accelerating. They were pulling away outside his missile range, just seconds before it would have been too late. And there was no way his fighters were going to be able to catch them—not without burning fuel they could not safely expend, not this far from their home base.

He shook his head in disbelief. This was a rat's nest.

How could the Poles already have so many of their best fighters in the air and waiting for them? First that group of twelve still holding over Warsaw? And now this squadron coming in from the south? Twenty-four F-16s was half the total in their whole damned air force! And where the hell were the Poles getting stealth fighters and weapons from? According to the briefings he'd been given, the Americans were supposed to be sitting this conflict out. Was that a lie?

But if the Americans were in the war, why had that second group of Polish F-16s suddenly turned tail and fled—especially before their radars could possibly have spotted his Su-35s? They must have been warned by that strange large aircraft orbiting around Warsaw, Filippov suddenly realized. After all, its high-powered APG-81 radar was still locked on to them. A secure data link could feed everything that system picked up to any allied aircraft within range.

He went cold. Oh, shit. Those F-16s had known exactly what they were doing. They weren't just running away. They'd already fired at him! "All Hunter Flights! Break left now! Break!" he shouted. "We're under missile attack!"

Without waiting for acknowledgments, Filippov threw his Su-35 into another high-G rolling turn. All across the sky, other Russian fighters—galvanized by their leader's roared orders—were doing the same thing. Decoy flares lit the darkness while chaff blossoms and jammers flooded radar frequencies with false images and static.

Their commander's abrupt order was almost in time. Almost.

Twenty-four AIM-120C missiles tore into the tangle of turning Russian jets. Most of the AMRAAMs were lured off target by chaff, blinded by jamming, or found themselves out of energy and unable to turn with their desperately maneuvering targets. But enough streaked through all the clutter and noise and exploded to send five more Su-35s tumbling out of the sky in spiraling plumes of smoke, fragments, and fire.

The nine survivors dove for the deck and raced east as fast as they could fly, heading home to Russia and safe haven.

Colonel Alexei Filippov was not among them.

Still more than a hundred kilometers from this scene of aerial slaughter, the twenty Russian Su-34 fighter-bombers were also ordered to abort their strike and return to base. Without fighter escort and left blind by the loss of the Beriev-100, pressing on into the heart of an alerted Polish air defense network would have been madness—especially one that appeared to be bristling with American stealth fighters and advanced weapons.

THE KREMLIN, MOSCOW
A short time later

Gennadiy Gryzlov listened intently while his defense staff and commanders summarized their findings. They were still analyzing the fragmentary recordings of radar imagery and other data obtained during the aborted raid on Warsaw, but certain conclusions seemed obvious. Painfully so.

"The Poles have obtained an arsenal of highly advanced stealth aircraft and weapons," Colonel General Valentin Maksimov said bleakly. "And it was this new technology which enabled them to successfully ambush our strike force."

"Now that we know this, can we go back again—to hit Warsaw with a more powerful attack?" Defense Minister Sokolov asked. His face was pale. The assumption that Russia would have absolute air superiority over Poland had been a key factor in all their war planning. "If we massed even more aircraft, with two or three Berievs along for support and control, surely we could overwhelm the Poles, even with their new stealth capability?"

"Not at a price we could afford," Maksimov said, sounding exhausted. "This failed raid cost us a third of our most advanced operational fighters from the western air division assigned to the Ukraine and Poland operation, without inflicting a single loss on the enemy. And we do not yet know what other improvements the Poles may have made to their ground-based air defenses. Without better intelligence, throwing more planes into Polish-controlled airspace would risk too much, for too little possible gain."

"But—" Sokolov started to protest.

Abruptly, Gryzlov's patience snapped. "Shut up, Gregor! And that goes for the rest of you, too!" He glared around the table. "Stop dancing around the real issue," he snarled. He tapped a key, bringing up some of the last data received from Filippov's Su-35 before the colonel was shot down. "Look at that!

An American-made aircraft using the same kind of radar used on their new F-35 stealth fighters! Do you think the Poles simply went shopping at some arms bazaar to buy aircraft like that?"

Grimly, Russia's air-force commander shook his head. "No, Mr. President."

"Of course not!" Gryzlov said. He scowled across the table at Sokolov and Kazyanov. The two men wilted. Gryzlov looked away in disgust, his mind racing. A moment later: "Wait. The American planes that were detected over the western Mediterranean . . ."

"Our naval vessels did detect an X-band radar several minutes after first contact," Sokolov said. "Now we know what the Americans were secretly flying across the Atlantic a couple of nights ago, don't we?" He stabbed a finger at the screen. "Those bastard F-111 hybrids! And God alone only knows what else!"

Russia's president turned his furious gaze toward Ivan Ulanov, his private secretary. The younger man swallowed convulsively. "Get that bitch Barbeau on the hot line," Gryzlov demanded. "She owes me the truth now! I will not tolerate any more lies!"

THE WHITE HOUSE, WASHINGTON, D.C.
Later that night

"No more bullshit, people," Stacy Anne Barbeau said icily. "No more 'we don't have a goddamned clue' disguised as 'our analysis is not yet complete, Madam President' crap. You hear me?"

Slowly, heads nodded around the crowded Situation Room. Although it was well past midnight, she had summoned the entire National Security Council and members of their staffs to this emergency meeting. Like her vice president and secretaries of defense and energy, most of them were loyal nonentities, political hacks selected to make her look good and to stay out of the way while she and her White House staff ran the government. Now, though, she wanted them present as a buffer against those—like the chairman of the Joint Chiefs and the CIA director—whose independent thinking she found galling and potentially dangerous.

"By now you've seen the transcript of my hotline conversation with President Gryzlov," Barbeau went on. She frowned. "A crisis we hoped would stay confined to Poland has now escalated into something one hell of a lot worse. The Russians are accusing us of providing covert military support to Warsaw. They're demanding our immediate withdrawal. And if we don't, that lunatic Gryzlov is perfectly capable of declaring war on *us*."

"But we're *not* helping the Poles," Secretary of State Grayson protested. "How can we withdraw support we're not giving?"

"Thank you so much for identifying the nature of the problem, Karen," Barbeau said acidly. "That's really a great help." There were moments when she wondered how the other woman had ever graduated from her Montana cow college, let alone won a senatorial election. This was one of those moments. She turned her irritated gaze away from the embarrassed secretary of state to Thomas Torrey and the other assembled intelligence chiefs. "Which brings me to you, gentlemen. I need solid information about what's really going on in Poland. And I need it now!"

"Fortunately, the intelligence picture we've been compiling is starting to come into clearer focus, Madam President," Admiral Caldwell said. The director of the National Security Agency brought up a set of charts on the Situation Room's large monitor. "This is where the trail begins."

Barbeau stared at what looked like a sea of numbers, large numbers, and three- and four-letter abbreviations. Colored arrows linked circled sets of numbers and letters. In a weird way, she thought, those charts resembled some crazed artist's rendition of the financial pages of the *Wall Street Journal* or the *New York Times*. Puzzled, she raised an eyebrow. "Go on, Admiral."

"Once we realized the Poles were buying refurbished F-111s from Sky Masters, my analysts started digging through the data we routinely and covertly collect from European and American financial computer networks," the NSA director told her.

"You were tracking the money," Barbeau realized. "The funds the Poles used to buy those planes and any other military hardware they've suddenly acquired."

"Yes, Madam President," Caldwell agreed. He shrugged. "But we found something more . . . interesting." He highlighted certain sections of the charts. "These show substantial investments made using Polish-government Special Economic Incentive Funds—investments in a wide range of smaller Polish industries and corporations."

"So?"

"What's interesting is that the shares purchased by the Polish government were then immediately transferred," Caldwell said.

"To Sky Masters?"

"No, ma'am," the admiral said. "These transfers were made to a variety of different companies and corporations, most of them headquartered in Europe, South America, and Asia."

"So it's a dead end," Barbeau said, not bothering to hide her disappointment.

"No, Madam President," Thomas Torrey said quietly. The director of the CIA looked her squarely in the eye. "When the NSA shared its findings, *my* analysts saw another pattern. We're fairly sure that at least several of those corporations serve as fronts, as shell companies, for a private American defense contractor called Scion."

"Kevin Martindale!" Barbeau spat out. "That sneaky rat bastard owns Scion."

"Our information does suggest that former President Martindale is significantly involved in the company," Torrey agreed, somewhat cautiously. "Which brings me to the next piece of the picture. And, in this case, it really is a picture, or rather, a series of them."

Impatiently, Barbeau waved him on. Inside, she was thinking fast. Martindale was a slick financial operator—and a dangerous political opponent.

What exactly was his game in Poland? Why was he buying up shares in their industries? Especially now, with the Russians raising all hell in Eastern Europe?

"We didn't have any satellites in position to see that first Polish attack, the one on the Russian air base at Konotop," the CIA director said. "But we were able to capture a set of thermal images from the raid on Baranovichi." He brought up a short video clip on the big monitor, showing close-ups of the action as Russian aircraft, armored vehicles, and hangars went up in flames.

Barbeau stared at the screen. Some . . . blurry thing . . . moved with astonishing speed across that Russian base—firing weapons with incredible precision. But her eyes couldn't focus on it. It was just an eerie jumble of random shapes.

"At first, our National Geospatial-Intelligence Agency specialists out at Fort Belvoir couldn't make heads or tails out of these images," Torrey said. "All we could pick up were occasional 'hot' and 'cold' thermal traces without any coherent shape. But then one of them had the idea of trying to connect up all the separate traces from different images—to see what they might look like if they were all somehow attached to each other. And this is what she came up with—"

The satellite pictures vanished, replaced by a drawing of a large, man-shaped machine, a robot equipped with a bewildering variety of weaponry.

Stacy Anne Barbeau stared at the screen in horror. Her skin crawled. "My God," she muttered. "It's one of those goddamned CIDs, one of those killing machines McLanahan used to—" With an effort, she stopped herself from saying anything more. Her past encounters with the Cybernetic Infantry Devices and Patrick McLanahan were decidedly *not* something she wanted in the public record.

"Yes, Madam President," Torrey agreed. "That's our assessment, too. The Poles are using combat robots originally developed for the U.S. Army."

"It's not just the Poles," Barbeau realized suddenly. "That son of a bitch Martindale is fighting a private war with the Russians." Her jaw tightened. "And now he's going to suck us in with him . . ." She whirled toward Luke Cohen. "I need to talk to Piotr Wilk, *now*, before it's too late!"

OFFICE OF THE PRESIDENT, BELWEDER PALACE, WARSAW
That same time

Piotr Wilk listened to the American president's tirade in mounting disbelief. How could the American people have elected someone so self-absorbed and seemingly unconcerned with their nation's historic role as leader of the free world? Gripping the phone tighter, he tried to keep an equally tight rein on his own rising fury.

"This war you've started has *got* to stop, Wilk!" Stacy Anne Barbeau said in exasperation. "I don't care what line of bullshit Martindale and his paid killers sold you. Thanks to the element of surprise, they may have won a couple of meaningless skirmishes, but that's over now. The Russians aren't screwing around anymore. The more you hurt them now, the worse this is going to get. And not just for Poland. For Europe and the whole world!"

"So you propose that I simply surrender my country to Moscow now, instead of making more trouble for you by defending our freedoms?" Wilk asked sarcastically.

"Christ, no!" Barbeau snapped. "This isn't a god-damned game. What I'm asking you to do is to stand your military forces down. Stop taking offensive action against the Russians while I see if we can negotiate a way out of this mess. But one thing's for sure, you've got to get rid of Martindale's hired Scion thugs and their killing machines. Gryzlov will never make peace with you until they're gone."

Enough, Wilk thought. He shook his head. "I will try to be very clear, Madam President, so that there is no room for any further misunderstanding. Even if your speculations about this company's involvement in this war were accurate, I absolutely refuse to surrender Poland's sovereign right of national defense. Not to the Russians. And not to any other foreign power, including the United States. When you wish to speak to me as an ally, as the leader of a nation ready to honor the solemn commitments it has made in the past, I will be here. For now, good-bye."

Then, without waiting for her reply, he cut the connection. He looked across his desk at Kevin Martindale. "It seems that Scion's service to my country is no longer a secret."

The American nodded. "It was only a matter of time before the folks in our intelligence community figured it out. At least we bought enough time to catch Gryzlov and his commanders with their pants down. And that's what really counts."

Wilk looked at the other man quizzically. "Do you not fear your president's anger?"

"I may not think much of Stacy Anne Barbeau as a national security strategist," Martindale said with a wry smile. "But I would never bet against her skills as a political survivor. If we win, she won't waste any time before figuring out some way to take credit for the victory. We'll both be her dearest friends and allies—at least while the TV cameras are on."

"And if we lose?"

Martindale shrugged. "Then what President Barbeau says or does will be the least of our worries."

THE WHITE HOUSE, WASHINGTON, D.C.
A short time later

For the second time that night, Stacy Anne Barbeau found herself staring at the stern, handsome features of her Russian counterpart on a secure hotline video call. This time, though, she shared his unmistakable anger. How dare that idiot Piotr Wilk dismiss her so cavalierly? Did he really believe that his pissant country could stand up to Moscow's armed might? Or had Martindale actually conned the Polish leader into believing that hiring his mercenary soldiers and pilots could drag the United States in on Poland's side—against her expressed will and America's own best interests?

Martindale, she thought viciously, had all the worst attributes of a megalomaniac and no saving virtues at all. At least Patrick McLanahan, his partner in so many dumb-ass geopolitical and military stunts, had finally had the grace to get himself killed taking one risk too many. Kevin Martindale, on the other hand, seemed to specialize more in leading others to death and then waltzing off unscathed himself. Well, not *this* time, she decided. One way or another, she would make sure that aging prick got what he so amply deserved.

With an effort she composed herself. "Thank you for agreeing to speak to me, Mr. President," she said, with just the faintest hint of sweetness in her voice. Before making this connection to Moscow, she'd discreetly undone the top couple of buttons of her otherwise businesslike blouse. There were rumors that Gennadiy Gryzlov had a thing for buxom older women—his own foreign minister, for one. Well, maybe she could play on that fixation just a little. It wouldn't be the first time that she'd used her attributes to gain an advantage, however fleeting, after all.

Gryzlov smiled thinly. His ice-cold, pale blue eyes never left hers. "Your message promised me answers, Madam President. Answers as to why the United States has secretly allied itself with Wilk's terrorist regime. Since I am a peace-loving man, I have agreed to do you the courtesy of trying to explain this act of insanity. And, perhaps, you can explain to me how you propose to atone for so large a mistake in judgment."

"That's just it, Mr. President," Barbeau said quickly. "You're misinformed. My government is *not*, absolutely *not*, supporting the Poles. Those advanced aircraft and the other high-tech military hardware your forces have encountered are definitely not part of our arsenal. They belong to a private mercenary gang, one masquerading as a defense contractor!"

The Russian arched a skeptical eyebrow. "Mercenaries? With so much power in their hands? In this day and age? Do you take me for a complete fool?"

"Not at all," she assured him. Hurriedly, she laid out the evidence the CIA and the NSA had compiled linking Scion and Martindale to the Poles and to Piotr Wilk's personal fortune.

When she finished, Gryzlov only snorted. "You seriously wish me to believe that a so-called private military corporation—a corporation registered in America and owned by a former American president—is acting without your knowledge or consent?"

"That's what I'm telling you, Mr. President," Barbeau said. "It's the truth."

"The truth is of no consequence whatsoever. Not now. Not after so many brave Russians have been murdered!" Gryzlov snapped. He shrugged, not even bothering to conceal his contempt. "Whether or not your absurd claim is accurate, Madam President, does not matter. I tell you this plainly: I hold you and your country directly responsible for this crisis. So you will begin cooperating with me to end these attacks on my nation's armed forces, or I will be forced to assume that a state of war exists between the United States and Russia."

By the time she finished talking to Gennadiy Gryzlov, Barbeau was pale and shaking. Damn the man, she thought furiously. How dare he threaten her like that? Unfortunately, that coldhearted Russian son of a bitch was right about the likely reactions of other world leaders. No other country would believe that a private American defense contractor could start a shooting war without at least a nod and wink from her administration. Years ago, the last time Scion's military contractors had screwed up—during that mess between Turkey and Iraq—it had taken months of careful diplomacy, and a lot of discreet payoffs, to sweep the real facts under the carpet.

But this was an even bigger mess.

The NATO alliance was hanging together by a thin thread as it was. Only the belief that Poland had miscalculated and deserved some punishment by the Russians was keeping Berlin, London, Paris, Rome, and others in line. If the Germans or the Brits and the rest started thinking she'd been secretly backing Wilk with equipment and military expertise all along, America's influence in Europe would melt away like a snowman dropped in the Sahara.

Well, not on her watch, she thought grimly.

Reaching into her desk, Stacy Anne Barbeau pulled out a piece of stationery, embossed with her official seal. She uncapped a fountain pen, rapidly scrawled a brief note, and signed it with a flourish. Then she picked up her phone. "Luke? Get in here. Now."

Luke Cohen appeared in her doorway within moments. The tall lanky New Yorker was hurriedly straightening his tie. "Madam President?"

"Listen up, Luke. When I'm finished briefing you here, you're going straight out to Andrews. An Air Force executive jet will be waiting for you. You're flying down to Tampa, to McDill Air Force Base. Understand?"

"Not exactly," he admitted.

"Then shut up and pay attention," Barbeau snapped. She took a breath, closed her eyes to regain control, reopened them, and then favored him with a sly, apologetic smile. "Sorry, Luke, honey. I didn't mean to jump down your throat like that. Things are just a bit *fraught* at the moment."

She handed him the note she'd just written. "First, you're going to take that written directive, in *person*, to General Stevens, the head of the Special Operations Command."

Cohen looked down at it. His eyes widened a bit as he read it out loud: *"By my order and for the good of the United States, the forces under your command will undertake a vital mission. The parameters of this operation will be orally relayed to you by the bearer, my White House chief of staff. To assure absolute security, you will discuss this mission only with the commanders directly involved. You will ensure that no relevant documents or orders are entrusted to any computer system in your com-*

mand. *And at no time will you discuss any of the proposed
details of this mission with anyone other than myself,
or with my personally designated representatives.*" He
looked up. "Good God, this is—"

"Your job, Luke," Barbeau told him bluntly. She
put a warm hand on his narrow shoulder. "You
wanted to play in the big leagues, tiger. Well, here
you are."

Swallowing hard, he nodded. "Yeah. I see that."
He looked closely at her. "So what exactly am I ordering SOCOM to do—in your name, I mean?"

Without mincing words, she told him. When she
finished, her chief of staff was the one who was pale
and shaking.

KIEV, UKRAINE
That same time

The newest and tallest office tower to grace Kiev's
urban skyline soared thirty-five stories into the
air—a shimmering monument in shining steel and
blue-tinted glass to optimism, or folly, depending
on one's view of Ukraine's long-term prospects.
Thanks to recent events, most of the office suites
were still vacant. But a few near the top of the building, those offering the best views of the city and its
surroundings, were occupied.

The engraved sign outside Qin Heng's private
thirty-fourth-floor office identified him as regional
managing director for the Kiev branch of China's

Shenzen Merchants Bank. That made him responsible for overseeing the equivalent of hundreds of millions of dollars of Chinese investments in Ukrainian corporations and government securities. Russia's effective annexation of eastern Ukraine had thrown Kiev's markets into a panic—a financial crisis made worse by the march of Moscow's armies toward Poland. If any excuse were really needed, this ongoing monetary meltdown explained Qin's well-known proclivity for working well past midnight.

In truth, most of his late-night work focused on the needs of his chief career—as a senior intelligence agent for China's Ministry of State Security. While Russia's military operations were costing the Merchants Bank and its shareholders millions in lost profits and declining values, they were providing Qin's primary employer with a wealth of information on Russian military technology and tactics. And, given the surprising events of the past two days, its unexpected weaknesses. Who could have imagined Poland's commando and air forces would prove so daring and so capable?

All things considered, the wiry, middle-aged Shenzen native suspected, his masters in Beijing probably thought the trade-off a bargain. China had no immediate need to confront Moscow militarily or politically. For now, they shared a general interest in further weakening the United States and the West as a whole. But the day was bound to come, in five years or ten or twenty, when it would be necessary to establish which nation—Russia or the People's Republic of China—was the real dominant world power.

Qin opened one of the encrypted files on his laptop and began sorting through a series of digital photos recently supplied by one of his paid Ukrainian informants. Taken at Konotop before Russian reinforcements arrived to secure the ruined base, they showed close-ups of wrecked aircraft and armored cars. Further enhancement and analysis should give the ministry significant clues to the types of new weapons used by the Poles. He attached them into the middle of his most recent report and began typing a quick summary.

Suddenly his office door burst open—smashed off its hinges by a battering ram. Armed men in *Militsiya* uniforms poured in through the doorway. "Hands on your head! Get your hands on your head! Now!" they screamed.

Qin barely had time to close and seal the file before the policemen were on top of him. Roughly, they dragged him away from his desk and slammed him back against the nearest wall. "What is this!" he demanded. "How dare you invade my—"

"Shut the fuck up, Slant-Eye!" one of them growled, shoving the muzzle of his submachine gun up under his chin. "No talking."

"At ease, Yuri," a smooth, cultured voice said. "There is no need for such violence."

Gritting his teeth against the pain from strained muscles in his back and shoulders, Qin looked up. A tall, square-jawed man with short gray hair looked down at him. The other man wore a police uniform with the three stars of a colonel on his shoulder boards. He also wore the insignia of Ukraine's State Security Service on his sleeve.

"I apologize for this intrusion, Major Qin," the Ukrainian said softly. "But I have my orders."

Qin felt cold. This Ukrainian counterintelligence officer knew his service rank. Which meant his cover was irretrievably blown.

Another man, this one in jeans and a brown leather jacket, leaned over Qin's laptop. After a moment's study, he spun the computer around and plugged a small thumb drive into one of its USB ports. The thumb drive clicked and whirred quietly for a moment and then a tiny light turned green. He took the drive out. Satisfied, he turned toward the State Security colonel. "We're set. No problems."

Qin looked at them in disbelief. "You cannot simply steal information from my computer like that! Not without a warrant from one of your courts."

"Steal?" the colonel said, pretending to be shocked. He shook his head. "My dear Major, we aren't *stealing* anything." He nodded toward the man in the brown leather jacket. "My colleague there has only added a few files to your machine. Nothing of significance to you personally. Merely a few payment vouchers for unusual services and equipment acquired here and in Warsaw. Anyone reading them will believe the Ukrainian terrorists who've been attacking the Russians were trained and funded by your country."

"What?" Qin stammered. "But my country is not doing any such thing!"

"True," the other man agreed easily. "But my client in Moscow wants Chinese fingerprints on this affair. *Your* fingerprints, my dear Major Qin."

Qin felt sick. "How can a Ukrainian intelligence officer have a client in Russia?"

The colonel smiled. "I'm afraid that you are operating under a misapprehension." He brushed a hand down the fabric of his uniform jacket. "This is not real. And I am *not* employed by the Ukrainian government."

His eyes went cold. He nodded toward the men gripping Qin's arms. "Dispose of him."

Qin was still screaming when they threw him out the window of his office.

THE PENTAGON,
WASHINGTON, D.C.
A short time later

General Timothy Spelling looked across his desk at his top aide, U.S. Marine Corps Brigadier General Rowland Hall. "The Russians have moved tactical ballistic missile units up to their border? How solid is this intel, Row?"

"It's pretty solid, sir," Hall told him. "We've got clear satellite pictures of some Iskander-type launchers on the move into the woods east of Kaliningrad."

"How many?"

"That's harder to pin down," the Marine officer admitted. "But we figure at least one brigade. And probably more." He frowned. "The Russians have done a really good job of hiding their launchers in among the trees. My personal bet is that we're looking at at least a dozen launchers spread out over four or five hundred square miles, plus reloads. One thing is certain: they've put in a serious shitload of work shielding that whole area with layered air defenses. Right now, outside of Moscow proper, I don't think there's a more heavily defended locality in all of Russia. But that's not all the bad news, I'm afraid." He shook his head in disbelief. "The NSA say it's picked up clear indications that the Russians have moved tactical nuclear warheads from their Zhukovka storage site into the same area."

"Good God," Spelling muttered. "Gryzlov *is* fucking nuts."

"Should I put out an alert to NATO headquarters?" his aide asked.

Spelling sighed. "No."

"Sir?"

"President Barbeau has ordered us to cease all military and intelligence liaison with the Poles during this crisis," Spelling said. "And since Poland is still officially part of NATO, any data we send to Brussels would get passed straight on to Warsaw—in direct violation of the president's explicit orders. So we have to restrict this news to our own chain of command. Is that clear?"

"Jesus Christ," Hall muttered. "President Barbeau *is* fucking—" With an effort, the Marine general closed his mouth before he slid into expressing open contempt for the command in chief.

"What you *are* going to do, Row, is put out an immediate and highly detailed alert to all potentially threatened U.S. commands in Europe and the Middle East," the chairman of the Joint Chiefs said. "Include the location, estimated numbers, and defenses of those missile units, along with the possibility that the Russians may plan to arm them with tactical nukes."

"Yes, sir." Hall hesitated. "But the NSA still doesn't know how Scion or the Poles or whoever hacked into our computer systems. They could be reading our databases and our mail."

"General Hall," Spelling said patiently, with the faintest possible hint of a smile on his otherwise stern face, "you're not seriously proposing that I withhold vital intelligence information from our *own* forces . . . just because there's an off chance that some other *unauthorized* group might pick up the same warning, are you?"

This time the Marine brigadier general got it. He grinned and snapped a quick salute. "Understood, sir. I'll send that alert out, pronto."

CHAPTER 12

*A hero is one who knows how to
hang on one minute longer.*

—NOVALIS, GERMAN POET

HIGHWAY M07,
WEST OF SARNY, UKRAINE
The next day

The muffled thump of distant mortars and the faint
rattle of machine-gun fire echoed across open
fields, clearings, and small thickets of trees. Columns of oily black smoke curled above the wreckage of armored cars and downed Kamov-60 scout
helicopters. Gray and white trails crisscrossing the
clear blue afternoon sky marked the firing of surface-
to-air missiles at fleeting targets of opportunity—
reconnaissance drones and other low-flying aircraft.

Not far off the main highway, a clump of wheeled
and tracked vehicles sheltered beneath camouflage

netting. Slender whip antennas poked discreetly through the camouflage. Heavy T-90 tanks, mobile SAM launchers, and other armored vehicles ringed the forward command post.

A BMP-3 turned off the road and clanked into cover. Its twin rear hatches popped open. Two Spetsnaz bodyguards jumped out, weapons ready. Behind them, Lieutenant General Mikhail Polivanov, commander of the 20th Guards Army, emerged. Seeing him, the little cluster of high-ranking Russian officers standing around a map table stiffened to attention and saluted.

Polivanov, tall and barrel-chested, strode cheerfully toward his waiting field commanders and staff. "So, gentlemen, is it true? The Poles have stopped running?" he asked, rubbing his hands together.

His operations chief, a major general, nodded. "It seems so, sir." He led the way to the map table. "Our reconnaissance units report contact with elements of Polish armor and infantry forces several kilometers west of here." He pointed at the map.

Frowning in concentration, Polivanov bent forward, studying the terrain it showed. Even after almost three days of rapid and unopposed movement, the bulk of his tanks and troops were still two hundred kilometers east of the Polish frontier. His army's scouts had first bumped into Polish recon units earlier that morning—lured into an ambush that had cost him a handful of wheeled BTRs and Tigr 4x4s. But since then the Poles had been steadily falling back, not bothering to make a fight of it even when the ground favored a defense.

"What is their estimated strength?" he asked.

His operations chief spread his hands. "That is difficult to say, sir. The Poles appear to be well dug in and camouflaged. Getting close enough to their positions to make an accurate count is difficult. Casualties among our scouts have been heavy. But our best estimate is that we face at least two battalions of tanks—including some of their German-manufactured Leopard 2s—and perhaps another battalion or so of mechanized infantry."

Polivanov grinned at him. "That is good news, Eduard! Very good news!"

The other man stared back. "Sir?"

Polivanov clapped him on the shoulder. "Cheer up, man. Don't you see? If the Poles are digging in that solidly, and if they're present in those numbers, then they've decided to make a first stand here. I was half afraid they'd keep dancing about in front of us, wheeling in and out to skirmish with our columns like Cossacks." He shook his head. "But that's at least a full brigade out there, according to your scouts. And no one plays hit-and-run games with that many troops."

"The Poles could still be trying to delay us," his operations chief warned. "If we deploy for a deliberate attack, we give them time to assemble more troops against us. But if we try to rush them now, without adequate preparation, this blocking force is strong enough to give us a real bloody nose."

"Indeed it is," Polivanov agreed, still smiling. "Which means my Polish counterpart has just made his first serious mistake." Seeing the bewildered looks on their faces, he explained. "Our primary objective is the destruction of Poland's armed forces, gentlemen. It is *not* the occupation of Polish territory for territory's sake. Once we eliminate their soldiers, everything else is ours."

He laid his hand on the map. "If they fight us here with only a brigade, we will destroy that brigade. And then we'll advance west against an enemy made that much weaker—an enemy already demoralized by defeat. If, instead, the Poles send more troops to oppose us, they make our task later that much easier." He shook his head. "No, gentlemen, we will do this properly. Our foes may think they have experience of war. But who have they fought lately? Only a handful of half-naked savages in Iraq or Afghanistan!"

Heads nodded at that. The Poles made much of their combat record against Islamist extremists in those two desolate, faraway countries. But those had been police actions fought alongside the Americans and other NATO allies—low-level counterinsurgency campaigns waged against ill-equipped guerrillas and terrorists. The lessons learned from those little wars would be of no use in understanding what it took to stand up against masses of Russian main battle tanks, infantry fighting vehicles, and artillery.

Polivanov's smile grew broader. "We will teach these amateurs what modern war is really like. No matter how deep they dig in, we will first pulverize them with fire and then obliterate them with shock action."

"We could hit the Poles with air strikes first," his operations chief suggested. "If the air force cut the roads behind them with bombs, they would be trapped and unable to reinforce or to flee. And then another wave of our fighter-bombers could smash their defenses from the air as we advance."

For the first time, Polivanov's smile faded slightly. "Moscow does not want to commit the air force to further offensive action—not while our flying comrades are still trying to figure out what went wrong last night." He shrugged. "They've sworn they'll keep Polish combat aircraft off our backs, but, for now, this war is all ours."

"So we bring up the guns," another of his officers realized.

"That's right, Iosif," Polivanov agreed. "And our rocket batteries." He looked around the circle of his subordinates. "Shake out your leading tank and motor-rifle brigades into combat formations on either side of the highway, gentlemen. And bring up the artillery. I want the guns up far enough to pound every square meter the Poles hold." He traced deployment zones on the map. "Once everything is set, we'll blow the hell out of them with a massive barrage and then send the tanks and infantry forward to finish the job."

His operations chief checked his watch. "That will take some hours, sir. Siting the artillery could take until dark. Perhaps even longer."

"It can't be helped," Polivanov said. He shrugged again. "If I have to trade time for more dead Poles, I'll do it gladly."

Several hundred meters in front of their prepared defenses, a small band of Polish soldiers crouched beside the burned-out wreck of a Russian BTR-80.

They were here to guard their commander, who had insisted on coming forward himself to see what the Russians were doing.

Major General Milosz Domanski lay propped up on his elbows among the rows of tread- and tire-flattened stalks of corn, studying his enemy's movements through binoculars. Thick clouds of dust hung over the distant woods, fields, and little villages, gradually spreading north and south as columns of Russian tanks and BMP infantry fighting vehicles deployed off the highway. He narrowed his eyes. From the amount of dust they were churning up, he would guess the Russians were swinging at least three full brigades into attack formations.

Another officer wriggled forward to join him. "We have new reports from those Iron Wolf scouts, sir."

"And?"

"Captain Schofield says the enemy is deploying large groups of self-propelled guns, towed howitzers, and Grad rocket launchers close behind their motor-rifle troops. He counts more than two hundred artillery pieces, so far—with more coming up the highway all the time."

Domanski grinned. "The Russians are buying it. Polivanov is setting up for a deliberate attack."

"And wasting all that precious fuel?" his subordinate mused. Main battle tanks like the T-72s and T-90s burned through more than two liters of diesel fuel for every kilometer they drove—and a lot more when moving off-road. The T-80s still in the Russian inventory were even bigger fuel hogs.

"It's not just the fuel, or even the added wear and

tear on their tank treads and engines," Domanski said. He lowered his binoculars. "Polivanov is following doctrine to the letter. Which means he's going to hammer us with his guns first."

"Two-hundred-plus artillery pieces firing six to eight high-explosive rounds a minute is going to make this a very uncomfortable place, General," the younger officer murmured.

Domanski nodded. "So it will, Krystian." He clapped the younger man on the shoulder. "All the more reason to follow *our* plan, eh? Let the Russians blow the hell out of a few square kilometers of empty Ukrainian soil while we watch the fireworks from a good safe distance back down the road."

"Not entirely empty soil," the other man reminded him. "Once the shelling starts, our screening forces are going to take casualties."

The Polish general sighed. That was true enough. Although his Russian opposite number might be acting as though he were a prisoner of his nation's military doctrine right now, he wasn't an idiot. The Russians would keep probing his defenses right up to the last possible moment. And if their recon troops penetrated far enough to see that the Poles had pulled back, Polivanov would call off his planned barrage—saving all those thousands of precious shells for another battle.

To keep the enemy in the dark, a few of his troops—elements of the 1st "Varsovian" Armored Brigade and the 21st Podhale Rifles Brigade— would have to hold their ground, continuing to destroy or drive off Russian scouting parties with tank and guided-missile fire. But no matter how well dis-

persed they were or how fast they retreated when
the time came, some of those Leopard 2 tanks and
KTO Wolverine armored personnel carriers were
going to take hits. Which meant a number of young
Poles under his command were going to die tonight.

Domanski's mouth tightened. So be it. But that
was all the more reason to make sure the Russians
paid even more dearly for their "victory."

FORWARD ECHELON SUPPLY LAAGER,
20TH GUARDS ARMY,
EAST OF SARNY, UKRAINE
Later that evening

Lieutenant General Polivanov and his logistics officers had taken great pains when positioning their
supply units. It was vital that their reserve stocks
of fuel, ammunition, and spare parts be positioned
close enough to the fighting troops to allow rapid re-
plenishment. But it was equally imperative to make
sure their vulnerable supply convoys were parked
far enough back to be safe from enemy artillery or
rocket fire. In this case, the 20th Guards Army had
decided to set up its forward supply echelon just off
the main highway—about thirty kilometers east of
the planned battlefield.

Dozens of tanker trucks and lumbering ammunition carriers sprawled across a wide expanse of open
cropland. Several small rivers cut through this part
of western Ukraine, flowing north into the boggy
tangle of the Pripyat Marshes. To make the natu-

rally soggy ground cultivable, drainage ditches ran through the fields, disappearing into concrete-lined culverts wherever farm roads crossed them. A platoon of three T-72 tanks, a detachment of mobile 9K35 Strela-10 SAM launchers, and two companies of motor-rifle troops mounted in BTR-80s provided protection for the widely scattered trucks and fuel tankers. It would have been easier to guard them if they were packed in hub to hub—but that would have been an open invitation to disaster if Polish planes broke through and bombed the truck park. Like so much else in war, finding the right balance between concentration to guard against one threat and dispersal against another was never easy.

In the growing darkness near the edge of the truck park, little groups of drivers gathered. Some of them shared cigarettes and swigs from carefully hoarded bottles. Everyone watched their army's massed artillery batter the Poles. Hundreds of flashes lit the western horizon, stabbing skyward in a continuous ripple of lightning and thunder. Smoke from the dozens of 122mm Grad rockets screaming westward blotted out the first stars. The ground shook and danced and trembled—quivering under the distant impact as powerful high-explosive rounds ripped and tore at the earth.

One of the drivers shook his head in wonder. "Poor dumb bastard Poles," he commented. "They won't last long."

"True," another agreed. Gloomily, he cadged a light and took a meditative puff on a foul-smelling cigarette before going on. "But then it's no more rest for you and me, tonight, eh? Every stinking tank commander and gun captain in the whole fucking army will be screaming his head off: 'Where is my fuel, Ivan?' and 'Bring me more shells, Dmitri!' And then once the trucks are empty, it'll be 'Off you go to the depots in Mother Russia, boys. But hurry back to the front with another load! Don't dillydally. Just eat and piss in your cabs while you're driving, can't you?'"

There were murmurs of disgruntled agreement and muttered laughs at this cynical depiction of their usual routine.

Curled up under the water flowing through a culvert on the northern edge of the truck park, Wayne Macomber listened with half an ear to his CID's running translation of the Russian driver's sardonic monologue and snorted in derision. REMFs were pretty much alike the world over, he decided. No one said driving a fuel tanker or ammo truck was an easy job, but at least they weren't shot at or shelled on a daily basis. A sudden, lopsided grin flashed across his face. Well, not usually, anyway.

The rest of his attention was fully absorbed in making sense out of the data flooding in from the robot's multiple sensors. One after the other, he pinpointed the prowling T-72s and other vehicles guarding the laager—feeding them into a program that would prioritize targets. As much as he disliked squeezing himself into this damned steel can, he had to admit that direct mental access to its computers made battle prep a hell of a lot faster and more efficient.

Maybe too easy, Whack thought somberly, and not for the first time. Christ, he mused, imagine pulling off this stunt like a regular grunt, lying half drowned in the stinking, muddy water swirling through this pitch-dark, cramped culvert. God knows he'd done crazy shit like that before during his time in the U.S. Air Force's Special Operations Command. Riding inside this CID cockpit was a piece of cake compared to that. But he couldn't shake the nagging worry that every time he sealed himself inside one of these war robots, he risked losing something—a connection to the sweat and blood and agony of real combat. When the CID's computer systems finished meshing with his nervous system, who was really in charge, the man or the machine?

A new set of sensor readings impinged on his consciousness, breaking him out of his nanosecond funk. Bright green thermal images showed a group of twenty to thirty men moving up under the cover of the woods about a kilometer away. They appeared to be armed with a mix of rifles, machine guns, mortars, and RPGs. Save the philosophy-seminar bullshit for your next bar crawl, he told himself. Stick to the business at hand, even if it means using an armor-encased hand.

"CID Two to CID One and support team," Macomber radioed, simultaneously relaying the sensor data to the other Iron Wolf units. "Looks like we've got some uninvited guests at this little party."

"I see them, Whack," Patrick McLanahan said. His robot was concealed on the other side of the highway.

"Copy that," Ian Schofield echoed. The Canadian and several of his recon troopers were in position in the same woods these new guys were prowling through. "They're moving up to the tree line about two hundred meters to my left."

"Are you at risk, Captain?" Macomber asked.

"Not unless they step on some of my lads," Schofield said. "We're rather well hidden among the undergrowth and fallen timber here."

"Can you get anyone closer to them without being spotted?"

"No problem," Schofield said, without hesitation. "Do you want them eliminated?"

"Negative," Patrick radioed back. "If they're hostiles, they can't stop us. And if they're friendlies, we don't need their help. But we do need a read on exactly who they are and what the hell they're doing here."

Fedir Kravchenko dropped prone at the edge of the woods. Faint lights glowed out in the fields ahead, dimly illuminating the shapes of large Russian trucks and fuel tankers. The ground under his belly rippled and quivered, transmitting the repeated seismic shocks inflicted by hundreds of artillery shells and rockets still tearing the earth far away to the west.

He grimaced, reminded too vividly of the suffering inflicted on his old battalion three years ago by those same Russian guns. But any trace of lingering guilt at luring those weapons into action against the Poles was drowned by a sense of deep satisfaction. Once the so-called Free World had stood idly by and watched Moscow slaughter his countrymen. Now, though, the United States and the others would have to act against Russia's invasion forces. Continued indifference and cowardice could not be an option—not when tanks and artillery barrages were crushing the soldiers of a NATO ally.

More partisans crawled into position on either side. Pavlo Lytvyn lay next to him, studying the Russian supply laager through the scope of his SVD Dragunov sniper rifle. Several of Kravchenko's men readied RPG-18 and RPG-22 launchers. On either flank, teams worked fast to set up a pair of RPK-74 light machine guns. A few meters back behind the main body, a four-man weapons team strained and sweated, connecting the separate components of their 82mm mortar—its heavy barrel, base plate, and bipod. The rest of his platoon-sized force carried AK-74 assault rifles, though two men had 40mm grenade launchers fitted to their weapons.

A massive squat shape clanked slowly down a farm lane several hundred meters away. Its long-gunned turret whined ceaselessly back and forth, in a strange parody of an elephant suspiciously sniffing the night air.

"T-72," Lytvyn hissed. "The gunner must be using his thermal sight to look for hidden enemies."

"Like us," Kravchenko murmured.

The big man nodded grimly. "The longer we wait, the more likely that one of those other Russian bastards will run a scan along this stretch of woods. And then we're screwed."

"Which is why we're not waiting," Kravchenko

told him. He glanced back at the rest of his men. "Listen up," he growled. "Remember your orders. Don't waste time firing at those Russian tanks or their APCs. Hit the soft-sided vehicles, the fuel tankers and ammunition trucks. Follow the plan. This is a hit-and-run attack. We fire for thirty seconds, do as much damage as we can, and then we run! Head for the rally point as fast as you can once I blow the whistle! Don't keep shooting too long! Our country needs live fighters, not dead heroes."

Pale faces nodded in the darkness.

Lytvyn gave him a skeptical look. Kravchenko shrugged. More than half of these raw, inexperienced partisan recruits were likely to die tonight. But he had nothing to gain from pointing out the obvious. Their sole duty to Ukraine was to kill as many Russians as possible, at any cost. Losing a handful of supply trucks would not seriously hurt the 20th Guards Army, but it would remind Polivanov and his thugs that they were deep in hostile territory. And every soldier, every tank, they deployed to guard their rear areas against future attacks was one less soldier, one less tank, available for battle at the front. Besides, any partisan who survived this raid would be a veteran—hardened to danger and ready for even more daring and complicated missions.

CCRRAACK!

Kravchenko swung back, startled by the unearthly, earsplitting sound. His eyes widened in surprise. There, on the far side of the Russian truck park, a T-72 tank sat motionless, engulfed in crackling flames. Closer in, the coughing roar of a heavy-caliber autocannon firing short, aimed bursts echoed over the pulsing, continuous rumble of the distant Russian artillery barrage. A BTR-80 ground to a halt. Smoke and fire boiled out through huge holes torn in its thin steel armor.

For more than a minute, Kravchenko lay frozen, watching in growing astonishment as more and more Russian vehicles blew up or were ripped to pieces. Antitank missiles, rocket-propelled grenades, and glowing incendiary rounds streaked across the laager, wreaking death and destruction. Slowly, a twisted grin writhed across his maimed face. Somebody had beaten him to the punch.

Eyes alight with maniacal delight, he saw metal-hulled fuel tankers and canvas-sided trucks set ablaze. Explosions rippled across the fields, sending shards of jagged metal screaming in all directions. Clumps of panic-stricken Russian soldiers turned to flee—and were ripped apart by rapid bursts of machine-gun fire.

"*Matir Bozha* . . . Mother of God," Lytvyn muttered, pointing toward a lithe gray and black shape stalking through the growing tangle of wrecked and burning vehicles and mangled dead men. It moved with eerie, murderous, machinelike precision—firing different weapons in every direction. "What is that devil?"

Kravchenko studied the creature hungrily. "That, Pavlo," he murmured with deep satisfaction, "is what all our attacks on the Russians were designed to conjure." He grinned. "And now it is time for us

to vanish. Our work tonight is being done for us—
and done well." Rising to one knee, he blew a series
of soft, piercing notes on his command whistle.

Quickly, in ones and twos and teams, the Ukrainian partisans gathered their weapons and gear and
melted away into the darkness under the trees. They
drifted past the motionless, ghillie-suited figures of
Captain Schofield and Sergeant Davis without spotting the two Iron Wolf scouts. Nor did Kravchenko
or any of his men notice the tiny low-light cameras
and directional microphones rigged to capture their
faces and speech.

Early-morning sunlight cast long shadows across
a landscape left churned, blasted, and burning by
last night's unrelenting artillery barrage. Craters
stained with acrid explosive residues carpeted once-
fertile fields. Long stretches of the M07 highway
had been smashed into slabs of broken concrete and
asphalt. Patches of woodland were now jumbled
heaps of shattered stumps and shrapnel-splintered
branches. Fires smoldered everywhere.

Lieutenant General Mikhail Polivanov cautiously clambered out of the BMP-3 he used as a
mobile command vehicle. His bodyguards, weapons ready, stayed close to him, tensely observing
the ruined countryside. Both of them looked grim
and nervous. There were too many potential hiding
places for stay-behind Polish snipers in this shell-
torn setting.

Ignoring them, Polivanov made his way gingerly
across the debris-strewn ground to where a group

of his army's officers and combat engineers stood studying two burned-out hulks—one a Leopard 2 tank, the other an eight-wheeled Polish APC, of the type they called a Wolverine. Heavy chains linked the two wrecks. Off to one side, blood-soaked blankets covered a row of mangled corpses.

An engineer officer saluted at his approach. "Sir!"

Polivanov gestured toward the pair of wrecked Polish vehicles. "What's the story here?"

The engineer nodded toward the Leopard 2. "One of our shells must have knocked a tread off that tank. The Polish infantry squad from that APC was trying to rig up a tow. From the look of things, they were all caught outside when our next salvo of 122mm rockets struck this area."

Polivanov winced, imagining the carnage. He sighed and turned away. "What a waste," he muttered.

One of his junior staff officers nodded sagely. "Those Polish soldiers were brave, but foolish."

"Idiot!" Polivanov snapped, scowling deeply. "I'm not referring to the enemy, Iosif. I'm talking about last night's little show by us."

"Sir?"

"We fired off more than ten thousand shells and rockets—a whole unit of fire for every gun and rocket launcher we deployed," the Russian general said heavily. "And for what?" He waved a hand around the artillery-blasted countryside. "To blow holes in empty Ukrainian farmland?"

"We did inflict casualties on the Poles, sir," the young staff officer insisted.

"A mere handful," Polivanov snorted. "Ten thousand shells to destroy three tanks and four armored personnel carriers? To kill or wound fewer than fifty of the enemy's troops?" He shook his head in disgust. "We wasted our barrage on a small screening force, Iosif. We were tricked. Made to look like giggling, trigger-happy fools!"

He pointed back the way they had come. A huge pall of oily black smoke hung low over the eastern horizon. "And while we pounded trees and cornfields, the Poles swung their commandos in behind us and kicked the snot out of our supply units. Every gallon of reserve fuel, every truckload of artillery ammunition . . . all blown to hell!"

"We still have enough fuel to continue our advance, sir," the younger officer said stubbornly. "Our artillery may be low on shells, but our tank and motor-rifle brigades still have enough ammunition for another battle."

"Certainly, we could chase after those bastard Poles," Polivanov growled. "But to what end? To walk into another ambush, and without artillery support this time? To bare our necks for these weird secret weapons the enemy is using against us so effectively?" He shook his head. "No, Iosif! A thousand times, no!"

His aide looked stricken. "But then what will we do?"

Polivanov sighed again. "We wait." He shrugged his shoulders. "We wait for Moscow to send us more fuel and ammunition. Once we're resupplied, we can push on toward Poland. But until then, we dig in deep here and protect ourselves."

MOSCOW
Several hours later

Looking for all the world like a well-dressed European corporate executive, former Russian President Igor Truznyev strolled out of the elegant five-star Ararat Park Hyatt hotel. He paused on the pavement, checking the most recent text message on his smartphone: KB 401 77.

Smiling, Truznyev looked up. There, coming toward him, was a yellow Mercedes taxicab, a cab with the license-plate number KB 401 77. He held up a hand, flagging it down.

The cab pulled up smoothly beside him. "Where to?" the white-haired driver asked.

"The Ministry of Industry and Trade," he murmured, sliding into the cab's rear passenger seat. Sergei Tarzarov was already there, waiting for him. They pulled away, back out into the busy Moscow midafternoon traffic.

"The driver?" Truznyev asked.

"Thoroughly reliable," Tarzarov said flatly. "One of the old breed."

The former president nodded his understanding. The taxi driver was ex-KGB, probably one of the agents the intelligence service used to plant in the ranks of Moscow cab companies. The KGB has used its "cabdrivers" to keep tabs on suspicious foreigners—and to serve as mobile contacts and drop points for Russian moles operating inside Western embassies during the old Cold War days.

"This will have to be quick, Igor," Tarzarov said, glancing at his watch. "Gennadiy has called another meeting of the security council for later today."

"The president's war is not going so well, then?" Truznyev asked brightly.

"There have been . . . *complications*," the older man allowed. He looked curiously at his companion. "How much do you know?"

"Enough," Truznyev said with a quick lift of his expensively tailored shoulders. "Enough to know that the Poles, with the aid of their American mercenaries, have not been cooperating with Gennadiy's precisely crafted military timetables quite as fully as he had hoped."

Sergei Tarzarov offered him both a thin-lipped frown and a reluctant nod, evidently not completely pleased with his somewhat facetious tone. "Our ground and air forces are meeting stiffer resistance than we had expected," he admitted. "But the correlation of forces still remains greatly in our favor."

"I'm very glad to hear that," Truznyev said. He smiled thinly. "Losing a war would be bad enough. Losing a war begun under false pretenses would be much worse."

Tarzarov's slight frown turned into a full-fledged grimace. "What do you mean, Igor?" he asked.

"It seems that some of my analysis was correct," Truznyev said, sounding pleased. "As were your earlier fears."

Tarzarov studied him. The other man did, in fact, look satisfied and smug, rather like a sleek wolfhound trotting back to its master with pieces of its prey dangling from its fangs. "In what way, Igor?" he asked drily.

"Gennadiy Gryzlov *was* manipulated into this war," Truznyev said. "Or so the evidence I've obtained strongly suggests."

Tarzarov sat up straighter. "Manipulated? By whom?"

"Beijing," the other man said calmly. "Though I cannot yet tell if the plot originated at the highest levels of the People's Republic. It may only have been primarily a local initiative by Ukrainian-based agents of the Chinese Ministry of State Security."

For a moment, Tarzarov sat transfixed. If what Truznyev claimed was true, a whole host of unpleasant possibilities presented themselves. "You had better explain that more fully," he said finally.

In answer, the former president opened his briefcase and took out a somewhat battered-looking laptop. "I come as a Russian patriot bearing gifts," he said blandly.

Tarzarov looked down at the computer. He raised an eyebrow. "Oh?"

"Some . . . people, shall we say . . . in my employ acquired this machine from a Chinese covert agent operating out of Kiev," Truznyev said.

"Voluntarily?"

"There were . . . *complications*," Truznyev replied, deliberately mimicking the older man's own earlier choice of words. "An intended discreet removal went slightly awry."

"Awry as in sudden death?" Tarzarov guessed, with a sardonic smile.

The former president had the grace to look abashed. "Unfortunately, yes. But the Ukrainian police have some reason to believe the Chinese agent—masquerading as an investment banker, by the way—may have committed suicide to atone for financial losses."

"His superiors know otherwise, I presume?"

Truznyev nodded. "Probably. I suspect the Chinese will begin silencing their intermediaries soon, if they have not already finished doing so."

"And this computer," Tarzarov asked, tapping it. "It contains evidence of a plot to lure us into conflict with the Poles?"

"I believe so," the other man replied. He spread his hands. "The technical people I hired were able to break into a few of the files—which discussed payments to Ukrainian insurgent groups."

"Ah."

"Indeed," Truznyev agreed. "But there is more. We found references to a plan to kidnap one or two Polish officers off the streets in Warsaw. And a few more bits and pieces which suggest a very covert arms-buying operation aimed at obtaining Polish and American military equipment."

"That is . . . suggestive," Tarzarov said grimly.

"There are more files on the machine," Truznyev told him. "But my experts were unable to decrypt them, at least not without risking triggering some kind of self-destruct program."

"So you brought this computer to me," the older man said flatly.

Truznyev nodded. "Of course, Sergei. You are the one who asked me to look into this possibility, after all." He smiled. "It also seemed best to let our government's own intelligence specialists try to crack the remaining files. Who better, eh?"

"Perhaps," Tarzarov said slowly. The somewhat pained expression on his face made it clear, though, that he suspected the best computer hackers no longer worked for the Kremlin. Why work for wages when you could, instead, sell your services on the slightly murkier, but considerably better paid, black market.

Privately, Truznyev was quite sure that was the case. He broke the uncomfortable silence by asking, "So, then, Sergei. What will you do now?"

The older man's expression was hooded, impenetrable. "I will consider that, Igor," he said. "In this case, thought before action seems indicated."

Truznyev pretended surprise. "You won't bring this to Gennadiy?"

"Immediately? No," Tarzarov said flatly. He picked up the laptop. "It would serve no real purpose now—not when victory is still likely."

"And if victory somehow eludes our young and oh-so-confident president?" Truznyev pressed. "By some unexpected and sadly unfortunate chain of events?"

"That would be a different question entirely," Tarzarov said. He sighed. "You have done well, Igor."

Truznyev nodded, pleased. "That is high praise indeed—coming as it does from a master, Sergei."

"You will gain nothing by flattery," Tarzarov said wryly. "Submit your list of expenses, and I will make sure that you're compensated. Discreetly, of course." He showed his teeth. "Neither of us would profit by revealing how this information came into my hands."

"No, indeed," Truznyev agreed fervently. "Let me stay in the shadows, my friend." He chuckled. "I find them far more comfortable than the limelight."

THE KREMLIN, MOSCOW
A short time later

Gennadiy Gryzlov listened in stony silence while General Mikhail Khristenko recited his litany of woes. To his credit, the chief of Russia's General Staff made no effort to cast recent events in a falsely positive light.

"Polivanov is being very cautious, but I cannot fault him for that," Khristenko said. "Until its tanks, other vehicles, and artillery are refueled and resupplied, the Twentieth Guards Army cannot continue its offensive. Not without courting serious danger."

Gryzlov nodded. He had been reluctant to believe Polivanov's claims, but the most recent figures transmitted by the general's supply officers painted a bleak picture. In effect, the 20th Guards Army had just enough fuel left to reach the Polish frontier—but not enough to advance any deeper into enemy territory. And while it had enough bullets and shells left for one big battle, last night's sneak attack by the Poles and their high-tech American mercenaries had destroyed all of the army's reserve ammunition. Under those circumstances, pushing ahead was not a sensible option. Fighting vehicles caught without fuel were reduced to immobile pillboxes—unable to maneuver or evade attack. And tanks, armored personnel carriers, and guns left without ammunition were nothing but targets.

"What about the Sixth Army?" he snapped. "Its commander has no such excuse!"

"General Nikitin and his troops continue their advance through Belarus," Khristenko said evenly. "Units of his advance guard have already made contact with Polish troops at several points along the border."

"Then tell Nikitin to press ahead faster and attack as soon as his forces are in position!" Gryzlov demanded.

"Such haste would be . . . unwise," Khristenko said. Aware suddenly of the long-suppressed rage beginning to distort his president's handsome face, he hurried to explain. "Intelligence and long-range reconnaissance reports indicate that Warsaw has deployed a large number of its available troops to confront our Sixth Army. Their positions are carefully fortified. Attacking them without careful preparation would be a prescription for probable failure . . . and heavy losses."

Curtly, Gryzlov nodded again, restraining his temper with difficulty. However unwelcome the older man's assessment might be, it was also undeniably logical.

"In fact," Khristenko said carefully. "I have cautioned Nikitin to slow his own advance—at least until the Twentieth Guards Army can resume its offensive."

"Why?"

"With Polivanov's forces temporarily halted, pushing farther west would only leave Sixth Army's left flank hanging in the air," the general said. "The Polish armor and infantry units that were facing Polivanov could swing north and surprise Nikitin's columns on the march."

Gryzlov frowned. "In other words, neither of our invasion armies can go forward without the other."

"That is correct, Mr. President," Khristenko agreed.

"Then you get those supplies forward to Polivanov without delay!" Gryzlov snarled. "I will not accept further excuses for inaction and failure! If your tank and motor-rifle troops cannot defeat the Poles, I will be compelled to use other means to destroy our enemies—means that would be far more lethal and far less precise. Do you understand me, General?"

"I understand you, sir," the chief of the General Staff said tightly. His president had just signaled his willingness to contemplate crossing the nuclear threshold. If Russia's conventional armies failed, Gryzlov would use his missile forces against Poland.

NEAR PYRIZHKY, UKRAINE
Later that day

Major Yevgeny Kurochkin banked his twin-tailed MiG-29M into a gentle left-hand turn. He glanced out through the clear canopy at the ground five thousand meters below. From this high up, the flat Ukrainian landscape was mostly a hazy blur—an alternating patchwork of light green, dark green, and earth-brown fields and woods. Thin gray lines, paved roads, sliced through the countryside in all directions.

One of those roads, the M07 highway heading west to Poland, was jammed with traffic. A kilometers-long column of cylindrical fuel tankers and canvas-sided trucks loaded with other vital supplies was slowly wending its way to the 20th Guards Army's stalled brigades. The supply vehicles could have gotten there faster on their own, but they were being shepherded by a battalion-sized task force of tracked T-72 tanks, BMP-2 infantry fighting vehicles, and self-propelled antiaircraft guns.

Kurochkin and his wingman, Senior Lieutenant Avilov, were assigned to fly top cover for the convoy, orbiting in a lazy, fuel-conserving racetrack pattern at medium altitude. If called on, their MiG-29s carried bombs and rocket pods for use against ground targets.

At least now he would be able to see well enough to hit something, the Russian pilot thought. The long supply column had spent most of the past hour driving through a wide belt of thick forest, closed up tight against the possibility of sudden ambush by Ukrainian terrorists or Polish Special Forces troops. Through his radio earphones, Kurochkin could hear the previously tense voices of the escort commander and his subordinates beginning to relax. As they moved out into more open country, their chances of fending off an enemy attack increased exponentially.

Not far off the highway, right in the middle of a field, there were two tiny, dazzling flashes.

Kurochkin frowned, keying his mike. "Avilov, did you see—"

Three seconds after they were fired, tungsten-steel alloy slugs sleeting at nearly six thousand kilometers per hour smashed through the two Russian MiG-29s. Both pilots were killed instantly, shredded by white-hot, razor-edged splinters torn from their own aircraft.

Riding with his head poking out through the turret hatch of the lead T-72 main battle tank, Captain Ivan Teplov adjusted his headset, trying to make out what his driver, seated below in the chassis, had just said over the intercom. Out in the open like this, the roar of the T-72's 780-horsepower diesel engine was almost deafening. Despite the distraction, he kept an eye on their surroundings. They were rumbling through farmland now, grinding slowly westward through fields planted in corn and sugar beets.

"Say again, driver," he growled.

"I said, we'll need to top up again sometime in the next hour, sir," the sergeant told him patiently. "We just hit the three-quarter mark—"

A sudden stuttering, clanging rasp of gunfire drowned out the intercom. In that same split second, a blast of heat washed across the back of Teplov's neck—scorching enough to make him yelp in sur-

prise. He swiveled to look behind them. His mouth
fell open in disbelief. They were under attack!

Fuel tankers and trucks were slewing across the
highway in all directions, already hit and burning. Soldiers fell away from the wrecked vehicles.
Many of them were on fire themselves, turned into
screaming, writhing human torches. More explosions tore at the long column—hurling smoking
pieces of trucks and crates of supplies high into the
air.

In all the chaos, a flash of blinding-fast movement caught Teplov's eye. There, racing along the
trapped convoy, came a tall, mottled gray figure out
of a nightmare. The weapons carried in its spindly
arms fired again and again, destroying trucks and
other vehicles with terrifying speed.

The Russian tank commander swallowed hard.
"Gunner! Target right rear! Range three hundred
meters!" he yelled.

The T-72's massive turret spun fast, slewing
toward the strange creature or machine. "Sir! The
computer won't lock on!" the gunner stammered.

"Idiot!" Teplov snarled. "Fire anyway!"

KA-BLAAMM!

The tank rocked backward as its 125mm smoothbore gun fired, propelling a round downrange in a
plume of brown smoke and orange flame. Teplov
leaned forward, clutching the rim of the turret
against the recoil.

The T-72's high-explosive round hit the ground
right beside the fast-moving enemy war machine and
exploded. A huge fountain of dirt and dust erupted.
Caught in the blast, the gray and black figure was

tossed backward, coming down in an awkward heap beside a burning Russian truck.

"Reload with armor piercing!" Teplov snapped into his mike, already swinging away to look for other targets.

Hydraulic system function severely degraded. Thermal camouflage off-line. Thermal sensors damaged. Weapons Pack One nonoperational, the CID's computer reported. *Fuel-cell power production down to forty-three percent.*

Patrick McLanahan ignored the cascade of damage and failure warnings flooding through his mind. Considering the sheer explosive impact and spray of fragments it had just taken at point-blank range, his Iron Wolf machine was lucky to still be in one piece. Without trying to get up, he turned his head to find the Russian T-72 that had just nailed him. Servos and actuators whined in protest. "Stop being such a big baby," he muttered. "You've been hit worse."

The enemy tank was about three hundred yards away, swinging around toward the rear of the supply column—where CID Two, piloted by Wayne Macomber—was still wreaking havoc. The imagery he was receiving was blurred and it flickered oddly. No surprise there, he thought. Half his visual sensors were just gone, ripped away in the blast. And with the robot's batteries and fuel cells damaged so badly, its computer was being forced to cycle its limited remaining power between arrays of critical systems.

"Dad? Dad? Are you all right?" Brad's worried voice flooded through his headset. His son was monitoring this attack from the Remote Operations Control Center back at Powidz.

"I'm fine, son," Patrick said. "Knocked around a little maybe, but otherwise intact."

Captain Nadia Rozek's voice cut in on the circuit. "*Dad?* Your father is *alive?* CID One is General McLanahan?"

Patrick switched frequencies with a pained smile. Let Brad handle the awkward revelation, he thought. He just hoped his son hadn't played the "my father is dead" sympathy card too hard while wooing that beautiful female Polish Special Forces officer. Right now, though, he had far more immediate problems.

Like that T-72. Its commander had damned fast reflexes and CIDs were not designed to stand up to 125mm armor-piercing ammunition. And from the limited information flowing through his data link, Whack already had a hell of a fight on his hands.

Slowly at first, and then faster as he overrode more and more of the computer's damage alerts and fail-safes, he climbed back to his feet. One rail-gun round should do it for that enemy tank. He started to uncouple the gun. *Electromagnetic weapon nonoperational*, the CID indicated.

"Shit," Patrick growled. He was going to have to do this the hard and ugly way, up close and personal. He detached his 40mm grenade launcher instead. *One thermobaric grenade remaining*, the computer reported.

He lurched into motion, unsteadily running toward the distant T-72 on wobbly legs. More actuators protested. Whole sections of his system schematics winked yellow and red—indicating a series of cascading failures. As his computer rerouted more and more power to movement, information from a variety of sensors vanished from his conscious mind.

Patrick's CID had covered two-thirds of the distance between them when the Russian tank commander saw it coming. Reacting fast, the other man yelled an order into his headset and fumbled for the grips of the 12.7mm machine gun mounted beside him. The T-72's turret whined frantically around, trying to bring its main gun to bear.

Too late, Patrick thought grimly. He bounded up onto the chassis, broke the tank commander's neck with one quick blow, and yanked the corpse out of the turret. In the darkened compartment below, he saw the gunner's face turn toward him, mouth opening in a panicked scream.

Without hesitating, he fired his grenade launcher directly through the open hatch and whirled away.

WHANG. WHOOMPH.

The thermobaric grenade's twin charges went off. A pillar of fire shot out of the tank turret's hatch, blindingly bright even against the afternoon sun. Already burning, the T-72 slewed sideways and clanked to a stop.

Patrick leaped off the smoldering tank, stumbling a bit as his leg hydraulics flirted with failure. He slid the empty grenade launcher back into his remaining weapons pack and took out his last functioning weapon, his 25mm autocannon. Time to get back into the hunt, he decided.

"Break it off, CID One!" he heard Macomber radio. "Repeat, break it off! Rally and recover."

Stubbornly, Patrick shook his head. "It's too soon, Whack," he said. "We're still meeting resistance."

"Bullshit," Macomber told him. "I know your sensors are fucked, but take a look around! We've already toasted ninety percent of their supply trucks and fuel tankers. So that Russian army up the road ain't going anywhere soon. Right here, the only Russians left alive are the ones who can fight back. And going head-to-head against alerted enemy armor when we can still back off is *not* in the damned plan!"

"Major—"

"I can see your robot's fricking damage reports, General," Macomber said tightly. "The way I read them, you've got a few hours max before the whole damned thing shuts down completely. Which means we are going to hightail it back to Powidz and swap you into my cozy little ride before that happens." Macomber paused. "Unless, of course, you're ready to just pull the plug and die. Right here and now. Because that's what staying amounts to."

Patrick laughed. "Point taken, Whack." He turned and limped away from the wrecked and burning Russian supply convoy. "CID One is heading for the recovery point. As ordered."

THE KREMLIN, MOSCOW
That evening

Sergei Tarzarov sat bolt upright in one of the plush chairs lining the walls of President Gryzlov's outer office. He was not alone. Defense Minister Sokolov,

Chief of the General Staff General Khristenko, and Colonel General Maksimov, head of the air force, sat around him. All four of them wore the same uneasy, nervous expression, as though they were small, errant schoolboys summoned for a beating by an angry headmaster.

But now, after having been ordered here on the double, they were being kept waiting.

"The president is in another meeting," his private secretary had told them apologetically. "He will be with you shortly."

Noting the absence of the foreign minister from this edgy gathering, Tarzarov frowned. Was Gennadiy foolish enough and reckless enough to waste time screwing Daria Titeneva while the rest of his national security advisers cooled their heels outside his door? At a moment when so much of Russia's war strategy appeared to be collapsing in ruin? It scarcely seemed credible, but then again, many of the younger man's actions often seemed rooted in instinct and impulse—rather than in cold calculation.

The phone on Ivan Ulanov's desk buzzed. Gryzlov's secretary snatched it up. "Yes, Mr. President?" He listened in silence for a moment and then nodded sharply. "At once, Mr. President!"

Ulanov rose from his desk and hurried over to open the door to Gryzlov's inner office.

"Very good. Then we have an understanding," Tarzarov heard the president saying. "Do not make me regret giving you my trust. You will ensure that your mistress understands this, too."

A second voice echoed his words, translating

them into a different language. Into *English*, Tarzarov realized abruptly. He stared hard at the two men who left Gryzlov's office. One he recognized, a translator attached to the Foreign Ministry. The second man, tall and thin and tired-looking, was a stranger. Something about him seemed familiar, however—as though Tarzarov had seen him before, perhaps on television or in the background at some international conference. Maybe in the entourage of a political leader? His travel-rumpled clothes marked him as an American, but not one of the sophisticated executives Gryzlov occasionally invited in to discuss old times in the international oil industry. What the devil was Gennadiy up to?

"Gentlemen," Ulanov said, breaking into his thoughts. "The president will see you now."

After being ushered into Gryzlov's unsmiling presence, the four older men were not asked to sit. Instead, they found themselves facing his desk, lined up like children—or like prisoners facing an execution squad, Tarzarov realized with a sudden shiver.

"This war has entered a new phase," the president said coldly. "Today's utter failure to resupply the Twentieth Guards Army leaves me no choice." He turned his pale blue hooded eyes on Khristenko. "You will transmit the necessary warning and preparatory orders to our Iskander missile brigade based in Kaliningrad."

"Sir!" Khristenko snapped to attention. "And the target sets?"

"I want every Polish air base, especially the nest of American mercenaries at Powidz, slated for destruction," Grzylov said. "You will also target the centers of governmental power and administration in Warsaw. Finally, additional missiles must be aimed at the most significant concentrations of enemy troops opposing General Nikitin's Sixth Army." He favored them all with an icy, predatory smile. "When our Iskanders have finished blowing a hole in the Polish defenses, I want Nikitin's tanks on the march toward Warsaw."

Khristenko looked worried. "The missile brigade we have assembled can fire a devastating barrage, sir," he said hesitantly. "But even nearly one hundred highly accurate conventional warheads may not be able to accomplish the objectives you have set forth."

"No?" Gryzlov said, with deceptive mildness. His eyes hardened. "Then you have my permission to include the use of tactical nuclear weapons in your attack."

Tarzarov decided it was time to intervene, to buy time to dissuade Gennadiy from this madness. "Mr. President, this may be most—"

"Enough, Sergei!" Gryzlov snapped. "The Poles and their hireling techno-soldiers have forced my hand. If their new weapons and tactics are beyond our ability to defeat with conventional methods, I am fully prepared to employ the only effective weapons remaining in our arsenal." With a dismissive wave, he turned back to Khristenko. "How soon can our Iskander brigade be ready to fire, General?"

"Within two to three hours after getting their target sets, Mr. President," the chief of the General Staff said quickly. "My staff has already prepared detailed plans which include most of the targets you have just assigned. The missile units move from their garrison locations to presurveyed launch positions for maximum accuracy. Once we have the most recent reports from Sixth Army's reconnaissance units, keying in the remaining target coordinates will not take long."

"Two hours, eh?" Gryzlov pondered that for a moment. "Very good, Mikhail," he said, smiling more genuinely now. Then his mouth thinned again. "But you will *not* fire those missiles without my direct order. And that order may not come until much later tonight. If *ever*. If we employ tactical nuclear weapons, we will follow all established execution protocols. I'm not afraid to use nukes, but I want to know precisely when and where all the detonations will be. *Precisely*."

For the first time since entering the president's office, Tarzarov felt a glimmer of hope.

Gryzlov must have seen it on his face, because the younger man nodded to him. "Yes, Sergei. I do have one more card to play." He showed his teeth. "Or, perhaps more accurately, I have one more card to watch someone else play *for* me."

SECURE HANGAR, IRON WOLF SQUADRON, POWIDZ, POLAND
A short time later

Piotr Wilk looked up at the Cybernetic Infantry Device. "I am very glad to see that you are unhurt, General McLanahan."

At his side, Nadia Rozek stiffened slightly. She glanced coolly at her president. "You knew that he was alive, too?"

"It was not my secret to share, Captain," Wilk said in apology.

To his surprise, the tall Iron Wolf robot inclined its head toward the Special Forces captain. "But it was mine to give, Nadia. And I made a mistake in not permitting Brad to tell you earlier—especially after we fought together at Konotop. I hope you will forgive me?"

Nadia's stony expression softened and slowly a smile crept across her face. "It would be wrong, I suppose, to hold a grudge against you for not really being dead." She tossed a mischievous look at Brad McLanahan. "So long as there are no *more* secrets being kept from me, that is."

"No, ma'am," the young American assured her hastily, grinning in relief. "One deep, dark McLanahan family mystery is the limit."

From his side of the conference table, Kevin Martindale cleared his throat. "Much as I hate to interrupt this touching scene of reconciliation and forgiveness, there is still a war on." He motioned toward the tall Iron Wolf war robot. "And while General McLanahan is very much alive in his new abode, the temporary loss of CID One's combat power is something we have to factor into our plans."

"How long will it take to repair the machine?" Wilk asked.

"At least forty-eight hours," Martindale said. "The robot took serious damage from that hit. And if that wasn't enough, the emergency overrides ordered by our friend here so he could keep fighting created a whole series of system failures and melt-downs. Some of my best Scion techs are going to have to strip CID One way down past the exoskel-eton just to get at some of its injuries."

"I see." Wilk nodded. He looked around the table at the Americans. "But perhaps this reduction in your Iron Wolf fighting force will not matter too much. So far, your campaign has been successful beyond my most fervent hopes and prayers."

"That is so," Nadia agreed with deep satisfaction. "The Twentieth Guards Army is stalled far from our border—unable to advance against us and unable even to retreat without risking further ambush." She grinned. "Our metal wolves have taught them to fear the dark . . . and now even the day."

"Unfortunately, we haven't been able to delay Gryzlov's other invasion army," Martindale re-minded the two Poles. "Its troops and tanks are still on the move."

"True." Wilk nodded again. "However, I believe my country's conventional forces can stop them cold, especially now that your earlier victories have made Moscow reluctant to use its airpower against us."

The Americans, including the CID, exchanged worried looks. The robot leaned down again. "With respect, sir, it's far too soon to pop the cork on any victory champagne. Gennadiy Gryzlov has other weapons at his disposal." His voice was somber. "And he is not a quitter." Martindale and Brad nodded their agreement.

"You refer to the Russian missile forces?" Wilk asked quietly.

"That's right," Martindale said. He reached into the briefcase at his feet and brought out a sheaf of printouts. With a flourish, he handed them to the Polish president. Other copies went to Brad and Nadia. "This stuff is hot, Piotr. As in practically 'burn *before* reading' hot."

Wilk glanced at the top page. It was marked *Top Secret CLARION—NOFORN* in bold red letters. He raised an eyebrow. "NOFORN?"

"No foreign national access allowed," Martindale explained. "Which definitely means you, and every other NATO ally, for that matter." He nodded toward the documents. "What you're looking at is an emergency alert sent yesterday to all major American military commands in Europe and the Middle East. The Russians have moved a substantial tactical missile force—possibly as many as three brigades of their Iskander-M and R-500 cruise missile launchers—into a position in Kaliningrad from which they can hit most of Poland's military and political infrastructure." He grimaced. "And if that wasn't bad enough, there are clear signs that Moscow has deployed tactical nuclear warheads to the same location."

"My God," Wilk muttered, staring down at the papers in his hands as if they had suddenly transformed into a nest of scorpions. "Are they insane?"

"The Russians don't think about nuclear weapons, at least tactical nukes, the same way we do," Patrick McLanahan said grimly. "They see them as potentially useful battlefield tools."

"That goes double for Gennadiy Gryzlov," Martindale agreed. His eyes narrowed. "His father taught him that much when he hit us thirteen years ago."

Heads around the table nodded. Nobody needed to dwell on the murderous attack Anatoliy Gryzlov had ordered against America's ICBM and long-range bomber forces. While the Russians had refrained from using high-yield strategic nuclear warheads, their smaller weapons had killed tens of thousands. With that history in mind, no one could doubt that Russia's current president might use the same kinds of weapons against a much smaller, much weaker country—especially one without a nuclear deterrent of its own.

"Then we must destroy these missiles before they can be launched," Wilk said.

"Yes, sir," Brad agreed absently, leafing through the pages of the Pentagon's warning. He stopped at a map showing the deployment zone for the Russian missile units. "Oh, shit . . ." He looked sick suddenly. "I have this really bad feeling that we don't have a lot of time left to take those launchers out."

"What do you mean, son?" Patrick asked sharply.

"Some weird new intel came through from Scion right before President Wilk arrived," Brad explained. "I was going to run it by you guys later, but now I'm afraid I know what it means." Seeing his father's CID give him a minute, encouraging nod, he went on. "Besides rifling through Pentagon databases, Mr. Martindale's computer specialists have been poking around inside Russia's Internet and telecommunications networks."

This time, they all nodded in understanding. Hacking Russia's communications had provided much of the intelligence they'd used to plan the Iron Wolf Squadron's raids on Konotop, Barano-vichi, and other targets.

He showed them the map of the Kaliningrad area he'd been looking at. "Well, they just spotted a weird pattern in the cell- and satellite-phone and Internet activity in this sector."

"What kind of pattern, Brad?" Nadia asked.

"About an hour ago, that whole region just went totally dark. There's zero communications activity. As in no wireless or satellite calls in or out at all. Every Internet connection is also down."

"Which means the Russian units stationed there have gone on total EMCON," Martindale realized abruptly. "Shutting down all outside communica-tions is pretty standard security practice before any big operation. So it's a safe bet that Gryzlov is readying his tactical missiles for a massive strike."

"Can our Iron Wolf ground forces destroy them?" Wilk asked.

"Not with just one CID operational, sir," Patrick said. Then, looking through the Pentagon's assess-ment of the missile deployment area's defenses, he shook his head. "Not even with two robots, really. Gryzlov has this zone ringed with troops and SAMs. If we were willing to take a one-way trip, we might be able to punch a hole—but not in time to stop him from launching. Before we broke through, his warheads would be raining down across Poland."

"Then we hit them with our remote-piloted XF-111 SuperVarks," Brad said. "They're the only weapons we've got that can get in fast and still have a shot at blowing those launchers to hell and gone."

"You believe your bombers can penetrate all those layers of antiaircraft defenses?" Wilk asked, unable to hide his disbelief. "How is that possible?"

"It'll be really tough to pull off," Brad admitted. "And we'll lose a lot of aircraft, maybe even most of them. But I've run our Iron Wolf crews through simulated attacks on complexes almost as heavily defended as this one. With the right mix of tactics and weapons, I think we can take those missile brigades out." He looked around the table at the others. "Anyway, what choice do we really have? We either go all the way in now with the XF-111s and Coyotes, or we might as well call Gryzlov and ask for surrender terms."

Wilk sat silently, deep in thought for what seemed an eternity. No one else spoke. Martindale, the two McLanahans, and even Captain Rozek could offer him advice. But this had to be his decision and his alone. Knowing now that the Russians might be planning the use of nuclear weapons—even so-called tactical weapons—against his nation and its armed forces, could he justify the risks involved in further resistance?

Nearly eighty years before, Poland had been crushed, partitioned, and enslaved by Nazi Germany and Stalinist Russia. Millions of her people had been murdered or starved to death. Even the end of the Second World War had brought only more decades of Communist oppression. But through all her suffering, Poland's spirit had endured—kept alive because so many of her ragged, brutalized people refused to kneel before tyrants. Could he do less?

For a moment longer, Piotr Wilk searched through his mind, trying to find the right words, words that would resonate with these brave American allies of his beleaguered nation. At last they came to him, in the ringing call to arms uttered by the American patriot Patrick Henry. He looked up, meeting their worried gaze with a defiant smile. " 'Is life so dear, or peace so sweet, as to be purchased at the price of chains and slavery?' " he quoted. " 'Forbid it, Almighty God! I know not what course others may take; but as for me, give me liberty or give me death!' "

Teary-eyed with pride, Nadia Rozek brought her fist down on the table. "Yes! We strike!"

"To win or lose it all?" Martindale asked softly.

Somberly, Wilk nodded. He turned to Brad. "Mr. McLanahan," he said solemnly. "You will carry out an attack on the Russian missile forces as soon as your aircraft can be prepared for flight and armed."

OVER POLAND
A short time later

The Polish Air Force W-3 *Sokół* VIP helicopter carrying Wilk and Martindale back to Warsaw flew low over the blacked-out countryside. Two F-16C fighters patrolled ahead.

Though he usually preferred flying in the co-pilot's seat, Wilk had decided to make this hop in the helicopter's passenger compartment. He and the American head of Scion needed to confer on alternative war plans in the event that the Iron Wolf strike failed or was only partially successful.

"Besides evacuating your cabinet officials and armed forces staff out of Warsaw, you'll need to disperse as many combat aircraft as you can as soon as possible," Martindale said. "It's a safe bet that your air bases are high up on Gryzlov's target list."

Wilk nodded, pulling up data on his personal tablet. "Not counting active military fields, there are another eighty or so civilian airfields with paved runways." He frowned. "Not all of them are suitable, and some, like our major airports, will also be hit in a first wave." He looked across the narrow space at Martindale. "Moving the fighters is relatively easy. I doubt we'll have time to shift much of our ordnance, fuel, and maintenance stocks."

"True," the American agreed. "But keeping something up your sleeve—even just enough F-16s and MiG-29s to make one or two combat sorties—is always better than nothing."

"Mr. President," the helicopter pilot's voice cut in through their headsets. "I am receiving an urgent encrypted radio transmission relayed through Warsaw. The American president is asking to speak with you immediately!"

Wilk exchanged a surprised look with Martindale. What more could Barbeau possibly have to say to him? Another patronizing suggestion that Poland yield to Moscow? More demands that he get rid of his so-called mercenaries? Well, he thought wearily, there was only one way to find out. "Patch her through, Jerzy."

Almost immediately, Stacy Anne Barbeau's

honey-sweet voice came through his earphones. "Mr. President? Piotr? Are you there?"

Wilk raised an eyebrow. *Now* she wanted to be on a first-name basis with him? "Yes, Madam President?" he said.

"Thank God, I was able to reach you, Piotr!" she exclaimed. "First, because I really need to apologize for believing that Russian bullshit about those terrorist attacks!"

"Excuse me?"

"My intelligence people just showed me new evidence that proves your country was framed," Barbeau said, speaking quickly. "Which means you were right all along. And it means I got terrible advice from the military and foreign policy folks I trusted when this crisis broke!"

"I am very glad to hear this admission of error, Madam President," Wilk said, more slowly. He raised an eyebrow at Martindale. New evidence? The American shook his head in puzzlement, indicating that his own intelligence analysts hadn't found anything resembling that kind of proof when prowling through CIA and NSA databases. Wilk frowned. "But while this news is welcome, it does nothing to offset the great peril my nation faces now."

"That's the second reason for this call," Barbeau told him. Her voice grew even more fervent. "My administration has to make this right! We have to stand with you against this unprovoked Russian aggression! And that's why I've authorized the dispatch of immediate American military aid to Poland. My hope is that our show of support will convince Moscow to back down before this war escalates out of control."

"What kind of military aid?" Wilk asked carefully.

"Not as much as I would like at first," Barbeau admitted. "It'll take time to ramp up the flow of supplies and weapons. But I've ordered my Pentagon people to do what they can as fast as possible. That's why we have a flight of C-17 transports in the air right now. They're loaded with supplies—mostly our best antitank guided missiles—and with some military liaison teams to help your troops use them effectively. Those C-17s are only minutes outside your airspace, on the way to that military base outside Warsaw."

"Mińsk Mazowiecki?"

"That's the one!" Barbeau said warmly. "Can you give our planes clearance through your air defense network?"

Inwardly, Wilk seethed. She thought the belated gift of a few antitank missiles and some Special Forces advisers would make up for betraying their alliance earlier—when it most mattered? Did she believe him to be that desperate? Or that naive? Or had Russia's recent battlefield defeats convinced Barbeau that it was time to jump on the victory bandwagon?

Then again, he reminded himself, Poland was still threatened by Gryzlov's missiles. His country still needed all the military help it could get—no matter how small or seemingly insignificant. "Very well, Madam President," he said. "I will clear your C-17s through to land at Warsaw."

THE WHITE HOUSE, WASHINGTON, D.C.

That same time

Quickly, President Barbeau cut the connection to her Polish counterpart. Then she glanced at her personal computer. Moscow time was eight hours ahead of D.C. It was already very late there.

For a moment more, she hesitated. What she was doing was risky, insanely risky. But what choice did she really have? Could she allow the Poles and Martindale to drag America and the rest of Europe into a wider war? A nuclear war? Pull yourself together, Stacy Anne, she told herself sternly. Of course not! Besides, it was too late to back out now. Events were already in motion.

She pulled open a desk drawer and took out a brand-new smartphone. It wasn't registered to her or to anyone in the White House. Years of political wheeling and dealing, often at or beyond the edge of strict legality, had taught her the vital importance of being able to communicate without being traced. One firm touch on the small screen dialed the number of another, equally anonymous phone. "Luke, honey," she said to the groggy-sounding man on the other end. "You tell our mutual friend that it's on. The Poles have just opened their back door."

Another firm finger press ended the call.

Then, unhurriedly, Stacy Anne Barbeau got up from her desk and headed for the White House Situation Room.

CHAPTER 13

*Courage is the capacity to
confront what can be imagined.*

— LEO ROSTEN, RUSSIAN
AMERICAN TEACHER
AND WRITER

OVER POLAND
A short time later

U.S. Army Ranger First Sergeant Mike Ikeda leaned close to his commanding officer, Captain Daniel Rojas, speaking just loud enough to be heard over the droning roar of the C-17's four big engines. "You know this operation is totally FUBAR'd, sir, right?"

Rojas shot him a tight, irritated grin. "As per usual, Sergeant? Or in its own very special way?"

"All on its own," Ikeda said. He shook his head in disgust. "First, because we're hitting the wrong side in this war. Second, because two platoons in one

C-17 isn't enough troops to safely accomplish the mission. And three, because the ROEs are screwy beyond belief." He tapped the M320 single-shot grenade launcher attached to his M4 carbine. "What is this 'nonlethal' bullshit? I'm really supposed to use this thing like it's a fricking giant Taser?"

Rojas frowned. "You've been trained in the use of the 40mm Human Electro-Muscular Incapacitation Projectile, haven't you, First Sergeant?"

"Sure thing, Captain," Ikeda said. "The damn HEMI thing works great for crowd control. I can reach out and zap some son of a bitch troublemaker with fifty thousand volts up to a couple hundred feet away." He glowered. "But I think it royally sucks as the weapon of choice when you're going up against fully armed troops."

Now Rojas sighed. "The rules of engagement specify nonlethal weapons use precisely *because* we don't want to kill anyone we don't have to. This is supposed to be a quick, tight, surgical operation with a very specific and very limited objective."

"Yes, sir," Ikeda agreed. He shrugged. "I just hope like hell the guys on the other side understand that."

"Amen, First Sergeant," Rojas said. "Any other complaints?" he asked drily.

"Just one for now, sir," the Ranger noncom said. He jerked a thumb back over his shoulder. "That AFSOC Zoomie gives me the creeps. The guy's so fucking gung ho that he's gotta be bucking for a goddamn medal. And that's the kind of shit that could get other people killed."

Rojas glanced back into the crowded troop com-

partment. Even among the tightly packed Army
Rangers and Air Force Special Operations commandos, he had no trouble spotting First Lieutenant William Weber. The tall, wiry young Air Force
officer wore thick horn-rimmed sports glasses and
his eyes gleamed with excitement. He was talking
animatedly to the members of his own team, jab-
bing a stiff finger into the palm of his hand to emphasize his points.

"Yeah, you may be right, Mike," the Ranger captain said slowly. "So we follow our part of the plan
and secure the perimeter. Let Weber and his guys
handle the technical stuff like they're supposed to."

"Yes, sir."

A red light flashed inside the darkened compartment.
The C-17's jumpmaster yelled, "Five minutes! Outboard
personnel stand up!" Struggling against the weight of
their parachutes and other gear, the Rangers and Air
Force commandos seated along the fuselage levered
themselves upright and turned to face the rear ramp.

"Inboard personnel! On your feet!" The troops
seated in two rows facing outward got up. Slowly,
the noise of the C-17's engines began diminishing.
The big plane was slowing toward jump speed . . .

REMOTE OPERATIONS CONTROL CENTER, POWIDZ, POLAND
A short time later

The eighteen men and women making up nine of the
Iron Wolf Squadron's ten XF-111 remote-piloting

crews crowded inside the ready room, listening intently while Brad McLanahan briefed them on the most recent intelligence affecting their mission.

"From the radar emissions our RQ-20 Vedette chain is picking up, we're pretty sure the Russians have a Beriev-100 up over Krylovo in south-central Kaliningrad, near the Polish border, covering the approaches to the Iskander missile field," Brad said, keying in the Russian AWACS plane's estimated position on the big wall display. He then keyed in another position on the map, not far outside the predicted maximum detection range for the Beriev-100's radar. "As per the mission plan, two Coyotes took off twenty minutes ago, heading for this point. We're positioning the third Coyote to the east in case it's needed against the Russian Army moving in from the east. They're armed with—"

A small cylinder hit the floor in front of him, bounced once, and then went off with a blinding, earsplitting *BANG*.

The explosion threw Brad back against the display. In that same moment, another flashbang grenade detonated at the back of the ready room. Smoke and bits of torn ceiling insulation swirled through the air. Before the stunned and disoriented Iron Wolf pilots and weapons officers could recover their wits, a sea of heavily armed men stormed through the gray haze—knocking them to the floor at gunpoint.

What the hell? Brad thought woozily. He tried to straighten up, and then went down hard when one of the invaders kicked his feet out from under him. With brutal efficiency, the other man yanked his wrists behind his back and secured them with plastic flexicuffs.

One by one, the Iron Wolf crews were hauled to their feet, cuffed, and prodded back against a wall by soldiers in battle dress and body armor. American soldiers, Brad realized groggily as the smoke cleared. He gritted his teeth. They were being held at gunpoint by U.S. Special Forces troops? This was just *wrong*—on so many more levels than his aching brain could count right now.

Slowly, his battered ears stopped ringing. Now he could hear more noises coming from the rest of the Remote Operations Control Center—the sounds of shattering glass and plastic. Overhead, the lights flickered and an acrid smell of frying circuit boards and other electronics rolled in through the open ready-room door. Oh, shit, he realized, these bastards are wrecking our remote-control stations.

A tall, lean U.S. Air Force officer with first lieutenant's bars on his collar strutted down the line of prisoners. Pale blue eyes gleamed evilly behind thick glasses. He stopped in front of Brad and looked him up and down. A sneer formed on his pale, thin face. "Well, well, well, what do we have here?" he said in a thick Alabama drawl. "I do believe this is that well-known, thoroughly useless piece of dog crap named Bradley J. McLanahan."

Oh, hell, Brad thought, suddenly recognizing him. Three years ago, then second-class cadet William Weber had goaded him into losing his temper during "Second Beast"—the three-week field training camp that every would-be cadet had to pass before starting the first academic year at the U.S.

Air Force Academy in Colorado Springs. Decking
that smug son of a bitch had felt really good at the
time, but it had also cost him his appointment to
the Academy and any hope of a career in the U.S.
military.

"Man, that's sure a slick getup," Weber taunted,
tapping Brad's dark, rifle-green Iron Wolf Squadron
jacket with a long index finger. "Does it help you sell
many Girl Scout cookies?" He snorted. "You and
your fancy-pants mercenaries aren't so tough without your big metal friends around to bail you out,
are you?"

With an effort, Brad kept his mouth shut. Did
Weber and his goons believe the Iron Wolf special ops
teams were still out in the field? Oh, man, he thought,
were they riding for a very unpleasant fall . . .

Weber adjusted the video cam on his helmet,
grinning nastily. "Say hello to the good folks back
in the States, McLanahan. Because here the party's
over. Your next stop is a cell in a federal maximum-
security prison."

POWIDZ FLIGHT LINE
That same time

Inside one of the camouflaged, bomb-resistant shelters built to hide and protect the Iron Wolf Squadron's aircraft, Captain Nadia Rozek kept tabs on
the fueling and arming operation for the XF-111
SuperVark Brad and she would fly remotely during
the attack. Moving smoothly, the Cybernetic In-

fantry Device piloted by Patrick McLanahan picked up one of the AGM-154A Joint Standoff Weapons, or JSOWs, and neatly slotted the thousand-pound weapon into place on one of the big plane's inboard pylons. Not nearly as long-ranged or sophisticated as the newer AGM-158 JASSMs, the stealthy glide weapon carried a warhead better suited to the task of nailing a large number of Russian missile launchers and support vehicles—a warhead packed full of 145 BLU-97B Combined Effects Bomb submunitions, complete with shaped charges to puncture enemy armor, a fragmenting case to spread deadly splinters, and a zirconium ring to set intense fires. All up and down the airfield's flight line, other Iron Wolf ground crews were equally hard at work in similar shelters, readying the rest of the strike force for its mission.

Suddenly the tall, man-shaped robot stiffened. Its head spun toward Nadia. "We may have trouble," its electronically synthesized voice said. "All my data feeds from the remote-control center just went down."

"Some kind of power failure?" Nadia asked.

The CID shook its head. "Not possible. The ROCC auxiliary generators are still running. But the problem may be inside the building, possibly just a wiring fault."

"Perhaps that is so," Nadia said, already moving toward the tall doors at the back of the aircraft shelter. She snatched up her MSBS 5.56mm Radon carbine on the way. "But I think I would like to make sure of that for myself. I don't trust so-called accidents so close to our takeoff."

"Neither do I," Patrick said, maneuvering his CID in the same direction. "Because the base control tower just went off the air."

Nadia flipped the shelter lights off and slid out into the black and silent woods behind the camouflaged hangar. The Iron Wolf robot, moving with astonishing grace and stealth, came with her. Together, they glided right to the edge of the forest, and went low—carefully scanning the runway and surrounding buildings.

"Those are not our people," Nadia murmured grimly, watching as a number of four-man teams of soldiers fanned out across the airfield. Despite being burdened by body armor, they moved quickly. They were clearly establishing a defensive perimeter.

"No," Patrick said tersely. "But they're mine." He paused. "Or, they used to be." The CID inclined its head toward hers again. "Those are U.S. Army Rangers. And from what I can pick up with my audio sensors and from their radio transmissions, their orders are to arrest Scion's mercenaries without seriously harming any Poles. If possible."

"How . . . polite . . . of them," Nadia said. Her bared teeth gleamed white in the darkness.

"Well," Patrick said, and she could swear she heard a grin in his electronic voice, "that bit of White House–imposed restraint does make our job a bit easier." He paused for a moment, mentally radioing messages to the rest of the Iron Wolf field teams as if playing a song in his mind. "I've alerted Whack Macomber and Ian Schofield and their special operations team, plus your own Polish Special

Forces units that were working with them. None of our guys are happy about this interruption."

That, Nadia suspected, was a massive understatement. Major Macomber, Captain Schofield, and the others had gotten back to Powidz only a few hours ago—after spending days behind enemy lines. Having their small sliver of much-needed rest and recreation interrupted by a treacherous American Special Forces raid—against one of their own ally's air bases—was definitely going to make them very angry. How would Brad put it? Oh, yes, she thought, it would "piss them off royally."

A worrying thought struck her. She looked up at the CID. "What about Brad and our other pilots and crewmen? They were in the ROCC when this attack started."

"They're being held as prisoners," Patrick said flatly.

"Then we must rescue them!" Nadia exclaimed.

"Indeed we must," the CID agreed. "But first we have to take care of the Rangers guarding the perimeter. Quietly. And without seriously hurting any of them. If possible."

SQUEEEEEEEEEEE.

Painfully shrill electronic noise spiked through First Sergeant Mike Ikeda's ears. He shifted frequencies. And again. No good. The mind-tearing noise was still there, on every channel. Someone was jamming their tactical radio net. Wincing, the Ranger noncom yanked his headset off. Blessed silence followed.

Swell, he thought. So much for stealth and surprise. Somebody on this Polish air base sure as hell knew the Americans were here. And without the ability to communicate by radio, the Ranger force was going to have to fall back on old-fashioned methods. As in the Mark I pair of legs issued to every soldier the day he was born.

Ikeda glanced at the Ranger private at his side. "We need to report in to Captain Rojas, Mulvaney. So follow me. Keep your eyes peeled and that dumbass Taser ready."

The other Ranger looked worried. "If the Poles are jamming us, Sarge, shouldn't we dump the nonlethal jazz?" He patted the butt of the M4 carbine slung across his chest. "This little beauty can reach out and touch hostiles a hell of a lot farther away."

Reluctantly, Ikeda shook his head. "You wanna start a firefight with a NATO ally on its own turf, Private? Because I sure don't." He scowled. "Not unless the captain says otherwise, anyway. So let's go find him, shall we?"

Together the two Rangers scuttled through the tall grass and brush lining the main runway. At last report, Captain Rojas and his command group were set up alongside one of those shelters the Poles had built for their F-111 fighter-bombers. That was a good central location for controlling their defensive perimeter and keeping watch over the runway. The C-17 that had dropped them over Powidz was already circling back to pick them up—using the excuse of mechanical trouble to explain its inability to fly on to Warsaw. And once they had those Scion mercenaries on board as prisoners, the plan was to skedaddle out of Polish airspace at high speed. There were U.S. Air Force F-22 Raptors and even a pair of brand-new F-35 Lightning IIs waiting over Germany to escort them to safety.

Feeling more and more exposed as they moved from shadow to shadow through the eerily quiet base, Ikeda led the way up to the front of the large camouflaged building. The big pair of double doors facing the runway were closed tight, concealing the aircraft parked inside.

Cautiously, the Ranger sergeant poked his head around the corner of the shelter. Through his night-vision goggles, he could see a small group of helmeted figures clustered together around a satellite phone dish. Whatever Rojas and his team were doing, they looked pretty focused. No point in startling the crap out of them by just dropping into their midst, he thought. And then probably getting Tasered by accident. Most Rangers had itchy trigger fingers and scarily fast reflexes. "Captain?" he hissed. "It's Ikeda. I'm coming in."

Nothing. Nobody over there even twitched.

What the hell? Ikeda swallowed hard. This op was going south really damned fast. He glanced at Mulvaney. The Ranger private looked as nervous as he felt. "Wait here and cover me," he growled. The other man nodded jerkily.

With a HEMI grenade loaded and ready to fire from his M320 launcher, Ikeda ghosted through the tall grass over to where Rojas and the others were huddled. He dropped to one knee and shook the captain by the shoulder. And then the others. No reaction. They were all out cold.

Thump.

Ikeda's head snapped back toward the aircraft shelter. What was that soft sound, something like a beanbag hitting a wall? His eyes opened wider. Mulvaney was gone. Just gone.

"There's a moment in any poker game where folding is the only good move, Sergeant Ikeda," a weird electronic voice said suddenly from somewhere close behind him. "This is one of those moments."

The Ranger noncom swiveled around again, weapon at the ready. There, only a few meters away, stood a tall, spindly-armed shape. Oh, fuck, he realized. That was one of those Cybernetic Infantry Devices they'd been briefed on—the creepy-ass war robots the mission planners had assured them would be hundreds of miles away, deep behind Russian lines. I was so right, he thought bitterly. This whole operation was totally FUBAR'd from the get-go.

He moistened dry lips. "What the hell did you use on the captain and the others?" he demanded. "Some kind of knockout gas?" Slowly, very slowly, he let his hand drift down toward the pouch where he'd stored one of the anti-CID weapons they'd been issued, a microwave pulse generator grenade. In theory, hitting a robot with one of those would be like nailing it with a lightning bolt—frying every one of its systems, including its life support, instantaneously.

"Nothing permanent, Sergeant," the machine assured him. "My CID carries a microwave emitter weapon. Basically, it heats up the fluids in the skin of any living target. The longer the beam is focused on you, the more heat, pain, and disorientation you feel, until finally you lose consciousness."

"Sounds like that would take some time," Ikeda forced himself to say calmly. His fingers closed around the microwave pulse grenade.

The strange machine nodded its six-sided head. "Several seconds at least, Sergeant," it said. "Maybe even long enough for you to load and fire that pulse grenade you just grabbed." Its head lifted slightly. "Now would be good, Whack."

ZAAAPP.

Ikeda felt himself knocked to his knees and then onto his back. Every muscle in his body locked up tight. He started twitching uncontrollably, utterly incapacitated and out of control.

Footsteps came closer and a big, powerfully built man loomed over him. "Sorry about that, sport," he said with a tight grin. "I guess those Tasers your other Rangers were carrying do pack a wallop."

REMOTE OPERATIONS CONTROL CENTER
A short time later

"Have you been able to reestablish communication with Captain Rojas yet, Lieutenant?" said a voice made familiar from a hundred political speeches and press conferences in First Lieutenant William Weber's headset.

Unconsciously, he stood up straighter. Having the undivided attention of the president of the United

States during a vital commando mission should do wonders for his career—unless he screwed up. "Not as yet, Madam President," he said quickly. "But we think the mess of electronics and shielding in this building may explain the loss of contact. As a precaution, though, I have dispatched a runner to locate Captain Rojas, and I expect to hear from him very shortly."

"Unfortunately, there may be other . . . snags . . . developing in the mission," Stacy Anne Barbeau said slowly, speaking from the White House Situation Room more than four thousand miles away. "We've lost contact with the rest of the assault force, too."

Weber felt cold. "Lost contact, ma'am?" he stammered. "When did—"

Just then the wall at the far end of the ready room burst inward in a spray of broken concrete and splintered wood. A huge, man-shaped machine stalked through the jagged hole it had opened and swiveled toward Weber, his stunned men, and their prisoners. The 25mm autocannon it carried on its right shoulder swung to cover them.

Reacting instinctively, Weber grabbed Brad McLanahan and swung the younger man in front of him for cover. He snatched the M9 Beretta holstered at his side and pressed it hard against Brad's head.

"Back away from my son," the CID said quietly. Its electronic voice was familiar, somehow.

Through his headset, Weber heard a startled gasp from President Barbeau. He ignored it. "What the fuck did you just say?" he snarled.

"I said, back away from my son, Lieutenant," the robot said again, louder this time.

For a moment, Weber froze. "General McLanahan?" he mumbled. His mouth was suddenly dry. "But . . . but you're dead!"

"Evidently not, Lieutenant," the CID said coldly. Its voice hardened. "Now follow my orders. Release my son, set your weapon down, and then put your hands on top of your head." Its six-sided head swung slightly from side to side, taking in the other American soldiers who were standing absolutely still, being very careful to make no sudden moves; the autocannon on the robot's shoulder swung around and pointed at the others like a serpent on Medusa's head. "That goes for the rest of you, too."

Recovering fast, Weber shook his head. "No way in hell!" He ground his pistol muzzle even harder into Brad's temple. This was his chance to show the president and her entire national security team how you dealt with a whack-job lunatic like Patrick God Almighty McLanahan. He smirked openly. "What are you going to do, shoot me right through your own boy? I know you're a coldhearted son of a bitch, but is that really how you want to play this?"

"I have no intention of shooting you, Lieutenant," the machine said calmly.

"I didn't think so," Weber sneered. This was how you played an ace, he thought gleefully. With Brad as his hostage and human shield, there was nothing that metal monster could do to him, or to his troops. And then he froze in horror as something cold and hard and round pressed against the back of his own skull.

"*He* won't shoot you, *dupek*," a low, husky woman's voice said sweetly in his ear. "But *I* will."

"You wouldn't dare," Weber stuttered, feeling his knees starting to buckle.

"Would I not?" the woman behind him asked, drily amused. "My country is under attack by Russia. My president has authorized me to free these men and women who are our defenders, using *any means necessary*. And you, *dupek*, asshole, are threatening the man I love. So just what do you think I will do?"

Numbly, aware suddenly of a sense of utter, irretrievable, and humiliating failure, Weber carefully moved the pistol away from Brad's head and thumbed the safety back on.

The woman behind him took the pistol out of his unresisting hand. "Thank you, Lieutenant," she said. "I guess you will get to live. This time."

She shoved him forward with the muzzle of her assault rifle as another group of armed men, most of them in Polish Special Forces battle dress, poured into the ready room. Within seconds, First Lieutenant William Weber and the rest of his dumbfounded AFSOC commandos found themselves being hustled outside under close guard.

As Weber was being hauled away, Patrick stopped him by snapping an armored hand on the Air Force lieutenant's chest—it felt like running headlong into a lamppost. Patrick put the fingers of his other hand under Weber's chin and raised his head so that the sports camera on his helmet was aimed right at the CID's head.

"You are a traitor to your country and to your allies, Barbeau," Patrick said into the camera, his electronically synthesized voice low and menacing. "If we get out of this alive, I'll make you pay. I promise."

Back at the White House Situation Room, President Stacy Anne Barbeau had risen to her feet in absolute shock, watching through the secure satellite video as her assault team moved with precision and sheer power . . . and then just as quickly and just as precisely got shut down. Now she and her national security staff were staring right into the blank, light gray sensor face of a Cybernetic Infantry Device robot, piloted by . . .

"McLanahan," whispered the president. "No. It can't be."

The robot's armored hand reached up, blocking the camera's view. They heard a very brief crackling and snapping sound as the robot's fingers closed over the camera, and then the view died away.

For several excruciatingly awkward minutes after the video feed from Lieutenant Weber's helmet cam went dead, none of the military officers or civilian officials in the Situation Room said a word. They sat in frozen silence, deliberately avoiding eye contact with President Barbeau. She stared at the now-black display in open disbelief.

At last, she looked away from the screen, turning a hard-eyed stare on her stunned advisers. "Did anyone in this room know that Patrick McLanahan was alive—instead of blessedly dead?" Her gaze focused on Thomas Torrey, the head of the CIA. "Well?"

"No, Madam President," he said, shaking his head. "None of my people had any idea that General McLanahan survived the grave injuries he suffered two years ago."

"Twenty billion dollars in funding a goddamned year and your spooks at Langley can't keep track of one shot-up, troublemaking flyboy?" Barbeau commented tartly. "I don't find that terribly comforting."

General Spelling sat forward abruptly, looking down the long table at her. The chairman of the Joint Chiefs was visibly angry. Finding out that the president had gone behind his back to order a covert commando raid against a NATO ally was reason enough. Being forced to watch in tight-lipped silence while that same ill-conceived raid failed so abjectly only made it worse. "McLanahan's death or survival is a minor issue in this mess," he said firmly. "Nearly one hundred American soldiers just went into the bag in what was once one of our closest European allies. Getting them home safely must be our first priority." His jaw was set. "Once that's done, we can start sorting out the leadership foulups and screwed-up decision making that led to this fiasco in the first place."

Barbeau glared back at him. The Air Force general wasn't even trying to be subtle. He was openly threatening to lay this disaster at *her* feet—rather than where it rightly belonged, with SOCOM's evidently piss-poor planning and mission execution. If push came to shove, party loyalty would probably keep any congressional investigations from getting out of hand, at least as long as Luke Cohen kept his mouth shut about her prior consultation with

Moscow. But the process would still be politically damaging and embarrassing.

Besides, she realized, Spelling was wrong about what really mattered. The capture of a relative handful of men, even elite Rangers and Air Force commandos, was nothing—not when the Russians were threatening to escalate their war with Poland into a war against the United States itself. "On the contrary, General," she snapped. "McLanahan's unexpected reappearance among the living lies right at the heart of this crisis."

Spelling opened his mouth to argue, but a tiny headshake from the CIA director dissuaded him. "In what way, Madam President?" Torrey asked quietly.

"I've read the psychological profile your analysts put together on Gennadiy Gryzlov," Barbeau said. "Did you?" Torrey nodded slowly. "Then you tell me, Tom," she continued matter-of-factly. "What happens when Gryzlov finds out the man who killed his father is actually still alive—and worse, running the mercenary outfit that's been kicking the shit out of Russia's armed forces?"

"Oh, hell," Edward Rauch muttered. Her national security adviser turned sheet-white. "He'll go totally fucking nuts."

"Which is exactly why we have to contain this situation *now*," Barbeau said. "Before the Russians put all the pieces together." She sighed. "At least, we've spiked McLanahan's guns for the moment by wrecking Scion's operations base. Whatever wild-assed stunt he was planning with those souped-up robotic F-111s will have to go on hold."

"I'm afraid not, ma'am," Spelling said flatly. "I know Patrick McLanahan. Sure, his original plan might have called for some kind of remotely piloted strike, but he's not going to let what our guys did to his ops center stop him. Not while he still has flyable aircraft and trained crews."

Stacy Anne Barbeau's eyes widened as she realized that the general was right. And there was no doubt that McLanahan would be right there with them, flying the lead F-111. That was his style. "What's his target, then? Moscow? Gryzlov himself?"

"No, Madam President," Torrey said. "Moscow is too heavily defended. And the odds against actually finding and killing Gennadiy Gryzlov with a small strike force would be astronomical." The CIA director looked thoughtful. "My bet would be the tactical missile brigades the Russians have deployed in Kaliningrad."

"Those Iskander units are the last real weapon left in Gryzlov's hands," Spelling agreed. "Between them, the Poles and those Scion aircraft and CIDs have already defeated Russia's readily available ground and air forces."

"Oh, Christ," Barbeau muttered to herself, imagining her Russian counterpart's likely reaction to another attack by Scion's mercenary pilots. She looked down that table at Spelling. "Could those Scion F-111s actually pull off a successful strike?"

The chairman of the Joint Chiefs shook his head. "Against the kind of defenses the Russians have deployed to cover their Iskanders? I seriously doubt it. I'd be surprised if any of those aircraft could even make it all the way to the target area, let alone inflict significant damage." Then he shrugged. "But I've been surprised by Patrick McLanahan before."

For a moment, Barbeau was strongly tempted to break away from the Situation Room and call Luke Cohen in Moscow. If the Russians knew for sure an F-111 attack was coming, their own fighters and SAMs could bushwhack McLanahan's air strike and stop it cold. But then she reconsidered. She'd already jeopardized her political future by letting Gryzlov know about her plans to hit Scion's operating base. Openly colluding with the Russians would be a step too far—even as a desperate attempt to preserve the broader peace.

No, Barbeau thought coldly, for now she would just have to hope that Gryzlov's fighters and air defenses could blast McLanahan and his F-111s out of the sky themselves. And if the Russians failed? Well, then all bets were off.

Brad stood rock-still while Nadia carefully sliced through the plastic ties cuffing his hands, completely unable to wipe what he was sure was a remarkably stupid, shit-eating grin off his face. When she finished, he gathered her in his arms for a heartfelt, passionate kiss. Grinning up at him, she kissed him back.

"Thank you," he whispered in her ear. "I owe you."

"Yes, you do," Nadia agreed, still grinning wickedly. "And I plan to collect my debt as soon as possible . . . and as often as I can!"

"Before you two get completely carried away,"

Patrick said, gently interrupting, "we have a serious problem."

Brad looked up at his father's CID. "Yes, sir. I'm afraid that we do." He glanced over at Mark Darrow. At his request, the ex-RAF pilot had gone to inspect their remote-piloting stations as soon as he was freed.

Darrow's face was grim. "The control cabs are totally buggered, Brad." He shook his head. "Those wankers ripped out every bit of circuitry and wiring, and, from the look of things, they smashed every monitor and display."

"Time to repair, Mark?" Brad asked.

The Englishman shrugged helplessly. "God only knows. Weeks, at least, perhaps months. I suspect it would be faster to fly in replacement equipment from the Scrapheap and rebuild from scratch, but if more of those Rangers are moving against us, that may not be an option."

"Which means the ROCC is down when it matters most, no matter what we do," Brad said, raising his voice so that everyone could hear. "So there's no way we can pilot our planned XF-111 strike remotely."

Nadia looked stricken. "Then we have no way to eliminate Gryzlov's missile force in time."

"Actually, we still do," Brad said quietly. Slowly, he looked around the room—meeting the eyes of every other Iron Wolf pilot and weapons officer. Several of them turned pale, realizing immediately what he proposed. But one by one, they nodded their agreement, however reluctantly.

"Hell, yes," Bill Sievert growled. "Why should Macomber and his guys have all the fun?"

Mark Darrow shrugged. "In for a penny, in for a pound, Brad."

Nadia just kissed him again.

At last, Brad turned back to his father. "Well, Dad, I guess the Iron Wolves will still fly the mission. But we're going to have to do it for real—inside the planes and not from behind a computer console."

CHAPTER 14

> *The true soldier fights not because
> he hates what is in front of him, but
> because he loves what is behind him.*
>
> —G. K. CHESTERTON

**SIXTY KILOMETERS SOUTHEAST OF THE CITY OF
KALININGRAD, KALININGRAD OBLAST**
Two hours later

"**S**ir, early warning radar reports a formation of high-speed aircraft bearing one-nine-five, direction of flight seven-nine-zero, range three hundred kilometers, speed eight hundred, altitude unknown!" the communications officer shouted.

"From the east, exactly as I guessed," Colonel Konrad Saratov, commander of the 72nd Tactical Missile Brigade, said aloud so all in the mobile command center could hear. He was standing behind a row of radar and radio operators inside a mobile command post trailer in the center of the Iskander missile force deployed to Kaliningrad Oblast. He stopped his pacing and stood behind the radar operator manning the feed from the 36D6 long-range radar site. "They obviously can see that we are prepared for an attack from all sides, but the west and south are too heavily defended. Lieutenant, sound air-raid alert throughout the force."

"Sound air . . . air-raid alert, y . . . yes, sir," Lieutenant Kararina Kirov, the deputy action officer, stammered. She tentatively pressed a red button on her panel, which sounded Klaxons outside. The warning would be relayed throughout all of the Iskander missile launch sites and S-300 and S-400 air defense emplacements throughout central Kaliningrad oblast. "Alert s . . . sounded, sir," Kirov said nervously.

"I can hear that myself, Lieutenant," Saratov said flatly. Good thing she was cute, he thought, because she was certainly skittish—that might be fun in the sack, but not in his command post. "Relax yourself. Our defenses are impenetrable. The Americans and Poles are flying right into my trap. Do we have an altitude on that formation?"

"Within range of 76N6 in one minute, sir." The 76N6 was an excellent radar for detecting low-flying, high-speed aircraft, but its range was limited. But once the altitude was determined, the handoff to the 30N6E target-tracking and missile-guidance radar was fast.

"Any IKS signals?" Saratov ordered. IKS, or *identifikatsionnyy kod samolet*, was a transponder and radio code used by all aircraft for identification by radar sites and interceptor aircraft. A missing or in-

correct IKS code usually meant a hostile aircraft . . .
or a friendly who deserved to die because he was not
following the proper identification procedures in a
combat zone.

"Negative IKS," came the reply.

"Number of inbounds?"

"Two separate groups, sir. I cannot break out the
numbers in each group. Close formation, perhaps a
kilometer or two apart."

That was not a very close formation, Saratov
thought—these must be the Polish Air Force, because he knew the Americans had better flying
skills and better combat tactics. "Very well. Break
them out as fast as you can. Where is my fighter
protection?"

"Voron flight is at seventy-five hundred meters,
fifty kilometers from inbounds, closing at Mach
one."

"Weapons tight—I don't want to shoot down our
own aircraft," Saratov said. "Looks like the fighter
boys will get the first shot. All units, acknowledge
my order."

"All units acknowledge weapons tight, sir," Kirov
said a few moments later. She was sounding better,
Saratov thought. "Voron reports he is tied on to our
target-tracking data uplink and will remain radar-
silent until after missile launch."

"Very good," Saratov commented. All frontline
Russian fighters could approach and attack a target
by many means other than using its own radar,
which was always a dead giveaway: they could use
an infrared tracker, or they could use the tracking
and targeting data uplinked from ground radars as

if it was their own onboard radar. The enemy could see the ground radar but wouldn't know that Russian fighters were in the air unless they used their own radars, which would expose themselves. "Time to attack?"

"Ten seconds, sir." He would have liked to listen to his beloved S-300s shoot down the Poles, Saratov thought, but this time the fighter boys could have their fun.

"Sir, Voron reports X-band radar detected! Suspect F-16 fighters inbound!" That confirmed Saratov's guess that it was Polish Air Force invaders—the Americans were flying AN/APG-81 radars in their refurbished F-111 bombers, which were very difficult to detect and track.

"Handoff to 76N6 complete!" a fire control officer shouted excitedly. "Hostile altitude is one hundred and fifty meters! Two groups, two aircraft in each group, now passing through nine hundred kilometers per hour! Solid lock, ready to attack!"

"Weapons tight, I said!" Saratov yelled. "Acknowledge!"

"All weapons tight, sir."

"Voron flight is missiles away, sir," the lieutenant reported. "Fighters engaging." In a head-to-head engagement the missile flight time was very short, and the fighters would probably turn on their radars in just a few seconds for more precise missile steering until the missile's own radar would activate for terminal guidance to the kill. Seconds passed . . . then more seconds . . . then fifteen seconds . . .

"What the hell is going on?" Saratov shouted. "What happened?"

"Sir, Voron flight reports their scopes are clear," Kirov said. "No contacts. All aircraft shot down!"

Saratov knew he should feel relieved and elated, but for some strange reason he didn't—not in the least. "Dispatch search teams to the site of that encounter—I want debris located and identified immediately," he told Kirov. "Then I want—"

"*Radar contact aircraft!* Bearing zero-nine-zero, range two hundred, low altitude, two aircraft, very large!"

They missed! Saratov thought to himself. The fighter pilots missed an easy engagement! Eyes bulging out of his head, he stared dumbfounded at the radar scope. Sure enough, there were two very large aircraft heading west at very low altitude. Were they heavy bombers? Few countries other than the United States, Russia, and perhaps China flew heavy bombers anymore. The planes were moving fast, as fast as a fighter. Did the Americans *send a B-1 bomber* in to attack? "Tell those fighters to clear out of the area until we attack, then return to base!" he shouted. "Double-check you have a solid IKS on our own aircraft! Release batteries! Release all batteries!" Kirov repeated the rapid-fire orders as fast as she could. "Sound the air-raid alert and—"

"Sir, 30N6 radar from Third Battery is off the air!" Kirov reported. Third Battery, with four S-300 launchers and four reload trailers each with four missile canisters, was the southern fire control radar controlling the four southernmost S-300 launchers.

"What do you mean, off the air?" Saratov shouted. "Is it being jammed? Has it malfunctioned? What in hell . . . ?"

"Sir, Third Battery reports it has been hit by a missile!" Kirov said. "Third Battery is under attack!

"Fourth Battery engaging inbound hostiles!" Kirov reported. "Solid lock on two inbound hostiles!"

Bombers! High-subsonic bombers! This was a major escalation! He went back to his own console and hit a button marked *OMY*, which was the direct secure line to his superior officers of the Western Military District.

"Major Kemerov, senior controller, go ahead, Seventy-Second Brigade."

"We are under attack, Major," Saratov said. "One air defense radar has been hit by a missile, and we have engaged two heavy bombers inbound from the east. I need permission to launch my air-to-ground missiles immediately!"

"Stand by, sir," Kemerov said, and the line went silent. Crap, Saratov thought, he'd better damned hurry!

"Inbound bombers down!" he heard over his headset. "Definite kill! Both targets down!"

Saratov wasn't going to buy that one for a second. "All batteries, weapons tight!" he shouted. "Get those fighters back out there to do a radar search! What about our ground spotters? They should have seen an explosion! Are there any visual—"

"*Sir, unidentified aircraft inbound, bearing zero-nine-zero, two hundred kilometers, low altitude, speed eight hundred, heading two-nine-five, two groups!*" came another excited report.

No! Saratov screamed at himself. Three separate contacts, all on virtually the same heading and altitude and almost the same range and speed? "It has to be radar spoofing!" he shouted. "We are being spoofed! Tell Fourth Battery to stay weapons tight! Tell Voron flight to search, but do not fire unless you have positive visual or infrared contact!

"Sir, Third Battery reports they can use their 3R41 radar to fill in for their damaged 30N6," Kirov reported. "Their tracking and fire control range will be reduced, but they will be back online in about ten minutes."

"Ten minutes, like *hell*," Saratov shouted. "If we are under attack, this will be over in *two* minutes!"

"Seventy-Second, this is OMU Alpha." Saratov recognized the voice of Major General Alexander Kornukov, commander of the Western Military District of the Russian armed forces, even over the pops, whistles, and wavering of the constantly encrypted-decrypted line. "What do you have, Konrad?"

"I've got a hatful of shit, sir, that's what I've got!" Saratov exclaimed. "One of my fire control radars was hit by a missile, but I've fired on two sets of radar targets to the east that turned out not to be there! Now I've got a third set of hostiles, but they're at almost the exact same position and track as the others. They're making us expend ordnance on shadows while they pick off our air defense systems, and I'm afraid we're going to lose all the S-300 fire control systems and eventually the Iskanders pretty damned soon. If you don't want to lose them, I suggest you get the order to launch them, sir, and I mean *now*."

"Relax, Konrad," Kornukov said. "As soon as I

got your initial report from the command post I requested an immediate conference with the chief of staff, and I'll speak with him shortly. For now, use your best judgment on your air threats. If you think you have legitimate targets, engage them. Order up reloads; I'll send them out right away. But shoot any bastard that looks like a legitimate hostile. Don't let a real hostile sneak past a spoof. That will land you in the shit with the Kremlin for sure. Copy, Colonel?"

"Yes, sir, I copy all," Saratov said.

"Anything else for me, Konrad?"

"Negative, sir," Saratov responded.

"Good, Konrad," Kornukov said. Saratov recognized a little bit of the helpful, sensitive, and friendly upperclassman comrade he knew during their years at the Yarolslavl Military Academy in the voice of his superior officer. In a much stronger commanding voice, Kornukov added: "Be aggressive and defend those Iskanders to the last missile. Venture on. I'll advise you immediately when you are authorized to engage your assigned ground targets with the Iskanders, but until then keep those slugs safe, secure, ready, and tight. Understood, old friend?"

"Understood, sir," Saratov responded, but the connection was broken before the words passed his lips. He punched the button on his comm panel from the command channel back to his brigade network with an exasperated stab. "Give me a status report, *now*," he ordered. "Surveillance?"

"Radar is tracking two hostle targets at bearing zero-nine-eight, range one-sixty, low altitude, speed eight hundred," the surveillance officer reported. "Voron flight of two is searching for the targets with airborne radar. All other sectors report clear."

"Air defense missiles?"

"Air defense is standing by and ready," the air defense brigade officer reported. "Battery Three is currently off-line but will be online with limited fifty-kilometer engagement range in ten minutes. Time to full combat readiness is approximately two days."

"Unacceptable," Saratov said. "Fly replacement 30N6 radar units in immediately. It has been authorized by the chief of staff. I want them up and ready in eight hours. Get them moving."

"Yes, sir. All other air defense batteries are fully operational, and we have reported negative enemy traffic."

"Get on it," Saratov said. "Ground attack, report."

"All batteries report fully operational and ready," the Iskander brigade commander reported. "Twelve Iskander-M and twelve Iskander-K extended-range launchers with two missiles each are ready for launch, plus another thirty-six missiles ready for immediate reload. Reloads can be ready to fire in less than an hour. All launchers have been deployed to presurveyed launch locations for maximum accuracy. Targets include Polish command and control sites, airfields, air defense sites, and headquarters locations. Our first strike will destroy Poland's ability to communicate with its remote units, and those remote units, in turn, will be unable to communicate with their subordinate units. Once we control Poland's airspace and destroy its air defenses, we can end its ability to conduct these ridiculous harassment attacks against our forces."

"Is it possible to disperse your forces in case your current locations have been targeted?" Saratov asked. "Can you move them to nearby locations and put decoys in their original locations?"

"Absolutely, sir," the ground-attack brigade officer responded. "We can accomplish this in a staggered schedule so we do not degrade more than two batteries at a time. Our decoys are inflatable, easily set up, and cost virtually nothing in manpower and equipment. Best of all, the decoys almost perfectly match the size, infrared, radio, and radar profiles of the real launchers—if they are detected, the enemy will undoubtedly be convinced they are genuine."

"Have them ready to deploy," Saratov said. "I want the Iskanders ready to fire as soon as we get the order."

OVER EASTERN KALININGRAD OBLAST
That same time

"It's obvious: the air defense radar site is processing bad dope, Vikki," Captain Pavel Ignatyev, the pilot in the lead of the formation of two Sukhoi-30 air superiority fighters said on intercom. "It's about time they let us do our jobs until they get their heads straight and get their gear fixed."

"They could be getting meaconed too," the front seat weapons officer, Senior Lieutenant Viktoria Gref responded. "I'm not picking up anything now, but I thought I saw an indication of something out there at twelve o'clock, sixty kilometers."

"We're not radiating now, are we?"

"No, but I'm ready to take a look," Gref said. "If it's a real target I'll see it at eleven o'clock, forty kilometers."

"Clear to radiate," Ignatyev said. On the air-to-air channel he said, "Voron Flight, Lead is radiating."

"*Two*," came the simple reply from the pilot of the second Su-30. As the old joke said, wingmen only had to say three things to their flight leader: "Two," "You're on fire, Lead," and "I'll take the ugly one."

"*Contact!*" Gref said. "Two targets, eleven o'clock low, range one hundred, speed seven hundred!"

"Finally we got the real bastards!" Ignatyev said. On the command channel: "Take spacing, we have contact."

"*Two*," his wingman said. The second Su-30 climbed a hundred meters and dropped back about half a kilometer, allowing the leader more room to maneuver while hunting down their prey.

"Radar in standby," Gref said. On her display, however, the fire control computer plotted the targets it had picked up based on their last speed and heading and displayed them as if the radar was still locked on. "Eleven o'clock moving to ten, ninety klicks."

Ignatyev thumped the channel selector on his control stick to the command channel and spoke. "Base, Voron Flight, we have an airborne contact, low-flying, heading westbound at seven hundred. Do you still want a visual?"

"*Affirmative, Voron,*" came the reply.

"Acknowledged," Ignatyev replied. On intercom: "Shit, they want a visual. At night, low altitude, fast mover—the worst setup."

"The infrared seeker will give us an image at fifteen klicks," Gref said.

"Yeah, but that's well within Sidewinder missile range and almost in gun range."

"That's why you wear the big-boy four stars, Pavel," Gref said. "If they fire at us, we nail them."

Ignatyev straightened his back in his ejection seat and tightened his shoulder straps. "Fuck yeah," he said. "Arm up the 77s."

Gref flipped a switch and checked her multifunction display. "Four R-77s prearmed, button set for single salvo. Your triggers are hot."

"*Odobryat,*" Ignatyev said. "Acknowledged. Light 'em up."

"Radiating . . . now." A second later: "*Contact,* ten o'clock low, sixty klicks, heading west . . . maneuvering, moving southwest, accelerating to nine-sixty . . . shit, he's right on the deck!"

"He's got to be a bad guy!" Ignatyev said. He flicked his channel selector again: "Base, Voron Flight, unidentified aircraft is at extreme low altitude and is almost supersonic. Do I have permission to—"

But his question was interrupted when Gref shouted, "Picking up multiple targets now, I've got four aircraft now. Two moving northwest, still at low altitude. The other two are heading south and accelerating . . . northerly targets turning northeast."

"Looks like they're bugging out to Lithuania and Poland, the cowards," Ignatyev said.

"Some may be decoys," Gref reminded her pilot. "Could be MALDs."

Ignatyev switched back to his air-to-air radio. "Two, we have contacts at three and eleven o'clock, about fifty klicks. Turn northeast and pick up those two. I'll go after the southerly ones."

"Two," Vonorov replied.

Ignatyev threw his Su-30 into a tight right turn, imagining exactly where the southbound intruders should be. He was rewarded with: "Targets twelve o'clock very low, fifty klicks, speed one thousand."

"That's no decoy," Ignatyev said. "How far away is the border?"

"About two minutes at this speed."

"He's not getting away," Ignatyev said. "Lock them up."

Gref finished programming the fire control computer, and a moment later: "Targets locked." But a half second after that: "Heavy jamming . . . shit, broke lock. Can't reacquire. Target is maneuvering . . . target now heading west-northwest."

"Turning back toward his original target . . . probably the Iskanders," Ignatyev said. "I'll close on him and nail him with the 73s if you can't break the jamming."

A tone sounded in their helmets. "Target-tracking radar, X-band," Gref announced. "He's got air-to-air."

"I think it's one of those F-111s with the F-35 radar," Ignatyev said. "But he's just giving away his own position. If he thinks he's going to fire a missile at us from two hundred feet above the ground, he's an amateur." The captain sneered. "Idiot. What's his range?"

"Range twenty," Gref said. "I've got an infra-red lock-on. Selecting the 73s . . . infrared missiles armed, your triggers are—"

At that instant, a tremendous flash of yellow fire burst less than a hundred meters to their right, followed by a huge explosion and burst of turbulence that threatened to twist the Russian fighter inside out. "*Presvataya Bogoroditsa!* Holy Mother of God!" Ignatyev shouted. "Where the hell did that come from?"

"My scope is clear!" Gref shouted, trying to blink away the stars from her eyes. "All I have is our target at twelve o'clock low, fifteen klicks! Check your readouts—I feel a vibration on the right."

"Do I still have a hot trigger?" Ignatyev asked.

"Stand by!" She had to strain to read the multifunction display. "Yes! R-73s are still armed, single shot. Your trigger is hot! Still locked on infrared, fifteen kilometers."

Ignatyev's thumb slid over to the missile launch button on his control stick. "*Do svidaniya*, Mother—"

The second flash of light was just as bright as the first, but instead of a hundred meters off to the right it erupted just centimeters in front of the Su-30's left wing. Both crewmembers saw the light . . . but saw, heard, or felt nothing else. Their fighter was blown to pieces in a millisecond.

"I'd like to bring a dozen of those Coyotes with me on every mission," Brad McLanahan said, bringing the throttles back and pushing the wing sweep handle forward to fifty-four degrees, the high-speed cruise setting. Seated beside him in the cockpit of their XF-111A SuperVark was Nadia Rozek, unrecognizable in her helmet and flight gear except for her voice, which was steady and sure even though they were flying at nine miles a minute just one hundred feet above the Russian countryside at night, with radars all around them and Russian fighters and missiles ready to blow them out of the sky. Brad glanced over at Nadia's multifunction display and punched up a different screen.

"I am so sorry I am not more familiar with these controls," Nadia said. "There was just no time to learn."

"That's okay, Nadia," Brad said. "Your original job wasn't to fly this mission. But I can use all the help you can give me. Besides, I'm pretty good at flying solo—I've got lots of simulator time pushing weapon buttons from the left seat." He read the new information on the screen. "Six minutes to the first launch point. We're prearmed and ready." Their SuperVark was loaded with two AGM-154 Joint Stand-off Weapons on external hardpoints on the wings, two AGM-88 High-Speed Anti-Radiation Missiles also on wing hardpoints, and four CBU-105 Sensor Fuzed Weapon munitions in the bomb bay.

A warning tone sounded. "Here we go," Brad said. "S-300 site. Swap screens for me please." Nadia hit a soft key, which transferred the weapon page from the right MFD to the left so Brad could see it. "Hit the top right button on your right screen to bring up the ECM status page . . . that's it, and it shows

SPEAR is active. But I have a HARM selected on the left screen, so SPEAR won't try to take down that radar. Consent switches up . . . that's it, you got it. Mine's up, and I hit the release button. That starts the launch countdown . . . we're climbing a bit to give the missile more room . . . five, four, three, two, one, watch for the flare . . . there she goes." A streak of fire and a loud *RROAR!* erupted from the left wing, and an AGM-88 antiradiation missile shot off into the darkness. "Descending back to one hundred feet."

"It is like a video game, is it not, Brad?" Nadia breathed.

"Except for the results," Brad said. Moments later they saw a bright flash of light on the horizon, and a cloud of fire rolled into the sky. "Splash one CLAM SHELL. SPEAR is active again." On the weapons page, he selected a Joint Standoff Weapon. "Now let's see if we can take out the launchers. Coming up on the first location. On your right screen, hit the button for the radar . . . that's it. Switch it over to the left." Nadia did so. "The computer has selected the last known location of an S-300 site, but the things are mobile, so we won't know if they're really there unless we spot it on radar. Hit the top left . . ."

But Nadia had already selected the proper button. The snapshot image showed a finely detailed, almost photograph-quality image of the target area . . . and, almost right in the center of the screen, was a large eight-wheeled vehicle with two large vertical missile tubes on the back. Another unit could be seen just a few hundred feet away. "There they are!" Nadia exclaimed.

"But notice that the computer didn't select either of them," Brad said. "That means the radar is not picking up some characteristic it expects . . . which means it might be a decoy. Let's search around a bit. Use your trackball on your right console and scroll around a little." Even though it was not a live radar image, Nadia was able to move the image from side to side to search the area . . .

. . . and sure enough, they saw another pair of S-300 launchers about a mile farther to the north. "Are those real?"

"Hit the radar button again and let's find out." Nadia hit the button to take another radar snapshot, and this time the computer had put a yellow box around each launcher. "The computer thinks they're good. Select that button there on your right screen to select a JSW . . . good, consent switches are up, just waiting for the in-range indicator . . . there it is, bye-bye." Brad pressed the button on his panel, and an AGM-154 Joint Standoff Weapon dropped free from the right wing. Brad banked slightly left to stay away from the glide weapon.

"Did it hit it?" Nadia asked a few moments later. "I did not see an explosion."

"The JSW carries bomblets, and they detonate close to the ground, so we probably won't see a—"

Suddenly off to the left the ground erupted with bright flashes of light, and tracers arced all around them. "*Shit!* We flew right into triple-A!" Brad shouted. He threw the SuperVark into a hard right turn, but they heard and felt several hard impacts on the left wing and fuselage. They had been in the gun's cross hairs for just a blink of an eye, but they had not come through unscathed. "Damn, that was close! Are you okay, Nadia?"

"Yes." She hadn't screamed or panicked, but there was definitely fear in her voice now.

Brad's fingers flashed over the multifunction display's soft keys, calling up status and warning pages. "Left engine looks okay . . . no, wait, hydraulic system is losing pressure, and we may have lost wing sweep and partially lost left flight controls. Can you call up the weapons page and check for warning messages?"

"Yes." She called up the correct page with a shaky gloved finger.

Brad scanned the page while testing the flight controls and autopilot. "Looks like we lost an SFW," he said. "We'd better jettison it." He selected the damaged weapon and had Nadia hit the "JETT" soft key. They heard and felt the bomb-bay doors open and felt a slight shudder as the bomb left the bay . . . but the noise from the open bomb bay did not vanish as expected. "Crap, the bomb-bay doors won't close," Brad said after scanning his status and warning page. "Not enough hydraulic power."

"What does that mean, Brad?"

"We'll be even bigger on radar and it'll be noisy," Brad said. "It probably means we won't get the landing gear fully down or be able to use flaps or slats, but that's a problem we'll deal with when we get home." Unspoken was the thought: You mean *if* we get home.

Minutes later they were over the first Iskander missile launcher location. As before, they took radar snapshots of each launcher, verified that it was real and not a fake. Nadia selected a weapon. Using cues provided by the attack computer, Brad executed a "toss" maneuver, pulling the nose up and banking hard left at weapon release so the bomb was flung through the air in a high, arcing path.

This time, Nadia could see the results, and they were spectacular. The CBU-105 Sensor Fuzed Weapon released ten submunitions over the target area. Each submunition had infrared and radar seekers and four explosive disks. When the sensors detected a vehicle within range, it set off the disks, sending a shower of molten copper slugs down on the targets it found. The slugs could penetrate armor up to two inches thick—the Iskander missile launchers and their missiles were no match for them. Two Iskander launchers, their missiles, support vehicles, and their nearby reloads were hit and destroyed in a blinding red carpet of fiery chaos.

"Good show, old boy," came a voice on the secure air-to-air channel.

"Where are you, Claw Two?" Brad responded.

"Just took out emplacement six," Mark Darrow reported. He had come into Kaliningrad from the north through Lithuania. "One more to go. I see you just attacked number five. Are you that far behind?"

"I had to drive a little south so a Coyote could take out a fighter for me," Brad said. "You're the first Wolf I've heard from tonight."

"I'm seeing a lot of targets taken out, so I think we've made quite a mess of Mr. Gryzlov's party down there, but I'm afraid I haven't heard from anyone else in several minutes on the channel,"

Mark said. "I'm afraid the butcher's bill is going to be rather high. Back to work. Good luck to you. See you back at the base."

"Luck to you, Claw Two. Fang One out."

The most difficult of Brad's targets lay ahead. Intel had reported that this was a field of three Iskander launchers plus the central command and control trailer, guarded by layers of S-300 missiles, antiaircraft guns, and short-range antiaircraft missiles. Between flying around towns and vehicles and responding to system warning messages, Brad had a few minutes to tell Nadia how he expected the run to go and what she had to do. While he spoke, he noticed she didn't move, just stared straight ahead, motionless. "Nadia?" he asked finally. "Are you okay?"

She was silent for a few moments; then she whispered, "I am so scared, Brad. I am afraid that I will do something wrong that will get us both killed. My own death I can face, but I do not want to be the one whose error kills you."

"Nadia, you are the bravest woman I know," Brad said. "We'll get through this. I'll talk you through it. You'll do fine." He took his right hand off the control stick and put it on her left hand. "You'll do fine. We'll—"

Suddenly the threat-warning system sounded: "*Warning, India-band search radar, S-300, twelve o'clock, forty miles . . . warning, Echo-Foxtrot band acquisition radar, one o'cl . . . warning, India-Juliett band target-tracking radar, S-300, SPEAR active . . .*"

"Here we go," Brad said. He pushed up the throttles until they were at six hundred knots, flying one hundred feet aboveground using the digital terrain-following system. He tried to pull the wings back to seventy-two degrees, but they wouldn't move. No time to worry about that now. "Bring up the HARM first . . . next page . . . one button down . . . there you go, Nadia, don't worry. Good. It's selected. You got it. A couple more miles . . ."

Seconds later, through another series of threat warnings, a HARM antiradiation missile leaped off the right wing, and seconds later they saw another brilliant explosion, along with a marked reduction in the number of threat warnings. Just a few moments later, they launched the last remaining external Joint Standoff Weapon at the surface-to-air missile emplacements in their path to the last of the Iskander missiles they had been assigned.

Brad made sure the navigation computer had cycled first to the decoy ground track and then the last target area. "Last run and we head home," he said. "We'll attack three Iskander emplacements in a row with the SFWs. We have no more antiradar weapons, so we'll have to rely on SPEAR, speed, and DTF to avoid any shots at us. After that, we make like a bat out of hell for the—"

"*Warning, X-band radar, Su-30, three o'clock, range forty,*" SPEAR announced. "*Warning, target tracking detected, SPEAR engaged . . .*"

Brad made a hard left turn and headed for the last target complex. "Call up the last bomb run, Nadia," Brad said. "Next page . . . you got it." He reached over and called up a page on Nadia's left multifunction display. "Good, all remaining weapons are automatically selected for each target. All we have to do is—"

"*Warning, missile launch detection!*" SPEAR warned. "*Maneuver right.*" Brad waited a few heartbeats for SPEAR to eject chaff and flares from the left ejectors, then did a hard high-G right turn at ninety degrees of bank. They saw a tremendous explosion behind them through their cockpit canopy mirrors.

"Countermeasures right!" Brad ordered. SPEAR ejected chaff and flares from the right ejectors, and Brad did another break to the left to line up on the attack run. "Sixty seconds to first release," he said. "Strap in tight, Nadia. Watch the left screen for any—"

At that instant a massive fireball exploded off the right wing—Brad didn't know how close it came, but the SuperVark felt as if it had been shoved sideways and was ready to depart controlled flight and do a flat spin—not that he had *any* idea what a flat spin was—before he regained control. Warning lights illuminated throughout the cockpit. "*Shit! Engine fire!*" he shouted. The computers had already initiated engine shutdown, fuel shutoff, and activation of fire extinguishers, but Brad could still see the bright flicker of a fire out the right canopy when he looked past Nadia's slumped head and . . .

"*Nadia!*" Brad shouted. She was unconscious. The canopy was cracked where her head hit. "Nadia! Can you hear me?" No answer.

Through all the warning lights and tones, SPEAR announced, "*Warning, warning, X-band target-tracking radar, Su-30, locked on, six o'clock, ten miles and closing . . . warning, warning, X-band search radar, unidentified . . . warning, warning, X-band missile guidance, warning, warning . . . !"*

Brad saw another huge flash of light in the cockpit mirrors, and he thought, Shit, here it comes. His right hand moved to the ejection handle while his eyes scanned for another fire warning . . . Should I pull it now or wait? If I wait, will the capsule survive . . . ?

But no other warnings came, and the SuperVark flew on at low altitude, and the attack computers were counting down to the first release.

"American bomber, this is Vanagas Five-One, *Lietuvos karinės oro pajėgos,* air force of the Republic of Lithuania," a voice on the air-to-air channel announced. "May I recommend that you climb to at least ten thousand feet to avoid the electro-optical guided antiaircraft artillery? You and your comrades seem to have all but eliminated all other radar-guided weapons in this area, so it is safe to climb. Your six is clear. I am at your eight o'clock position, moving forward."

As he began a shallow climb, Brad looked to his left and saw a dark shape against the background of fires and lights below. Just then a tail recognition light snapped on, showing a blue shield and a white hawk emblazoned with a castle crest . . . on the tail of a Lithuanian Air Force F-16 Fighting Falcon! He was never so happy to see another aircraft than right now, and it wasn't even American! "Thanks for the help, Five-One."

"You are most welcome, sir," the Lithuanian pilot

said. "We could not allow you Americans to have all the fun. I can escort you to the Polish border, and then I must return to base."

"Roger," Brad said. "I'll be releasing on my last series of targets in a few seconds."

"Then I will hang back a bit and watch the fireworks," the pilot said. "*Sėkmės, geras medžioklė.* Good luck, good hunting."

RUSSIAN 72ND TACTICAL MISSILE BRIGADE COMMAND TRAILER, SOUTH-CENTRAL KALININGRAD OBLAST
That same time

"All communications to district command headquarters have been cut, sir," Lieutenant Kararina Kirov reported. "We have also lost contact with all air defense batteries!"

Colonel Konrad Saratov could not believe what he was watching . . . or, rather, *not* watching. One minute he was preparing to wreak havoc on the Polish Army and Air Force, and the next he had . . . *nothing.* "What *do* I have contact with, Lieutenant?" he shouted.

"Iskander Flight Fox," Kirov reported a few moments later. "Flight Jupiter reports that two of his launchers are out of commission and he has no contact with the others. No reports from any other flights."

"None?" Saratov groaned. "Out of two dozen launchers, I have only *three remaining*?" Kirov wouldn't dare answer—she had never seen that wild-eyed look in her commander's face before. He pounded the console so hard that coffee cups overturned and pencils jumped. He was silent, leaning against the console, his head bowed . . .

. . . but he said in a low, almost inaudible voice, "Order Fox Flight to launch immediately."

"Sir?"

"I said, *launch immediately*!" Saratov screamed. "Release all batteries and attack *immediately*! Then put out a call to the entire brigade in the clear to launch all active missiles!"

"But we do not have launch authorization from district headquarters, sir!"

"If we don't get our missiles downrange immediately, we won't *have* any missiles to get authorizations for!" Saratov exclaimed. "Order all available units to launch *immediately*!"

OVER SOUTH-CENTRAL KALININGRAD OBLAST
That same time

Brad's attack from ten thousand feet was almost like being in the simulator again: quiet, no bouncing-around terrain following, smooth, almost relaxing. The first Sensor Fuzed Weapons left the Super-Vark's bomb bay as commanded; Brad could no longer feel the detonations at his altitude.

"Good impacts, good detonations, good secondaries," he heard on the air-to-air channel.

It was not the Lithuanian pilot—he recognized

the electronically synthesized voice right away. "Thanks, Dad," Brad said.

"I'm picking up telemetry from your aircraft," Patrick said. "I think you'll make it back just fine. I see no other fire indications. I also see no other antiair threats. Congratulations. How's Nadia?"

"Unconscious," Brad said. "I can't see how bad."

"Bringing back a loved one from a bombing mission seems to be becoming a habit for you, son."

"That's one habit I'd rather not have," Brad admitted.

"I'm thankful for it, son. Nadia will be, too."

"How bad were our losses?"

"Pretty bad, but we did a hell of a job on the Russian rockets and air defenses," Patrick said. "I'll brief you back on the ground. You should be coming up on your second target now. I'm about ten miles south of—"

And at that instant, off on the dark horizon, Brad saw a large rocket streak away in a bright trail of fire. "*Missile launch!*" he shouted.

Patrick's CID sensors detected the missile launch a millisecond before he heard Brad's warning. "*Missile attack!*" he radioed back to the Iron Wolf command post. "Take cover *now!*" He raised his electromagnetic rail gun, followed the cueing signals, and waited for the gun to charge. The missile disappeared from sight, but not from his sensors. As soon as the gun was ready, he fired. The projectile sped off into the night sky, spltting the air with a loud supersonic *CCRACKK . . . !*

. . . but the Iskander had accelerated to well over five times the speed of sound, easily outrunning the electromagnetic projectile. It had taken too long to charge the weapon, and he had been taken completely by—

This time Patrick's sensors detected a second missile launch, and he whirled north, acquired the rapidly accelerating missile immediately, and fired. The projectile penetrated the missile, ignited the solid fuel propellant, and exploded the Iskander missile in a massive orange and red fireball, growing to at least a half mile in diameter before disappearing into the night.

"Good shot, Dad," Brad radioed. "I got the second launcher. Man, that was one hell of a fireball."

"Thank you, son," Patrick said. "I wasn't able to track the first missile, but its initial flight path indicates it was headed for Powidz, not Warsaw. I hope the guys took shelter in . . ."

. . . and then he stopped, because his sensors had picked up another terrifying reading . . . "Base, Wolf One, I'm picking up low levels of strontinum and zirconium from that Iskander missile explosion. I think that missile had a nuclear warhead on it!"

**IRON WOLF SQUADRON SECURE COMPOUND,
33RD AIR BASE,
NEAR POWIDZ, CENTRAL POLAND**
That same time

"*Shit!*" Wayne Macomber swore. He was piloting the damaged Cybernetic Infantry Device, limping on patrol around the base until the entire area could be cleared by Polish Special Forces of any remnants of American troops. He instantly raised his already-charged electromagnetic rail gun and scanned the skies for the incoming missile. Behind him on the base, men and women were scrambling into basements and bomb shelters, wanting desperately to be anywhere but aboveground.

They were not going to make it in time.

"Whack . . . ?" Patrick radioed.

"I'm on it, General," Macomber said. "I've got nothing so far."

"You'll have less than a second when it appears."

"I don't need the coaching, General," Macomber said. "What I need is a fistful of—"

The missile appeared on his sensors almost directly overhead at an altitude of thirty thousand feet, heading straight down at four thousand miles an hour. Macomber centered the missile in his sights and fired. The Russian missile exploded at twenty thousand feet in a spectacular globe of fire.

"Luck," Macomber said, finishing his prayer.

THE KREMLIN, MOSCOW
A short time later

"You lied to me, Barbeau!" Gennadiy Gryzlov ground out through gritted teeth. "You promised to eliminate Poland's American mercenaries for me. And yet these same mercenaries have just killed hundreds of brave Russian soldiers and destroyed precious equipment!" He slammed a clenched fist down on his desk, rattling the video monitor carrying their secure link. "So why should I not order an immediate nuclear strike against your European bases—as revenge for this treacherous sneak attack?"

"My special operations troops *were* able to wreck Scion's remote piloting center," Barbeau snapped back. "The rest of their mission only failed because they ran into a complication nobody anticipated!"

"What complication?" Gryzlov demanded.

"Patrick McLanahan," the American president said bitterly. "We all *thought* he was dead. Hell, we all *hoped* he was dead. But we were wrong. Somehow, that bastard is still alive. For Christ's sake, who do you think just led that F-111 strike on your missiles?"

For a long, blinding, dizzying moment, Gryzlov saw nothing but red. A wave of pure rage roared through his mind, threatening to drown all rational thought and any semblance of physical control. Shaking wildly, he gripped the sides of the monitor, tempted to hurl it through the nearest window.

"Mr. President? Gennadiy?" a voice said urgently in his ear. "Gennadiy!"

Slowly, with enormous effort, Gryzlov regained some measure of command over himself. Blearily, he looked up into the worried face of Sergei Tarzarov. "Did you hear that?" he growled to his chief of staff. "McLanahan is alive. That murdering piece of *shit* is still alive!"

"Yes, Mr. President," Tarzarov said. The older man leaned forward over Gryzlov's shoulder. "A moment, please, President Barbeau. I must confer privately with my president. But I assure you that he will return shortly, to continue discussing this difficult and unfortunate matter." Before the clearly shaken American political leader could interrupt, he pressed a control button—putting the secure link to Washington on hold.

"Why should I say anything more to her?" Gryzlov snapped, gesturing at the static-laden screen. "We have been lied to and stabbed in the back at every turn. By the Poles. By that fat American whore Barbeau. But at least now we know the true author of this evil plot: McLanahan! We must destroy him and all those around him, no matter how much it costs!"

"Our defenses inflicted very heavy losses on those bombers," Tarzarov reminded him. "The American may already be dead—and this time at our hands."

Gryzlov scowled. "I doubt it. That would be too convenient. Too easy." He shook his head. "No, Sergei! I feel it in my bones. McLanahan is still alive and flying back to Warsaw to boast to his new masters. So this war must go on until we've ground the Poles and McLanahan and his mercenaries into dust."

"Go on? How can we continue this war, Gennadiy?" Tarzarov asked. "Our armies are stalemated, short on fuel and ammunition. Our air force has suffered serious losses. And now the Iskander missile units that were our last resort have been annihilated. This is the moment to salvage what gains we can before—"

"We have other armies, Sergei. And additional

aircraft. And more missile brigades," Gryzlov snapped. He shoved his chair back and stood up. "Get Khristenko, Sokolov, and the others in here! We can strip troops and tanks and bombers from the Far East to assemble an invasion force so powerful that not even McLanahan's secret weapons can stop us!"

"You would weaken our defenses in the east, those facing the People's Republic of China, to continue this war? That would be a catastrophic error, Mr. President," Tarzarov said flatly. His eyes were cold. "And it would be a mistake you might not survive."

Gryzlov froze. He glanced narrowly at the older man. "Are you threatening me, Sergei?"

"No, Gennadiy," Tarzarov said in exasperation. "I'm trying to save you." He sighed. "The Poles and their mercenaries are not the true authors of this war. They were tricked into it. Just as we were. We have all been manipulated—tugged about like puppets on a string."

"What the devil are you talking about?" the Russian president demanded. "Manipulated? By who?"

"By the Chinese," Tarzarov told him.

Gryzlov listened in silence and growing consternation while the older man quickly ran through the new intelligence he'd gained from secret sources of his own—intelligence that strongly implied that agents of China's intelligence services were the ones who had been arming and equipping the terrorists, not the Poles. When Tarzarov was finished, he dropped back into his seat. "My God . . . that treacherous snake Zhou. I would not have thought him so . . . clever."

"Zhou or some of those around him," Tarzarov said evenly. "Which is why we must stop playing this destructive game Beijing set in motion—and instead turn it into one played for our own advantage."

"Advantage? How?"

"Think of what you have already won, Gennadiy," Tarzarov urged. "The eastern Ukraine is ours. Who will take it back from us? Kiev? Warsaw? The Americans?" He shook his head. "If we offer them peace now, on the basis of the status quo, they will trip over their own feet and tongues to agree."

"True," Gryzlov said slowly. Regaining permanent control over all of the Russian-speaking, heavily industrialized regions east of the Dnieper could certainly be presented as a great victory to the Russian public.

"But even that pales beside your greater victory," Tarzarov told him. "A victory of more lasting significance."

Gryzlov stared up at him, unable to hide his lack of understanding. "What greater victory?"

"You have broken NATO beyond repair," the older man said simply. "After seeing Washington abandon Poland—not just abandon them, but attack them—in its hour of need, who will trust the Americans now? And as the alliance splinters, we need only sit back and gather up the pieces as they fall into our lap—into our sphere of influence. Think of it, Gennadiy, *you* have accomplished what generations of your predecessors have failed to achieve!"

For the first time, Gryzlov began to smile. What Tarzarov said was true. Stripped of any belief that the Americans would protect them, Europe's smaller nations would gravitate—of necessity—into the orbit of the strongest remaining power, Russia.

But then his grin faded. "All of this is true, Sergei. But declaring an end to this war now would leave McLanahan alive. And that I will *not* accept!" He looked at Tarzarov. "This American is dangerous beyond belief. How many times has he robbed us of victories we believed were already ours? How many times has he bombed and killed and maimed our countrymen, with impunity?" He shook his head forcefully. "McLanahan *must* die."

"Yes, Mr. President," Tarzarov agreed coolly. "The American must be killed." He smiled. "But not by us."

Briefly perplexed, Gryzlov stared back at him. Then, as he understood what the older man intended, his cold blue eyes began to gleam. He swung back to the video monitor and reopened the connection. "President Barbeau, are you still there?"

Stacy Anne Barbeau's drawn and nervous face looked back at him. "Yes, I am!" she said. "Mr. President, it's crucial that we—"

"Be silent," Grzylov snapped, hiding his own inner amusement. "You have claimed that your government only seeks peace. Very well, I believe you. But I tell you this plainly: if you would have peace, then you must buy it . . ."

OVER CENTRAL POLAND
A short time later

Gritting his teeth, Brad held their badly wounded XF-111 SuperVark on course. The big fighter-bomber had so many holes in its wings and fuselage—and so much damage to its avionics and control surfaces—that his hands were kept busy on the stick and throttles. The XF-111 juddered and shook and rattled, constantly threatening to fall right out of the air. Jesus, he thought, the Super-Vark's flight controls were triple-redundant digital fly-by-wire. From the feel of things, this bird was down to about half redundancy and the "wires" must be frayed really thin . . .

With one engine dead and half their electronics out, it was a miracle they were still flying, he knew. It was way past time to set this sucker down. Sweat stung his eyes. Impatiently, he blinked it away. He looked over at Nadia. She still hadn't moved.

"Claw Two to Fang One," Mark Darrow radioed. He and Jack Hollenbeck were flying several kilometers ahead, nursing their own badly damaged XF-111 northward. "We're coming up to rendezvous with you and lead you to base. How is she handling?"

"Getting worse," Brad said. "I'll be landing with wings swept to fifty-four, no flaps, no slats, no spoilers."

"You'll need a very long runway, no doubt."

"I don't think so: I'll probably be landing with no landing gear."

"Marvelous," Darrow said in a reassuringly jovial voice. "How is Nadia?"

"Can't tell," Brad said. "She hasn't moved."

"She'll be all right. She's one tough lady." There was a moment's pause; then: "I'm picking up another plane north of you. It's a friendly, not Russian.

It might be Claw Four, or the Lithuanians. No radio or transponder, but he's got his radar on. Got him?"

"My SPEAR gave up the ghost twenty minutes ago," Brad replied. "I'm on essential bus only, and I might be on battery bus only in a few minutes."

"We'll have you on the ground in no time, One. Break. Southbound aircraft northeast of Barcin, this is Claw Two, come on up on tactical freq or on GUARD. Over." No response. Darrow tried again—still no . . .

Just then Brad saw a streak of white light slash across the sky from the northeast. Oh God, that was a *missile* . . .

A huge flash lit the darkness ahead of them. Darrow's XF-111 blew up in an enormous cloud of fire. There was a tremendous fireball and shock wave that seemed to engulf Brad's SuperVark, but it lasted only a second, and then the darkness closed in again.

Brad swore under his breath, desperately wrestling his damaged XF-111 into a tight, rolling evasive right turn. "Unknown aircraft, this is McLanahan!" he yelled into his mike. "Break off your attack! We're friendlies! Repeat, friendlies!" But just then, another bright burst of light and streak of white fire arrowed straight toward them, growing bigger with every second.

Game over, Brad thought. He calmly took his hand off the throttles and control stick, straightened his back, pressed his head back against the headrest, grabbed the yellow-and-black-striped handle by his right knee, squeezed, and pulled.

WHAAAM!

An explosive cutting cord around the XF-111's cockpit ejection capsule detonated, separating it from the rest of the aircraft, and then a powerful rocket motor at the capsule's base ignited, hurling it skyward. At that same instant, a missile slammed into the SuperVark and went off, sending the bomber spiraling out of control. Fragments smacked into the capsule with tremendous force, tearing holes into the partially deployed capsule parachute.

Brad was stunned, but awake enough to realize that the capsule seemed to be falling at a very high rate of speed. He couldn't see the parachute. The cockpit was filled with smoke, his back and neck were aching from the ejection, and he couldn't feel his legs. But he had enough consciousness to reach over and take Nadia's gloved hand . . .

. . . just before the capsule slammed into the earth at high speed and began to tumble, and then everything went black . . .

SECURE RECOVERY WARD, MILITARY INSTITUTE OF MEDICINE, WARSAW
Two days later

Wearily, Brad drifted along a darkened coast, letting the current take him where it would. Swimming seemed like too much work, especially with his arms and legs tangled so tightly in floating coils of seaweed. Better to lie back in the water's warm embrace and rest, he thought. Struggling against his bonds would be too much work.

A light blinked suddenly on the horizon. And again.

Almost against his will, Brad turned his head toward the flashing light. Must be a lighthouse, he decided drowsily—a beacon perched high on the cliffs to warn off passing ships.

But, damn, that light was bright. So bright that it was almost blinding.

Brad blinked away tears against the dazzling, painful glare. And then he realized that he was looking up into the beam of a small penlight. It clicked off, revealing a stranger's face peering down at him. A doctor, by his white coat.

"He is conscious, Mr. President," the doctor said in accented English. "And there are no immediate signs of neurological trauma."

Slowly, Brad became aware that he was sitting propped up in a hospital bed. Bandages swathed his head and chest and his left arm and both legs seemed to be stuck in casts. The memory of those terrifying last seconds before their XF-111 ejection capsule slammed into the ground rushed back at him. "I'm alive?" he croaked.

The doctor raised a bushy eyebrow in wry amusement. "Yes, Mr. McLanahan, you are. And lucky to be so." He shook his head. "Remarkably, however, your injuries, though serious enough, are not life-threatening."

Alive, Brad thought; now, there was a surprise. Then panic seized him. "Nadia? What about Nadia?" he demanded. "Is she . . ." he swallowed painfully, unable to go on.

"I am right over here, Brad," he heard her say.

Wincing against the pain involved in moving, he turned his head. Nadia Rozek smiled back at him from a chair by his bedside. A pair of crutches were propped up beside her, gauze bandages covered the right side of her cheek and head, and she had a massive black eye. But she appeared otherwise unhurt. He sighed in relief. "Did you know that you look beautiful even all banged up?"

She laughed. "Flattery will get you everywhere." Then she inclined her head toward the door. "But at the moment, we have distinguished visitors."

Reluctantly, Brad looked away from her lovely face. Both Piotr Wilk and Kevin Martindale stood there, watching him with thoughtful expressions. "I'm sorry about the rest of the squadron," he said slowly. "We knew it would be bad . . . but I really didn't think we'd lose every plane."

"That will be all for now, Doctor," Wilk told the Polish physician quietly. The white-coated doctor nodded and left the room, closing the door behind him.

"Did anyone else make it out alive?" Brad asked, feeling a tightness in his chest.

"We don't know yet," Martindale admitted. "Macomber, Schofield, and their teams are out in the field now, looking for other survivors." His shoulders slumped a bit. "Without any luck, so far."

Brad closed his eyes briefly, fighting off a wave of sorrow and regret and guilt. Memories of smiling faces flashed through his mind—Mark Darrow, Jack Hollenbeck, Bill Sievert, Smooth Herres, Karen Tanabe, and all the others. How could he have lost them all? "Christ, I got everyone killed," he muttered.

"On the contrary, Brad," Piotr Wilk said gravely, coming forward to stand by Nadia's chair. "If there are other survivors, we will find them—no matter where they are. But the courage and self-sacrifice of all of those who died will be honored forever." His expression was serious. "Your mission was successful. Your Iron Wolves destroyed the Russian missile force before it could launch."

"Then we have won," Nadia said softly.

Martindale nodded. "To a degree. The Russians have offered a cease-fire and we've accepted it. Their armies are pulling back." He smiled thinly. "Leaving an embarrassing trail of broken-down and out-of-gas tanks and other vehicles in their wake, I might add."

"Gryzlov is backing down?" Brad asked, surprised. Based on painful personal experience, he wouldn't have expected Russian's egomaniacal leader to accept defeat so easily.

"Not quite. Friend Gennadiy is proclaiming victory," Martindale said drily. "Moscow has started signaling that its so-called Zone of Protection over eastern Ukraine is likely to become permanent."

Wilk nodded. "Eastern Ukraine is the bone Grzylov will throw his people, hoping to distract them from their other military defeats."

"Unfortunately, that's not the only success he can claim," Martindale went on relentlessly. "There's also the win that Stacy Anne Barbeau just handed him on a silver platter." He shook his head in disbelief. "In just a few weeks, she's managed to do what the Russians have been trying and failing to do for more than sixty years: she's destroyed the NATO alliance."

"Oh, crap," Brad murmured. "She has, hasn't she?"

"I am afraid so," Piotr Wilk said. "President Barbeau's cowardly refusal to help us in the face of Russian aggression was damning enough. Deciding to actually side with Moscow—by attacking our base at Powidz and then ordering her F-35s to shoot down your surviving aircraft?" he frowned. "That is treachery beyond my ability to forgive."

"No other nation in Central or Eastern Europe will be able to trust the United States now," Martindale agreed. "Not with Barbeau in the White House. And without the United States as its linchpin, NATO is effectively dead."

"Then how will we defend ourselves in the future?" Nadia asked. Her voice was troubled. "We stopped the Russians this time. But like all barbarians, they will be back."

Wilk nodded. "It may be time to try reviving the old dream of *Międzymorze*, the Intermarium." He saw the puzzled looks on their faces and explained. "From the end of World War One to his death, Józef Piłsudski, the founder of modern Poland, tried to form an alliance of all the newly free nations from the Baltic Sea to the Black Sea. He failed then. But perhaps the time is riper now. Together with forces like your Iron Wolves and Scion's technological wizardry, such a coalition might give us all a fighting chance to survive Russia's continued menace—at least until the United States awakens from its torpor and folly."

Martindale, Brad, and Nadia all nodded.

"It's worth trying," Martindale said. A wry grin crossed his face. "If nothing else, it'll give Brad and me and the others meaningful work during our exile."

"Our what, sir?" Brad asked carefully.

"We seem to have seriously pissed off Madam President Barbeau," Martindale said cheerfully. "She's labeled you and me . . . and everyone who works for Scion or who joined the Iron Wolf Squadron . . . as fugitives from justice. Last I heard, she was on the warpath up on Capitol Hill pushing legislation to strip us of our American citizenship. And failing that, she's demanding that President Wilk extradite us immediately for criminal trial back in the States."

Brad took that in silence. Then he asked, "What about my father?"

"Barbeau thinks Patrick McLanahan is dead, for real this time," Martindale said. "She's sure he was flying one of the XF-111s she ordered shot down." He shrugged. "For obvious reasons, we're allowing her, and Gennadiy Gryzlov, of course, to go on believing that."

Brad nodded. In a sad way, his father was safer and freer "dead" than he was alive.

"Naturally, I have refused President Barbeau's ridiculous demands," Wilk assured him. "In fact, I am offering all of those who fought so valiantly Polish citizenship. If they wish it."

Feeling suddenly dazed by all of this, Brad leaned

back in bed. Barbeau wanted to put them all in prison? And strip them of their citizenship? He shook his head in dismay. He'd been proud to be an American all of his life. If he lost the right to call himself that, what would he do then? Could he really become a citizen of Poland and be happy?

Nadia must have seen his confusion and concern because she leaned forward and took his hand. "Don't worry, Brad," she told him gravely, but with the hint of a smile in her eyes. "A mere scrap of paper does not determine who is a *real* American. That is a question of courage and determination and optimism. Those are what truly matter. And those qualities you have in abundance. You will always be a *true* American." She kissed his hand gently and then looked deep into his wondering eyes. "*My* American."

EPILOGUE

KIEV, UKRAINE
A few days later

This late at night, the sidewalk outside Fedir Kravchenko's dingy, run-down apartment building was empty—dimly lit only in places by the murky glow of a few unbroken streetlamps. Rusting, broken-down cars and stinking piles of uncollected garbage lined the street. Rats scurried back into the pitch-black alleys, momentarily alarmed by the sound of his reeling, drunken footsteps.

"Major?"

Scowling, Kravchenko turned around. "What?" he slurred through vodka-numbed lips. He peered uncertainly at the shadowy figure who'd just stepped out onto the pavement a few meters behind him. "Who the fuck are you?"

The tall, square-jawed man came forward a bit into the dim glow cast by a streetlamp. Light shone dully on close-cropped gray hair, dark jeans, and a black leather jacket.

Suddenly Kravchenko recognized him. He was the nameless go-between used by the similarly anonymous patron who had funded his failed campaign against the Russians. "You were better dressed the last time we met," he growled. "Come down in the world, have you? Like me?"

The man smiled gently. "No, Major. I simply choose my clothes to suit the job at hand."

"Which is what exactly?" Kravchenko asked, feeling himself starting to sober up just a bit.

"Garbage removal," the other man said. In one quick, smooth motion, his hand came up holding a silenced 9mm Makarov pistol. The muzzle centered on the former partisan leader's forehead.

Phut.

Kravchenko crumpled. Blood, black in the dim light, trickled away into the gutter.

With a nod of satisfaction, the gray-haired man slid the pistol back into his shoulder holster. No fuss and very little mess, he thought. His employer would be pleased. He turned to go—

And large, articulated metal fingers abruptly tightened around his neck, hoisting him high into the air. Another metal hand reached under his jacket and plucked out his Makarov. Casually, it tossed the weapon aside.

Struggling and choking, the gray-haired man found himself staring up at a six-sided head studded with lenses and other sensors. One of the lenses whirred softly. The metal fingers relaxed slightly, allowing him to breathe.

"My name is Patrick McLanahan," a cold synthetic voice said. "And, according to the scan I've just run, you are Dmytro Marchuk—formerly a colonel in the Ukrainian special police, the Berkut."

The machine shook its head slightly. "Not a very pleasant bunch, Mr. Marchuk. You and your former comrades once did all the dirty work for the crooked Kiev politicians backed by Moscow. Not to mention the brutal tasks assigned by any number of crime syndicates."

"What do you want with me?" Marchuk gasped, still futilely straining against the robot's implacable grip.

"We're going to have a little talk, Mr. Marchuk," the machine said coolly. "A talk about all the people who died. Plus all the damage done by Major Kravchenko and the other fanatics you've now silenced. And when that's done, we'll talk about who you really work for."

"And then you will kill me?" the onetime Ukrainian secret policeman stammered, unable to conceal the abject terror crawling through every part of his body.

"Kill you?" the machine echoed. It shook its head again. "Only if you are very, very lucky." And then it turned, striding away into the darkness with Marchuk still desperately kicking and struggling in its grasp.